EYES OF THE ETERNAL

EYES
OF THE
ETERNAL

G.E. WHITE

BOOK ONE OF THE REALMS OF REBIRTH

Doll House Publishing
Hamilton, Ontario, Canada

Eyes of the Eternal

Category: Urban Fantasy, Greek Mythology, New Adult, LGBTQIA+

For all inquiries, including media queries, please contact the publisher directly at dollhousepublishing.com

Library and Archives Canada Cataloguing in Publication

Title: Eyes of the eternal / G.E. White.
Names: White, G. E., author.
Description: Series statement: The realms of rebirth ; book 1
Identifiers: Canadiana 20210288892 | ISBN 9781775223832 (softcover)
Subjects: LCGFT: Novels.
Classification: LCC PS8645.H528 E94 2021 | DDC C813/.6—dc23

Author: G. E. White
Editor: Theron O. Pierce

Cover Art: Hoàng Lập (Solan)
Book and Cover Design: Frank Lawrence

Promotion: Christina Kolombos
Publisher: Rebecca Doll

Special Thanks to: Kiran Massey, Marcus Sarpong, Robert E. Newton, France Fontana Hart, Glenn Lowson, Steph Forrest, Ainsley Sanderson.

To all the kids who were told they dreamed too big,
talked too much, and had too many stories to tell.

PROLOGUE

ARGES SAT IN the back of the pub, nursing his gin. He wrinkled his nose as he took in the scent of the humans around him. With his heightened senses, it was as though he were drowning in their petty little world. The pub was filled with the sounds of their pool tables and darts games. They chatted to one another while buying drinks at the bar and attempted to recreate lost youth as they listened to eighties rock pour out of the vintage jukebox.

To the other patrons of the Fox and Fife pub, Arges looked like any other human. His true form was hidden behind a barrier of magic, but no illusion could completely conceal his oversized frame. His brown hair was closely cropped to his skull and framed two dark gunmetal eyes that moved quickly as they worked to counteract the glamour concealing his true facial form.

The brooding man sneered. Why his contact had insisted on meeting in the Second Realm was beyond him. Not only would he stink of humans by the end of the night, he now had to spend a tediously long evening masquerading as one of the vermin.

Most daimons were capable of limited transformation, shifting from a human-looking form to their more beastial shapes. Arges and his brothers however preferred to use glamours as any true transformation was disorienting as their vision would change. True, many of his kind had made this realm their home, though Arges could not understand how they could constantly demean themselves by wearing human forms. Speaking of his kind, his contact should have been here half an hour ago.

The worn chair creaked as he turned to survey the pub. He was rewarded with the sight of his sister-in-arms entering through the wooden doors, followed closely by a dark-haired man Arges did not recognize, due in part to the newsboy's cap shadowing the strange man's face.

Upon catching sight of Arges, the woman slid up to meet him at his small table in the back of the establishment. She appeared to be in her early to mid forties, and time had been kind to her, leaving her ageless face free from scars and other misfortunes. Her dark, shining hair was piled loosely on her head, and a few wayward strands fell down around her dark-green eyes to frame her slight, Mediterranean features.

Her companion trailed behind her. He seemed younger and appeared as if he were of Asian descent, tall and lean—no match for Arges' intimidating size, the giant thought smugly. However, as he thought of his own single eye, the Cyclops grudgingly admitted that appearances could be deceiving.

"Arges, good to see you," the woman said, her voice easily cutting through the steady murmur of human conversation.

"You as well, S—"

"Scarlet," she interrupted.

"Scarlet," Arges echoed. "Is that what you're calling yourself these days?"

"For now, well at least around mortals. I think it fits, don't you?"

Scarlet neatly folded herself into the chair opposite the hulking giant. Her silent companion remained standing, his attention focused on the crowd around them.

"I wouldn't know, seeing as the day you invited me to take part in your...scheme, was the first I'd heard from you in over twenty years." Arges gestured to the man behind her. "Who's the stooge?"

"A new business partner. He's provided some detailed information and access to our targets."

Arges sniffed. "He's not one of us." Another sniff. "Not exactly human either."

"It doesn't matter what he is," Scarlet answered sharply. "I'm vouching for him. That should be enough for you and your brothers. Now, I suggest we get on with it before that flimsy glamour of yours wears off and we have human hysteria on our hands."

The Cyclops grunted. He and his brothers may have had reputations for not being the most cunning creatures across the realms, but he knew how to put on a simple human glamour. Her implication chafed at him as she sat comfortably in her human skin, but he'd come here to hold up his end of their bargain, so he swallowed his pride and allowed her to continue.

"Fine."

"So, did you bring it?" Scarlet asked, urgency creeping into her voice.

Arges pulled an item out of his breast pocket that was dwarfed by his massive fist. He neatly tossed the object to his visitor with a certain grace that contradicted his appearance.

Scarlet caught the item with ease and began her inspection. It was a heavy metal cuff bracelet with a watch-like dial and only two visible settings.

"I take it you had no trouble getting the materials?"

"While Hephaestus hasn't changed his scrap heap locations in centuries, they're still pretty well guarded. It wasn't easy, but I was able to scrape up enough pieces to put it together." Arges grinned, taking a certain amount of satisfaction in stealing from a god. "He really should keep track of what he throws away."

Scarlet nodded absently, her attention still fixed upon the device in her hand. "And you're sure it works?"

Arges grunted in irritation. *What did she take him for? An idiot?* "Of course, it works. My brothers and I tested it thoroughly. Those magi won't know what hit 'em."

Scarlet ran her finely manicured nails over the merchandise, her appraising eyes seeming to be pleased with what she saw. "All right then, make me sixty more."

"Sixty?!" he hissed, incredulous. "It took us months to cobble up enough *aetherum* to forge just one! Do you know how long it would take to skim that much without Hephaestus catching on? Not to mention the time needed to forge them all. It would take months, or more likely years! One is more than enough to move ahead with your plan."

Scarlet scoffed at his indignation, "You're starting to sound like a mortal. As *if* a couple of years would make much of a difference to us. We have to do this right. Yes, one is more than enough for the initial stage of our plan, but to secure what we need for the end goal, we will need many more. You need time? Take it. I'm in no rush."

Arges' gaze trailed over the woman's face. He knew that look: jaded yet determined. The plan she had described to him over the phone was far from inconsequential. It could change everything. Obviously, she had been patient in getting this far. What were a couple more years to eternal beings like themselves?

"Fine, sixty it is. So, you really want to do this?" he said. "Just wipe them all out? Do you know what this would do to the gods?"

"Make them obsolete," she answered.

"That's not all."

"I know what it would do!" The nails that had just been caressing the cuff now dug deep into the wood of the table. "I've been thinking about this for a long time—ever since the last job we pulled together," she continued.

"The Soul Calendria?" Arges huffed. "I knew going after that magical paperweight was a mistake. What's in it that has you so agitated?"

"That's none of your business. All you need to know is that once this is over, they will be gone, and things will go back to the way they were."

"You do realize that the Fifth Race was here before us," he said.

Scarlet shrugged. "Fine. Then, back to the way things should have been." She focused once more on the cuff before her. "I take it, once you and your brothers have finished with this project, you'll be ready for the final stages?"

"That's a given," Arges replied, flicking his gaze over Scarlet's companion once again. "Your new acquaintance might be giving you some access, but without me and my brothers, your plan falls apart."

"A fact I don't deny. I still need you."

"And when you don't need us anymore?" he quipped. Arges might have said it lightly, but he wasn't joking. He'd known her long enough to earn his skepticism.

Scarlet leaned back in her chair to fully observe the giant sitting before her.

"We are of the same kind, and not many of us exist anymore," she said. "Do you honestly think I'd betray you or your brothers?"

"Can't be too careful nowadays." Arges' glamoured eyes narrowed as he looked down his nose at the woman before him.

"No, I suppose you can't. But don't worry. If something does go wrong, I'll look after you," she assured.

Scarlet gave a jerk of her head, now gesturing to her silent companion. The slight man pocketed the cuff and stood at attention, waiting for his mistress' word.

Scarlet stood. "Once you're done with the next shipment, I'll make sure they get passed on to our other…compatriots. Contact me once you secure the needed materials."

Arges nodded his head toward the tavern door, and Scarlet and her companion moved as one toward the exit.

Despite her words, he knew she was dangerous. Treachery ran in her blood, as the last man in her life could attest. Or at least the man could have, were he still alive. Scarlet's assistant would be wise to be on his guard.

As for Arges, he had his brothers to help watch his back, as he would theirs.

Family came first.

☙

Scarlet and her partner exited the pub. She hissed as the spitting rain caught her in the eye, prompting her to dig into her purse, find her sunglasses, and slip them onto her face. The man at her side opened a compact umbrella, sheltering them both as they strolled toward the parking lot.

"You actually trust him?" Scarlet's companion asked, finally breaking his silence.

"I don't trust anyone, Victor. Not even you," she replied.

"And yet, you're willing to work with us." Victor's eyebrow raised.

"I am. Only Arges and his brothers can build what I need. And so far, only you can give me access to where we need to go."

Victor's dark eyes trailed over Scarlet's slight form, narrowing as he scrutinized her, studying her motives. "You really hate the gods that much?"

"It's not so much about hate as it is about necessity," she answered casually. "I've lived much longer than you, and after seeing the gods make the same mistakes over and over, I've grown to pity them. I've realized that they don't deserve the curse of mortality."

"You've known that for a while and have been content to do nothing. What's changed?" Victor asked as they approached his car. He stepped to the passenger side and held the door open.

"They tried to take my family from me." Scarlet dropped her voice as she sank into the car seat.

Victor closed the door behind her and made his way to the other side of the car.

From inside the vehicle, Scarlet watched the dark-haired man's fluid movement and choked out a humourless laugh. "No one steals from a daimon."

CHAPTER ONE

Quinn Smith had never considered himself a criminal mastermind. In fact, he supposed he couldn't be considered a criminal by any stretch of the imagination.

The somewhat gangly seventeen-year-old youth was slight of build with bright grey eyes. His ash-blond hair feathered about his face, blinding his vision briefly as his slender fingers, now shaking slightly, forced a paperclip into the front door of the Ashdale Public Library. The library had been closed for hours, its patrons and staff long since departed.

If he had been asked to describe his state of mind as he jostled the clip into the tarnished lock, Quinn would have been hard pressed to articulate the enormity of the compulsion he was feeling. In a way, he couldn't even describe what he was doing there himself.

G.E. White

It wasn't as if he had gone out with the intent to break and enter on this muggy, late-August evening. No, Quinn had just felt restless. It was a feeling that had been haunting him for a little while now, slowly ramping up like a pot beginning to boil on a back burner of his brain. But it had never felt this urgent and intense. Almost as if his life depended on something his mind couldn't quite remember.

He had spent the past few days at work helping his boss, Mr. Reynolds, clean and set up some of the classrooms at the Lakeshore Community College. With a brand new school year around the corner, the maintenance manager had him working overtime to prepare the small collegiate institution. Finishing late, he had simply planned a stroll in the quiet evening hours back to the group home where he lived. He had figured the fresh air would do him some good.

But Quinn's walk had done nothing to relax him. He felt more on edge with each step, almost as if he were about to leap out of his own skin. During his less-than-ideal upbringing, he'd been exposed to the horrors addicts endured as they detoxed from drugs. The sweating, shaking, panic that made the stomach twist in agonized knots. When he reached for the words to describe the feeling that wracked his body in this moment, all he could think was that he must be suffering some form of withdrawal, though he'd never once touched an illicit narcotic himself.

In his darkest days, he'd always found refuge in books. They were his drug of choice when life became too chaotic. Now, he hoped that some late-night reading would act like a balm applied to his frenzied mind. So, when the young man had seen the sign for the local library, his growing anxiety had driven him toward the now-closed building. If Quinn could have thought clearly, it might have occurred to him just how bad an idea that was.

His breathing now coming in ragged, sharp pants, Quinn soon felt the lock beneath his fingers give way with a faint click. The library's front door swung inward, and as if he were being led along a puppet master's string, Quinn stumbled through the door frame and across well-worn tiles to the stairs leading up to the second level. He bypassed the fiction sections he normally frequented in favour of the instructional books. Stories wouldn't suffice tonight. He wanted—no, needed—information.

He continued up the two flights of stairs undeterred, numb to the possibility of any security cameras or silent alarms. Reaching the instructional section, Quinn turned into the first row and pulled several books down at random. Maybe if he were to read them, then this strange compulsion would be satisfied. Collapsing to the floor, now sitting within a ring of hardcover books, Quinn picked up the tome nearest to him and began to read.

The book was a manual on home renovation, and he soon became completely immersed in learning about load-bearing walls, feng shui, and the benefits of cork flooring. Quinn read faster than he ever had before, faster than humanly possible. If he'd had the wherewithal to process what he was doing, he might have been astonished by the fact that he was retaining the information despite his quickened pace. The knowledge satiated him completely, like warm broth might a starving man.

Absorbed in his frantic reading, Quinn failed to notice the blue and red flashing lights that shone through the library window several minutes later.

༺༻

A career cop in his mid-forties, Officer Kendry had been surprised to get the dispatch call to check out the local library. The silent alarm had been triggered a few minutes ago, but a burglary seemed unlikely—the books were already free to borrow. Maybe a couple of kids had broken in to vandalize the place for kicks.

Kendry had asked his younger partner, Officer Fields, to wait outside should anyone try to slip past him. She nodded, content to stay by the patrol car.

The police officer entered the library silently, noting that the lock had been picked, if the unfolded paper clip jammed in the keyhole was any indication. "Police! Show yourself!" he called, his gun and flashlight drawn.

Hearing the rustling of pages and a faint voice murmuring from upstairs, Kendry ascended the worn wooden stairs, creaking and groaning with every step he took. He noted that the noise did not seem to alert the intruder.

As he reached the top of the second story landing, Kendry could see a young man sitting on the floor, dozens of books scattered around him. The boy's lips moved slightly as he muttered softly to himself.

Stepping onto the landing, Kendry swung his flashlight over the intruder. The young man in front of him did not stir from his position on the floor, between the large bookcase and the railing.

"Hey, kid!" the officer called. "What are you doing?"

Receiving no reply, Kendry cautiously approached the frantic-looking young man. Discerning that the boy was no immediate threat, he holstered his weapon, watching the teen flip through his book's pages at an alarming speed. There was something wrong with him.

He's not hurting anyone. Doesn't appear to be armed, or bloody...or high...could he be mentally unstable?

"Hey kid, are you all right?" he asked the boy, his voice softening as he stepped closer. Met still by silence, Kendry placed a hand on the reader's shoulder.

ᔕ

Intently focused on the words in front of him, Quinn did not hear the officer speaking to him. With the large book in hand, the hyper focused young man felt as if he were tightly wrapped within a cocoon of knowledge and safety—one that the outside world could barely touch. When the officer touched his shoulder, the teen was jerked back to reality with an unsettling jolt.

Suddenly disoriented, Quinn glanced up to see a shadowed figure looming over him. It terrified him before his brain could process what his eyes were actually showing him. His reaction was instinctive: he threw out his arm, the large book still clasped in his hand as he attempted to fend off the threatening presence. It was a fight or flight response. Something that had been etched into his muscle memory since his very first childhood bully, in that very first foster home.

Surprised by the combination of the fearful cry and powerful shove, Quinn's assailant stumbled back onto the old railing. The brittle wood split with a loud crack, giving way under the figure's weight as he crashed to the lower level. Quinn hadn't even registered what was happening until it was too late.

The sound of flesh hitting tile woke Quinn from the remnants of his trance. He blinked away the fog from his mind and lowered his arms, realizing that whatever pressure or compulsion had possessed him was gone. Unsettled by the sight of the missing guardrail, Quinn crawled to the edge and peered over the landing.

What just happened?

A uniformed police officer lay flat on his back, his head lolling back and forth, with shattered bits of the guardrail trapped underneath him. A piece of the man's shin bone jutted out of the navy blue fabric of his pants, and a darkening burgundy puddle began to pool around the grotesque injury.

Wait... Did... Did I do this?

Quinn stared in horror, unable to look away or even move. His chest heaved as he tried to catch his breath. Realization and guilt ripped through him. It felt as though he were under water. The disfigured policeman flailed on his back, crying out in pain. Quinn watched as the fallen officer's partner, drawn by the sound of the crash, entered the building. She stopped short upon seeing Kendry, raising her flashlight and gun to the floor above, pointing them both at Quinn, who blinked owlishly in the sudden light.

"You! Hands where I can see them," she ordered.

Stunned, Quinn complied, raising his hands in a submissive gesture.

Keeping her eye on the frozen young man, Officer Fields raised her two-way radio to her lips. "Dispatch, this is Patrol Officer Three-One-Eight-Five at Ashdale Public Library, requesting back up and an emergency bus. I have an officer down... Hang on, Kendry, they're on their way!"

The other cop began to approach Quinn, her gun still trained on his shivering form. "You some kind of junkie or something?" Her accusation was met with silence. Quinn couldn't even bring himself to formulate an answer. The anxiety that had possessed him before had left his body a clenching, shaking mess.

"All right, take it easy, get down on the ground, hands behind your head. Now." She was assertive and Quinn instinctively acquiesced, his faculties slowly returning to him. Cold metal slid over his wrists as the handcuffs clicked down.

"You're in big trouble, kid."

The rest of her words blurred together in Quinn's racing brain as he gazed down at the fallen man.

Something is wrong with me. Why did I do that?! Why did I even come here in the first place! Part of him wanted nothing more than to run away. Another hoped this was all some kind of waking nightmare. More than anything, though, he wished desperately for his late father to come and make it all okay again.

How had the night come to this?

CHAPTER TWO

"It'll all be okay soon." Quinn had repeated those words to himself for the last several months, in the hopes that if he said it enough, he could one day believe it. In truth, the oft-whispered mantra was probably helping to keep him from completely breaking down, despite his lack of faith in its veracity. He had no idea if anything would ever be okay again.

The past five months had felt like a blurred state of limbo. His arrest back in late August had been disorienting, and he only remembered fragments from that fateful night. The musty smell of the library carpet he had been forced to lie upon as an officer handcuffed him, the wail of the ambulance upon its arrival, the bright flash of the camera as his mug shot was taken, and the slick texture of the ink as he was fingerprinted.

But above all, it was the image of Officer Kendry, laying on that library floor, that haunted him every time he closed his eyes.

Dazed as a deer in headlights, Quinn had gone along with everything asked of him as the cops booked him. It was as if he were unable to think for himself, and when he was placed in the precinct lock-up, he had simply stared into space, thinking about the man he'd hurt. It wasn't until the next morning that he was able to formulate a coherent sentence, and he ended up using one more often than any other while giving his statement to the police: "I don't know."

And it was true. Quinn didn't know why he had been at the library that night. He didn't know how he had gotten into the building, and he certainly didn't know why he had pushed Officer Kendry. He couldn't explain the feeling that had taken hold of him. He could barely remember it. To make matters even more confusing, the interrogation had left him with more questions than answers. The detective forced him to verbally retrace his actions, from picking the lock, to his assault on the officer, yet it offered nothing to explain his behaviour.

With every *I don't know* that left Quinn's lips, the detective grew angrier. Quinn had had no intention of frustrating the cops this much. He'd always been good about respecting authority figures, and aside from the occasional jaywalk, he'd never knowingly broken a law. The library incident had been his first and only criminal offence. He wanted to comply, but he couldn't exactly tell them things he himself didn't know.

After the prosecutor arrived and had grilled him with the exact same questions Quinn had been unable to answer for the detective, he finally gave up and asked to see a lawyer. They left him to sweat it out all alone in the interrogation room for about two more hours before a legal aid attorney was finally called. An hour later, a plump, balding defence lawyer named Artie McMullin arrived and sat down with him.

In the beginning, Artie had been a blessing. The stocky man had had a calming effect on Quinn. When Quinn had explained his side of the story as best he could, it became obvious that Artie truly believed that the confrontation with Kendry had simply been an accident. Their conversation filled Quinn with hope. He had already confessed to the crime, despite his shoddy memory and had not resisted his arrest. And to make up for what he'd done, he told Artie he was more than willing to do community service or be placed on house arrest in his group home. He was so sure that Artie could make this right, that this would all be seen as a very unfortunate accident and a big mistake on Quinn's part.

Unfortunately, the arraignment had been postponed by almost a month due to the backlog of cases. This left him cooling his heels in the lock-up at the local police station.

As prisons went, Quinn supposed it could be worse. His youth would have paid him no favours in General Population at an actual provincial penitentiary. But it wasn't exactly a picnic in the park either. During his first week, the police officers treated him like he was scum. They cast cutting glances and muttered curses toward the strange boy in lock-up. Sometimes they would hit the holding cell bars if they noticed he was about to drift off, preventing him from sleeping. After all, he'd hurt one of their own. In their eyes, he needed to pay for it. Quinn understood their anger toward him. The guilt he felt at the thought that he was the one responsible for Officer Kendry's injuries gnawed away at him every single day, like a corrosive acid.

It drove Quinn to ask one of the cops for a pen and paper. Without his lawyer's knowledge, Quinn wrote Officer Kendry a letter. In it, he took responsibility for hurting the man and expressed his sincerest regrets for what he'd done. He still couldn't explain why he'd done it. But he couldn't live with himself if he didn't apologize. He even asked if there was anything he could do to make amends.

Officer Kendry's partner, Officer Fields, was the one to deliver

Quinn's letter. She'd read it over beforehand with a surprised look on her face. Word must have gotten out around the precinct, because Quinn noticed a shift in how the officers treated him after that.

They moved him out of the shared holding pen into a private cell. This one had real walls with a barred window, a padded cot and his own toilet and sink. It wasn't much, but it was nicer than where he'd been before, so he took the victory, sure that he wouldn't have to stay here for much longer.

And he kept telling himself that, until September 22, when everything changed.

It was Quinn's eighteenth birthday. He was supposed to be starting his internship at the local community college that month to help cover his tuition fees. Instead, Officer Fields showed up with a cupcake, a single light blue candle stuck into the buttercream frosting. She also explained the new wrinkle in Quinn's case.

Since he was now eighteen, he was too old to be tried as a juvenile and thus would not be sent to a juvenile detention facility. It also meant that he'd lose his government-provided housing, since he was neither in school nor working. His room in the group home would be reassigned, and what few possessions he had would be boxed up and stored away until all this ugliness was over. Quinn cried himself to sleep that night. Artie often visited, keeping him informed. Apparently, Quinn's case had quite a bit of local media coverage; there likely wasn't a single adult in the tricity area who didn't know the details. Whenever a cop was killed or seriously injured, people took notice.

Quinn guessed he should consider himself lucky that his situation was the latter. If Kendry had died, he would surely be rotting in a provincial prison, alongside hardened murders and rapists instead of his small-town precinct jail.

Even though the officer had lived through his severe injuries, the prosecutor wanted to make an example of Quinn. After all, he had done damage to public property and attacked a police officer, causing him a grave injury. He would have to be punished to the fullest extent of the law. That could mean up to seven years in hard lock-up. Being tried as an adult would mean that his criminal record would follow him for the rest of his life, and finding a job or rental living accommodations would be next to impossible. No plea deal was offered.

It left Quinn no choice but to take his chances at trial.

After the arraignment, a trial date was set for the beginning of March. To his credit, Artie fought to keep Quinn in the precinct rather than in a provincial prison while he waited for his day in court, as he didn't have the financial means to post bail.

Remarkably, both Officers Kendry and Fields had written recommendations on his behalf. Given his youth, the fact that the toxicology report showed he didn't have any drugs or alcohol in his system, and that this was his first offence, the judge saw fit to grant his request, much to Quinn's relief.

Throughout the autumn and into the winter, Quinn earned the trust of the police in whose precinct he'd become a de facto resident. During the day, he volunteered to help the office administrator with her paperwork and filing. He also assisted the janitor in keeping the bathrooms and break room clean and always made sure to keep the precinct stocked with freshly brewed coffee and tea. As a reward for his hard work, they'd given him an air mattress, hand-me-down blankets, and a pillow. They let him use their showers and gave him police-issued sweats and t-shirts to wear. Instead of the disgusting mush that passed as food for the prisoners, Quinn got semi-decent, frozen microwavable dinners. They'd even stopped handcuffing him.

Around Christmas, Officer Fields brought him a stack of old paperback novels. She explained that the collection of mostly mystery thrillers had been some of her favourites when she'd been Quinn's age. The sweet gesture brought tears to Quinn's eyes.

For all this, the young man was grateful. His time here could have been a lot worse, and he was acutely aware of that. The only issue was, he knew this couldn't last. After the trial, there was no telling what his future could hold. That terrified Quinn most of all.

☙

At the beginning of January, Artie had come to break the bad news.

"Listen, Quinn. I know you meant no harm that night, nor even meant to be there. But that leaves me wondering what you *were* doing there. You say you can't remember, and I'm inclined to believe you, but honestly, the whole thing makes me think there's something wrong with you, medically speaking. When they brought you in, despite the fact there were no drugs in your system, you were disoriented—almost non-responsive—but certainly not violent. I even talked to Officer Kendry, and yeah, he was pissed at you initially, but he seems to have warmed up to you somehow. Even he says there was something strange going on with you that night. He said he'd never seen anything like it before in all his years on the force."

"So, what are you saying?" Quinn nervously felt his fingers rise to twist his hair as he listened to his defence attorney. "You think I'll be free to go soon?"

"No, thing is, this is still a serious offence. They have you on video, son. There's no denying that it was you who shoved Kendry. Our only option, if you don't want to end up in prison—and I mean *real* prison—is if we plead not guilty by reason of mental disease or defect. I've already contacted an old friend to do an evaluation. She'll be here in two weeks."

Quinn had been unable to say anything else after Artie's announcement. What could he say, really? Either he had attacked the officer on purpose, or there was something wrong with him.

Quinn realized it was the latter. He knew in his heart that something was very wrong. He just didn't know what it would mean for his future if he admitted that to the authorities. Artie's words "mental disease or defect" rang in his brain at all times like a taunting bully. Somehow, they felt ominous. Like a death sentence.

Couldn't the judge see the last several months I've spent at the precinct as time served? I could volunteer for more community service too. They already know me, and I know my way around here. I could get back to the group home. I just have to restart my internship with the college at the start of the next semester, and then I'll get my housing back. Quinn strategized to himself as he waited for the meeting to happen.

I just have to convince this friend of Artie's that I'm no threat, that it was an accident and it will never happen again. And then this whole nightmare will be over. Everything will go back to normal.

☙

Quinn's plan stayed at the forefront of his mind as he was led from his cell, exactly two weeks after Artie's visit. The guard inside the visitors' room swung open the door at the end of the hall upon Quinn's approach and steered him toward a seat opposite an older woman, whose steely gaze bore holes through Quinn as he sat down. The officer made to handcuff Quinn to the table, as he would any other criminal under these circumstances, but the woman told him not to worry about that and shooed him away.

Pointedly avoiding eye contact, Quinn's gaze followed the back of his security escort as they left the room. The cop on the inside of the visiting chambers shut the door behind him and leaned against it. Knowing there was now no escaping this evaluation, Quinn turned to face the woman. He swallowed the bile that rose in his throat. Broken fragments of memories flashed through his mind of the day he had become a ward of the state. There had been a woman then that reminded him very much of the one in front of him. Only that woman had been a social worker. She'd wanted to help him and assured him over and over that everything would be okay. But that was the day his life had changed for the worse. With a clenched jaw and balled fists, he did his best to push all of those thoughts and feelings aside and deal with the problem at hand.

Likely in her late forties or early fifties, this new woman had pinched features, made all the more so by the tight bun pulling back her greying, dark hair. By the look on her face, Quinn guessed that he wasn't exactly what she had expected. She'd probably been anticipating some burly, tattooed punk with a shaved head, or at the very least, someone easily capable of overpowering a seasoned police officer. Acutely aware of Artie's absence as the woman scrutinized him, Quinn cleared his throat and voiced his concern. "I hate to be rude, but where's Mr. McMullin? Shouldn't my lawyer be present for this conversation?"

The woman blinked, apparently surprised at his civility. "Your lawyer thought it would be best if the two of us could talk alone. I'm Dr. Joan Lisbon," she said. Her practiced tone was soothing and reassuring as she offered her hand, now that she had decided the young man in front of her was no threat. The smile twisting her thin lips, however, didn't quite reach her coldly analytical eyes.

"Quinn, Quinn Smith, but you already knew that," he responded, taking her hand and giving it a professional shake, as if he were at a job interview. "So, based on what Artie said and the fact that you called yourself *doctor*, I take it you're some sort of therapist?"

"Psychiatrist, to be precise, but good guess," she corrected. "You seem like a smart kid. I'm guessing you know why I'm here."

Quinn instinctively crossed his arms tightly across his chest but tried to keep his voice as steady as possible and his tone cordial. "I understand that Artie needs you to speak with me to help my defence. I take it from your presence here that must mean he thinks there's something wrong with me, mentally. That I'm crazy." He knew the man was trying to help him, sending this woman to evaluate him, yet he couldn't shake the insult he felt levelled at him through the action.

"Not crazy," Dr. Lisbon adjusted herself slightly in her seat. "We're just trying to make sense of what happened that night, I suppose; find out why you did what you did."

Quinn kept his cool, despite the growing knot of anxiety in his chest. "I already told him and the cops and the prosecutor. And after more than four months, my answer is still the same: I don't know."

"That's why I'm here." Dr. Lisbon looked downwards to a file laying open in her lap. "I've done a bit of research on you, Quinn, and I have to say, I'm a little confused by what I've found."

"What do you mean?" Quinn asked the question, but he understood what she meant. He knew that there were holes in his life. Things from the past, when his dad and mom were alive, that he couldn't seem to remember, no matter how hard he tried.

But he also hoped that those memory gaps wouldn't matter. After all, he knew he was a good person and was certain that anyone who knew him well would agree. He worked hard, got good grades in school, and if the library situation hadn't happened, he would have been halfway through his internship and on his way to college.

Dr. Lisbon shuffled her papers. "Well, let's see. According to your file, you lived in a series of foster homes since you were six years old. There was a short time—I believe you were about fourteen—when you were classified as a runaway. Is that correct?"

Quinn bit back the sarcastic commentary that he normally used as a shield in these situations. He wanted to approach this interview with some kind of strategy. Instead, he found himself lost in the memory of Andi, his best friend and foster sister at the time. They'd run away from an abusive group home together.

Every day was a constant struggle to feed themselves, find shelter from the elements, and keep up with basic hygiene. After about three months, Andi couldn't take it. He'd tried to stop her, to lift her spirits, and give her hope that their situation would change, but she lost herself in a needle and then disappeared entirely. He finally found her, a few months later, in his new panhandling spot, strung out and shaking from an overdose. He'd done his best to save her, put her into a rusty, abandoned shopping cart and wheeled her to the nearest hospital. Due to their age, social workers were called, and Quinn found himself in a new foster home by the end of the week. Andi, on the other hand, didn't make it out of her hospital bed. She was buried in a government-run cemetery days later.

"Quinn?"

Dr. Lisbon's voice shook him from the memory. "Sorry, Doctor. One year. That's how long I was homeless. My foster sister Andi and I thought we could do better on our own. We learned within a week that we couldn't."

"And you now live in the suburbs, at a group home for those transitioning out of foster care?" she prodded.

"Yeah, I've got government housing until I graduate from college or, at least I did. I'm not so sure what happens now. And honestly, I hope when this is over that I can get back to my life there. I mean, it's a pretty good arrangement," Quinn rushed to say. He'd had some rather ugly experiences in the past, but this was one of the few times he could remember since entering the system that he was genuinely happy with where he lived. "The building was decent, I liked having a manager rather than a foster parent, and the other tenants were actually pretty nice. I even liked my room. I would be there right now if it weren't for…the stuff that happened in the library…" Quinn trailed off, suddenly seized by his guilt over the incident that had landed him in this mess in the first place.

"Yes, we'll get to the library incident in just a minute. For now, I'd like to focus on the past. I think it holds the key to understanding what happened that night in August." Dr. Lisbon said, her voice bordering on clinical. "While your life is well documented from your time in foster care until today, there are no records before that. No birth certificate, no hospital or school records. Nothing. Why is that?"

"I don't even know what to tell you. I was just a little kid. I don't know what happened to my birth certificate or any of that other stuff," Quinn kept a respectful tone despite his discomfort. "You're the expert, Doctor. You must have the police report and medical records from when I was handed over to Youth Services."

Dr. Lisbon shook her head. "I don't. Would you mind filling me in?" she asked.

Quinn had a persistent feeling that she might indeed have the information, but if this was how she wanted to play the situation, he would tell her what he knew.

"Sure, I guess," he said with a shrug of his shoulders. "No one really knows who I am. Not even me. Apparently, some old man found me washed up on the side of the river when I was six. Well, that's what they guess, anyway. The police were never able to track down my parents or figure out where I came from."

The doctor scribbled notes in her file but didn't respond. Quinn tried not to let her pen scratching against the paper fray his nerves. Instead, he waited to continue until after she'd finished writing.

"When I was pulled from the riverbank, I had no idea who I was or how I got there." Quinn cocked his head to the side thoughtfully as he recounted the events that had landed him in foster care. "Still don't, actually. I believe they call it acute amnesia. The doctors thought over time I'd remember, but it's been over a decade, and I don't remember anything specific. I have impressions, though, like the vague memory of having a father. I wouldn't be able to tell you his name, where he worked, or even what he looked like, only that I knew him and was safe then. Memories of my mom are pretty much nonexistent. I was found wearing a jacket with my first name printed on the tag in permanent marker. You know, like how some parents write on their kids' clothes so they don't lose them at school? That's the only reason I know my name is Quinn."

Dr. Lisbon listened intently, flicking her nails against her thumb in between her note-taking as she took in his story.

"Seeing as they never found out who I really was, there were no birth or medical records, or any official documents of any kind," Quinn concluded. These details of his past profoundly upset him. Or rather, not being able to remember much more than what he'd shared already was a sore point for him. But in the intervening twelve years, he'd learned to deal with it well enough to give this virtual stranger a rough play-by-play of his most guarded and sacred memories.

"Yet there seemed to be a few medical events that popped up afterward," the doctor noted, tapping the paper in front of her.

"I broke my arm once when I fell from the school jungle gym, if that's what you're talking about. I would hardly call that 'a few events.'" Quinn was confused; why was she so concerned with medical records?

"I have two boys of my own." Dr. Lisbon smiled genuinely for the first time since meeting him. "Breaks and bruises are to be expected from an active child, but that's not what I'm referring to."

Anxiety crept along Quinn's spine. Here they finally were, getting to the main reason she was here: to confirm if he was mentally unstable.

"Then what are you referring to?" he asked.

Dr. Lisbon readjusted her bun, her expression puzzled. "You honestly don't remember?"

"Remember what?" Irritation was beginning to seep into Quinn's voice. Why couldn't she just spit out what she wanted him to know and get it over with? He couldn't explain why, but this line of questioning was making him feel nervous.

"I was talking to Carol Thompson. You remember her, right?"

Hearing the woman's name helped calm Quinn down as he recalled her round, freckled face and wild cascade of frizzy red hair. "She was one of my foster parents," he said slowly, a small, inadvertent smile gracing his features. "I liked her, she always smelled like sugar cookies. And she'd bake each of her foster kids our favourite kind of cake for our birthdays. Nice lady."

"Seemed she liked you too," Dr. Lisbon observed. "Said you were one of the best-behaved boys she ever cared for: quiet, often kept to yourself, but still played with others. If reminded. You had a very active imagination and spent most of your time reading."

"Lots of kids did there," Quinn replied. "Ms. Carol didn't believe kids should be raised on cable, but there was always the library. She encouraged all of us to love reading."

"Yes, but unlike the others, you didn't just read story books or novels. You read textbooks, instructional guides, cookbooks, electronics manuals—not exactly kid reading." Dr. Lisbon looked at him over her notes, her gaze fixed upon his eyes.

Quinn's lip curled slightly as he shifted in his seat, attempting to appear less slouched. "I like to know how to do things. Is that a crime?" he tried to keep his tone light and appropriately humorous. He didn't want her to see how much this was starting to bother him.

"Only if it results in you breaking and entering, causing significant damage to public property, and assaulting a police officer." Dr. Lisbon shot him a look that Quinn could only interpret as disapproval wrapped in professional condescension. And she had a point. Accident or not, he had caused someone to get badly hurt.

He hung his head, defensive posture draining from him like a punctured balloon. "I didn't mean to do that. I hope you know that. I hope Officer Kendry knows that. I have been working in whatever capacity I can to prove to everyone just how sorry I am for what I did."

The cloud of disapproval that hung about Dr. Lisbon seemed to dissipate as she spoke. "Yes, I heard about your volunteering around the precinct, and Officer Kendry showed me the letter you wrote him. I know you didn't mean to hurt anyone. But I'm not going to lie to you, Quinn, he damaged a few of his vertebrae, and the break in his leg was quite messy. It's going to take a lot of physical therapy for him to be able to walk normally again."

Quinn instinctively drew his arms and legs closer to his chest as guilt swept over him in a wave. "I'm so sorry," he whispered, every word sincere.

"I know you are, Quinn." Dr. Lisbon shifted in her seat. "However, I think that what happened that night wasn't your first episode."

"Episode?" Quinn echoed. He did not like the sound of that word in the slightest.

"Ms. Carol told me about an incident that happened during your first year with her. You would have been about ten. It was early March, spring break, and the older kids at the house were spring cleaning. Apparently, you were all so busy, most of you didn't have much time for anything else, especially not reading for pleasure. You were all too tired each day to do anything but sleep. It took about five days to get the whole place clean. At the end of it, you stole all the textbooks in the house, including those of the other children, which you apparently snatched right out of backpacks and bedrooms. You took them all to your room and locked yourself in." Dr. Lisbon paused, noticing the confused expression moving across the young man's face. "You don't remember any of this, do you?"

Quinn's eyes slid away from her, his thoughts far away as he tried to recall the incident. He shook his head. He had no idea what she was talking about.

"You wouldn't leave your room for anything other than the bathroom. In fact, you barely seemed to realize that anyone else was there," Dr. Lisbon continued. "Ms. Carol brought you your meals, which you barely touched, and when she sent you to bed, you took the books with you and continued reading through the night. When she found you still reading the next day and tried to make you stop, you lashed out at her."

Quinn tensed in his chair. He would have never hurt Ms. Carol! It disturbed him to consider that he could have injured her, whether he was aware of it or not. Why couldn't he remember this?

"You didn't hurt her. It was just verbal," Dr. Lisbon answered his silent question. "But right after, you fell into an almost...catatonic state. You were taken to the hospital, but doctors couldn't find anything *physically* wrong with you. You recovered quickly, and the doctors concluded that you had just exhausted yourself. Similar incidents happened on three more occasions during your time in foster care. It's one of the primary reasons you were bounced around so much. No one had any idea what was wrong with you or what to do with you."

Quinn shook his head, still in denial. "I don't remember any of this. I—I'm sorry, Doctor. I really don't remember."

"To be honest, that's not surprising. Can you describe what you felt leading up to the night of your arrest?"

Quinn furrowed his brow as he tried to recall the events. "I was tired. I'd been helping Mr. Reynolds fix up some of the classrooms at the skills centre. I have—had a job lined up with him, helping some of the instructors, cleaning classrooms, doing errands. Anything I was set to earn would have gone toward my tuition. Mr. Reynolds said I might be able to start taking classes come September. Or, at least I would have if, you know, all this hadn't happened." Quinn gestured to the police precinct walls that surrounded them.

"What about the library?" Dr. Lisbon pressed. "How did you end up there? Help me understand."

Quinn rested his hands on the table, steepling his fingers as he spoke. "I was walking back from the skills centre, and I suddenly felt...I don't know, anxious. Restless. Or, like I was going to be sick."

"So you went to the library, even though it was closed?"

"I saw it just up the block, so I went," he answered, as if it were the most logical of explanations. "I guess I didn't think about whether it was open or closed."

"Why?" she prodded. "Why the library in particular?"

"Because I thought it would make me feel better," Quinn replied honestly. That sounded strange, and he knew it. But at the time, it felt

G.E. White

right. "Reading also makes me feel calm."

"And after that? What happened after you decided to go to the library?"

Quinn shrugged and shook his head. "No idea. That's when things get hazy."

Dr. Lisbon closed Quinn's medical file, shuffling it to the bottom of the documents in her lap before opening up another folder.

"According to the police report, you picked the lock with a paperclip. The door was pretty old and could have been kicked in with enough force. So why did you pick the lock?"

Quinn turned his gaze toward his fingers, seemingly inspecting their length as he spoke. "This might sound far-fetched…" Quinn started, unsure if the doctor would take him seriously or not.

"Try me."

"Okay, so when I was younger, I was really into how magicians pulled off their illusions. I remember reading about how they used to pick locks to pull off those crazy escape tricks. That sounds unbelievable, I know. But I can remember everything I read. It stays etched in my brain." Quinn shifted in his seat embarrassed.

"And that's how you knew what to do?" Dr. Lisbon pressed forward, confident she was getting close to the reasoning behind Quinn's night at the library and clearly intrigued by his confession.

"I think so. It's not like someone randomly taught me how to pick a lock. And as I already told you, I don't remember what really happened that night. This is my best guess," Quinn replied.

The psychologist sighed. "You remember how I called the incident when you were ten an 'episode'? Well, I think that what you experienced the night of your arrest was another of these episodes."

"Episodes of what?" Quinn swallowed heavily as he asked, his heart starting to pound in his chest.

"That, unfortunately, is not as easy to diagnose. What people witnessed that night, and what you described, have the markers of several different disorders," she explained. "First, you display overt obsessive-compulsive tendencies when it comes to books. You said you became anxious and felt unwell until you gave in to your urge to read. Your obsession almost borders on bibliomania, though your focus is on reading, not collecting books. But what really concerns me are your periods of catatonic excitement and the stupor that follows."

Quinn recoiled, almost as if he had been struck. "What exactly does that mean?"

The doctor grimaced, and Quinn was sure he would not like what she said next.

"Your sudden compulsion to read books is not normal," she stated. "When you enter into one of your reading fugues, you become frenzied in your movements: talking to yourself and disregarding anything that doesn't have to do with what you're reading, including food, hygiene, sleep, even human contact."

She continued somberly, not meeting his eyes. "You build a wall around yourself that you can't seem to escape from. The only options for your relief seem to be you feeding this compulsion until you crash, or someone pulling you out of it, leaving you manic and disoriented, which is what I believe happened that night," the doctor elaborated.

Quinn's blunt fingernails dug into the soft tissue of his palms, leaving crescent-shaped wounds behind as his body clenched in tension. "So, what does it all mean?" he asked.

Dr. Lisbon bit her lower lip. "I believe that you're showing the early signs of catatonic schizophrenia, and don't let the name fool you," she said, stumbling over her words. "It doesn't mean that you become unresponsive. If anything, you seem to display frequent episodes of catatonic excitement, instead of stupors—at least to begin with."

"Catatonic excitement?" he echoed, trying to keep the tremor from his voice.

"Well, it's as I described, basically, it's how you become frenzied in your pursuit to read, and when your movements are harried and sometimes purposeless." Dr. Lisbon sighed. "Your susceptibility to agitation is high, and you're likely to turn violent when interrupted," she continued. "The disorder usually manifests in people in their teens to early twenties, but with the right..."

As Quinn listened to the diagnosis a wave of dread and despair washed over him. His shoulders hitched as he cradled his face in his hands and sobbed, his breaths heaving with short gasps. Dr. Lisbon fell silent as she listened to his weeping.

Mentally cringing at his weakness as the last remnants of his emotional control crumbled, it took several minutes for Quinn to regain his composure. Objectively he knew that suffering from mental illness was nothing to be ashamed of. Like cancer, or heart disease it could affect anyone and no one was a fault for the illnesses that befell them. Still the social stigma of mental illness that would now follow him weighed heavy on Quinn. He wiped fruit-lessly at his eyes, the tears continuing to well and occasionally slip down his cheek.

He hated to admit it, but her words made sense. His past actions combined with the library incident were all pieces he had desperately been trying to fit together these past long months. Perhaps he had known that something was not normal with him this whole time but needed a professional voice to fully accept the truth about his mental health. It was time he faced this head-on.

"What do I do now?" he croaked.

"You shouldn't be in jail," Dr. Lisbon stated with certainty. "You need help."

"You're saying I should agree with McMullin's motion, that I should take the insanity plea?"

Dr. Lisbon's fingers twitched, as if itching to reach out and grasp his hand. Her professionalism kept her actions in check. "I hate the word *insanity* because it's a legal term, not a medical one. But yes, I believe it would be the best course of action," she replied.

Quinn nodded mechanically, his brain still straining to fathom what he had just heard.

The guard by the door made eye contact with the doctor and tapped his watch.

"It looks like I have to go. Perhaps I could come back," she said, attempting to be reassuring.

"That's okay, you don't have to," Quinn replied. This wasn't her problem to carry, he reminded himself numbly. And to be honest, he felt that another visit with her would only depress him further.

"Well, I could at least contact Mr. McMullin if you want." Dr. Lisbon was resolute in her sincerity.

Quinn bobbed his head in agreement. "Okay. Tell him to do it, please."

"You mean, go through with the motion?"

"Yeah," he replied as the doctor stood and pushed in her seat.

She nodded her head in acknowledgement and turned to leave.

"Oh, and Dr. Lisbon?"

She paused. "Yes?"

"Thanks for being honest with me," Quinn said sincerely. "And for offering me help. I just want this to all be over soon."

The doctor's lower lip trembled for a moment as she gave a stiff nod of her head before turning and leaving the room.

Quinn slumped farther into his seat, heart beating heavily in his chest.

What was going to happen now? Would he ever be okay again?

G.E. White

CHAPTER THREE

THE PATIENTS IN Cedar Hills Mental Health Facility shuffled aimlessly across the activity room in their hospital-issued scrubs, dressing robes, and slippers. Quinn stood beside the portly Nurse Belamy, watching their slow progression. He shuddered, thinking of the endless monotony of their days. Nurse Belamy gave him a pat on the shoulder, one Quinn supposed was meant to be reassuring. "Don't worry, honey, it's not forever," she said.

He nodded solemnly. No, technically it wasn't forever; just until he was deemed to no longer be a threat to society or himself—a lifetime, perhaps.

Artie McMullin had done his job. Quinn had been found not guilty on all charges of breaking and entering, destruction of public property, and assaulting a police officer. Unfortunately, this was all due to his insanity plea.

Quinn reflected on these turns of events solemnly as he looked over the activity room of Cedar Hills, which was located just outside of town. The drained faces of the other patients filled him with mounting dread. Many reflected pain, while others were seemingly resigned to their fate.

Quinn stepped away from Nurse Belamy to wander over to the window, her earlier words of comfort ringing in his ears.

☙

"This will be your room," Nurse Belamy said cheerfully as she swung open a door to reveal a sparsely furnished room with two narrow cots and a pair of rickety dressers. "We're a little crowded at the moment, so you'll be sharing with Jeremy."

"And why is he here?" he asked.

She shot him a curious, wary look.

"I'm just wondering if I'm sharing a room with Hannibal Lecter or something," he said. Quinn knew he was in no position to judge another for their mental illness, but a heads-up would be appreciated.

Nurse Belamy gave a dark chuckle. "Jeremy may have an eating disorder, but not a taste for human flesh."

Quinn placed his small duffle bag, carrying the few possessions he had been allowed to bring, on the end of one of the battered cots.

"Now, as you're still fairly young, the doctors have decided to refrain from prescribing any antipsychotic medication, however, they do want to start you on a regimen of medication for anxiety and depression. They will review this decision when you turn nineteen, or in the case of your episodes turning violent again."

Quinn's stomach lurched at her words. He wasn't sure if it was the fact that he might be put on a powerful medication or the news that he would be here until he was at least nineteen, an event six months away. Nurse Belamy continued her tirade, unaware of Quinn's inner turmoil. "All meals are served in the cafeteria down the hall. Breakfast is from seven thirty to nine, lunch from noon till one, and dinner from five till seven. You'll be having group therapy sessions every other day, starting tomorrow, in the Wittman Lounge at eleven o'clock. The dress code is casual, though we would prefer you to be out of your pyjamas. Unfortunately, we couldn't locate your personal effects, so we've provided scrubs, towels and your basic toiletries."

"You'll also have one-on-one therapy sessions with Dr. Salazar every Monday, Wednesday, and Friday at one thirty," she continued. "Other than that, you'll be free to roam the halls or make use of the activity room, courtyard, lounge, or library. As long as you behave yourself," she added as a grimly amused afterthought.

Quinn tried to smile at the jibe, though it probably came out as more of a grimace. He supposed he should get used to the verbal barbs and reminders of his epic cock-up, as this was his life now.

☙

Nurse Belamy led him from the room for a tour of the rest of the facility. Along with the resident doctors' personal offices, there were a handful of conference rooms where group therapy sessions could be held. There was also a large cafeteria, a rec room that housed some games and a single bookshelf, a visitors' area, a couple nurses' stations, and dorm-like bathrooms with multiple stalls and showers. The basement housed the laundry, boiler room and, to Quinn's grim surprise, a morgue. Having finally been shown all the areas accessible to him, Quinn took some time to study the other patients.

They varied in age, race, and gender. A Japanese woman with a blank expression on her face silently worked on a jigsaw puzzle, while her visiting male relative looked on encouragingly. An elderly white man in his eighties was parked in front of the television in a wheelchair. His head was thrown back and his mouth gaped as he slept through the opening theme of *Law and Order*. Another man, probably not much older than Quinn himself, paced the room and muttered. Outside in the courtyard, two women sat on one of the benches. The older of the two, a Black woman, perhaps in her late thirties, puffed a cigarette, while the other, a pale and weary-looking blonde woman, kicked dispassionately at the soggy grass beneath her feet. Quinn saw his future self reflected in their faces and grew cold with fear.

He trudged back along the corridors toward the room he was to share with the still-absent Jeremy. Quinn lay on the covers of his bed, his head turned sideways on the pillow as he stared at the muted olive wall before him.

It was over.

Everything that Quinn had worked for: his good grades, the home he'd been living in, the job that would have helped him go to college one day—all gone. Who knew when he'd get out of this place? Any hopes and dreams he might have had were permanently on hold. Even if he got out of here in record time, there would be few doors still open for a man who had been incarcerated at a mental facility.

Quinn felt the back of his throat begin to close as he thought about the future he no longer had. He buried his face in the pillow and choked back a sob, praying for the oblivion of sleep. Perhaps then he would wake to find all of this was no more than a horrific nightmare.

❧

The cold city wind whipped against his cheeks as Quinn was pulled through the streets by an older man. The latter's features were hard to discern as he continued to face forward, his hand clasped tightly around Quinn's as he tugged the boy along.

And a boy he was, Quinn realized, as he looked up at the back of the man's head. His small legs pumped hard to keep up with the man's pace as his equally small lungs struggled for air.

G.E. White

Quinn noticed that his other hand was squeezing something soft and fluffy. Looking down, he could only make out a small, white and yellow plush toy—a stuffed animal.

"What's going on? Where are we going?" asked Quinn's child self, worriedly. The tall man didn't answer, occasionally glancing behind them as they hurried along. Quinn looked over his shoulder, too, but saw nothing—just an empty street, tapering into darkness. So what were they fleeing from?

The man put on a burst of speed as he and Quinn approached a long bridge connecting the mainland and what appeared to be a barely visible island in the distance. A dog growled in front of them, and the man stopped short, pulling Quinn to a sudden halt.

Quinn trembled at the sight of the large dog and a human-like figure standing behind it. Though they stood directly before him, a haze seemed to block Quinn from seeing the details of their features, making their identity a mystery.

"Please," the man holding Quinn's hand rasped. "You don't need to do this. You can pretend you never saw us."

The shrouded figure silently stared at Quinn's protector, immobile.

The man grasping Quinn's hand faltered.

"That's not all you're here for, is it?"

This time, the figure looked away, almost ashamed, as the dog's growl dwindled into a whine.

Quinn's companion bowed his head. "That's okay. I'm ready. But please, pretend you didn't see him."

The sound of multiple footsteps approaching quickly from behind caused the man to tighten the grip on Quinn's hand. They would be there soon.

The shadowy figure lowered its head for a moment but then waved a hand in a dismissive gesture. What did that mean? Was he letting them leave? Why were they being chased in the first place?

"Thank you," the man holding Quinn's hand said, before crouching down to the boy's level.

Quinn could make out the stubble on the face in front of him, but not much else. The tall man seized the boy in a fierce hug and brushed a kiss on top of Quinn's head.

"I need you to do something for me," he croaked. "You have to swim; swim as hard as you can till you reach the shore."

Quinn dropped the stuffed animal onto the ground and returned the hug, nodding his consent. It was strange, his mind was racing, telling him not to obey, to rail against the request, but it was as if he had no control over his actions and was simply a puppet in some pantomime.

The man pulled away, his lips trembling as he attempted to hide his grief.

"I'm sorry," he choked out.

But before Quinn could ask what the man was sorry for, he was lifted and dropped over the side of the bridge. The water below rushed toward him.

⁊

Quinn was jolted awake by cold water dripping down his face. Sputtering, he wiped the water from his eyes to see a bug-eyed man in his late twenties looming over him with an empty plastic cup in hand.

"Oh good," the mystery man said wryly. "I thought you were dead."

"What the hell?! I was sleeping; didn't you notice I was breathing?" Quinn shouted as he dried his face with the sleeve of his hoodie.

"Sometimes, after a person dies, the air vacating the body makes it look like it's exhaling," the man explained.

Quinn opened and closed his mouth soundlessly, the words he had been thinking refusing to pass his lips. *Was this guy for real?*

He blinked up at the skeletal young man with thinning brown hair. "And you didn't think to wait and see if I inhaled?" he asked, reaching

G.E. White

to grab his facility-provided towel from the night stand.

The other man cocked his head to the side, bird-like. "I guess I didn't think that far. Regardless, I'm just happy you're alive. If you'd died, I'd probably end up sharing a room with Paul again, and that man is a slob. But then, what do you expect from a hoarder? I'm Jeremy by the way."

Did this guy even pause to breathe? "I'm Quinn."

"Yeah, I know," Jeremy said, moving to sit on his own bed. "This is my first time rooming with an honest-to-god schizophrenic."

Surprised, Quinn stopped towelling off his shirt. "You know about that?"

"Oh please. Everybody knows."

The utter dread that Quinn had felt before intensified. Great, not only was he stuck here, but he was also gossip fodder for whatever passed as a social circle here.

"Anyone who is not *completely* off the deep end makes it their business to know what everyone else's problems are. Keeps our minds off our own problems for a while," Jeremy explained.

Quinn studied the older man in front of him, wondering just what sort of problems he suffered from.

Jeremy rolled his abnormally large eyes, giving a huff of exasperation. "Before you ask or jump to conclusions, I am not anorexic or bulimic. I don't have body-image or self-esteem issues. Yes, I do have an eating disorder, but not because I'm worried about getting fat."

"Then what exactly is your deal?" Quinn was still annoyed by the cup of water his new roommate had dumped on his head, so he let his words come out as blunt as they were in his head.

The thin man sulked. "I'm just worried that there might be something sharp in my food that could cut my throat."

Quinn nodded, gazing down at the blankets he was sitting on, instantly aware of the reality of Jeremy's issue and slightly guilty for snapping at him. It probably would have sounded silly to most people, but Quinn took it seriously—he had seen what fear and anxiety could do to a person. After a moment, he suddenly looked up. "Have you tried mashed potatoes?"

Jeremy barked out a laugh. "That's what they've been using to keep me up and running, but I think they switched the actual mashed potatoes for some sort of high-protein gruel."

The other man's wry humour earned the first genuine smile from Quinn since he had arrived at Cedar Hills.

"Speaking of which, it's six o'clock. Mealtime," Jeremy continued, gesturing for Quinn to rise.

Quinn furrowed his brow. "You have a problem with eating, yet you want me to go down to get dinner with you?"

"If I didn't, I'd get in trouble from Nurse Carl." The shudder that coursed through Jeremy's frame signalled that was one of the last things they would want.

Quinn nodded absently as he stood and followed Jeremy down the hall. "Is that the only reason? To stay out of trouble?"

Jeremy had the decency to look guilty. "Well, there is one thing I could use your help with."

CHAPTER FOUR

QUINN DRAGGED HIS spoon through the puddle that had once been Jeremy's mashed potatoes. "Dude, I don't see anything," he said.

"You're sure?"

"These are no longer mashed potatoes, this is potato soup. There is nothing even remotely sharp in this," Quinn assured his roommate.

Jeremy raised his gaze from the plate before him, his expression solemn. "You think so?"

"Yeah, I'm pretty sure," Quinn said, trying to give the other young man an encouraging smile. "Now, if we're done dissecting your food, perhaps, I can eat mine?"

"Oh, yeah, sure, go ahead," Jeremy replied, eyeing his spoonful of liquid mashed potatoes with suspicion.

Quinn sighed heavily; he figured he wasn't in any position to judge.

He bit down on his own spoonful of peas and twisted his face in displeasure.

Great, they were already cold.

Quinn dropped his spoon, dejected, and turned toward the garden just outside the cafeteria window.

It was almost the end of March, and there were still some small piles of snow left over from the last death throes of the Canadian winter. Already, plant life was awakening, weeds springing up between the yellow blades of grass. Quinn tried to take comfort from the view before him. Perhaps he should be resilient in the face of his confinement, just like the stubborn little sprouts, but truth be told, he could hardly bring himself to care.

Dusk was starting to fall, so when he noticed a small light fluttering around from leaf to leaf, Quinn took notice. March was hardly the time for fireflies, and the strange blue light didn't seem as if it belonged to the luminescent bugs.

Quinn peered intently at the light as it drew close to the window glass.

It was at this point that he began to seriously consider the possibility that he was right where he belonged, for there, as if stepping directly from the pages of *Peter Pan,* stood a faerie on the windowsill.

Cloaked in fresh green leaves, the fae's tiny body gave off a soft blue glow that enhanced the sheen of his sapphire hair. The faerie plastered himself against the windowpane as he looked over the patients. Making eye contact with Quinn, the tiny man waved his hand in greeting.

Quinn tore his eyes away from the window, his heart racing. This couldn't be happening. *This must be the result of stress or sleep deprivation,* he reasoned to himself. In his peripheral vision, he saw the little fae tap on the window again in an attempt to regain Quinn's attention. No one else appeared to hear or see the creature, and after a minute or two of being ignored, the faerie shrugged and

G.E. White

flew from the windowsill.

Quinn took a quick glance at the window to make sure his visitor was gone and whipped around to face Jeremy.

"Did you see that?"

"See what?" Jeremy asked, raising his gaze from his plate.

Of course, Jeremy hadn't seen anything; Quinn was the one with schizophrenia, not him. Did he really expect the man to confirm his vision? And even if he did, also being a patient here, would his confirmation make him feel any better? After a long moment, Quinn simply shook his head. "Nothing, never mind."

Jeremy's face lit up. "You just had a hallucination, didn't you? That is so cool! What was it?"

"Cool?! I just sat here and accommodated your psychological hang-up and you think that the slow deterioration of my mental faculties is cool?!" Quinn hissed, the anger at his situation boiling to the surface. Jeremy stared at him as if he had grown a second head.

Jeremy's shoulders slouched in apology. "Sorry, poor choice of words."

Quinn rolled his eyes as he sighed. "But seriously, how is hallucinating cool, especially when we're in here?"

"It's not, really," Jeremy conceded, his expression turning sympathetic. "Actually, it's a pretty bad sign, but I've never met anyone who's had them before and I've been here for four years."

Jeremy's words only further reminded Quinn that even among the patients of Cedar Hills he was an anomaly. Quinn slumped into his seat, the realization that something was truly wrong with him darkening his mind.

☙

The following days and weeks passed in a blur of inane chatter and cold meals, courtesy of Jeremy's need to have his food thoroughly inspected before being consumed. The dream that Quinn had on his first day kept repeating over and over, never any clearer or different from the day he first arrived.

Quinn found himself passing most of his free time in what the facility had the audacity to refer to as a "library." The single book-shelf unit held maybe a hundred and fifty books, consisting mostly of novels and the odd self-help book. Any time he felt himself beginning to fray around the edges, or becoming overwhelmed by the reality of his situation, he would retreat to the corner of the recreation room where the bookshelf was located. With a book in his lap, he'd escape, at peace for a short while. He dove into them with wild enthusiasm only to find that many were missing pages or deliberately censored to keep the more fragile patients from being triggered by some of the harrowing plots.

To compensate, Quinn attempted to develop his own version of how the stories were meant to end or what happened in the missing pages, but soon even that game became dull. Nevertheless, while Quinn might claim to be horrifically bored, at least he was able to remain calm. And for that he was grateful. Books had occasionally triggered bouts of mania and catatonia, and in fact, his last such episode had seriously injured a cop. Knowing that he could retreat into his reading without hurting anyone was a huge relief to him.

The only real threat to Quinn's sanity was the persistent visions of the small fae creatures out in the garden and courtyard. At first he had stayed quiet about the visions, hoping they were merely the product of his new drug regimen that would go away as his body adapted to its new chemical balance, but after two months, with no change, he finally confided in his psychiatrist Dr. Salazar. The answer, of course, was more drugs, a low dose of some antipsychotic he couldn't pronounce. Quinn had been thankful at first, hoping the drug would banish the strange creatures from his mind, but the hope appeared in vain. Truthfully, the only things the drugs seemed to do was give him dry-mouth and a recurring case of the shakes.

G.E. White

Dr. Salazar ended up taking him off the medication after a month with no improvement. The shakes and the dry mouth went away, but the fairies still remained. Another antipsychotic replaced the first, and compared to the last one, these meds weren't a problem, though he found himself feeling sluggish at times and having a hard time with memory recall and attention span. And while the fae-creatures still lingered, they didn't seem to appear as often. As for the catatonic episodes of aggravation that had landed him in Cedar Hills, Quinn had not relapsed once since arriving at the facility. No matter how many triggering topics the therapist asked about in their sessions, it failed to induce such a relapse.

However, the sessions with Dr. Salazar presented their own pitfalls. Much like Dr. Lisbon, Salazar constantly attempted to dredge up the past, picking at the once-healed scars of his myriad past traumas. He reminded Quinn of all he had lost: his parents, his childhood memories, Ms. Carol, Andi. The list went on and then repeated itself until it felt like the papercut-thin psychic wounds had become substantial trenches of a torn soul. It was supposed to allow him to grieve for these losses. While there might have been some truth in Salazar's claims that acknowledging what he had lost was the first step to recovery, it left Quinn feeling raw.

Weeks turned into months and before Quinn was even aware, over a year had passed with him behind the walls of Cedar Hills. Still, despite everything he had been through, and other than some bouts of depression and his strange hallucinations, he considered himself a fairly sane individual.

A sunny afternoon in mid-June soon shook this belief to the core.

Quinn had fallen into a routine after lunch, of playing chess with Jeremy in the courtyard. Like many of the games left in the rec room, pieces were missing so a few pebbles stood in as pawns, while an eraser took the role of a white bishop. Quinn was now a year and three months into his residence at Cedar Hills. By now, the young man knew the names of the patients, nurses, orderlies, doctors, and the regular visitors who passed through Cedar Hills. So when an unfamiliar man appeared in the courtyard one day over lunchtime, Quinn noticed him instantly.

With his stylish raven locks, steely blue gaze, and designer clothes, the young man stood out among the placid Cedar Hills patients. If he had to guess, Quinn would place the visitor in his early to mid-twenties. A strange cloak hung over the man's shoulders, with its hem resting mid-thigh. The cloak was so complete in its darkness that it seemed to suck all light from around it, save for strange gothic-style white embellishments on the shoulders. The cape was so incongruous to the rest of the young man's attire—it wasn't at all in keeping with the trendy, designer clothes he wore below the fluttering black fabric. Quinn thought that the whole ensemble might look like a garish costume, if it didn't appear to be so finely made.

Despite the visitor's striking appearance, no one else at Cedar Hills seemed to pay him any mind. He moved silently as a shadow as he approached an elderly patient, Marvin Jacobs.

The visitor said nothing but placed a hand on Marvin's shoulder and smiled. Marvin looked up from where he sat in his wheelchair, startled.

"I didn't know Marvin's grandkids were into cosplay," Quinn commented as he continued to stare at the stranger across the courtyard. "I wonder who he's supposed to be?"

Jeremy scowled at the chessboard. Quinn had to give his companion credit for his determination. In all the matches he had played against Quinn, he had yet to win a single one, but it never stopped him trying.

"Marvin doesn't have any grandkids," Jeremy replied, still concentrating on the game pieces in front of him.

"Then who's that?" Quinn asked, gesturing with his chin to the dark-haired visitor.

G.E. White

Jeremy followed Quinn's gaze and frowned. "What are you talking about? There's no one there."

The words hit Quinn in the chest like a sledgehammer. The other young man was there, plain as day, Quinn was sure of it. "But—"

"Dude, you are losing it." Jeremy picked up a bishop from the board, using it to take one of Quinn's pawns. "If I were you, I'd seriously consider asking Salazar to up your meds."

Quinn pulled his feet up onto his seat, hugging his legs closer to his chest. He glanced over at Marvin, and sure enough, the young man was still there.

Almost as if feeling Quinn's gaze upon him, the stranger looked up, his blue eyes locking with Quinn's grey ones. The stranger gave Quinn a rakish smile that caused a fluttery feeling to ripple through his stomach and his face to flush with heat.

While Quinn had never had the opportunity to date thanks to his constant shifting between foster families, he had long come to terms with his pretty much exclusive attraction to men. The man before him looked as though he'd stepped right out of a daydream or a fantasy. As if he were the very manifestation of Quinn's idea of a perfect guy. Sudden shyness overtook him and Quinn was the first to look away. The stranger returned his attention to Marvin.

The elderly man smiled up at his mystery visitor as if he were greeting an old friend. The stranger leaned forward, whispering something in the old man's ear. Marvin's smile grew. The young man then turned and walked away, around the corner of the building and out of sight.

Once he could no longer see the cloaked figure, Quinn looked over at Marvin. The old man was slumped in his chair and appeared to be asleep, save for the fact that he didn't stir.

He just had company. How did he fall asleep so quickly? Something feels off...

"Marv?" Quinn called from across the courtyard.

Marvin remained entirely still. Dread started to creep up Quinn's spine.

"Marv!" Quinn felt his voice crack as he sharpened his tone, trying to get Marvin's attention.

"Geez, Quinn, let him sleep," Jeremy scolded.

"He's not sleeping," Quinn insisted, worry evident in his voice.

Quinn's voice attracted a couple of nurses, who now rushed to the still man.

"Mr. Jacobs?" one of the nurses asked, lightly shaking Marvin's shoulder. The gentle woman's face drained of colour as she received no reaction.

"Jenny, I need you over here!" she hissed to the older nurse.

In a matter of minutes, several orderlies ushered the other patients indoors. The doctors who followed placed a white sheet over the now-deceased Marvin, in preparation for the morgue.

CHAPTER FIVE

SEBASTIEN AZERI WAITED with a feeling of ill ease. The sketch he had been working on lay forgotten in his lap as he listened to the gentle patter of rain against the window. He wished he knew what time it was.

Raising a tanned hand, he brushed some of his wavy brown hair away from his cloudy golden eyes, more so out of habit than of any obstruction to his sight, which he had lost years ago.

Sebastien stood, placing the sketch on the end table to his right, and approached the floor-to-ceiling windows. Twenty stories below his vigil, the citizens of his city stumbled through their lives like newborn fawns rising to their feet for the first time, searching for some stability. If he was being honest, he almost envied them. They still believed that they were the true masters of their own destiny, unaware that many of what they saw as their own choices were hardwired into the path that would be their life.

He knew them, all of them: who they were, where they'd been, and where they were going. He knew them from birth, and he would until their death. Only on the rarest of occasions would a person break from their fate onto a new path not even he was aware of. Those were the people who interested him the most. But while gifted with this knowledge, he was still troubled by the hush of his apartment and the feeling of helplessness that clouded it now.

It was a hot and humid July day in Toronto, Ontario. The air had been heavy and damp since the beginning of the week, and today was one of the rare days when the clouds saw fit to release their tears onto the city below. The busy streets seemed even more congested with hundreds of umbrellas carried by the hurried crowds.

Sebastien marvelled at how business went on as usual: appointments were made and broken, luncheons were held, money was exchanged for goods and services—some legal, others less so—yet high above the city streets during all this chaos, tucked safely away in his penthouse apartment, he was still idly awaiting his companion's return.

Suddenly, Sebastien heard muffled cursing as someone struggled to unlock his door. He tensed, the small hairs on the back of his neck prickling as he waited to confront whoever fought with the lock on the opposite side.

The door flew open, slamming against the interior wall. Sebastien heard a sound of irritation before the familiar voice of Surina Malik muttered, "Who the hell drives a car in this city?"

The tensed muscles of Sebastien's shoulders uncoiled with relief. He should have known it was her—he always knew. So, what had changed? The feeling of being surprised or caught unaware was foreign and unwelcome. But ever since he'd received the news from the Earthen Temple, his thoughts had been preoccupied with fear and a growing sense of anxiety.

"Commuters, cabbies, delivery people," Sebastien answered his visitor's question, attempting to tamp down the slimy sensation of uncertainty that rose in his gut with his usual dose of dry humour. "But I'm guessing that's not what you meant," he continued, teasing her gently in his lilting Cuban accent.

While it was true that Sebastien was blind, he also happened to be the physical reincarnation of the Moirai, more commonly known as the Fates. Every sentient creature possessed a Thread of Fate within them that contained the circumstances of their origin, the timespan of their life, and their inevitable death. As the plural Fates bound into a single being, Sebastien oversaw the spinning, measuring, and harvesting of the Threads of Fate. But he did not work alone; he did not create life or worry about conception—that was Hera's domain. His job was to observe and guide each life along its path, drawing the important stories from the Threads of those people who would impact the world in significant ways. As for the end of life, he knew where the Threads must be cut, but he did not act alone. Working in tandem with Thanatos and his reapers, Sebastien instructed them on what mortal Threads would be cut and which souls were to be collected to be deposited in the Underworld.

Sebastien's responsibility for the Threads of Fate was part of him—a kind of symbiotic relationship. Thus, he still possessed a certain "sight" beyond his ability to see the past and future.

While he would never again see the luminescence of a person's skin or the colour of their eyes, Sebastien's own eyes sharply regarded the strands of Fate contained within each living being. If someone stood before Sebastien, he could see their Threads, twisted and coiled into a vague outline of the body in front of him. Each Thread was a unique combination of colour, length, and brightness, and helped Sebastien to identify just who or what was in the room with him at any given time. For example, the woman now standing in front of him possessed a deep-teal-and-blue coloured Thread that gave off a soft silvery glow as it illuminated her tall frame.

Surina Malik clucked her tongue irritably. "Traffic jam stalled the streetcar for over thirty minutes. I decided to walk the last five blocks. Obviously, that was a mistake."

He could hear water dribble on the floor as she wrung the excessive rainwater from her soaked, dark hair to illustrate her point.

Sebastien had never been able to see Surina's features, but he had received information from her with which he often imagined her appearance. The way she talked made it seem like she wore a permanent sneer of annoyance on her face. Early in the days of her duties to him, she had allowed him to trace his hands over her heart-shaped face as he followed the lines of her Grecian nose and almond eyes. Her athletic build was only a couple inches shorter than his own five-foot, eleven-inch frame. He knew she was beautiful, and her near-constant state of irritation and snarky wit, was all part of her charm. He also knew by now that all that attitude was a carefully cultivated front to the empathic, generous woman underneath. And he had to admit, he rather enjoyed their spiked repartee. She never used kid gloves with him, like everyone else did.

Surina also always did him the courtesy of filling in his unspoken questions before he even thought to ask them. She inherently seemed to understand how much easier it made things for him not having to constantly play catch-up or guess what she was talking about. It was one of the reasons he valued her company.

He could hear her flipping her long, dark wavy hair, which she left loose and parted to the side—she'd worn it the same way since the day they met. Her skin was also tanned, though hers was due to her Pashtun heritage on her Afghani father's side, while Sebastien's own similar skin tone originated from his Hispanic, African, and Taíno roots. These were facts he knew more by supposition than by observation, but her complaints of racial profiling and his own experience of that blight had made it abundantly clear how true his assumption was. Surina had once said that her eyes were a dark hazel green, but few people could claim to have seen them, thanks to the dark sunglasses constantly shielding her eyes.

Sebastien heard Surina kick off her waterlogged boots, and he tracked the wire-like frame of her Threads as she entered the alcove kitchen and dropped the bag of groceries on her arm onto the countertop. "I warned you to take an umbrella, Surina," Sebastien stated as he watched her outline move over to the bathroom, snatch a towel, and began to dry her hair.

"It was sunny this morning," she reasoned, leaning in the bathroom door frame, "and the forecast promised it would be clear, so why would I listen to you? Are you also a meteorologist?"

"Of course, Surina. What could I possibly know about the weather forecast?" Sebastien asked with a long-suffering sigh, while tucking a piece of his hair behind his ear. Sometimes he swore she ignored his predictions in some vain attempt to spite him, though it was usually only to her own detriment.

"Mind toning down the sarcasm just a tad?" she retorted.

"You first."

She snorted. "Touché. Besides, aren't you the one who always says that knowing changes nothing?"

"I used to say that. Though, over the years, some people—and I'm not naming any names—have caused me to reconsider my way of thinking. Now I have a new saying."

"Oh really?" Surina scoffed as she threw the now-damp towel onto the bathroom counter.

"*Si.* Knowing doesn't change anything, it changes little."

"That's nice to know." Surina's tone suggested it was anything but.

Sebastien smiled. "Did you bring what I asked for?"

Surina let out an irritated sigh and returned to the kitchen. She pulled something from the grocery bag and dropped it onto the countertop.

"Mangos, just as you requested," she said. "Please tell me you're making your *mamá's Pastel de Mango*. It's the least you could do for sending me out in the rain."

Her words caused a warmth to bloom in Sebastien's chest. Even though Sebastien was technically Surina's employer, he couldn't help but worry at the thought of just how much he relied upon her. During their time together, they had developed a teasing, complex friendship, yet Surina had never once made him feel like an invalid. While she would often mock his predictions with skepticism, she marvelled at and even tried to exploit Sebastien's talent for art, cooking, and baking. Never once did she question his abilities, condescend to him with pity, or try to baby him. It was a refreshing change.

"It was supposed to be a surprise," he grumbled good-naturedly as he approached and opened the fridge with practiced precision, retrieving a can of iced tea from the door.

"And it was supposed to be sunny today, but here we are. You know, I've been working for you for how many years now?"

Sebastien pursed his lips in thought. "About four."

"It's already been that long?"

"Ever since you left the temple."

"I didn't realize I was getting so old." Surina huffed dramatically.

Sebastien rolled his eyes, a gesture that stayed with him even after he lost his sight. "Hey! I'm only a few years older than you, and I'm definitely not old, so neither are you. Twenty-seven isn't ancient."

"Maybe not for your kind. But for someone who only gets one ride on this rotating ball of dirt, let's just say my days of being called young are running out. Anyway, you're getting off topic. I was saying, I've been looking after you for four years now. When I got assigned this gig, I was under the impression that I was going to be your bodyguard, not your errand girl."

Sebastien winced; this was technically true. Sebastien hadn't hired Surina directly; the woman had been assigned to him by the temple.

Not all beings in the Three Realms were pleased with how the gods governed things, and Surina's main job had been to keep him safe. With what had been required of her in her past position, she was more than capable of the job. Luckily, very few threats had surfaced in the time she worked for him. As time passed, her job skewed more toward errands and companionship, with less active vigilance over his safety.

"Keeping me well fed is essential to keeping me alive, you know. So technically, you are doing your job," Sebastien argued, cracking open the can of iced tea and taking a sip. "The other gods and goddesses wouldn't want me to starve," he added wryly.

"Bizcochuelo mangos, straight from Cuba, and only sold in, like, one specialty store in the city, are a luxury, not a necessity. I'm starting to feel like a husband going out to satisfy my pregnant wife's food cravings. You want some fancy Italian gelato and Kosher pickles next?"

"And why not enjoy a few luxuries, eh? This body doesn't afford me much in the way of luxuries. So why not indulge?"

"Damn, I hadn't thought of it like that."

"Don't worry about it. Hey, at least it comes with its own benefits." Sebastien gestured to his sightless eyes. "I never have to look at Leo's idiotic face, for one."

"You've never seen his face before," Surina said, pretending not to laugh at his jab.

"Doesn't matter. I've heard him talk. I know it's dumb."

Another suppressed giggle. "I'm gonna tell him you said that."

Sebastien gave an amused snort at Surina's nonthreat, turning once more toward the window. He could feel the warmth of the July sun coming through the glass as it broke through the clouds. However, the welcome heat and the always-lively banter with Surina did little to lighten his mood, with the information he received that morning clouding his thoughts once more.

Sebastien could tell that what he had heard was just the beginning of what could become a much bigger problem if events were simply allowed to play out without interference. He was hesitant to bring it up to Surina, but then again, she would be the best person to deal with the news he had to share—that is, if she could hold her temper.

"Something wrong?" Surina's question pulled Sebastien away from his musings. "I was joking about the errand girl stuff. Really, you know I don't mind—"

"It's not that," he said, cutting her off.

"Then what?" Surina took a step toward him.

"The Earthen Temple…" Sebastien trailed off. He had been debating whether to even tell her about the situation, given her history with the three Celestial Temples. But the mere mention of one of them was enough to pique her interest.

"What about it?"

"Someone broke in."

"That's impossible," she said, her voice tight with anger and righteous certainty.

"Obviously not." Sebastien swallowed on a dry throat, feeling suddenly uncertain of telling his companion what she least wanted to hear. Taking another sip of his tea, he decided it was unavoidable. "Thuban was stolen."

The nearby couch creaked as Surina sank onto its arm. Sebastien knew that his information must be a hard pill for her to swallow. A theft at any of the temples was a serious matter, but the stolen artifact's importance made it even worse.

"It had to be an inside job," she said.

"I agree, but you know as well as I do: that means people at the other temples are suspect too."

Sebastien could practically hear Surina's frown. Thuban was part of a valuable and powerful artifact, one of three pieces guarded by the Celestial Temples. Should all the pieces be collected and the artifact reforged, they would all be in serious trouble.

Surina raised the braided structure of Threads that made up her arm as she ran a hand restlessly through her dark waves. "So, what's going to happen?"

"No lo sé." Sebastien shook his head as he slipped into his native tongue.

"You don't know?!" she exclaimed, jumping to her feet and marching to where he stood, hunched and pensive by the window. "You see the past, present, and future, and you don't know?"

"The future isn't absolute," he countered. "Something is blocking me, or clouding me. Things were messed with in the past, making things unclear in the present regarding the future. It's all in flux and I can't make heads or tails of it. First the Soul Calendria, now Thuban."

Surina sighed heavily. Sebastien imagined her rubbing at her brow as it furrowed with tension. There was a moment of silence as she seemed to consider her options. "Count me out."

"Pardon, *qué dijiste?*" Sebastien was taken aback by her words. He had assumed that once she learned of the Celestial Temples' connection to Thuban's disappearance, she wouldn't be able to resist the mystery. Surina was dogged in her pursuit of the truth. It was one of her defining traits. For better or worse, she couldn't, or wouldn't, lose sight of her goal.

"I said, I'm out. I'm not getting involved. I know what you're thinking, and no. Have someone else look into it. I've got my hands full as it stands now, just looking after you."

"But you know them; you've worked with the temples before," Sebastien felt as if he was proverbially trying to wrangle an angry cat into a tiny carrier.

Stubborn like a burro...

"Yes, but we didn't exactly part on good terms, if you remember." Her words were practically dripping with self-recrimination. "So, why would I willingly go back there? They wouldn't want to see my face."

How could he forget? It was true, Surina's history with the Celestial Temples was complicated at best, but she was the only one Sebastien trusted who had the inside knowledge and the wherewithal they would need to flush out the thief and retrieve the priceless artifact.

"It's been a long time since your...difficulties," he assured her. "Maybe—"

"Four years!" Surina scoffed, her voice raising slightly in an attempt to mask her pain at the recollection. "Four years and the Zodiac Council still haven't elected new members to the House of Gemini— it's considered cursed! I think they remember."

As much as he tried to understand her misgivings, Sebastien couldn't help the flood of frustration that washed over him at her inflexibility on this front. They'd talked about it many times before, going round and round in circles for hours, and still, he could never understand her reasons for not facing her past and resolving things with the Council. Instead, she pushed herself into a kind of self-imposed isolation as a form of punishment. Only at this point, Sebastien couldn't tell who'd been hurt more by that decision: Surina or the Three Realms. She was one of the most cunning warriors, with a keen mind and yet she decided to give up and hide out on the sidelines when they needed her the most. He knew from experience that she could not be reasoned with and he was exhausted with the argument before it had even happened. "Fine."

"Fine?" Surina's voice escalated as she asked the question, her tone coloured with surprise that he had given up so easily.

"Yes, fine." Sebastien turned from the window and crossed over to the chair he had previously occupied. He gently picked up the sketch he had been working on.

"No pleading? No Reverse Psychology? No pulling rank?" she prodded.

"If you won't do it, I'll just have you find me someone who will."

"And what does that mean?" Surina's tone was combative, but he refused to be drawn into a fight. Not again. There just wasn't enough time to change her mind. Her Threads were clear: she did not want to face the Celestial Temples—not alone.

"All right, let me spell this out for you." He let his frustration out with a sigh and a shake of his head. "Someone needs to take on the responsibilities that you've decided to abandon. So, if you won't do it yourself, then, as your boss, I order you to go find me the person who will. Why do you always have to make things so difficult?!"

Spinning on his heels, Sebastien thrust the sketch into Surina's hands, before retreating to his bedroom and slamming the door behind him.

∽

The reverberations of the slammed door and the sting of Sebastien's words caused Surina to wince.

Perhaps she was being unreasonable, but the thought of returning to the Solar, Earthen, and Lunar Temples made her gut clench with anxiety. Besides, it seemed likely that the temples wouldn't even allow her to conduct the necessary investigation in the first place. And despite the hurt his implications caused her, Surina also couldn't help but wonder who Sebastien had in mind to take her place.

She glanced down at the picture in her hand, which seemed as detailed as a photograph. It showed a blond, teenage boy with weary grey eyes, dressed in hospital scrubs, reading a battered copy of Aldous Huxley's *Brave New World*. The expression he wore spoke of a deep-seated pain. The image filled her with a lingering sense of pity. Why did this young man appear so beaten down?

"What is this supposed to be?" she called after him, but only silence, not Sebastien, responded.

∽

As Sebastien entered his study, the subject of his latest drawing weighed heavily on his mind. As of late, his visions had revolved around the young, blond man, and Sebastien knew there could be no coincidence that he was thinking of the boy—not with the timing of Thuban's theft. The two were connected somehow. The Threads of Fate within him hummed with a feeling of familiarity that he could not ignore. This boy was one of them.

Ever since the Soul Calendria was stolen almost thirty years ago, tracking down the newest incarnations of the gods had been difficult, to say the least. Only a handful of gods had been awakened since the theft, mostly those who were already related to a current god, or promising individuals Sebastien had been blessed with visions of. Still, the number of awakened gods was dwindling. It was an increasing concern. If he and the other gods didn't find them soon, by the time the present generation of gods passed on, all would be forgotten. Sebastien couldn't let that happen.

Crossing the study to his bookshelf, Sebastien reached up to the third shelf and felt until his hands encountered what he was looking for. The smooth, hard metal of the ancient helmet was in shockingly good condition, despite having been used in the Imjin War of the late 1500s.

The helmet was one of many artifacts his various incarnations had collected over the centuries. At some point, each item had belonged to one of the dozens of gods throughout history.

While many of the items—a book from India, a necklace from Sudan, a doll from the French Revolution—belonged to gods who were not currently accounted for, it was the helmet that seemed to call out to Sebastien the most. Granted, it had been worn by several gods, but only one was its true owner.

Plucking the helmet off the shelf, Sebastien set it on his desk. He couldn't shake the feeling that the god this relic once belonged to was the boy in his vision. And if the theft of Thuban was a sign of things to come, they certainly would need him.

CHAPTER SIX

I N T H E D AYS following Martin's death, it was said that the old man had died of natural causes. Knowing that no one else had seen the blue-eyed visitor, Quinn didn't mention him again. Depression weighed heavily on him as the thought that he truly was losing his mind persisted.

The days turned monotonous as Quinn went through the motions of living in this institutional purgatory. He had lost interest in reading, having gone through all the books in the sparse library, and had begun to forgo his daily chess matches with Jeremy. Salazar added medication to help with his growing depression, but it just made him feel queasy and mentally hazy.

The fae creatures continued to visit Quinn but often left disappointed in the young man's lack of attention given toward them. Assuming that the faeries were a symptom of his decreasing mental stability, it soon became obvious to Quinn that he would not get better on the low dose of meds and therapy alone. The next Friday was his twentieth birthday. Quinn abandoned any thought of celebration and prepared himself for his private therapy session. He would confess his persistent hallucinations and ask Dr. Salazar to increase his medication.

Part of him argued this wasn't the way forward, but what other options did he have? This place was draining him; he needed a way out. Perhaps a change of medication would help him convince his doctors that he was ready to leave Cedar Hills. If he continued to stay here, there was no possibility of him getting better. So, he would grit his teeth, take the antipsychotics and hopefully one day get out of Cedar Hills, or he would slowly fade away behind these institution walls.

However, it seemed that whatever hand wove his fate had a different plan in store.

At ten minutes past eight in the morning, on September 22, Nurse Belamy approached the listless man and spoke words he had never expected to hear: "Quinn, honey, you have a visitor."

℥

Quinn scratched at the back of his hand as he entered the visitation room. Had the judge reconsidered his sentence? Maybe they were letting him go. With the luck he had been having lately, it was more likely that Officer Kendry's condition had worsened, and they were now going to send him off to prison. He shook his head. That couldn't have happened—Kendry had to be getting better. And more importantly, he had already been sentenced.

Besides, even if this meeting was to change his sentence, Quinn wasn't sure whether a shorter incarceration term would be an improvement or not. There was no denying he wanted to get out, but he wanted to leave in control of his own mind. After all, what sane person saw faeries or trashed libraries for no reason?

As he walked in, Quinn couldn't help but compare the visitation room at Cedar Hills to the visitors' room at the precinct lock-up, where he had awaited trial almost two years ago. While this space had windows toward the outside world and was much more accommodating than prison, the plain tables and chairs scattered throughout the room betrayed its purpose.

What *did* surprise Quinn, was the person waiting for him. Nurse Belamy had told him his lawyer was here to see him, so he expected to see his balding public defender, Artie McMullin. There had been a time when he had been truly angry at his lawyer for talking him into the insanity plea, but considering what he had seen and experienced since then, Quinn was inclined to agree that the decision to send him to Cedar Hills was fitting.

Instead of Artie, a dark-haired woman sat at the table closest to the windows. She was likely in her late twenties. Her dark hair had lighter highlights that shone almost silver in the spring light. A pair of nearly opaque sunglasses, set with slick oval frames, obscured her eyes.

The business suit she wore had been evidently tailored to fit her sleek frame—yet, she wore it with the awkwardness of a football player in a tutu, occasionally shifting and pulling at the skirt hem. Quinn slid into the chair across from her, his eyes narrowed in suspicion.

"You're not my lawyer."

"You were expecting Mr. McMullin. Unfortunately, he was called away. I'm your new lawyer, Surina Malik," the woman explained, extending her hand. Quinn noted that her voice had an almost lyrical lilt to it. Taking her hand and shaking it, he felt calluses on her palm that were incongruous to her tailored outfit and job title. Her hands felt more like those of a bare-knuckle boxer than a lawyer.

"So why exactly are you here?" he asked, choosing to keep his observations and reservations to himself for the moment. "Is there some change in my case?"

"You're being released," she answered as if it was the most obvious thing in the world.

"Released?" Quinn asked, skeptical.

"Yes. The terms of your incarceration were that you would stay here until you were deemed well enough to reenter society."

He knew of the terms of the plea, but Dr. Salazar was well aware of his continuing hallucinations, that while seemingly harmless, still left Quinn with a feeling of dread. He also couldn't shake the feeling of injustice if what this Surina woman said was true. To Quinn, the past year and a half felt like a life-time, but when he thought of the pain and injury he had dealt Officer Kendry his time here barely seemed like adequate penance. "I doubt Dr. Salazar would have signed off on that."

"He already has," she replied, fetching his release papers from her briefcase and presenting them to him. Quinn snatched up the papers, his eyes speed reading over the document's contents before zeroing in on Salazar's now familiar chicken scratch signature.

"But how?"

The woman shrugged, "My boss can be very persuasive."

He shook his head, an uncomfortable feeling settling in his gut, "It's not right."

Surina threaded her fingers in her lap, seeming to find no issue with his statement. "Don't you want to get out of here?"

"Of course," Quinn said, standing and moving to the window. Outside in the garden, he saw one of the small fae creatures who had been plaguing him over the last year and a half. The little figure out-side took notice of his staring and flew closer. Now pressed against the glass, the fae began contorting her face into mocking expressions.

Quinn sighed. "I'm just starting to think this might be the best place for me."

"Why? Because that stupid faerie out there keeps making faces at you?" Surina's eyes were covered by the sunglasses, but Quinn could

G.E. White

hear the amusement in her voice.

He whirled around to face her, his eyes wide as hope welled in his chest. "You can see her?"

Surina sneered. "Of course I can see her. And if she knows what's good for her, she'll beat it—*before* I come out there and rip her wings off," she said, directing the comment to the tiny figure outside. The crimson-haired faerie on the other side of the glass squeaked in indignation and stuck her tongue out at the woman, before flying off.

Quinn gaped at Surina in disbelief as she glared after the retreating figure. "Yeah, get outta here, Red!" she called after the retreating fae. "Whimsical-ass, little bitches. Man, I hate those things."

"You've seen them before?"

She nodded. "They're not overly common in the Second Realm, but they usually hang around places like this. People here are more likely to see them and interact with them, but they obviously won't be believed if they talk about them."

Quinn noted that the way Surina spoke about the strange and fantastic creatures seemed similar to an exterminator giving a consultation on household pests. *Just who was this woman?*

"Is this where you tell me I'm a wizard? Cause I gotta say, you're like nine years too late with my Hogwarts letter," Quinn couldn't help the snarky tone that escaped his lips. It seemed like all his interactions were determined to further undermine his sanity—why not roll with it?

Maybe this is just a dream? Or maybe I'm in a coma? Or maybe I've truly gone and lost it...

Surina snorted. "Great, another smartass," she muttered to herself. "No, you're not a wizard, but it's obvious you're not like other humans."

He shook his head in disbelief and gave the woman a bemused half smirk. "Listen, girl, I'm starting to think that you belong here just as much as I do," he said.

Adjusting her sunglasses, Surina kissed her teeth and leaned across the table. "I'm perfectly sane, as are you. You just have a keener sense of perception than most people. When a dog can hear things we can't, do we automatically assume it's crazy?"

Quinn slowly sank back down into his seat, his grey eyes narrowing as they scrutinized Surina's athletic frame. "I'm getting the distinct impression that you're not actually a lawyer."

"And what makes you say that?"

She couldn't be serious, could she? "The fact that we're having this conversation, for starters. But there are other signs."

"Really? Like what?" she asked, intrigue and amusement both evident in her voice.

Quinn figured he might as well indulge her. "Well, you're not comfortable wearing a suit, which, if you were a lawyer, would feel like a second skin. Then there's your hands, you obviously work a lot with them—not exactly typical for someone who spends most of their time behind a desk or in a courtroom. Plus, you've got this whole Agent Smith thing going on with the sunglasses. I'm thinking you're with the military or some other government agency, or more likely just some crackpot who thinks they are. But that's probably just the schizophrenia talking."

"A small dose of paranoia is good, now and then," the woman chuckled. "But no, I don't work for a government agency, pretend or otherwise. Or at least, not any you would be familiar with."

"Interpol?" Quinn asked, tilting his head.

"No. While I'll admit one of our numbers does hold an office with them, she and my other bosses wield a lot more influence."

What did that even mean? Quinn asked himself. This whole conversation was getting stranger by the moment. "And these people are interested in me?" he asked, disbelief colouring his words. Nevertheless, he smiled at the strange woman, still amused at the ridiculousness of the situation in which he'd found himself.

At least it's a break from the monotony…

"Is that so hard to believe?" Surina countered.

G.E. White

Quinn snorted. "Completely. Up until the last two years, my life has been pretty uneventful. I mean, my last name is Smith." Even as he said the words, he could hear the lie behind them. Knowing that there was such a huge gap in his memory had often spurred fantasies for his younger self in foster care. In these fantasies, his parents were spies or secret nobles, waiting for a safe moment to return to claim their son. But as the years passed Quinn started to realize that his lost memory didn't mean he was special, only that he was alone and gifted with a last name as plain as he felt: Smith.

Surina scrutinized him closely. "According to your file, it might not be your real last name."

Quinn shrugged. "Youth Services gave it to me. They said I had acute retrograde amnesia—memories from the first six years of my life completely wiped out. All they had to go on was my first name, written on the jacket I was wearing."

"And no one came looking for you? No family? Friends? People who wanted to talk about your past?"

Quinn shook his head again. "Some couples came by and considered adopting me, but it never went anywhere." The teen paused, gazing intently at the woman. "Did you know my parents?" he asked. The hope that he had first felt when Surina noticed the fae creature started to grow inside him anew. He had long given up on finding out his past, but perhaps this woman held the answers he so desperately wanted to know.

Surina's gaze fell. "No, sorry. At least, I don't think so."

"Oh," he said, hunching his shoulders, trying to hide his disappointment. "So why all the questions?"

Surina scratched lightly at her temple. "That's going to be a bit difficult to answer. The truth is, I've been trying to piece your story together, but I don't have any answers—not yet. But perhaps this might help."

Surina reached down to the bag at her feet and pulled out a large, round object wrapped in a dark cloth. She held the parcel out to Quinn, who took it suspiciously.

"There had better not be anything scary or threatening in here—or I *will* scream and make a scene to end all scenes," he warned her as he began to peel away the fabric from the object in his hand. Polished metal revealed itself with each tug until he cradled a helmet in his hands. Quinn stared at his reflection in the metal dome. This thing was ancient. What possible answers could it reveal? Still staring at his reflection, Quinn blinked and instantly found himself somewhere else.

℘

The eyes staring back at him from the helmet blinked in unison with his own, and though they were the same colour, they peered out from a very different face. The face reflected in the helmet was older, in his forties or fifties, and East Asian.

Quinn looked up to ask Surina what she was trying to pull, only to see that wherever he was—whenever he was—was as distant from the visitors' room as woolly mammoths were from rocket ships. Laid out before him was the rampart of an old fortress, or maybe a castle. Jinju Castle, his mind supplied as everything came rushing back to him.

The year was 1592, and he was Korean commander Kim Si-min: protector of this fortress and leader of the 3,800 men who defended it.

Looking out to the surrounding land, he could make out a dark line on the horizon, growing larger and thicker by the moment as the Japanese invasion marched toward the castle. Both dread and fierce determination swept over him at the sight. He and his soldiers were outnumbered once again, but this castle guarded Jeolla province—they couldn't let it fall.

Earlier that morning, he had laid hands on every one of his soldiers, imbuing them with the strength and battle knowledge needed to see

G.E. White

them through this war. He remembered seeing the light of his magic entering their very core and now the soldiers, whose hearts had quivered at the sound of war drums, stood tall and ready for battle.

The magic that Kim had passed into his soldiers didn't guarantee their victory, but as Kim/Quinn placed his helmet on his head, he vowed they would make it a battle the world would never forget.

 e/s

Quinn blinked once more and found himself back in the visitors' room, the old helmet now on his head. It fit perfectly. Jolting fully back to the present, he scrambled to remove the metal headgear, tossing it onto the table with a loud clatter and throwing himself back in his chair, as if the object had physically attacked him. His heart raced as the strange vision lingered, the emotions of Kim so close to his own that he struggled to extricate himself from them.

"What the hell was that?!" he screeched.

"A memory," Surina replied.

"So, what, it's haunted by the guy who used to own it?"

"No," she replied, shaking her head. "It's yours."

The words caused Quinn's quickened thoughts to grind to a halt. "What do you mean, it's mine?"

"The helmet is yours, and the memory is too. A vision of your former self. Your past life. Sebastien was right," she said, muttering the last sentence to herself.

"What do you mean, he was right? Who's Sebastien?" With each question he spat out, Quinn felt panic bubble inside him. *What did this all mean?* Surina had said the helmet might help give him answers, but all he had now were more questions.

"Sebastien is the man I work for. He's the one who gave me the helmet and sent me to find you. Took a lot longer than I had hoped, but all I had to go on was a drawing." As she spoke, she pulled a folded piece of paper from her briefcase. She passed it to Quinn across the table. The young man unfolded it to reveal a hyper-realistic sketch of himself reading in the Cedar Hill's rec room. He recognized the novel in his image self's hands as the same one he had started in September. Yet, a mark at the bottom claimed the sketch was dated sometime in July.

Despite the madness he was feeling, Quinn could discern the honesty in her voice. "But why?"

Surina glanced away, turning her head to the side. "That's not an easy thing to answer. Or at least, the answer isn't easy to swallow."

"Then start small," Quinn challenged. "Tell me why I saw the memory of some Korean warrior from the sixteenth century."

"It's *your* memory—or former incarnation's memory, anyway."

"So, reincarnation is real?" He found the idea kind of romantic—the ability to try to be better in the next incarnation, to perhaps chase a loved one through the ages. It had its appeal.

"Yes, but not for everyone." Surina plucked an old-fashioned pocket watch from her blazer, clicked open the front panel, and checked the time, before dropping it back into her pocket. "Tell me, do you know anything about Greek mythology?"

Quinn nodded. "I used to read all about it when I was growing up."

"Okay, that will make this a little easier. You've probably heard about the twelve Olympian gods," she said, counting them off on her fingers as she named them. "Zeus, Hera, Poseidon, Hades, Hestia, Ares, Athena, Apollo, Hermes, Aphrodite, Artemis, and Hephaestus. Of course, there are many more gods, but they are usually considered 'lesser' gods, though that's not really true. Many of them have more power than the Olympians. And every one of them is real."

"You're saying that the Greeks were right about the whole deity thing?"

"Yes, and no," Surina said with a wave of her hand. "You see, these so-called gods and goddesses aren't really gods, at least not in the way most people understand the word. They've got a boss, just like everybody else. Think of gods as more like governors than actual deities, ensuring the world remains in balance. Well, as best as they can. Gods are not all powerful or omnipotent. If they were, there'd be no suffering. But unlike the myths, gods have mortal bodies, and they live and die just like regular humans. Unlike humans, they have to come back and live again and again."

"They reincarnate." Quinn exhaled, rolling this new information about in his brain. "So, you think I'm one of these reincarnated gods?"

"I wasn't sure before, but I am now."

She was talking about him, right? Him? Quinn? "You do realize how crazy that sounds, right?"

Surina gave a soft huff of amusement. "I'm not the one who had the vision. So, who are you trying to convince? Me or you?"

And that was the real question, wasn't it? Sitting there, his mouth gaping, Quinn struggled to find an answer. But Surina didn't need to show him any more evidence. After coming in contact with the ancient helmet, his own mind had supplied the answers for him.

"I know this isn't easy to process," Surina reassured him. "We used to know which god or goddess would be reborn into particular bodies. But our records of reincarnation were stolen almost thirty years ago, and several of the gods are still unaccounted for."

Surina paused for a moment. Quinn couldn't see her eyes behind the darkly tinted sunglasses, but he knew the woman was scrutinizing him intensely.

"My boss, Sebastien Azeri, sent me here to find you," she continued. "He's one of these gods and thinks that you might be one of his kind. Your reaction to that helmet just about proves it, though, who you are exactly is still up for debate."

"What do you mean?"

"That helmet has been in the possession of a few different gods over the centuries, so finding out which god you are will require a little more investigation."

Quinn raised his eyebrows. Despite what he had experienced, he still had trouble accepting her words as truth. "You can't be serious, right? This all has to be some big joke."

"Do I look like I'm joking?"

The young man shook his head. It would be easier to tell how truthful she was if he could see her eyes, only those damn glasses she wore obstructed her pupils and irises. The shape of the frames allowed him to see that she had no facial disfigurement to hide, and based on her behaviour, he could tell she was sighted. He guessed that the sunglasses were like a shield for her. Perhaps she had an adverse reaction to light, photosensitive? Or maybe she preferred to keep the world at bay, keep her inner thoughts and feelings to herself? Either way, it would have been rude to ask or comment.

"I don't know. You're a little hard to read." His tone was sarcastic, but he kept it purposefully lighthearted.

"Or maybe you just don't want to see what's right in front of you. Maybe you've spent so long thinking you're crazy and that you deserve to be here that you actually believe it."

Quinn slumped down in his seat feeling completely overwhelmed. Rationally he knew that there was something behind his vision and the fact that they both could see the strange fae creatures that had pestered him this past year and a half. However, another part of him warned him to get his head out of the clouds. This was a *folie à deux*—a madness shared by two. "I don't know what you want from me."

"I want you to hear the truth," Surina hissed, her statement punctuated with her hand slamming down on the table.

Quinn recoiled, which caused Surina's shoulders to slump and her tone to lighten. "Think about it. My boss prioritized finding you over everyone else when we have all this other stuff on our plate to deal with. It took us a couple of months to track you down. You and I can see things that others can't. And you can't explain away the vision you had when you touched that helmet. So why else would I be here telling you all this? You think I enjoy messing with you? That I like coming here?"

Quinn folded his arms tightly across his chest, his lips pursed in obstinance.

Surina sat back in her chair, weary of sparring with him. "Look, I'm just trying to do my job. The guy who sent me drew your likeness perfectly without ever seeing you before. As he learned more about you, your past was revealed to him."

He made a disbelieving sound in the back of his throat. "Ridiculous," he muttered.

"Really? Then how come he knew that when you were twelve, you put worms in Jamie Cowen's backpack for calling you a coward during recess? If he isn't what I say he is, how would he know that?"

Quinn's eyes widened as she continued to speak. He had never told anyone about the worms. The fact that this Sebastien character seemed privy to one of his best-kept secrets sent chills up his spine. Part of him wanted to leave this little room at that moment, to call Surina and her employer out as unhinged stalkers and have security escort the strange woman out of the building. Yet there was something about Surina's direct, no-nonsense tone that made Quinn believe she was telling the truth, even if he couldn't see her eyes to judge how honest she was being. She was right about one thing, though: he couldn't ignore all the evidence.

"I hear you, and that's all really compelling and everything. But I'm not well. Mentally. That makes most of what you're arguing circumstantial. It doesn't prove anything. And let's pretend for a minute that what you're saying is true—at the end of the day, that doesn't mean I am who your boss thinks I am." His voice came out weak, suddenly tired by the exchange, the spark of hope within dimming.

"That's very true," Surina conceded. "There *is* a chance that you're not one of these gods, but just someone who is...magically sensitive, to put it in layman's terms. But wouldn't you like to find out for sure?

Think about it. Your whole life could change. Right now."

Quinn didn't answer, and Surina pressed on.

"If Sebastien is right, you're not crazy. You'll be free to leave this place and will never have to worry about money again. Gods are a pretty well-off lot, what with their centuries of accumulated wealth. Give me the rest of today to help me figure this out, and if at the end nothing comes of it, I'll drop you back off here, and you'll never hear from us again."

It was a simple proposition, but the unknown possibilities threw Quinn off-kilter. So many different feelings churned inside him: fear and disbelief, especially. But it was hope—hope that his life could turn around—that rose to the forefront. Originally, he thought that he had escaped prison by taking Artie's deal, but the monotony, medication, and rehashed trauma were slowly grinding him down as surely as any prison sentence would. He had awoken this morning resigned to a life of heavy medication or a slow withering in Cedar Hills.

He glanced down at the scrubs he wore, then at the outside world beyond the window. What harm was there in taking a chance on this strange and wild story? Even if this all turned out to be nothing, and that Surina would return him here, deeming him just as plain as he imagined, at least he would have had one last day of freedom. And why shouldn't he? It was his birthday, after all.

Quinn squared his shoulders, turned to face Surina, and whispered softly, "All right. It's better than staying here."

The hard lines of Surina's face relaxed at his answer, and a genuine smile graced her lips. "Good choice." Adjusting her collar as she stood, she gestured for Quinn to stand as well. "Come on; let's check you out of this dump. We should get moving while it's still early."

The young man stood and followed her out of the visitation room doors. "Where exactly are we going?"

Surina gave a short snort of amusement, before calling back over her shoulder. "To meet your true self."

CHAPTER SEVEN

When Surina told him they were going on a journey to discover his true self, Quinn had expected something a little more...mystical. As he squinted at the sign hanging over the stairs leading underground, he couldn't help but feel a slight pang of disappointment.

"This is the subway," he pointed out.

"Yes, I can read," Surina replied. "Now, are you coming or not?"

Quinn pouted but said nothing as he and his guide descended the steps leading into James St. Station.

Before leaving Cedar Hills, Quinn had taken a moment to say his goodbyes to Jeremy. As strange as his roommate was, Quinn was grateful for the companionship. Jeremy seemed more concerned with the immediate problem of who would check his food for him every day. He barely registered Quinn's exit.

Both he and Surina had also taken the time to change: Quinn into the faded jeans, plain white t-shirt, scuffed, off-white, shell-toe sneakers, and rust-brown hooded utility jacket he had entered the facility in, while Surina had ditched the lawyer getup for a more comfortable pair of jeans and a tank top she'd paired with army surplus combat boots. Over her top, she wore a faded, hunter green bomber jacket, which helped Quinn follow her as she slipped gracefully past people in the subway station.

Personally, Quinn had never had much patience for the subway. During the long year he had lived on the street, he had made friends with several homeless men who had occasionally taken shelter here. He had never understood why they preferred the underground stations; the constant coming and going of screeching trains created a harsh blast of air that sent a chill through clothing and flesh alike.

"So, where exactly are we going?" he asked, struggling to keep up as they maneuvered through the throngs of commuters. "I mean, what train are we taking?"

Surina glanced over her shoulder. "Who said anything about taking a train? We're heading to a place a little off the beaten path."

"To do what?"

"To confirm my boss' suspicions about you."

Quinn stopped short as Surina turned down a corridor just off the main platform. "About me being some sort of god? Yeah, I got that. But just how are we going to prove it? You're not planning on pushing me in front of the train to see if I survive or something, are you?"

Surina snickered. "No. These gods aren't immortal—tougher than most humans, yes, but getting hit by a train will still kill you." She turned to inspect a door marked *Employees Only*.

Quinn moved to stand beside Surina as she dug into her pocket in search of something. His lips pursed in irritation, realizing that she hadn't actually answered his question. He decided to let it go, in favour of asking a more pressing query.

"What if he's wrong?" he asked.

"Ah-ha!" she said triumphantly, pulling out a large ring of odd-looking keys and beginning to flip through them. "What do you mean?"

"Your boss, Sebastien. What if he's wrong about me? You said you'd just take me back, but how do I know you won't just kill me to keep me quiet?"

"Who says I can't just erase your memory, like in *Men in Black?*" Surina replied, stone-faced.

Quinn paled, the subject of memory still a sore one.

Surina's aloof mask cracked, giving way to an upward twitch at the corners of her lips. "I'm kidding. I wouldn't worry about it, anyway," she assured him. "You'll soon discover Sebastien is never wrong."

Surina found the key she was looking for and unlocked the door, quickly waving Quinn inside. Ahead lay another, longer, dimly-lit corridor.

"Oh," he said. "Must be nice—to not be wrong, that is."

"Actually, he's pretty damn annoying. Useful, but annoying," she replied as the door shut behind them, the lock snapping securely into place. "Just don't ever tell him that I said he's useful. It'll just make his giant head even bigger."

Quinn smiled slightly, starting to get a feel for his new companion's sense of humour. He followed Surina through the long brick corridor and down a winding staircase that led them down two levels. At the bottom of the landing, an ornate iron door loomed ahead of them. The sliding speakeasy grille reminded him of the cheesy gangster flicks he used to watch at the Watsons' house. His memories of his third foster family's weekly movie night rituals seemed, in that exact moment, as if they belonged to someone else's life.

Surina rapped her knuckles against the weathered iron, the sound echoing along the spiral staircase. A few moments later, the grate of the grille slid open. A pair of irate brown eyes glared down at them. "Password?"

Surina threw the voice behind the door an unimpressed scowl. "Leo, open the damn door before I bust your knee caps in."

Leo's glower dropped in an instant, revealing a much more relaxed and pleasant gaze. His now-relaxed voice—light, jovial, and tinged with a distinct New York Italian accent—matched his new demeanour. "Eh, close enough," he said, before stepping back to unlock the door for their entrance.

Quinn heard several heavy bolts being thrown back before the large door swung open, allowing him and Surina to enter.

The room behind the door looked nothing like what Quinn had expected. Instead of another dark and grimy hallway, they now stood in a chamber that resembled a warm living area. The left wall was lined with heavy doors, similar to the one they had just passed through. A charming and cozy-looking couch sat in front of a beautiful stone fireplace, the red-brown, wood-panelled walls reminding Quinn of a log cabin. The built-in bar along the back wall appeared well stocked. Quinn thought that it could have belonged to the frat houses he used to see in raunchy comedies.

If nothing else, the man who had let them in certainly fit the stereotypical frat-boy image. Leo was six feet five inches of athletic muscle, with a mop of curly red hair and a face full of stubble. Likely in his early to mid-thirties, he still had a youthful energy about him. He wore a navy button-down flannel shirt with a bright red t-shirt underneath, featuring a logo Quinn recognized as sports related but he couldn't quite name the team. Quinn could almost feel the warmth of the man's smile as he closed the door behind them.

"Surina," he greeted. "Long time, no see."

"Leo," she returned with a subtle bow of her head. "I see you didn't waste any time fixing this place up."

"Figured I might as well make my exile comfortable. I'm sure old Janus wouldn't mind me fixing up the place while she's on vacation," he said with a shrug.

G.E. White

"Janus?" Quinn asked. How many more gods would he meet today?

"Leo is referring to Erica. She's the current incarnation of Janus, God of Beginnings and Endings, Gateways and Halls," Surina said, before addressing the other man. "And I don't think she'd appreciate being called old, Leo. You know she's always been particular about her age."

"Whatever," he muttered. He turned to Quinn and gave a questioning look. "So, who's the kid?"

"I'm twenty," Quinn protested, attempting to keep the pout out of his voice. He knew his features weren't the most chiselled or manly, but he was still an adult.

Surina moved her hands between the two men as she did the introductions. "Leo, this is Quinn. Quinn, this is Leo Russo."

"Is he one of us?" Leo asked her.

"One of you," she corrected, "and Sebastien's convinced he is, so I wouldn't talk about him like he's not here."

"One of us?" Quinn asked incredulously. "You mean, Leo's a god?"

"Yeah," Leo impatiently cut Quinn off. "Let me properly introduce myself: Leonardo Vincent Russo, 634th incarnation of the God of War, Ares. But you can call me Leo."

Quinn took in the laid-back demeanour of the man. "You? You're the God of War?" he said, disbelief contorting his features.

"Yeah, you got a problem with that?" Leo's tone seemed cheery, but Quinn heard the edge underneath. Quinn felt a momentary shift in the room, as if the air had become infused with a fiery energy that seemed to radiate from Leo himself. If he didn't know better, he swore he could taste the metallic tang of blood in the air. However, just as quickly as the sensation came, it left.

"Well, it's just hard to believe it, when you're acting as a doorman," Quinn replied, giving his head a shake to clear the last of the hostile feeling from his mind.

Surina stifled a snort of laughter.

"That's Cosmic Doorman to you," Leo corrected, placing his hands on his hips and puffing out his chest dramatically. "Look at this," he said, waving his hand to the other strange doors lining the empty walls. "It's not as if I'm just watching this one door. This is some pretty serious business. You see these doors?" Leo gestured widely around. "All these are actually entrances into the lower levels all over the world. Gates are the main mode of transportation for our kind. You might still think that you're under—uh, where did you guys enter from?"

"Toronto," Surina replied.

"Right, so you might still think you're under Toronto, but this place exists outside of mortal concepts of space and time, which means each Gate can instantly teleport you from one end of the world to the other, even to a different realm completely—and I'm in charge of it."

"Still, it seems to be a strange thing for the God of War to be doing." Quinn was still reeling from the fact that he was out of Cedar Hills, let alone that he was some kind of god or that he'd just walked into a place that apparently ignored the laws of physics, but this felt as though it defied all logic.

Surina smirked. "Leo here has been put on probation since his last...job."

"Job?"

"He'd been working with a small African tribe in Angola who were trying to put pressure on the local government due to some questionable laws. It didn't go very well..." Surina trailed off as she noticed the look on Leo's face.

"Hey, it went as well as could be expected," the burly man defended. "Those people were losing their civil rights. I just made sure they stood up for themselves, you know?"

"Even though dozens of them died in the conflict?" Surina questioned.

Leo gave a dismissive wave of his hand. "All wars can get a bit bloody, and sometimes they go on longer than people like. Everyone forgets that."

Quinn scratched the back of his head. "Well, no one really likes war."

"That's debatable," Leo replied. "But whether you like it or not, sometimes it's unavoidable, even necessary. What'd'ya think would have happened if no one fought the Nazis? Let me tell you something, it would be a very different world than the one we got now."

Quinn nodded. "I see where you're coming from. That doesn't mean I like it."

"Every person to his pie," Leo chuckled.

"I wouldn't know—haven't eaten much pie," Quinn said, smiling.

"Well, that's just sad. My nonna used to make the best apple walnut pie in the Second Realm. My family owns a restaurant in Queens where they make her recipes. I'll get you some next time I go visit."

While Quinn appreciated the offer of dessert, it was another one of Leo's words that truly captured his attention. "That's the second time you've mentioned the word *realm*. What exactly do you mean by that?"

Leo turned on Surina with a huff. "You didn't explain the Three Realms to him?"

"I was trying to convince him to come with me. I didn't really have time for a history and geography lesson," she replied.

"So, what does he know?"

Quinn stepped between the bickering adults, irritated. "I know that supposedly the gods of the ancient Greek pantheon are real and have been reincarnated many times over the centuries. Maybe."

"We got ourselves a skeptic here, huh, Surina?"

"Do you really blame him?" the woman retorted.

"I suppose not," Leo conceded. The large man was about to say something else when one of the other doors burst open, and another man appeared accompanied by a gust of wind that disturbed the papers on the coffee table and billowed their clothes.

The young man who entered the strange way station was a touch shorter than Quinn's own five-foot ten-inch frame, though he appeared fit and tightly muscled like a decathlete. He wore a loud yellow moto jacket, white jeans, and a pair of gold running shoes with wing-like embellishments that folded over the tongue of the shoe to feather along the outer side. His skin, while originally white, had been tanned a radiant gold by hours in the sun. Green eyes sat in a symmetrical face, crowned with a perfectly feathered shock of golden brown hair that wouldn't look out of place on the cover of the latest boy band album. The stranger's eyes were focused on the cellphone in his hands as he typed a message into it at lightning-quick speed. Attached to his head was a Bluetooth earpiece, while a black leather messenger bag was slung over one shoulder.

"Leo, I'm gonna need those three Gates I ordered ASAP. I'm hoping to deliver the last of these packages by six. Gotta date with this hot little *mami* in Miami tonight and I—" As the man looked from the phone he cut himself off. "Oh, I didn't know you had company!"

"They're just passing through, Carter. I'll go get those Gates for you," the War God replied, before disappearing into one of the rooms at the back of the hub.

Carter's green eyes sparkled with mischief as he took in the two other people in the room. Quinn blinked and with another gust of wind the stranger was suddenly in front of him, though Quinn had yet to see him move. "Hey, Carter, my pleasure," he said by way of introduction, giving Quinn a rakish smile and a quick handshake.

"Uh, Quinn, likewise. Did you just teleport?"

"Nah, I'm just really fast," the other man replied.

Beside him Surina cleared her throat, drawing Carter's attention toward her.

"And Surina, how is my favourite demigod? You look ravishing as always. Sebastien still running you ragged?"

"No more than usual," she said with an easy grin. "Hope that 'little mami in Miami' doesn't keep you too busy; Sebastien's got some messages for you to relay to some key mortals. Should have them ready for you by Sunday."

"Will do. So," Carter said, pointedly looking at Quinn. "Haven't seen you around. You new to the club?"

"We're on our way to the Hall of Erebus to confirm, but if I were to guess I'd definitely say that the gods' ranks will be growing by one today," Surina answered for him.

Carter's eyes narrowed as he regarded Quinn with growing intensity. He pushed his face forward, getting right up into Quinn's personal space. While Quinn didn't step back, he did lean away to keep their noses from colliding. Carter's scrutinizing gaze was unnerving but it allowed Quinn to make his own observations about the other man.

If Quinn was to guess, he thought Carter was about his age—maybe a year or two older, it was hard to tell. He couldn't help but feel a bit intimidated by being so closely studied by a man who could pass for a fashion model, with his trendy clothes, square jaw, and smouldering eyes. As Carter cocked his head to the side in contemplation, Quinn once again took note of the Bluetooth earpiece sticking out from his head. Up close, he could make out the details of the gold-plated bit of metal and plastic that was in the shape of a winged staff with two serpents twined about it.

The realization of Carter's true identity struck him like a clap of thunder.

"Hermes." The Messenger of the Gods. Said to be quicksilver fast, Hermes was the God of Communication, Languages, Trade, Travel, and the patron God of Thieves. Quinn blinked, realizing he had said the name aloud.

Carter pulled back as a knowing smirk crept across his face.

"Well aren't you clever. Yeah, that's me," Carter said, his eyes narrowing as he gave Quinn an appraising look. "Well, that settles it," he proclaimed more to himself than anyone else, a smug grin easing across his roguish features.

"Settles what?" came Leo's voice as he reentered the hub with a couple of manila envelopes, held in a bundle with a rubber band, which he then tossed toward Carter as if it were a football. The younger man caught the package with a laugh.

The look on Carter's face practically oozed with self-satisfaction. "I know who Quinn is," he remarked confidently.

Surina's eyebrows raised from behind the rim of her dark glasses. "Bullshit. Just from looking at him and a few exchanged words? I don't buy it."

Quinn couldn't help but doubt the man's words as well, but he would be lying if he said he wasn't curious about Carter's deductions.

"Oh, I'm 100 percent sure."

Leo snorted. "Well don't keep us in suspense, out with it!"

Carter shook his head, "Nope. I'm not going to ruin the surprise. Besides, there is, like, a 0.1 percent chance that I'm wrong and no need to give the guy a complex for no reason. Don't worry, I'll text it to you later!"

The War God gave a grunt of irritation. "I swear, Carter, you're the biggest tease in all of the Second Realm."

The words reminded Quinn of his earlier query. He decided to speak up before the two gods got distracted by yet another tangent. "Hey, you never did finish explaining what you meant by *realms.*"

Carter furrowed his brow as he turned to regard Quinn once again. "You don't know what the different realms are?"

"I was just about to give him a history lesson when you barged in," Leo explained.

The Messenger God shook his head in dejection, his nose wrinkling at the thought, as if he'd smelled something foul. "Nope, you suck at telling stories. You're gonna grab my new friend a drink, and *I* will give the history lesson." He wandered over to one of the couches and flopped into it. Leo glared at Carter but did as he asked, retrieving a couple bottles of sparkling water from the minifridge behind the bar.

"Quinn, Surina, take a seat," Carter encouraged them to occupy the loveseat opposite him.

As Quinn sank into the small couch, Surina gave a huff of irritation. "We really don't have time for this."

Carter smirked as Leo moved to pass the two of them the bottles of water. "Well it's either I tell him now, or you leave and get to field his thousands of questions when you leave."

Surina seemed to realize when she was beat. Swiping the bottle from Leo, she sharply twisted off the cap and started to drink. Quinn had never seen such a simple act convey so much annoyance, yet Surina raised no more objections. "Just hurry it up, okay? There are only so many hours in a day and not all of us have super speed."

Seemingly pleased with himself, Carter leaned back in his seat. "Now, how'd it go again?" he asked, apparently to himself. "Oh, yeah…"

༄

"In the beginning, there was the Creator, without gender or form. This being was the spark of what would one day be known as the Big Bang. Filled with love, knowledge, peace, wisdom, and understanding, it is difficult to believe that the Creator could feel incomplete.

But the universe can be a lonely place, even to the one who created it.

So, the Creator looked out across the galaxies and planets and chose one as Their child—an experiment. This planet became what we know as Earth.

The Creator sowed the seeds of evolution over Their chosen planet and watched Their children grow. The first fruits of Their labour were creatures of beauty, strength, and brutality—you knew them as the dinosaurs. But while the Creator had set all things into motion, They could not control all potential outcomes. Calamity struck when an asteroid hit Earth. And thus, the eldest of the Creator's children left Earth forever.

But all was not lost. To fill the void that grew within Them after the loss of Their children, the Creator tried again, and what we now know as the five races were born.

First born were the centaurs: wisest of the races, half beast, half man, who looked upward toward the stars.

The Creator's second children were the fauns: creatures of the wild, diverse in appearance, filled with a wild energy and a love of art.

Next came the merfolk: dark creatures of the deep, full of jealousy and secrets.

Fourth, the fae: varying in size and stature, they were the swiftest of the races, blessed with magic, though prone to mischief and curiosity.

And lastly, humans. They were known as the race of chance, as they held the most potential for good and evil.

For a time, the five races existed together in harmony.

But all that is different, or unknown, breeds fear.

An unheard-of love between a nymph and a human prompted scorn and fear in a world that had always upheld a segregation of the races. And when the couple was found murdered, growing flames of distrust and anger were fanned into an unquenchable blaze. War broke out among the races, giving birth to torture, grief, and hatred that lasted generations.

Yet in this destruction, some were conceived who thrived. These creatures were known as the wrathborn, but soon earned names of their own: harpies, goblins, revenants—among others. They were birthed from mutilation and rape between the different races, while others were created after using dark magic to manipulate the dead and experiment on their enemies.

The Creator looked down on Their children, who had cloaked

themselves in hatred, blood, and fear, and They wept. They could not allow the races to murder one another, so They selected a few dozen individuals, all humans, and changed them. They became immortal and more powerful than any other creature. These individuals became the titans and the gods. Unfortunately, these beings, though immortal and powerful, were young and impetuous.

The gods were supposed to be impartial but ended up choosing sides, and the wars continued. Worse still, their fighting turned inward. During a great battle many of the titans and even some of the early primordial gods such as Uranus, Nyx and Hemera were destroyed. In the end, humans—the last race to evolve before the wars broke out—were labelled the instigators. The Creator didn't have the heart to destroy them. Instead, They divided the world into three separate realms—dimensions that would overlap one another, but forever be separated.

In the First Realm, the Creator placed the first four races, along with the wrathborn.

The Second Realm became home to the fifth race: humans. Members of the other four races would sometimes slip through cracks into this realm.

What had once been the home of the gods, Mount Olympus became the Third Realm: Olympia. It was originally created to be a place where the gods could pass judgment over the other races, should anything monumental happen in the world, but since the splitting of the Realms, Olympia has been shuttered, locked away so enemies of the gods could never access its secrets. Not a single god has set foot in Olympia since.

However, as an eternal lesson to the gods for their mistakes, the Creator stripped the gods of their immortality and cursed them to die and be reborn for all eternity. For a while, the gods had been mortal, but they had never died and thus did not fear death. This fear—this knowledge of the swinging pendulum—is what motivates all life to survive at its core. The gods now shared this dreaded knowledge of mortality with the mortal creatures they watched over.

And so it has been ever since. The gods live, serve, die, and live to serve again, standing as the few pillars of order against the ever-present chaos of life."

❧

Carter's words rolled off his tongue with a practiced ease. Each sentence unfolded in a direct simplicity but almost had the feel of a magical tale shared about a campfire. Quinn found himself enthralled by the story. Yet he couldn't shake the sense that something wasn't quite right. It was like listening to a song you knew forward and backward, but with some notes changed at the end. The sense of discord scratched at the back of his brain, but he couldn't find just what it was in Carter's tale that set it off.

So wrapped up in the sensation, he also missed the fact that the story was now over. He was brought back to the present by the obligatory but unenthused slow clap Surina gave. "Excellent history lesson, Professor," her words came out gently teasing as her smile betrayed her approval.

"I try," Carter replied.

"Is that all?" The second the words were out of Quinn's mouth, he realized just how rude they sounded. "Sorry, I mean, is that all to the story? It kind of feels like something is missing."

Carter apparently took no offence to Quinn's belligerent question, as the pleased grin on his face only grew. "Oh yeah, I'm totally right about who you are," he said to himself, before addressing Quinn's query. "Is there more to the story I just told you? Maybe? There was a lot of chaos in the splitting of the realms, and it took awhile for the gods to get things under control. They started to experience their first cycles of death and rebirth. It's possible that some things or events got lost or forgotten over time. But as far as we can tell, this is our history. So, does that story help make things clearer? Or just crazier?"

Quinn considered Carter's words carefully. If you'd asked him a few hours ago if such a story could be true, he would have outright denied it. Yet the strange visions, secret tunnels, and man before him with superspeed made him pause.

"Overall, it does seem kind of crazy," Quinn said. "But I could see it making sense. Science has explained a lot; the formation of the universe, evolution. Your story gives it a *why*."

"So, you're willing to believe us?" Surina pushed.

Was he truly willing to believe in the fairy tale these people had spun? Only a few short hours ago, he was sitting in Cedar Hills wondering if he'd spend the rest of his life there, slowly deteriorating into a babbling, incoherent mess. And even if he'd managed to get out on his own, where would he go? He knew intimately well how hard it was to survive on the streets. And without group housing or even a single penny to his name, what could he possibly do but follow these strange people? Even if that meant he would have to find a way to wrap his still-skeptical mind around the crazy magic crap they were trying to peddle to him.

"I'm willing to see this through. What have I got to lose?" Quinn said, deciding on the spot. He hoped he had made the correct decision.

Leo gave Quinn a hearty slap on the back. "That's the spirit! Now, let's all have a drink. Erica has some craft beers on tap—"

"We're fine with the water you already gave us, Leo," Surina interrupted. "Besides, we've spent more than enough time here," she continued with a pointed look to the hanging cuckoo clock on the wall that proclaimed it to be almost one in the afternoon.

The God of War groaned. "Spoilsport. It's always business with you, isn't it, Surina?"

"Unfortunately, one of us has to get some work done."

Carter rose from his seat on the couch. "I should get going too."

He tapped the bag hanging off his hip. "These packages won't deliver themselves." He crossed over and offered his hand once again to Quinn. "It was good to meet you, Quinn. I'm sure I'll be seeing you around."

"Glad one of us is sure about this. Don't suppose you'd tell me who you think I am?" Quinn asked.

The other man shook his head. "Trust me, this type of information is best discovered on one's own."

Quinn snorted. "Leo was right, you are a tease."

"True, but most people don't complain." Carter's words were accompanied by a saucy wink that prompted a flush to spread across Quinn's cheeks. "All right, gods and demigods, catch you later." There was a gust of wind, the slamming of one of the other Gate doors, and suddenly Carter was gone.

Having watched the Messenger God go, Leo then turned his attention back to Surina. "So, onto the Hall of Erebus?"

"If you'd be so kind," she replied.

Quinn watched the exchange with growing curiosity. So far, the three individuals he had encountered today were all so different. Surina appeared calm and collected, yet she had a streak of sarcasm that dwarfed his own. Leo on the other hand was boisterous and almost jovial, yet a simmering aggression lay just beneath the surface. And though he knew Carter the least, much was apparent about the man. As fast with his words as he was on his feet, the Messenger God was an unrepentant flirt. His new acquaintances obviously knew each other well enough, but were they actually friends or just work associates? And what was this Hall of Erebus they were talking about?

"Hey, Quinn, let's get a move on."

Quinn pulled out of his musings to see his companions waiting for him at one of the doors. As he stood a wave of dizziness swept over him, followed by an uncomfortable feeling of nausea. Fighting down the urge to vomit, his mind went to the meds he should have consumed a few hours ago. If what he was feeling now was a result of a withdrawal, the drugs must have been a lot more powerful than he realized.

Glancing over at the others he was glad to see they hadn't noticed his discomfort. Taking a fortifying breath, he jogged up to them as Leo swung an ornate door open and beckoned them through with a sweep of his well-muscled arm.

"M'lady," the man said as Surina stepped past him, snorting in exasperation as a reply.

"Good luck, man," Leo said as Quinn approached. "Next time you stop by, we'll have that drink. Hopefully by then, we'll both know who you are."

What a strange thing to say, Quinn thought to himself, before grinning at Leo. "Sounds good!"

"And don't let Surina here scare you too much. She's okay when you get to know her," Leo assured him.

"Whatever you say. Oh, by the way, Sebastien says you have a dumb face," Surina called from ahead of them.

Leo snorted. "How would he know?"

"I mean, he's heard you talk," Surina replied, pulling a scowl from the War God. "Come on, Quinn, let's go," she called.

The young man gave a small bob of his head in farewell to Leo, before moving into the cramped corridor behind Surina. The door closed swiftly behind them, leaving them in the dark, save for a small light at the end of the tunnel.

CHAPTER EIGHT

As they exited the dark hallway, Quinn paused in awe. The chamber they entered sprawled out for almost a mile and was vastly cavernous, with enormous rows of stone pillars supporting the roof overhead. Through a large circular window in the ceiling about twenty feet in diameter, Quinn saw the late morning sky, bright with golden sunlight. The position of the sun seemingly at odds with the clock back in the Gate hub.

"Where are we?" he asked.

"Somewhere under San Francisco, I believe," Surina replied as she consulted a series of directions written on her phone. "Never actually been to Erebus, so I'm not completely sure."

That made sense, Quinn reasoned, what with the three-hour time difference between the east and west coast. "But, that skylight," he said, stumbling along behind her. "Doesn't anyone notice it?"

"Sadly enough, no," she breathed a sigh. "And to think that only a small glamour conceals it."

"Glamour?" Quinn echoed.

"A special kind of magic that hides the true form of a person or thing. Remember that *Employees Only* door we went through in the subway station?"

"Yeah."

"Well, any normal person would have just seen a wall."

Quinn paused as he took in Surina's words. "Wait," he called after her. "If I can see the door, doesn't that already prove that I'm...you know..."

"A god?" Surina supplied. "It's okay to say it. Remember, we don't mean 'God' the way other humans mean it. No need to worry about getting struck down for blasphemy, or anything."

"Is that my answer?"

"Not only gods can see through glamours—well, most glamours, that is," she explained. "I mean, I'm not a god. Technically I shouldn't even be called a demigod, as my genes only stand at 25 percent. Still, I could see it, so it's possible you just hold some sort of connection to the magical world. As for everyone else, there are some things that people shouldn't know about, and this is one of them."

Rolling this new bit of information around in his head, Quinn posited another question. "If you only have 25 percent god genes, that would mean a god was your grandparent."

"That's correct," she said, offering up no further details.

"You're really gonna make me ask, who is it?"

"You'll find out soon enough."

Figuring this was the end of the conversation for now, Quinn turned his attention once again to the giant space they now walked through. "So, this is the Hall of Erebus?"

Surina shook her head. "Not yet. This used to be one of the gods' meeting halls, but we had to move the gatherings around to accommodate those living farther away. In the end, it was forgotten, I guess. The Hall of Erebus is up ahead."

"I see. So, what exactly is the hall?" Quinn asked.

"You said you've read quite a few Greek myths. Tell me, what do you know about Prometheus?"

Quinn wracked his brain. Within a couple of seconds, he could recall everything he had read about the titans.

"There are several different versions of the stories. Some say he was a Titan who created mankind out of clay; others, that he tricked Zeus and the other gods into accepting the inedible parts of a sacrifice, like cow bones. That last story claims that Zeus took back the gift of fire so that humans would be unable to cook their food, and Prometheus went on to steal the fire back from Olympus for the humans. In other versions we didn't have fire in the first place, and we only do now thanks to Prometheus' theft. Either way, Zeus punished him by chaining him to a rock and sending a bird every day to peck out his liver, but it would just grow back during the night so the bird could return the next day to start again. Seems like a pretty harsh punishment for just trying to help people out."

Surina's brows furrowed under her sunglasses. "It's not that simple, Quinn. Prometheus didn't bring ordinary fire to mortals. We'd already figured out how to make fire on our own; we're pretty resourceful."

Quinn cocked his head to the side, confused. "Then what happened?"

"Prometheus took *the* fire. The Olympian fire, only found in the Third Realm of Olympia. And he was punished for good reason. Olympian fire is pure magic; it's made up of the remnants of the souls of the gods. A living soul is represented as a spark or flame, and when a mortal—who is not a god—dies, that flame goes out and becomes something else. The souls of gods are different, they don't extinguish or transform. It's more like...how hermit crabs abandon shells they outgrow for something new. The 'shells' that are left behind become part of the Olympian fire and help cleanse the gods' souls on their way to their next life."

"Then what do mortal souls become?"

Surina shrugged her shoulders gracefully. "No clue. Only the Underworld gods would know. Anyway, Olympian fire burns the hottest, and it can never be put out. It's a dangerous weapon that could end everything if it fell into the wrong hands. Not only is it unquenchable, but once it's unleashed, it has the power to show us for who and what we truly are. Can you imagine how humans would react, seeing monsters and powerful beings everywhere?"

Quinn wondered for a moment if Surina had meant to give away as much as she had in her few words. Strangely enough, he had begun to accept that there were gods walking among them—even if he wasn't sold on the idea that he was also one of them. Despite his interactions with the small fae buzzing around Cedar Hills, he had never considered his own abilities until Surina had mentioned them. And then, she described monsters. *Monsters are real!*

He shook his head. "What do you mean, the fire shows us for what we truly are?" he asked. "I've been thinking about this ever since meeting Carter. He's inhumanly fast. How could anyone, human or not, overlook that? If gods are capable of powers like that, shouldn't they be fairly easy to spot? Why would you need to use the Olympian fire at all?"

"Ah, yes, I see why you might be confused by that," she said. "Okay, so visiting Olympian fire and connecting with it is kind of like a ritual. When gods die, they shed most of their memories and powers from their last incarnations. If they didn't, there would be no way for a regular mortal human to carry that baby to term. So, when the gods are reborn, they are diminished. They have a spark of their abilities, but nothing that would make others believe they were superhuman. Carter probably just came off as the fastest kid in his county growing up—super talented for sure, but nothing completely out of the ordinary.

"That spark of talent would remain, unless that individual came in contact with Olympian fire. Reconnecting with the fire is like blowing on an ember and starting a bonfire. It's from that interaction that someone like Carter would receive his superhuman speed. It's also what makes gods more durable. Although not immortal, a god's body can put up with a lot more punishment. Still, we can't just allow anyone to just stumble upon the Olympian fire, god or not, they wouldn't be able to handle it."

He glanced over at his guide. "You don't give people enough credit; they're more intelligent than you think," he commented.

"No," Surina corrected. "Individuals are intelligent, but in a group, they become panicky beasts—slow to think, but quick to act. As a race, humans have forgotten too much of their histories to be able to handle the truth. As for Olympian fire, it's a miracle that we've been able to contain it away from human hands."

"And that's what's in the Hall of Erebus?"

"Well, yeah, but it's not actually a hall, not like this one. The Hall of Erebus is actually an offshoot of the Underworld, though no one is buried there. It's a place of complete darkness. At one time, the dead would pass through it on their way to the Underworld. Now only the souls of the gods pass through it on the way to their next incarnation. Olympian fire is the only light in the hall, and like all light, it creates one very important thing."

"What's that?"

"Shadows."

Surina turned and continued walking toward the doors at the other end of the large room. Quinn took this as a sign that the conversation was over and stayed silent, aware of Surina's apparent impatience to get to their destination.

Exiting the entrance hall after Surina, Quinn found himself in a much smaller room, with a single set of stairs leading down. Police tape hung over the stairway's entrance, and a sign attached to the tape

G.E. White

read, *Stairs Out of Order. Sorry for the Inconvenience.*

"Great. Just great," Surina grumbled.

"I don't get it; how can the stairs be out of order?" Quinn asked.

"Probably a body jam on levels three and four."

"Body jam?" he croaked.

"An overload of people burying their dead. It's pretty common, unfortunately. It's like humans have never heard of cremation. It's so much more sanitary and keeps people from resurrecting the dead."

Quinn's eyes widened. "People can do that?"

"Well, not many. Only those trained in god magics, mostly magi and the like. It doesn't happen very often, as it's some seriously dark magic, not to mention downright illegal. Anyway, that doesn't matter," she said, shrugging it off. "We need to keep moving."

He gave her a puzzled look. "And how are we going to do that without stairs?"

"We'll just have to take the elevator," she said.

Quinn watched Surina retrieve an old-fashioned, gold pocket watch from her jacket. She clicked the faceplate open, revealing the intricate pattern etched around the front: tiny murals representing the twelve signs of the zodiac. The middle of the plate was glass, allowing half of the clock face to be seen. Quinn had never seen a watch like it before and could not help but stare.

"You like it?" she asked. "It's a protean watch—a gift from my father. Said it belonged to my grandmother. I've never seen anything with such amazing craftsmanship. I almost refused to take it, but he insisted."

Quinn tilted his head to view the watch's inside face. Small sections on opposing sides of the face had been cut out, presumably to reveal the inside workings of the machine. The hour marks were laid in gold Roman numerals, and each number appeared to have some sort of image behind it. A fourth hand pointed straight up to the number twelve and the image of a watch.

Surina paused to wind the watch, changing the extra hand to point to three o'clock and a symbol of a weapon. The watch began to contort and elongate, morphing into a full-length sword. Quinn's brain recognized it as a rapier, and his jaw dropped as he gazed at the weapon. "Huh," he choked out, temporarily at a loss for words.

"The watch can change into a dozen different weapons or tools, depending on where you set the extra hand," Surina explained. "Kind of like the ultimate Swiss Army knife. Stand still."

To Quinn's surprise, Surina began to mutter to herself—an incantation in Latin, a language that he had encountered in biology, botany, and legal texts, though he had heard it spoken in movies and occasional sermons from the time he lived with the Johnsons.

"Rectis per aetheris parte aditus mihi. Et revelata est via et ostium."

As she spoke, Surina used her sword to carve a circle around the two of them, engraving the number seventeen into the circle's centre. Quinn couldn't help but wonder why this seemingly magical incantation was in Latin. With the gods' connection with Greece, shouldn't it be in ancient Greek?

As he considered the conundrum, the thought came to him. It was most likely any spells originally written in ancient Greek were lost during the Great Fire of Alexandria, or other events like it, based on the Christian religious zeal of the times. From there, most books were only written down after the Romans took over most of the ancient world. Therefore, it would make sense that their spells would be written in Latin.

He thought about asking his companion about it, but Surina didn't seem like the kind of person who would tolerate a bunch of questions. And he had already asked about a million since meeting her, so it was probably best to save his questions for later. Besides, she seemed to have her hands full with her ritual.

Once Surina's work was complete, she gripped the hilt of the sword tightly and stabbed the tip of the blade deep into the stone floor. "You might want to hold on," she warned.

Unsure of what was happening, Quinn nevertheless obeyed and clenched the sword's hilt into his right hand.

The floor shifted beneath them, and suddenly they were falling. Quinn let out an undignified scream as they plummeted downward, still miraculously standing on a section of the floor.

Surina appeared unfazed as she counted aloud.

"Thirteen...fourteen...fifteen...sixteen...seventeen, this is our stop."

And just as suddenly as they had started falling, they stopped. It took a moment for Quinn to realize that he couldn't see what was keeping them aloft. As far as he could tell, it was just them, the stone circle, and the hole they had fallen through. The thought alone was nauseating.

"Why doesn't it keep going?" he asked.

"Why doesn't *what* keep going?"

"The floor. Why does it stop when we stop?"

"Well, you see," Surina began, only to stop mid sentence, her mouth hanging open as she racked her brain for the answer. "Huh, well, I guess I just never really thought about it."

"Probably best not to," Quinn replied.

"Probably."

It was at this time that Quinn's earlier nausea decided to rear its head. He turned away just in time to avoid barfing all over Surina's shoes. Out of the corner of his eye he saw the woman cringe in sympathy before awkwardly patting him on the back.

"You okay there?" she asked, offering him a tissue from her pocket.

Feeling a touch better, now that his stomach was empty, Quinn nodded, taking the tissue and wiping his mouth.

"Come on, I'll make us a door, and we'll be on our way."

"Yeah," he said with a tremulous laugh. "I'd like that."

Surina's sword cut through the wall stone like wind over a faerie's wing. Carving out a door, she pushed it open to reveal another dark tunnel. They stepped from the stone and started down the corridor toward a light shimmering in the distance. It grew brighter as they walked until eventually the tunnel opened up into a large circular room.

The Hall of Erebus.

Quinn was overwhelmed with a feeling of déjà vu. He had been here before. The feeling should have instilled a sense of confidence, but he winced at the sudden sensation of icy fingers clutching around his heart.

How did he know this place? Was Surina's boss right? Was he really a god?

He took in the room around him. Huge Greek columns formed a circle in the centre, disappearing upward into the ceiling's inky heights. Several openings led off in different directions—tunnels, similar to the one they had just exited.

Within the circle on a low dais sat a marble pedestal with out-stretched arms and cupped hands cradling a brilliant ball of fire. The hands were remarkably detached from the flame, which flickered red, then orange, then yellow—through all the colours of the rainbow.

Quinn was mesmerized, drawn to the fire like the proverbial moth.

"Olympian fire," he breathed.

"All right, Quinn. Enough gawking, it's time," Surina called, pulling him from his trance.

Quinn turned from his thoughts to Surina, who now stood on the other side of the fire, the flames reflected in her dark glasses. But despite the beautiful colours falling across her lenses, his attention was immediately drawn to the shadows Surina cast.

Even though she stood directly in front of the fire, no image was

        G.E. White

cast behind her. Instead, two distinct shadows branched out to her right and left. The shadow on the right seemed to resemble a stag with its front legs reared back, preparing to strike. Despite the shadow's fierce demeanour, Quinn felt no threat when he gazed upon the stag.

The shadow to the left, however, filled him with dread. The dark figure twisted and turned to reveal a large hooded serpent with its fangs bared. The shadow of the enormous snake swayed gently in tandem with Surina's shifting feet.

"But...but how?" Quinn asked.

She smiled. "This is the real me. I'm human, yet at the same time, I'm also a descendant of an incarnation of Artemis," she continued, pointing at the stag. "The stag is one of her symbols."

"But I thought that Artemis was a virgin goddess."

Surina placed her hands on her hips, her head dropping down as she emitted a laugh. "You weren't kidding when you said you read a lot. The incarnation that the name Artemis is tied to was indeed a virgin. Accounts of her life described her as someone you would call asexual, but each incarnation changes both the body and soul of the god. Yes, many things stay the same between lives. But not everything."

"I guess I understand. So what does that stand for?" Quinn pointed to the serpent.

Surina's lips tightened into a thin line. "It represents the bloodline I inherited from my mother. I'd rather not talk about it."

Quinn lowered his gaze. "Sorry. I didn't mean to pry."

"It's fine," she said sharply. Her tone indicated she wouldn't allow any further questions. "It's not important, anyway." Surina's attention shifted from Quinn's face to the still-formless shadows behind him, reminding him of his purpose.

"Step forward," she said, beckoning with her hand.

Quinn did so, anxiety creeping through his stomach as he approached the flames. The heat radiating from the fire was almost too much to bear, but he had to see this through. As he stood by the brazier of Olympian fire a strange wave of energy washed over him, stealing his breath away. The sensation wasn't painful, but invigorating. Any hint of hunger, thirst, or weariness was banished as he stood in the blazing heat of the flames before him. The experience was cleansing—any lingering feeling of nausea or chills from his lack of medication was now gone. Quinn couldn't help but wonder if the flames could give an addict the detox their body so desperately needed. Though from Surina's words it was also possible that the flames would consume anyone who wasn't a god. It made sense to him that this was how the gods awakened their superhuman abilities. Still, he had no idea who he was. He twisted his upper body slowly to see what lay behind him.

Unlike Surina, Quinn cast only one shadow, yet it was not his own. Spread behind him was the inky visage of a great owl, its wings unfurled as if in flight. The sight felt at once foreign, but deeply familiar.

"Athena," Surina whispered.

Quinn spun around to face her. "That can't be right, I can't be... *her.*"

Athena was a goddess, not a god, and Quinn had no doubt in his mind he felt male. But what shook him the most was knowing what Athena stood for.

Athena had been a symbol of hope and wisdom: the patron Goddess of Heroes, a master strategist, and the Goddess of Knowledge. Quinn considered himself a quick study and well read, but brave or heroic? Hardly. He hadn't even been able to speak up for himself at his own trial.

His shadow seemed to mock him, showing him everything that he never was and couldn't be.

"Quinn? You okay?" Surina called out to him.

He shook his head from side to side, failing to supply words for his distress.

G.E. White

Surina stepped around the pyre to place a hand on his shoulder. He could tell that neither of them was truly comfortable with the gesture.

"I know it's overwhelming, but trust me, this is a good thing."

Quinn tensed. True, this development meant he wouldn't have to go back to Cedar Hills, but it felt as though it brought as many problems as his time in that institution had, if not more. His whole life was about to change, and he had a strange feeling that not all of it would be for the better. Yesterday he had known who he was and what was expected of him. Now he felt hollow. It was as if someone had scraped his soul of everything he was and thrown it into the fire before him.

He glanced back again at the winged shadow. This wasn't him. It couldn't be. This had to be some kind of mistake. He'd wake up soon and realize that this was all a dream. But for now, what could he do but go along for the ride? It's not like he had any other options.

"Yeah. Sounds great," he said, his tone making it clear it was anything but. "So, now what?"

Surina pulled out her cell phone and quickly typed out a message, before sliding it back into her pocket.

"I just let everyone know that you're Athena. They'll be so excited to know they've finally found you. Athena's a big player, a key piece of the puzzle, if you will. But for now, we head topside. It's already late afternoon, and this is a lot to take in."

"Okay," Quinn hung his head, still having a hard time trying to swallow this pill.

Surina frowned. "It won't be that bad. Promise."

"Easy for you to say," he grumbled. "At least you were born into this. I'm basically getting thrown headfirst into the deep end."

"Well, then you'll learn to swim fast. It's like remembering how to ride a bike—in a badly mixed metaphor kind of way," she said, stumbling over her words.

Quinn chuckled, which put a smile back on her face.

"Come on, we should blow this place before…" Surina trailed off.

The young man looked at her intently, but then he too heard it. The rustling of movement.

Picking up on Surina's unease, Quinn moved closer to her, frantically searching for the source of the noise. "What is that?"

Both Surina and he looked upward to see the twinkling of over a dozen pairs of catlike eyes. Surina slowly reached for her watch, her eyes fixed on the ceiling. She turned the watch's hands to five o'clock. The watch shifted and morphed into a blade heavier than the rapier she had had before. She lifted the broadsword in her hand and shouted, "Artemis, *lumen!*"

A gentle blue light pulsed outward from her body, illuminating the room for an instant. In that moment, Quinn saw creatures he could only loosely identify as women. Their tattered and blood-stained rags draped about them, and their hair laid tangled and horribly matted against their scalps. Seemingly infinite pairs of eyes glinted hungrily as the women-creatures crawled, spider-like, toward the two companions.

"Danaids!" Surina gasped. "Run! Now!" she commanded, shoving him in the direction of one of the tunnels.

The creatures sprang from their perches in the shadows. Quinn faltered, noticing Surina made no move to follow him.

"I said, get going! We'll meet up later," she shouted. One of the women-creatures launched herself at Surina. She leapt aside with incredible speed, swinging her sword and taking off one of the creature's arms. "I can handle this! Go!"

Blood splattered across the stone floor as the arm flopped lifelessly to the ground. Quinn gagged at the sight. He had never witnessed such gore in real life. Surina turned from him just in time to behead another of the creatures as she tried to snap at her shoulder.

Quinn ran toward one of the tunnels. *They all must lead to the surface eventually,* he told himself. He tried to block out the sound of metal severing flesh and the shrieks of pain as he ran.

G.E. White

The tunnel became darker and darker. Quinn could barely see his feet in front of him, but the sounds of something pursuing him kept him moving.

Suddenly, there was nothing in front of him or below him. Fear and adrenaline overcame him as he fell, tumbling head over heels. He fell for what felt like an eternity, only to scream in terror as the ground rose up to meet him.

CHAPTER NINE

THE FIRST THING that Quinn became aware of as he came-to was the discomfort running through his senses. The uneven ground he lay upon dug into him at odd angles, and the air hung heavy, dank, and full of despair.

Quinn cracked his eyes open and beheld a large cavern, stretching out for miles. A dim light emanated from strange lanterns jutting out from the stalactites above the massive room. There seemed to be a path winding its way through the craggy terrain, flanked on either side by rows of crumbling, white marble columns, resembling bleached bones jutting from the ground like spines.

Quinn sat up and ran a quick triage of his body, both relieved and confused to discover nothing appeared to be broken, though he did sport a new and throbbing lump on his head. The fall should have killed him. But here he was, relatively unscathed. He thought back to Surina's proclamation that connecting with the Olympian fire would make him far more resilient to injury. Is this what it means to be a god? He glanced upward into the darkness of the gaping hole. It was obvious he wasn't getting back to Surina that way.

Quinn shuddered, remembering the shrieks of the rabid women that attacked them. He hoped Surina was all right. He might have just met her, but she was his only point of contact in his new world, other than Leo and Carter, and he had no idea how to get in touch with them. The idea that Quinn was all alone without Surina to guide him through whatever mess she'd dragged him into was terrifying.

It didn't help him to mope around in some dark cave. He needed to be smart about this to avoid getting trapped here.

The cavern was way bigger than Quinn initially realized, and somewhere off in the distance, he swore he heard the sound of flowing water.

Quinn pushed himself to his feet and looked around. The path appeared to go on for miles in either direction. Taking a few steps, then stopping to listen carefully, Quinn chose to follow the path to his right. The sound of rushing water was stronger on that side, and he reasoned that he might stumble across an underground river or spring that could lead him back to the surface world.

This place is so unnerving. I would hate to get lost. And if Surina comes down this way, I need to let her know what direction I went in.

Quinn cast his gaze around the area and smiled with relief as he found a piece of charcoal-like rock. He tested it on the nearest marble pillar and sure enough the dark grey *Q* he'd etched stood out in high contrast to the stark white. Now he could be relatively sure Surina would be able to find him.

If she survived those creatures attacking her, that is.

The thought propelled him to keep moving. He couldn't dwell anywhere. It was clear he was in a world where he didn't know the dangers or the rules and he felt overwhelmed by it all. He knew just how in over his head he was, but the only thing he could do was try his best to survive. Foster care hadn't done him any favours, but at least he'd learned how to adapt to whatever messed-up situation he'd found himself in.

With a determined resolve and pounding headache, Quinn took off on his trek.

Hours later, the hunger and thirst caught up to him. The water sounds he'd been following seemed no closer, and the terrain all blended together in a homogenous blur. He'd not yet come across a pillar marked with one of his *Q's,* which gave him hope that he was still at least moving forward. If it weren't for that, he could have sworn he was going in circles.

He stopped for a moment and did the math. He'd made a game of counting the columns a while back. Based on a rough estimate of the distance between each marble spine, the rough number he'd trekked past, and the walking speed of an average human being about four miles an hour, he guessed he'd already covered twelve miles in about three hours. For a second, he was stunned. Quinn had always considered himself a bright individual, but coming up with such a calculation in a matter of moments was usually beyond him. Was this Athena's power making itself known?

Shaking his head to clear the thought, he focused again on the twelve miles he must have covered. *That can't be right! This place is massive! And I can't keep wandering around indefinitely, god or not. I need some kind of vantage point to see if I'm even going anywhere!*

Seeing no other option, Quinn decided to try his luck climbing the tallest of the hills just off the pillar-lined path. Quinn tried not to let his dust-dry mouth and grumbling belly get the best of him as he climbed. Luckily, on the other side, at the foot of the hill, was a wooden pole with several signs attached, each pointing in a different direction.

With a whoop of joy, Quinn jogged down the rest of the hill, anxious to see where he should go. *Surely, one will lead me back to the surface!* But his spirits fell once more after reading the five wooden signs. "Acheron, Cocytus, Phlegethon, Styx, Lethe. What the hell do those mean?" he muttered to himself.

"Means you're lost," hissed a rough voice behind him, close to his ear.

Quinn whirled about, coming face to face with three emaciated figures, who most certainly hadn't been there a moment ago. Yet as he took a closer look, he realized that they weren't only thin but also translucent.

The voice by his ear appeared to belong to a man, his beard and dark hair peppered with grey. The clothes that he wore looked like the old confederate uniforms Quinn had learned about in school, from the age of the American Civil War. The man sneered at Quinn, his teeth crooked and yellow with grime.

"No need to be rude, Harold," scolded the female apparition at his side. Blonde, almost white, locks floated around her face, which appeared deeply hollow in places. Her glamorous appearance was heightened by her flapper dress, similar to ones Quinn knew starlets had worn in the 1920s. While her accent was decidedly British, and her tone was warm, the cloying scent of cloves clinging to her caused Quinn to lean away from her in distaste.

She turned milky blue eyes toward him and smiled, though there was no warmth in the gesture. "It's okay, darling, we'll help you find your way," she drawled, her voice slow and syrupy with artificial concern.

"Kind of fleshy, isn't he, Rosa?" the third spectre finally said.

He was young—perhaps only a few years Quinn's senior. The military-green fatigues he wore were stained with blood, and his eyes danced with a strange hunger.

"That's not exactly a bad thing, now, is it, Jimmy?" Rosa asked.

"Besides, the boy obviously needs our help. And it would be nice to have some new company."

Rosa reached a bony hand and gripped Quinn's upper arm tightly. "Come on, dear, we'll take you somewhere nice and quiet."

What had started off as an uneasy feeling turned to full-blown terror. As Quinn tried to pull away, he found Rosa's grip much stronger than her appearance belied. "No, that's all right," he assured, attempting to keep the tremor from his voice as he finally slipped his arm out of the woman's surprisingly firm hold. "I'm just waiting for a friend, and she'll be here any minute."

Jimmy pushed his face against Quinn's and stared into his eyes. "You're lying," he said, sounding disappointed.

"Aw, look at him. He's scared," Harold chuckled, taking in Quinn's trembling.

Jimmy reached out toward Quinn's face. "Don't you want to be our friend?" he asked.

Quinn jerked back from the ghoul's reach. "Don't touch me!"

Harold's face twisted into a snarl, his hand painfully gripping Quinn's forearm. "No need to be rude, boy."

Fear morphing into adrenaline, Quinn wound back his free hand and delivered a solid punch to Harold's chin. The ghoul fell back, releasing him as Harold's companions looked on in disbelief. Quinn's fist connecting with Harold's transparent form had stunned them into silence.

Harold staggered to his feet. He, Jimmy, and Rosa advanced on Quinn, who stumbled back, frantically looking for a way out. Just as the three were closing in, a new voice echoed across the cavern.

"That's enough, you vultures!"

The three apparitions shrank back, allowing Quinn to fall backward. He was unsure from where this newcomer had appeared, but grateful nonetheless.

Quinn's rescuer stood solid in contrast to his ghostly assailants, the

G.E. White

former's shock of black hair slicked away from his face in a stylish coif. Quinn blinked in surprise. Standing before him was the mysterious stranger he had seen at Cedar Hills, just before Marvin's death. He hadn't gotten this close a look at him before, but he was so strikingly beautiful, it would have been impossible to forget his face.

The young man's ice-blue eyes glared daggers at the spectres. His sleek attire of black slacks and a fashionable grey sweater would not have looked out of place on the cover of *GQ* magazine. In fact, the man looked as though he could be a cover model himself. Chiselled features, a piercing gaze, full mouth, and the kind of body that people spent hours at the gym hoping to achieve. Quinn hoped he wasn't blushing like an idiot, but the characteristic burning of his cheeks told him that his body had betrayed him.

"Jared," Harold wheezed, "We didn't know he was with you."

"And that should make a difference?" Jared challenged. "Did you even stop to think what a mortal would be doing here, with his flesh still attached?"

"We're sorry, my lord. We promise it won't happen again," Rosa pleaded.

"Damn straight it won't. If it does, all three of you will find yourselves at the bottom of the Phlegethon faster than you can say Tartarus. Now get out of my sight!" he bellowed, throwing out his arm in the direction of the cavern's entrance.

With an anguished wail, the three spectres vanished, like ashes cast into the wind.

Quinn stood stiffly, his gaze fixed on his saviour, who continued to glare in the direction of the vanished apparitions. Once again, a strange fluttery feeling raced through his stomach. "Thank you," he said softly, suddenly shy.

Jared's once-fierce expression softened as he turned toward Quinn. "No problem. Lousy ghouls don't know when to quit. I thought they knew that only gods can physically connect with spirits. Looked like that right hook of yours hurt Harold too."

"Uh, thanks, I guess," Quinn replied, scratching the back of his hand. As Quinn looked up at Jared, he realized that the other god was younger than he first thought. Jared was probably in his early twenties, only a few years older than Quinn. He just carried himself with a maturity and confidence that Quinn found both alluring and intimidating.

As Quinn inspected Jared, the other man returned the gesture. "You're Quinn, right? The new Athena?" he asked.

"Yeah, how did you know?"

Jared smiled gently. "Carter got a message from Surina and gave us a call to say you might be down here."

"Us?" Quinn asked.

"My family and I. Oh, I'm sorry. Where are my manners?" the dark-haired man mused to himself. "I'm Jared Doyle, the current incarnation of Thanatos."

"Thanatos?"

"God of Death."

Quinn felt his face give an involuntary twitch. *The God of Death? Could this day get any crazier?* A part of him wondered if he was experiencing all of this in his head while he was safely tucked away in Cedar Hills, finally lost in his illness. But he doubted that his head would hurt as much as it did if all of this was a hallucination. However, as he attempted to process Jared's words in his head, something didn't quite make sense.

"But I thought Hades was the God of Death."

Jared chuckled good-naturedly. "Technically, Joseph—uh, that's my brother; he's the current Hades—is God of the Underworld. That means he deals with the administrative stuff—where dead souls end up, things of that nature. Me, I handle the part where people actually die. Think of me as the Grim Reaper, though I like to think I'm more handsome than how most people picture Death. Little less skeletal, better hair and wardrobe." Jared's explanation was accompanied by the perfunctory smoothing of his perfectly arranged hair and a self-satisfied grin that belied his sense of humour. Quinn found himself unable to resist returning the smile. *Who would've guessed that Death would be so charming?*

"One second," Jared said, holding up a finger with his left hand and pulling out a cellphone from his jacket pocket with the right. "I've just gotta make a quick phone call." He flicked through his contacts, before finding and selecting a number. Quinn listened intently to Jared's side of the conversation as the person on the other end picked up.

"Hey, yeah, I found him... Yeah, he's okay," Jared said into the receiver, giving Quinn a once-over. "Got a bit of a lump on his head, maybe a little shaken up, but otherwise he's fine. So, what do you want me to do? ... Uh-huh... Oh..." The God of Death paused before his voice dropped lower, making it obvious he just received some unwelcome news. "I see. But you've got it under control? ... Uh-huh... Yeah, I can do that... Okay, just let me know if anything changes. Bye."

Jared placed his phone into his jacket and peered at Quinn's questioning face. But instead of asking who Jared had been speaking to, Quinn found another comment pressing against his lips.

"I've seen you before," he said.

Jared tensed, his forehead creasing. "You have?"

Quinn nodded. "At Cedar Hills, back in June."

Jared's frame relaxed as he laughed. "Oh right, Marvin Jacobs. I thought I was imagining that you saw me. But you *were* there!"

Quinn's eyes narrowed at the other man's odd behaviour, he was certain the two had made eye contact, but let it slide as he waited for answers to his questions. "No one else could see you. Why is that?"

"Oh! Probably because of *this,*" Jared reached out, the gothic-looking cloak Quinn had previously seen at Cedar Hills appearing from thin air like a veil of smoke. With a flourish, Jared set the cloak about his shoulders. "My cloak of invisibility," he explained proudly. "That's why I didn't think you saw me."

The words sparked a memory in Quinn. "I thought it was a helmet."

Jared gave a snort. "And cover up this hair?" He ran his hand across the glossy locks. "No, my helmet days are over—a former Athena saw to that. I wear this on the job. Makes me invisible to everyone but the soul I'm collecting. Well, except for gods and animals, of course."

"Animals?"

"What can I say? They like me, or is it that they fear me? No, they respect me." Jared concluded.

The mention of animals brought Quinn's thoughts back to the creatures who had attacked Surina in the Hall of Erebus. "You said Carter contacted you about me. What about Surina? Was that her on the phone?"

"Ah, no. That was Carter. Surina's a little indisposed at the moment, but don't worry, she'll be fine," Jared reassured him. "She's tougher than some of the actual gods. It'll take more than a few Danaids and a case of miasma to take her down."

"Miasma? Like Asthma?" Quinn echoed, unfamiliar with the term. "Is that some sort of breathing problem?"

Jared cringed. "Uh, yeah, something like that," he replied, his eyes shifting away from Quinn's.

Quinn scowled. There was obviously something the other man wasn't telling him, but before he could voice his skepticism, Jared continued.

"Surina was more worried about *you*, but who wouldn't be, when their charge is in the Underworld."

Quinn's heart stopped briefly when he heard Jared's words. "The Underworld?"

"Where did you think you were?"

Quinn shook his head. "Not there, but I guess I should have figured it out." He gazed up at the road sign, realization finally clicking in.

"These paths lead to rivers, don't they?"

"Yep, the five rivers of the Underworld. Let me guess, Styx gave it away."

"Oh, yeah, duh. Almost everyone's heard of the River Styx. I don't know how I forgot," Quinn said, feeling foolish for not recognizing his surroundings sooner.

Jared waved it off. "Hey, you did just bump your noggin; I think you're allowed a little memory slip. Plus, didn't you just find out that you're one of us? That's gotta be a mindfuck."

"I suppose." Quinn wanted to quip about how much of an understatement that was, but kept it to himself. "So how come you came to get me, and not Surina? I mean, miasma aside."

"Let's walk and talk, okay Quinn?" Jared said as he started walking down the path toward the River Styx. Quinn quickly fell in place behind him, willing his legs to match Jared's longer stride.

"You see, while it's not officially a rule, there is an understanding that mortals who aren't gods shouldn't be allowed in the Underworld. Unless they're dead, of course. We've had a few incidents—Orpheus and Eurydice, Izanaki and Izanami, to name a couple—and they've never ended well. That, and then there are a few gods who don't exactly trust Surina."

"Why is that?"

Jared shook his head. "It's not really my story to tell. Let's just say that it has something to do with her heritage and leave it at that."

Though Jared's tone was soft, Quinn could tell that pressing the matter would be fruitless. He walked alongside Jared until they reached the bank of a wide river. The water ran grey and quick, and a light mist blanketed most of its surface. Despite his extreme thirst, Quinn had read enough Greek mythology to know better than to drink from the rivers of the Underworld. While water from the Styx may have made Achilles invulnerable, others found it poisonous. Supposedly some of the rivers could induce memory loss or a sensation of endless burning.

He just hoped he could bug Jared for a bottle of clean water whenever they got to wherever they were going.

As their path brought them closer to the river's edge, Quinn could make out a ghostly blue arm that rose, as if pleading for rescue from the depths, before sinking back beneath the surface. He soon noticed that the river was filled with many such souls: some wept, others raged, but most just floated as if asleep, apparently at peace as they moved along the Styx's currents.

Quinn tore his gaze from the river as Jared pushed something into his hand. "Here, you'll need this."

The items in his palm were two silver coins with an olive branch etched onto each tarnished surface.

Out of the mist floated a small boat ferried by a looming and cloaked figure. The boatman's face was impossible to see under the cloak's hood, but the hands that gripped the long pole were a dull, white hue—the colour of ancient bone.

The boat pulled up to the bank of the Styx and Jared calmly stepped in, handing the ferryman his own coins. Quinn moved as if to follow, but his feet wouldn't shift, leaving him standing on the river's edge.

"Come on, hurry up," Jared called. "Don't let this guy scare you; Charon here is just an old softy at heart," he reassured, patting the skeletal figure on the shoulder.

Charon groaned in irritation but remained immobile. Hesitantly, Quinn stepped into the boat and approached the ferryman, who held his skeletal hand out to the young man. After a moment of staring into the dark abyss behind Charon's hood, Quinn remembered his coins and placed them in the boatman's open hand.

Charon grunted in approval and pointed to one of the seats in the boat.

Obviously not much of a talker.

Quinn sat, apprehensive, as Charon used his long pole to push away from the shore and began steering them across the River Styx.

The journey along the water was made in silence. Quinn huddled, crouching inward on himself to avoid getting too close to the edge of the boat. Jared leaned against the side, head propped up with his hand, appearing uninterested as he stared out at the river. The ghostly apparitions floating around the boat paid them no mind, each disappearing into the currents of the dark water as the waves pulsed around them.

With expert steering from Charon, the ferry pushed against the white sand of the opposite bank several minutes later.

Jared stepped out of the boat with an ease born of repetition and gave a casual wave. "Thanks, man," he said to the ferryman.

Quinn was not quite as graceful as he disembarked, catching his foot on the rim of the vessel. He would have fallen flat on his face if not for Jared's quick reflexes as he caught Quinn about the shoulders and put him to rights. Heat flushed across his face at the close contact as he muttered his thanks to the other man, all the while mentally berating himself for being such a klutz.

Once on solid land, he offered his thanks to the ferryman as well, but Charon just grunted in acknowledgement, before shoving his craft back out into the river's murky depths, disappearing once more into the mist.

❧

As the two gods walked together in silence, his whole situation struck Quinn as odd. They soon approached the grounds of a sprawling mansion, surrounded by impressive gardens. The vast grounds, stretching as far as Quinn's eyes could see, were surrounded by a towering fence and main gate constructed entirely of bone.

Strangely enough, Quinn noted, this usually morbid material didn't seem grotesque or out of place; in fact, the gate could be considered beautiful. The bone's surface was completely flawless—

white, smooth, and gleaming like marble. Quinn paused at the imposing gate to take it all in.

"Come on, hurry up," Jared ordered. "My brothers and sister-in-law are desperate to see you."

"What do you mean?"

"Well, you *have* been missing for a while," Jared replied.

That wasn't right. Quinn hadn't been missing; he had just never met these people in his lifetime. For some reason, the thought tugged at him and made him feel slightly insecure. Did these people care about who he was, or were they more preoccupied with who he'd been?

Noticing Jared's genuine smile, Quinn hoped the man wasn't just seeing Athena when he looked at him. He spent the last three hours, which felt like an eternity, hiking through this barren wasteland, wrestling internally with what it all meant and he still hadn't quite come to terms with who he was meant to be. To some degree he supposed it made sense. Goddess of Wisdom. He could be described as someone with a good head on his shoulders, a careful planner. And given his ability to speed-read and retain extraordinary amounts of information, that registered. If what Surina had said was true, his abilities would now only get stronger, having connected to the Olympian fire.

But he was also just...Quinn. His life was the sum of his own experiences; the good, the bad, the sublime, and sublimely stupid. He owned his triumphs and his failures. He was more than just a shell to house this entity called Athena.

With every new god he met, he might always have that question in the back of his head... *Are they going to see me for who I am, or are they just going to see her?*

It bothered him to some degree with the others, but with Jared, that feeling was so much more intense. He couldn't explain it, but it mattered to Quinn that Jared knew him for who he was, not just who he was supposed to be.

As they moved past the gate, the garden—neatly constructed in symmetrical circular patterns on either side of the main path—led up to the raised two-story mansion. Unlike the terrain they had navigated through earlier, the grounds of the mansion were vibrant with deep green grass and a wide array of colourful flowers and fragrant fruit trees. He marvelled at this place. There was no visible sunlight, yet these plants were clearly thriving.

How were they managing that without the means for photosynthesis?

Quinn decided to chalk it up to magic. Though if you'd asked him this morning, he would have told you how bizarre it would be for him, a scientifically literate person, to chalk anything up to magic, let alone gods.

Still, the sprawling gardens were magnificent. Magic or not, he could appreciate the beauty here. Surprisingly, that sense of appreciation sparked a tiny twinge of déjà vu. He shook his head and jogged to catch up with his host.

Why does this place feel familiar?

As he moved, he caught a flash of scarlet at the corner of his eye. Quinn wondered if the Underworld's famous pomegranates had originated from the paradise where he now stood.

Despite being the home of the death gods, there was little about the place that seemed macabre. Even the figures of leaping fauns and nimble dryads that were sculpted into the fountain were radiant with their smiles, each one garlanded in ropes of real, blossoming flowers and appearing to be in the midst of a joyful dance.

Quinn walked behind Jared at a slightly slower pace, taking in the gleaming white-washed exterior walls of the Mediterranean-style villa as they ascended the stairs toward the front entrance. The large, turquoise glass doors swung open on their own, allowing the pair into an elegant foyer. Quinn noticed that the bone forming the guardrail lining the upper level and twin staircases had flowers wound around the banister, almost at odds with the austere paintings hanging on the faded parchment-coloured interior walls.

Jared had passed ahead of him and now stood in front of another set of doors under the second floor overhang. Quinn subconsciously tried to wipe his face with the back of his jacket sleeve and combed his hair with his fingers, just as his companion pushed open the right door and stepped inside.

Taking in his surroundings, Quinn noted that he was in some sort of dining room, filled with paintings of men and women he didn't recognize. For some strange reason, he felt a twinge of familiarity while gazing at them. A velvet-soft, burgundy carpet led from the door to a long wooden table. On the far side of the table, on a slightly raised dais, sat two imposing thrones: one made of bone, the other seemingly constructed of interwoven wood and flowers.

Sitting on the throne of bone was a man with dark, closely cropped hair, a short, meticulously groomed beard, and a crisp black, clearly bespoke, tailored suit. There was something both fierce and kind about his gaze, and his features were much like Jared's. The slightest hint of crow's feet appeared at the corners of the man's pale blue eyes as he smiled, amused at being the subject of Quinn's stunned perusal.

To the left of the throne, a heavily tattooed man sat perched on the edge of the table. He could have been Jared's double, but his hair was pulled away from his face, arranged in a style Quinn had once seen in a historical depiction of a Viking. The plaits joined into a pony-tail of dyed white hair that fell down to the middle of his back. His angular jaw and chin were shadowed in dark stubble. The darkness of the stubble and the visible roots of the man's bleached locks showed that, like Jared and the enthroned man, this man's hair was naturally jet black. His hairdo suited his well-worn Blue Oyster Cult t-shirt, ripped black jeans decked out with swinging metal chains that hung from his front and back pockets, and scuffed combat boots. His hand-some features were lively and animated as he talked with the equally attractive, impeccably dressed older man.

Quinn was taken with how the two younger brothers looked so similar and yet so different. He didn't know much about Jared, but he inherently knew the man would never be caught dead with earlobe spacers, lip ring, and tattoos. But on this other man, they looked really good.

On the throne of wood to the right sat a woman with dark, ink-black eyes, framed with thick lashes and eyebrows. Her black hair was braided tightly against her scalp in neat rows, before winding into a larger plait that curled over her shoulder. Tiny flowers and glittering jewelled beads decorated the elaborately twisted coils, and her baby hairs were expertly styled into sweeping waves that graced her forehead. Her dewy, warm mahogany black skin was complemented by her sleeveless black satin dress. The fabric was accented in delicate floral lace and embroidered with the same flowers she wore in her hair . Her entire demeanour radiated a regal serenity that took Quinn's breath.

The three were having a hushed conversation—one that died off as they took notice of Jared and Quinn. Each of their expressions morphed into a genuine smile, even if Jared's twin looked like he was barely holding back his amusement.

The thought struck Quinn like a bullet. They were happy to see him; they wanted him there. It was strange, but Quinn couldn't help but feel the same way as he gazed at the idyllic family image they presented. It almost felt as if he was returning home. For a lost orphan, the feeling was one he'd desperately chased for as long as he could remember, and to be getting it from strangers, out of the blue, in the Underworld of all places, was shocking.

Part of him wanted to run toward the woman. Something about her screamed *family*, like they were old, dear friends. Hell, the way the woman was staring at him made Quinn think maybe she felt the same way. He could feel the warmth and happiness bursting forth from her, like spring sunshine melting snow.

But he had to keep his cool. He already knew he would be mortified if he embarrassed himself in front of the disarmingly handsome God of Death.

Jared smirked, gazing at his overwhelmed companion. "Quinn, I'd like you to meet my family."

CHAPTER TEN

Surina dropped her sword and leaned against the wall of the Hall of Erebus, exhausted. She fumbled with the sunglasses in her pocket, before slipping them back on. All that remained of the Danaids were their lifeless, limbless bodies—plus several mounds of rubble, some still retaining their humanoid shape. A feeling of disbelief washed over her. This was her first visit to the Hall of Erebus and it seemed that the Olympian fire also invigorated demigods. Without the new-found strength and focus that the flames had given her, Surina never would have been able to take out the dozen Danaids she had encountered. She certainly didn't escape the skirmish unscathed, as her various cuts and bruises could attest, but she and Quinn were lucky to be alive to tell about it.

Her charge at the forefront of her mind, Surina collected her sword, pushed off the wall, and stumbled toward the tunnel she had last seen Quinn enter.

"Quinn!" she called, walking down the darkened path. The sound of her boots echoing against the stone floor mocked the lack of response she desperately wanted to hear.

In the dark, she could make out the faint outline of a body lying on the ground. Apprehension overwhelmed her as she knelt to get a better look. She exhaled in relief. The body wasn't the one she was looking for, but one of the Danaids she had wounded. The feral woman was obviously dead and missing an arm. She must have stumbled there after battling with Surina, lost too much blood, and died.

On her remaining arm was a strange bracelet—a metal cuff with a sort of dial or clock face on the side.

Finding jewellery on a woman so savage she could no longer speak seemed odd indeed. But then again, the Danaids' presence in Erebus was odd as well. Perhaps the clunky piece of jewellery could give Surina and the gods a clue as to how and why they came here.

Surina slipped the cuff off the dead woman's wrist and tucked it into her jacket pocket.

She continued to move down the tunnel in search of Quinn. She kicked some of the pebbles at her feet and heard them tumble down a steep incline in front of her. Casting a small spell to illuminate the dark tunnel, she saw Quinn's footprints in the floor dust disappearing into the gaping pit below.

"Shit, this is *not* good," she muttered to herself.

Yet Quinn's disappearance was not the only thing that the light revealed.

Surina's eyes widened behind her dark glasses as she took in the blood drying on her coat and hands—Danaid blood.

Fuck.

G.E. White

She rushed back along the way she came. Her concern for Quinn was overwhelming, but she knew if she didn't get treated soon, she would be of no help to him.

Surina ran as quickly as she could across the Hall of Erebus. She knew that Gates in the Underworld were few and far between, and so her only option was to run. Spying another tunnel leading upward, she used another burst of speed to ascend the stairs.

She pulled her smart phone out of her pocket and scowled—no Gate could penetrate this place, but she could still get a cellphone signal. She hit the speed-dial for Leo, growing more anxious with each ring.

"Hello?" she finally heard on the other line.

"Leo, I'm heading back to you. I need you to get a priest there *now*," she commanded as she continued to climb the stairs with feverish haste.

"What? Why?"

"Things went bad. We got attacked by Danaids, and Quinn is somewhere in the Underworld."

"Danaids!" he exclaimed. "What were they doing down there?"

"No time to explain. You have to find Quinn, he's Athena."

"Right," Leo replied, quickly falling into his accustomed role as a soldier, carrying out his orders. "Don't worry, I'll have the Doyles track him down."

"There's more," Surina admitted. "I killed the Danaids."

"All forty-nine of them?!"

"No, maybe twelve—it doesn't matter, their blood is all over me."

"You gotta be kidding," Leo said, horrified. "Has the miasma hit you yet?"

"If it had, I wouldn't have the foresight to call you, genius! I'm compromised with Danaid blood. I need a priest, priestess—anyone who can perform a proper cleansing ritual."

"Okay, I got you. Just get here as soon as you can."

"I will, but just in case, be prepared. You know, should the worst happen."

There was a moment of silence as Leo took in her request.

"Leo!" she prompted.

"All right," he agreed. "See you soon. And good luck, because I don't want to have to kill you," he added, before ending the call. Surina still had a dozen more flights of stairs to climb. The trip would probably take her another ten minutes, if she kept up this speed. She could only pray that she could fight off the miasma until then.

ℰℑ

Sebastien took in the dark, blood-red Threads that shifted inside Leo as he moved to stand beside Sebastien. The War God was gripping something in his hands, but it wasn't a living creature whose Threads he could read so Sebastien couldn't tell what the object was. However, he could clearly smell the scent of metal and gunpowder and hear the sound of a gun being loaded as he and Leo waited for Surina to arrive. "Is that really necessary?" Sebastien asked the God of War.

"Surina said to be prepared," Leo replied.

The Seer ran a hand through his hair. "Don't you have a tranquiliser gun or something?"

Leo shook his head, his eyes constantly flicking up to the Gate Surina was expected to come through. "No can do. If the miasma *has* taken hold, a tranq would barely make her flinch before she ripped us in two."

Sebastien turned toward Leo's voice; his eyes narrowed. It was the closest act his cloudy eyes could manifest into a glare.

"If it makes you feel any better, I'll aim for a leg first," Leo conceded.

"You do that."

Leo opened his mouth to retort, but Sebastien threw up an arm, demanding his silence. The two men heard quick, staggered steps coming from the other side of the Gate. Sebastien approached the door and grasped the handle. The steps grew closer. The current incarnation of Ares raised his weapon.

"Do it," Leo ordered, and Sebastien complied, pulling the door open.

☙

Surina entered the room, caked in the blood of the Danaids—her movements slightly off-kilter. Sebastien stepped away from the door, returning to his previous position beside Leo.

Her head was down, and her hands hung at her side—one clutching her bloodied sword, the other occasionally twitching with nervous energy. Her breaths came in heavy pants as she turned her gaze toward them, her eyes still hidden by the dark glasses.

"Surina, are you okay?" Leo asked, his weapon still at the ready.

"What's he doing here?" she ground out.

Leo looked over to Sebastien, who didn't appear to be upset by her tone. "You said you needed someone who could perform a cleansing ritual. He was the only one I could think of."

"It doesn't matter who it is now; we don't have time." Sebastien gripped Surina's arm and dragged her over to another Gate, shoving her inside. He turned to Leo once again. "I've got everything ready. I can take it from here."

"You sure?" Leo asked, genuine concern in his voice.

Sebastien nodded. "I'm sure. Besides, she has to take everything off—glasses included."

"She could just close her eyes," Leo reasoned as the slighter man entered the Gate he had just pushed Surina through.

"Yes, but I doubt you would. I'll alert you when we're done," Sebastien quipped, shutting the Gate in Leo's face.

The God of War felt indignation rise in him from the insinuation, but the gravity of the situation made him hold his tongue. His feelings didn't matter at this point—he just hoped that the young Seer could save Surina. He had questions about how the Danaids could have found their way into the Hall of Erebus. But for now, Quinn was still lost somewhere in the Underworld, and Leo needed to get the Underworld gods to investigate while he concentrated on the situation at hand.

So Leo pulled out his phone and called Carter.

☙

On the other side of the Gate lay a large ceremonial bathtub—part of a larger temple the Gate was connected to. Sebastien heard Surina's weapon clatter against the tiled floor as she dropped it, followed by the rustle of fabric as she attempted to disrobe. The bath behind her was sunken into the floor and already filled to the brim with water Sebastien had blessed before her arrival. Two ornate shower heads loomed over the basin, pointing in opposing directions.

Sebastien heard Surina's frustrated growls as she struggled to remove her clothes. He stepped forward and placed his steady hands over her shaking ones.

"Let me get this," he said calmly.

"I can take off my own shirt, damn it!" she snapped back.

"Normally, yes, of course you can, but right now you're having trouble focusing, so just let me do this. I promise I won't peek," he joked, hoping to lighten the mood.

Surina gave a shaky chuckle as he peeled off her shirt and began fumbling with her belt and pants.

"This might sound horrible," she said as she moved to unhook her soiled bra, "but right now, I am very thankful that you're blind."

Sebastien finished with her pants and moved down to her socks. "No offence taken." His nearly absent vision wasn't something that the two of them talked about much. Sebastien moved with such ease and grace that it was almost impossible to tell that he had a disability. He had described the reality of his sight to her early on in their arrangement, pointing out the shifting blue and teal of her own Threads.

He had always thought that her colours complemented his own yellow and gold Thread and had once hoped that they might someday intertwine. Part of him realized that under different circumstances this scene could have been charged with sexual energy or tension. Once upon a time that would have been something he wanted, yet as he learned more about Surina he discovered that would never be. Over the years, he'd made peace with that.

The demigod before him was a singular being, sharp-witted and sharp-tongued. Though their Threads had intertwined, their connection was never romantic or sexual, no matter how he might have felt about it at the beginning of their acquaintance. There was true love between them, but they loved each other as friends, and Sebastien was grateful that he had the foresight to not push for more than Surina was able to give. Being privileged enough to have held Surina's Thread in his hands, he knew her intimately. However, it wasn't his place to expose her to the part of herself she wasn't ready for.

In fact, there were things about her that even he couldn't access. It was the most bizarre thing he'd ever experienced as the reincarnation of the Moirai. The only problem was he felt it would be unethical to explore those hidden depths when the woman was so against exploring her past. It felt like a violation, so he waited and let her lead. He just hoped that one day she would come to embrace their friendship enough to trust him. They could face whatever secrets he dug up, together. And maybe then she'd be able to embrace herself as she truly was, with no regrets.

❧

Surina quickly placed her glasses on the floor beside her clothes, before stepping back from Sebastien to remove her underwear. After her bra and underwear joined the rest of her clothes on the floor, she turned her emerald gaze to her employer. Even though he was blind, Surina couldn't stop the flush flooding her cheeks. She knew that this was a necessary evil and that Sebastien would never take any liberties, but she still felt vulnerable to be so exposed. She did have to admit, however, that it was nice to be able to meet another person's eyes without her usual glass barrier—and without anything terrible happening to them.

"I'm getting in," she told Sebastien, climbing down into the bath and submerging herself in the water to her shoulders. Sebastien kneeled at the edge of the tub, cupped the water in his hands, and poured it over her head, washing off the blood and grime.

She closed her eyes as she became fully submerged in the water. When she had entered the bathroom, she had felt the irrational anger, bloodlust, and rage within her waiting to be set loose and wreak havoc, but Sebastien's voice crooning the Latin incantations for the purification rite seemed to drain those feelings away from her body.

Sebastien picked up a small ceremonial dagger he had placed at the edge of the tub and paused. "Are you feeling okay? If I do this, you won't freak out on me, right?"

Surina nodded. "I should be okay. I feel a bit more in control."

Sebastien dipped his head in acknowledgement, before bringing the blade to his hand. He pricked his right index finger and, with extreme care, he smeared a small amount of his own blood on Surina's forehead and cheeks.

"Blood spilled in anger, be cleansed by blood spilled with compassion. May you be released from this rage," Sebastien said, his hand now resting on Surina's head.

He pulled back, giving a soft tilt of his head and gesturing for her to rinse off any remnants of the Danaid blood.

G.E. White

Surina drained the tub, turned on both shower heads, and used the soap that was left beside her to clean herself off. When she finished, relief flooded through her entire body. The hatred and violence that she had fallen prey to were now washed away. Had Sebastien not done his ritual, Surina would have soon succumbed to the miasma. Her companions would have been left with no other option than to put her down, like the rabid dog she would have become.

Sebastien stood at the side of the tub, a bathrobe in one hand and her glasses in the other. Surina bypassed both offerings and embraced her employer, her friend. The relief of being free of the miasma's influence brought a strange but welcome sense of euphoria that buzzed throughout her being. "Thank you," she said simply, gratitude choking her. She knew that Sebastien would understand the weight of her words.

Surina had always prided herself on her self-restraint. Of course, there were times when certain behaviours were beyond her control, but the possibility of losing her mind was a truly terrifying thought, and this man had saved her from it.

Sebastien stood stock-still for a moment, before his arms slowly moved around her to return the hug. *"De nada,"* he replied, heat flooding his cheeks. "But while I might not be able to see, I can tell that you are very wet, and uh, very naked."

Surina had forgotten her state of undress in her desire to make her gratitude known. "Sorry," she mumbled as she pulled back, taking the robe and throwing it over her dripping body.

"No problem," Sebastien said, attempting to shrug off the awkwardness of the situation. "I'll leave you to finish up in here."

"Thanks. I'll be out in a few minutes."

"All right," Sebastien said, the blush on his cheeks still present as he exited the bathroom.

As the door clicked shut, Surina let a smile tug at her lips. She had been aware of Sebastien's interest earlier in their partnership, and while he was handsome and fun to banter with, going any further didn't feel right. It might have been that she worried that they would ruin the connection they currently held if they tried and failed at a romantic relationship. Surina's relationships had always been complicated; there were few people who she truly connected with. In the past there had been those who wanted things from her, things she didn't know how to give.

The thought of how she had disappointed others in the past left her cold to the touch. But knowing she had a true friend in Sebastien gave her hope. Perhaps it was time to make more connections.

❧

A few minutes later, Surina returned to the Gate hub, wearing her robe and glasses and carrying a bag holding her soiled clothes. She dropped the bag by the door she had just exited and basked in the sudden warmth of the room. A crackling fire now blazed in the fireplace of the large and cozy room. Her hair, while no longer dripping, was still damp and hung in waves about her shoulders.

Sebastien and Leo were sitting in the lounge by the fire: Leo in the reclining chair, Sebastien on the couch opposite him. Each cradled a cup of coffee, while a mug, presumably for her, sat on the table between them. She picked it up and claimed the seat next to Sebastien. "Any word about Quinn?"

"Jared called to say he found him. Said he's a little shaken up and has a new goose egg on his head, but otherwise, seems fine. I told him to take Quinn back to meet the folks for the time being, as you two were dealing with your own problems. Said you'd call him back when everything was straightened out," Leo told her.

"And you were fine with leaving him in the care of that peacock?" Surina asked Sebastien, humour in her voice.

Leo shrugged. "Jared was the one who found him. I was gonna

call Carter, but you said Quinn fell into the Underworld, and only an Underworld god can freely enter or exit that creepy place. Besides, next to Hermes, Thanatos is the fastest of the gods," he reasoned.

"He'll get him back safely," Sebastien assured her. "By the way, you shouldn't call Jared a peacock. Just because he's concerned with his appearance doesn't make him a coward or any less deadly. Literally. You're lucky you're on good terms with him. You should know better than to make fun of a god."

Surina sighed, running a hand through her still-damp hair. "I know. I just hate sitting here, doing nothing. Quinn was counting on me to have his back, and I almost got him killed. Not only was I starting to like him, but I almost inadvertently committed deicide."

"So, Quinn is Athena for sure?" Leo asked. "I mean, you're 100 percent sure, right?"

"I wouldn't say it if it wasn't true," she replied.

"Just wanted to make sure. I've already told the Doyles. I kinda figured that if anyone would wanna know that Athena was back in the fold, it would be them. Honestly, glad to have her back...or I guess him, in this incarnation." The God of War made a sound of approval. Over the centuries, Athena had been the only god capable of keeping up with him on the battlefield. Quinn might not enjoy war's inevitable bloodshed, but Leo was certain that he would make a fine strategist and competent warrior in due time. "Anyway, Quinn's in good hands, Surina. I wouldn't worry about it," he said.

"You wouldn't worry about a lot of things," Sebastien muttered under his breath.

Leo glared at the blind man, but otherwise ignored him. "Plus, you should take into account that you were in a very unusual situation; it's not like you could have foreseen this."

"Yeah, well. *Someone* should have," Surina muttered darkly, before taking a sip of her coffee.

"I told you to be on your toes this morning. As of late, some of my visions have been murky. I knew that something was going to happen, I just didn't know what." Sebastien put down his mug with a sigh of frustration.

"Why didn't you tell me you were having trouble with your visions?" Surina asked him, concerned.

Sebastien waved away her worry. "Because there was nothing you could do about it, and it would only cause you to stress over something you couldn't change. Besides, there are two other things that concern me more at the moment."

Leo and Surina both raised an eyebrow in curiosity, waiting silently for the Seer to elaborate. "The first is the item you had in your pocket when you first came in," he said to Surina.

Surina pursed her lips as she tried to recall what he might be referring to. Suddenly, she was reminded of the strange cuff.

Surina shuffled back to her bag, taking care to use a washcloth to pick up the cuff from her pile of soiled clothes. She returned to her seat and held out the bracelet to Sebastien, who recoiled.

"That's it. I could sense the strange aura from it the moment you stepped in the door. What is it, exactly?"

Surina shrugged as she placed the cuff on the table. "It's some sort of bracelet I found on one of the Danaids. In fact, I think all of them wore one. I've never seen anything like it. I'm not sure what it's made of, but it has a round dial, like a watch, but with only two settings. Right now, it's set to the side with two notches, and the other side only has one."

Sebastien nodded his head during Surina's description. "There's something off about it—a mixture of old and new magic, and something else. It feels somewhat familiar; I just can't put my finger on it."

"Who cares what it does, or how it was made. I think the bigger mystery is, how did the Danaids get into Erebus? We all know that Erebus is a special part of the Underworld," Leo butted into their conversation. "It only exists in the Second Realm, and last time I checked, the Danaids are in the First. The miasma fried their brains; they can't think past their next kill. They're not smart enough to get into the Second Realm on their own—at least, not without anyone noticing."

Sebastien's face turned grim. "So, we just need to figure out who sent them here, how they did it, and for what purpose."

Surina's lips pursed in thought. "Well, the miasma has made them eternal like the daimons. It's not unheard of for daimons to keep an eye on anything that can live as long as they can. Maybe some of the local friendlies have information."

Leo snorted. "Too bad there ain't many daimons willing to play nice anymore. Though, it's not like they were the most cooperative to begin with. No offence, Surina."

"None taken."

"I wouldn't bother with that right now. Keep an eye and an ear out for any information, but I think my second concern takes precedent for now," Sebastien said.

Surina shifted in her seat to look at him head-on. "And what could be more concerning than eternal bloodthirsty monsters rampaging through the Second Realm?"

"War."

Leo's eyes widened. "What did I do?"

"I'm not talking about what you've done, but what might come next," Sebastien said, before turning to face Surina. "After the theft at the Earthen Temple, I warned both the Solar and Lunar Temples to be careful."

"But?" Surina prodded.

"There was a break-in at the Solar Temple. Vega was stolen."

"Leaving only Polaris," she said. "Do we have any idea who the thief is?"

Sebastien rubbed at his forehead, trying to ward off an inevitable headache. "Well, that's the problem."

"We have no clue?" Leo asked.

"Actually, it's the opposite," Sebastien countered. "In fact, both the Earthen and Solar Temples have a good idea who's behind this. Too bad they can't agree on the same group or person."

"So, what does that mean?" Surina asked.

"It means that I want you to investigate it, Surina. Leo, I know you're just a stand-in, but I want you to arrange a Gate for Surina, Jared, and Quinn to travel to Delos," Sebastien ordered. "Surina, I know you have your reservations, but this is more important than your history with the Celestial Temples. I want the three of you to examine the Solar Temple, while the crime scene is still fresh."

"You want me to take Quinn along? Are you sure that's a good idea?" she snorted in disbelief.

"You said it yourself—you'd have a difficult time dealing with the temples, but no one knows temple politics better than you. That being said, we both know you're not the most tactful person, but Jared has enough charisma to charm the robes off a priestess of Artemis. As for Quinn, with so many gods unaccounted for, we need him fully tapped-in to his abilities as soon as possible. He's going to get a crash course with some on-the-job training. Besides, Athena has always been the cleverest of us—perhaps he'll catch something the two of you might miss."

Surina twisted her lips in a pout, seeming younger than her years.

"Don't make that face at me—this is not up for discussion," Sebastien's tone was irritable.

Surina scowled. "How did you know?"

Sebastien ignored the question, shaking his head. "It's getting late. We should all get some sleep. Contact the Doyles and inform them that they are responsible for Quinn for the night. Surina, you and I will head back to the apartment tonight; you can pick up Jared and Quinn around noon."

"Can I take the Phantasm?" she asked.

Sebastien gave an indulgent sigh. "I suppose."

His assistant silently pulled her arm down into a fist in a gesture of victory.

"Don't look so excited," Sebastien warned, standing at last. "You get one scratch on it, and I'll know."

Sebastien wandered off into the kitchenette near the back of the lounge to rinse out his mug.

"How does he do that?" Leo whispered to Surina.

"I don't know, but I'm starting to wonder if he's as blind as we thought."

Sebastien's voice drifted back to them, cutting across the sound of running water. "I heard that."

CHAPTER ELEVEN

Q_UINN STOOD ROOTED to the spot as he took in the sight of Jared's family. He raised his hand in a small wave. "Uh, hi."

Quinn was already scolding himself the moment the words were out of his mouth. *Hi? That's the best I could come up with when greeting this... royalty? Way to make a good impression—they're gonna think you're an idiot.*

Surprisingly, his simple words were well received as the woman with the braids was the first to break the silence. "Oh, he's adorable!" she cooed, her bright, cheery voice at odds with her gothic clothes.

"Justine, do *not* start," scolded the man on the throne.

The woman—Justine—glowered. "What do you mean, don't start? Don't start lightening the mood?" She gestured to Quinn dramatically. "I can see the poor boy is petrified by your gloomy ass, so I'm making him feel welcome."

"Yes, and he's probably had a very long day, and he doesn't need you cooing and fawning over him like he's some kitten on YouTube. You're making him uncomfortable."

Justine crossed her arms and snorted. "You're just jealous that I don't spend my whole day 'fawning' over you, Joseph." She turned to Quinn. "Am I making you uncomfortable, honey? If so, just tell me and I'll back off."

Quinn blinked in surprise, before giving a shake of his head. "Uh, no, it's fine."

Justine shot a mischievous glance at Joseph. "See, Joe?" She then turned and smiled at her guest, vindicated. "Come, come, sit down." With a wave of her hand, two thick, leafy vines sprang from the ground and wove themselves into two chairs.

Quinn hesitantly shuffled forward. He was still unsure what the protocol for something like this was. Justine and the bearded man—Joseph—were seated in thrones. Should he bow? Justine had already invited him to sit, so it was probably rude not to follow her instructions. As he sat down at the miraculously conjured chair, he couldn't help but marvel at how comfortable it was. "Thank you, ma'am."

"Ma'am? Oh my lord, you are so precious! Call me Justine. 'Ma'am' is for grandmothers, school principals, and church deaconesses," she said, giving a dismissive wave.

"Well, you are getting up there," said Jared's double, who had been watching the exchange with an amused smirk.

"Uh, excuse you," Justine exclaimed, indignant. "First of all, my melanin keeps me looking fresher than you could ever hope to look. Second, real smart move to piss off the woman who does your hair. Joseph," she spun around to face her bemused husband with a roll of her eyes, "come collect your rude-ass brother."

Joseph gave a half-hearted sneer toward the long-haired man. "No one asked for your opinion, James." Jared groaned as he sank into the remaining chair as James brushed it off and immediately made amends with his irritated sister-in-law. Quinn got the distinct impression that this was a common occurrence. While he might have grown up in a series of foster homes, he still knew what playful family squabble looked like. He'd seen it on TV sitcoms and imagined it for himself many times over the years.

"Let's stop referring to him as adorable and precious, he's not a puppy. He has a name. Everyone, this is Quinn. Quinn, this is my twin brother, James," Jared said, gesturing to the ponytailed man.

James gave a half salute, his smirk permanently etched across his face. Pointing to the man sitting on the throne, Jared continued. "My older brother, Joseph, and as you've probably guessed, this is his wife, Justine."

Quinn nodded and softly murmured his hellos. He was struck by how elegant they all appeared: Justine in her black satin and lace dress that accentuated her graceful movements and fresh loveliness; Joseph, sitting regally on his throne, in his suit with a dark wine-red button-down shirt ; and James, even in his gothic rock-star attire, looked like he commanded respect. Their arresting appearance filled Quinn with a sort of awe. And yet, at the same time, they all seemed so *human* as they bantered with one another.

"So, you are all gods, but you're also a family?" he asked tentatively, not wishing to interrupt or upset anyone, though he was not entirely sure he had cause to worry.

Joseph inclined his head as he met Quinn's gaze. "Yes, although it's a pretty rare occurrence for a group of gods to reincarnate into the same family. Well, except for these two," he intoned as he gestured to Jared and James. Quinn's brow shot upward in confusion as Justine leaned across the table to explain.

"Thanatos and Hypnos have always been connected. The polite way of putting it is, they're two sides of the same coin. I always thought it was because they only had so many brain cells to share between them. Though, between you and me, I'm pretty certain Jared got the lion's share."

James melodramatically clutched his chest. "You cut me to the quick, dear sister-in-law. But I'm the one you hang out with, 'cause I'm the most fun. We all know Joe's a workaholic and Jared's a killjoy. Literally." Justine rolled her eyes, but her slightly curled lip betrayed her.

Quinn turned to James. "Hypnos. God of Sleep, right?"

"Got it in one," James said, winking at Quinn. "There's that Athena brain we've all grown to love."

James' statement about Quinn being Athena and them knowing Athena in some capacity threw Quinn for a loop.

"And Joseph over here is the big, bad Hades, Lord of the Underworld! Ooooooooh," the God of Sleep said, shuddering in pretend fright.

Joseph glared at his younger sibling. "I swear, James. Can you take even one thing seriously? In your whole life? Just one thing?"

"What?" James asked, feigning innocence.

"We're trying to make a good first impression here and you insist on acting like a twelve-year-old."

"Oh, don't worry about Quinn! He's gonna love us!" James shrugged, wearing the same rakish grin that Quinn had seen on Jared before. "Athena is one of ours."

"Yours?" Quinn echoed the word, unconsciously posing it as a question. It sounded foreign in his own ears. "What do you mean *yours?*"

"Guys, knock it off," Jared warned. "You're gonna scare him off! He only just found out he's Athena."

"Don't worry, I'm not that creep, Bram. He's not scared of us— right, Quinn?"

"Uh, right...umm, who's Bram?" Quinn asked, still confused.

"Oh, yeah, you haven't met everyone yet." James snorted, a snarky look on his face. "Bram's kinda like us, in that he's another

Underworld god. But the important thing to know is that he sucks. He's the God of Fear."

"God of Fear..." Quinn's magical memory banks pulled up the relevant information, like a computer. "Phobos, if I'm not mistaken, right?"

"Yep. In this incarnation he's named Bram. And he's the worst!" James dramatically rolled his eyes and sighed.

"Ugh, stop being such a dick, James! He's really not that bad!" Justine protested. "He's just...a little different."

"Justine is being nice. As per usual," James started.

"You should try it sometime, asshole!" Justine shot her brother-in-law a withering glare. "I swear these Underworld gods—"

"What? We're gonna be the death of you?" James teased, clearly amusing himself. Justine shook her head, but cast a bemused half smile toward him.

"All right, all right, we've all had our fun. We need to—" Jared's thought was cut short by his cellphone ringtone. He perused the caller ID and stood up in a single, fluid movement. "Sorry. I've got to take this."

Justine tapped Quinn's hand as Jared moved to the far corner of the room, speaking in hushed tones.

"So, what do you think of the place? Not the *Addams Family* realness you might imagine when you think of Hades' palace, is it?"

Quinn had to agree. "It's very beautiful, the gardens especially. They're remarkable."

"My handiwork, naturally. When it comes to decorating, I like a gloom and bloom light touch, not a full gothic vampire aesthetic, but I'm so glad you approve. I don't get many visitors when I'm down here so I'm the only one who seems to enjoy them." Justine's face glowed with pride as she pushed her thick braid behind her shoulder. It was as if a light bulb was illuminated in Quinn's mind. "You're Persephone, aren't you? I mean, you're married to Hades, so of course you are.

Goddess of Spring, Queen of the Underworld."

Justine turned to Joseph and grinned. "Ooh, he's smart too. I like him. But I guess that's to be expected—from an incarnation of Athena."

Though Quinn flushed slightly under the compliment, he also felt a pang of that same insecurity he'd felt before. Why did everyone act like everything he did was just a reflection of the goddess? Couldn't he have deduced that using his own wit or intelligence?

"You should come stay with us sometime," Justine continued. "As long as that's cool with your parents of course."

"Well, I'm twenty, so it's not like I need parental permission. Besides," Quinn muttered. "I don't have any parents, anyway."

He instantly felt guilty as he watched Justine's excitement drain away. Her smile fell as she looked to Joseph for something to say.

"Well, he's going to have to stay with someone," Jared interrupted, dropping his now-silent phone from his ear and wearing a slightly troubled expression.

"That was Surina," he explained, "She said she won't be able to pick you up tonight, Quinn, as something has come up."

"She's okay, right?" Quinn asked.

"Yeah, she's fine," Jared assured. "The miasma's been cleared up."

"Miasma!" Joseph exclaimed. "How on earth did she get infected with miasma?"

"Danaids."

Quinn slouched down into his chair as the sinking feeling he often associated with being lied to rose in his stomach. "Would someone mind telling me what the hell that really means? Please? I'm starting to guess it's nothing like asthma."

"You told him it was *asthma?*" Justine cried.

Jared awkwardly waved his hand through the air in a dismissive gesture. "I might have implied that it was *like* asthma."

"Which is still a bald-faced lie," James interjected. "Great job, by the way, you meet your version of Athena and the first thing you do is lie to him?"

Quinn was struck by James' choice of words. What did he mean when he said that Quinn was *Jared's* version of Athena? Why would he specifically refer to him as belonging to the gorgeous Death God?

"He'd just been attacked by ghouls," Jared explained, cutting off Quinn's internal inquiry. "I didn't think that it was the best time to tell him that his guardian might be infected by tainted blood and was likely to become a murderous, wild woman."

Quinn sprang from his seat, horror rushing through him. "What?! What do you mean infected by tainted blood?!"

Jared raised his hands in a plea for order. "Relax, I said she's all right. No harm, no foul."

"I bet the Danaids would say otherwise," James replied, smirking.

The intense sensation of being in over his head began to bubble up in him again. It felt as if the family was speaking a different language. "Again, with that word! Please, I just need to understand what's happening. So, what exactly are these Danaids, anyway? They looked like women to me—feral, maybe, but still women." His curiosity overpowered his frustration as he slowly sunk back into his chair. He needed to know the answers to all his questions. It was an almost supernatural need to get to the bottom of things. Now that he knew he was an incarnation of the Goddess of Wisdom, he supposed that made a lot more sense.

The twins exchanged a look. "Do you want to tell him?" Jared asked his brother.

"No, I think you've got this one," James said.

Jared sighed, taking the seat Justine had provided.

"The story of the Danaids is not very well known in modern mythology; at least, it's not one of the famous ones, and it's rarely ever remembered correctly. Danaids was the name given to the fifty daughters of Danaus, the King of Libya. His twin brother Aegyptus,

G.E. White

the King of Arabia, also had fifty children, all men. Aegyptus suggested that they wed their children to one another."

"Incest, ew," James chimed in, earning him a scornful look from his brothers.

"Yeah, we know. But things were different back then," Joseph chided. "All the gods practiced consanguineous relationships to some degree or another in those days. Even Hypnos."

James grimaced. "I still stand by what I said, gross."

Jared rolled his eyes and continued his story. *"Any*way, Danaus refused, suspecting that the only reason his brother suggested the mass marriage was to gain control over Libya. But after being pursued across the sea by his brother's army, Danaus finally agreed. Only, on the night of his daughters' weddings—yes, they were all wed on the same night—he gave each of them a dagger and told them to kill their new husbands. The next morning, forty-nine of his daughters presented the heads of their husbands to Danaus. Or at least, that's how the myths remember it."

True to Jared's words, Quinn was completely ignorant of the story. It had never been mentioned in the few mythology books he had read as a child. But there was something about hearing this story that oddly *warmed* Quinn. It wasn't a very happy story, but it seemed to invigorate him somehow. He furrowed his brow as he considered Jared's tale. "But I'm guessing it didn't go down like that—in reality, that is."

"Well, nothing was planned in terms of a slaughter; Danaus never ordered his daughters to murder their new husbands. But when forty-nine out of the fifty men took what each of them thought their new wife owed them, the Danaids lashed out, each refusing to be their husband's bed slaves. Lynceus, who truly loved his new wife and respected her choice to not consummate the marriage, was spared."

Quinn cocked his head to the side. "So was it a revenge killing or self-defence?"

"Neither," said Jared. "It was an infection. When the forty-nine other Danaids killed their husbands, they were consumed with anger—the violence and disregard that the sons of Aegyptus showed them infected their very beings." Jared paused briefly, frowning. "That is the core of miasma; call it a taint, an infection, a virus, whatever you wish. It's a condition that spreads with the shedding of blood in a violent and hateful manner. So technically, it was the sons of Aegyptus who were the original carriers of the miasma, which they spread through the rape of their wives. The miasma caused the Danaids to turn on their husbands, and once they had spilled that blood, the infection grew.

"People who come into contact with miasma need to be cleansed of the blood they've spilled or else the violence and bloodlust will consume them, which is what happened to forty-nine of the fifty Danaids. After slaughtering their husbands, they turned their anger on innocent men, killing complete strangers in revenge. The miasma continued to feed and grow on their hatred, and soon enough, it didn't matter who they attacked. Men, women, children—all the same to them. All that was left for them was bloodshed."

"You see, they used to be human," James jumped in. "You know, before the murders. But the miasma had one so-called positive side effect: though their minds are lost, their bodies become tougher, stronger, unable to age. Some people say that they drink the blood from their kills, keeping them young."

Quinn listened intently, his head bobbing occasionally. "Kind of like vampires."

"Yes. Minus the charm, comprehension, communication skills, ability to blend in, and, according to recent literature, glittery complexion," James snorted.

"So, when Surina fought them off—"

"She was tainted by their blood and would have regressed to being just like them," Jared interrupted. "But she was able to get to a priest in time to perform the cleansing ritual."

Quinn rolled the new information around in his head for a moment. Violence as an infection wasn't an entirely new concept to him. He had seen how violence often begat more violence. Yet, there were definitely some questions he still had. "What about soldiers who kill during war? Wouldn't they get infected with miasma as well?" he asked.

"Not exactly," Justine joined in. "Miasma is created by blood spilt in absolute hatred, malice, or joy. Most soldiers don't have a personal connection with their enemy that would enable them to truly hate them, nor do most enjoy killing others. For pawns of your great wars, it's just an act of survival. And even then, they might not be completely spared—as you see in traumatic after-effects, like post-traumatic stress disorder."

"So, are you saying that Surina *enjoyed* killing those wom— Danaids?" Quinn felt ill at the thought.

"No! No, definitely not," Justine said, sounding slightly panicked. "It's just that miasma is spread in two very different ways. It's first created by those who take joy in their violence, but once they are infected, their blood becomes tainted, and whoever comes into contact with it will also contract the illness."

Quinn's shoulders relaxed as Justine explained the virus' transmission. It was strange; he had only known Surina for a short while, but the idea of her losing herself to some magical infection was painful to him. He knew somehow that she mattered to him, even if she was little more than a new acquaintance. "Oh. Well, it's good to hear that Surina is okay. If she can't pick me up, I'll just—" he suddenly realized he really didn't have anywhere to go, except back to Cedar Hills. "I just realized I have nowhere to live...I don't suppose being a reincarnation of a god comes with a free apartment or anything like that?"

"You could stay here," Justine offered.

Joseph shook his head. "It's not safe for him here. Athena or not. The dead will be a problem for him. If he wandered off the palace grounds, he'd be fighting off armies of ghouls. He'd need one of us to chaperone him at all times. Besides, the boy needs fresh air, and he certainly isn't going to get it down here."

"It does get quite stuffy down here," James griped. "Almost stale or something."

"You can move out whenever, you know," his brother replied. "It's not like you're doing me any favours sitting around my palace, annoying my wife, playing your music loudly at all hours, while you and your girlfriend eat me out of house and home…"

James threw his hands up in surrender. "Okay, okay, message received! I'll shut up."

"Wait, you have a girlfriend?" Quinn jumped in, before quickly backpedalling. "Not that I doubt you have one, I just thought mortals weren't allowed to know about god stuff."

"They're not. Lucky for me, Sofia isn't a mortal. She's a god too. Pasithea, if you want to know."

Unfortunately, the name failed to ring any bells for Quinn. "What's she the god of?"

Joseph fielded this question. "Technically, relaxation, mediation, and rest, though her realm of influence also includes some substances of the, uh, mind-altering variety," he finished awkwardly.

"Huh?"

"Drugs," James clarified. "A lot of her work centres around drugs. Natural stuff that is, weed, shrooms, and the like. Trust me, she is not pleased with where the chemical market of psychedelics and opioids has gone. It's a pretty big mess up there, what with the opioid crisis. She's trying to get a handle on it, so it might be a while before you get to meet her."

"I'm sure she and Quinn will hit it off once they have the opportunity. However, we still don't have a plan for tonight," Joseph stated.

"What about your place, Jared?" Justine asked.

Quinn watched as Jared stiffened under her question. Quinn tried to suppress a cringe at the other man's reaction. For some reason it stung a little that Jared appeared to not want to spend time with him. But Quinn also hated the idea that he could be a nuisance or imposition on someone else. Of course, someone as cool as Jared wasn't going to want to share his place with him. He probably had a model girlfriend, or boyfriend, or a girlfriend and a boyfriend waiting for him back home. Quinn suddenly became very aware of how dusty his clothes had become during his trip through the Underworld. *Gods, do I smell?* He was about to attempt making a quick sniff check when he heard Jared's reply.

"Yeah, I guess. I haven't vacuumed this week, but I guess that would be okay—"

"Good, problem solved," Justine replied, seeming to cut him off before he could change his mind.

"Oooh," James cooed in a teasing tone. "Is it your guys' first date in this lifetime?"

"James. Drop it." Jared's tone was hard, his voice strained.

But his twin was a relentless tease. He leaned over the table toward Quinn, a conspiratorial grin on his face.

"You know, I used to tease Jared when he first came out that he was gonna have to explain to Athena one day that he really liked other dudes, but look at fate. Athena's a dude now!"

"Seriously, James, I will end you. Don't think I won't." Jared stared daggers at his brother.

"Wait," Quinn interjected, finally fed up with the comparisons to the goddess, but also deeply confused by the insinuations that there was something between him and Jared. Sure, he thought Jared might well be the most insanely beautiful man he'd ever laid eyes on, but they were acting like there was something already happening between them. "I don't get what you guys are talking about. Ever since I got here it's been Athena this, Athena that. And you keep teasing Jared about me. I'm beginning to feel like you're all in on the joke and I'm the butt of it."

The Doyle family looked at each other sheepishly. It was a few seconds before anyone spoke.

"You...you don't know, then, do you?" Joseph started, glancing over at his wife.

"Know what?"

"Athena and Thanatos," Justine said. "Back in the days of the first gods, the two of you were lovers. Husband and wife. Inseparable."

"Um, what?" Quinn simultaneously felt his heart leap into his throat and his stomach fall to his shoes. He looked at their faces to see if they were pulling his leg, but all he saw in their expressions was concern. He had never read about such a pairing in mythology, but he was inclined to believe them. Now, at least the jokes and pointed comments made sense.

"You and my brother used to be together," James explained, a warm smile on his face. "And in just about every lifetime, you find one another. Since the beginning, you've always found your way into this family. And you and I have always become really good friends."

Quinn's mouth hung open for a few seconds, before he remembered to breathe. He ran his hand over his face and through his ash-blond hair.

"Quinn," Jared started, his eyes stormy with suppressed emotion. "I...you...I mean, that doesn't mean anything. You're not obligated to be or do anything that you did in the past. You're your own person."

"Yeah," Justine interjected, clearly attempting to dissipate the air of awkwardness that had descended on the room. "We're individuals. Each incarnation is like starting a human life all over again. But there are some things—some quirks—that we carry with us from incarnation to incarnation."

She smiled, her face softening as she played with the golden band on her finger. "Some of us...have habits we can't break." She cast a look at the strong, handsome man beside her and winked. To Quinn's surprise, the large man's cheeks reddened as he shook his head and returned his wife's smile.

Of all the surreal things I've seen, watching the Lord of the Underworld blush has got to be one of the more unexpected, Quinn mused to himself, still in shock at this latest revelation.

"Jared is right, things don't always go down the same way," James chimed in. "I'm sorry for teasing. I thought you knew about the history. But you aren't obligated to join our family or date my ugly brother. You might not even be into guys. It's totally okay either way. I'd still be friends with you even if we're not in-laws this time around."

"It's okay," Quinn responded, suddenly overwhelmed once again. "I just... This has just been a lot to take in. And I don't mean you guys and the Underworld. Although, I did not imagine this is how my day would go when I woke up this morning. But this whole finding-out-I'm-a-god thing..."

Justine got up and crossed the room to pull Quinn into a warm hug. The gangly young man's chin could sit on top of her head, and the sweet scent of tropical fruit washed over him.

At first, he just stood there, almost letting the embrace happen to him. After a few seconds, he realized how stiff he was acting and politely returned the hug.

"I'm sorry, honey," Justine began, letting him go and allowing him to sit. "You're probably so tired and overwhelmed. And here we go, running our mouths and stressing you out."

"It's...just been a lot," Quinn confessed, a surprising tremor of tears tickling his throat as he spoke. It had been so long since anyone just hugged him and tried to comfort him. If he stopped to think about it, he worried that he might genuinely break down and cry.

Justine seemed to realize what was happening and immediately snapped to her senses, like a drill sergeant. Wiping a stray tear that had wound its way down Quinn's cheek, she straightened her shoulders and began to boss her family around.

"Gentlemen, Quinn is going to need some help. We live in a fricking palace. Go find him some clothes, shoes, and whatever else he's going to need. Jared, you have the safest place, so you're going to take him in for now until we can get his living situation sorted for the long term."

The three Doyle brothers just stood there looking dumbfounded for a second before Justine snapped them out of it. "Move, damn it! Don't make me repeat myself!"

Jared cast Quinn an apologetic look and opened his mouth as if to say something but was quickly ushered out of the room by his brothers, who hustled to obey their queen's orders.

Quinn stood to join them, but was halted by Justine's hand on his arm. "I didn't mean you, honey. You're our guest." He watched the three men exit the room, unsure of what to make of the situation. He didn't want to impose upon Jared, though he *would* prefer to sleep somewhere topside, and having a roof over his head that didn't have bars on the windows seemed like it would be a nice change.

The only issue was the whole Thanatos-and-Athena thing. It was clear that Jared was uncomfortable with the idea of Quinn staying with him.

And who could blame him? I mean, look at him. He's so stylish and hot... What a cruel trick for fate to play on him. He's gay. I'm gay. But he'd never like a loser like me. And yet, I'm the reincarnation of his soulmate or something.

"Don't let Jared bother you," Justine said soothingly, seeming to pick up on Quinn's unvoiced fears.

"Umm, he seems pretty hesitant to let me stay with him and honestly, I feel like...he must be kinda disappointed in me or in this whole...thing."

"I promise, It's nothing like that. I can see it in his face. He's definitely not disappointed in you. He just doesn't know you and you don't know him.

"And our not knowing each other is precisely why I don't want to impose on him."

"Oh, his hesitation is not related to you specifically. I know him. Or I know this incarnation of him better than you do at this point. He's probably just worried you'll look down on him when you see his place."

"I usually sleep on a hospital cot, in the same room as a man obsessed with finding sharp objects in his food. I'm sure his place will be fine," he said, smiling sadly, though he tried to keep the conversation light.

Justine shrugged. "He might also be worried about how you judge his particular eccentricities."

Quinn raised an eyebrow. "Eccentricities? Like what?"

Justine threw up her hands and shrugged. "Don't get me wrong," she said. "Thanatos—not just Jared, I mean all the incarnations of Thanatos—form a habit of being close to the living. He has a bit of a soft spot for them. So, while Jared has the means to live the high life, he would rather live with them, as one of them. That said, he does have an art critic's eye and a fashion editor's taste, so he does indulge in at least some luxuries. Anyway, it's his whole philosophy. He might be a reincarnated god, but he's also human now, so he's gonna live like it—he wants to be their equal. For it is only in death we are made as such."

Quinn grinned. "You should have been a poet."

"Who says I'm not? Come, we should get going. I'm sure they're waiting for us in the foyer."

CHAPTER TWELVE

By the time Quinn and Jared arrived at the latter's apartment, the sun was well on its way to setting, painting the vault of sky overhead in ever-darkening jewel tones, streaked by clouds of coral orange and magenta pink. It was a beautiful evening, and had Quinn not been so preoccupied, he might have noticed it.

Their journey up from the Underworld had been much less eventful or dangerous than Quinn's fall downward had been. One of the many luxuries to be found in Hades' palace was a magical elevator, which deposited the pair into the basement level of an underground parking structure. When they stepped out into the cool air of the late-September evening, Quinn looked around and couldn't help but notice the large reflective bean sculpture in the park across the way. *We must be in Chicago.*

Jared flagged down a taxi and soon they were on their way again. Quinn took his seat next to Jared, a messenger bag slung over his shoulder and a duffle bag laid across his knees, both of which had been provided to him by the Doyles. He waited for Jared to give the driver instructions before he decided to speak.

"So, I just wanted to say thanks. You and your brothers didn't have to give me so much stuff. It was really generous of you. Once I get on my feet, I'll get a job and pay you all back somehow." The words tumbled out of Quinn's nervous mouth, and he only inhaled after he'd finished speaking.

"Don't worry about that. Justine would have flayed us alive if we didn't." Jared smirked, attempting humour. But Quinn felt so awkward.

What if he hated having to give up his stuff to me?

"I really hate to be an inconvenience…" he started, his face flushed.

"Shit. I keep doing that. I keep making you feel bad. I promise I don't mean to. I'm sorry. It was just a joke." This time it was Jared's turn to blush. If Quinn wasn't already so mortified by the situation, he would have found it adorable.

"It's okay. I guess we're all still figuring this whole thing out." Quinn kept things vague so that the cab driver wouldn't overhear anything crazy. That was the last thing he needed on the very day he'd gotten out of Cedar Hills. With a start of shock, Quinn realized this whole adventure had only taken place over the course of a day.

Jared opened his mouth to speak but was interrupted by a text message. "Goddammit." He sneered at the glowing smartphone screen. "I need a few minutes to get my…employees…straightened out. I rarely take a few days off from my…job. You'd think they'd be able to handle it!"

"Sorry to hear." Quinn didn't want to disrupt Jared's frantic texting. *Besides,* he reasoned, *it's not like I'd even know what to say.*

The whole Athena and Thanatos as lovers who found their way to each other in each lifetime was a lot for Quinn to process. He'd gone from having no one in his life, to finding himself sitting next to the man who was supposed to be his soulmate or something. The weight of it made Quinn feel like he was shrinking into himself.

After nearly half an hour of cutting through city traffic, they reached a modest-sized apartment building in the quiet, affluent neighbourhood of Lakeview. The building was one of the older ones, a monument to the neo-Gothic, art deco architecture for which the Windy City was famous. Jared paid the driver and stepped out, without saying a word to Quinn. The younger man took his host's cue, thanked the cabbie and got out gracelessly, still encumbered by his donated bags.

The pair practically flew through the black marble foyer, past gleaming silver fixtures and green velvet drapes. The cut crystal chandeliers cast shimmering rainbows of light over papered walls streaked with silver and gold lattices of geometric shapes.

Another elevator ride, this time to the thirteenth floor. Quinn's eyebrow cocked as he noted the numbered button Jared pushed.

"Huh. Thirteen. You don't see that too often, do you?" he noted, suddenly nervous that he'd say or do something humiliating now that he was alone with Jared.

"You mean the floor number?"

"Yeah, you know the whole unlucky thirteen thing? Most buildings this age skipped the number thirteen to accommodate people's superstitions. But, oddly enough, this building has a thirteenth floor."

"Oh, yeah, I guess I'm used to it. The last Thanatos changed it when he bought the building. I kinda liked it so I kept it when I inherited it from him. Now that I think about it, I do have a rather hard time keeping renters on that floor, even though I keep the rates very low. *C'est la vie.* Besides, the fewer people to observe me and the odd hours I keep, the better."

"So, you own the building, but you don't live in the penthouse?"

Quinn remembered Justine's words only after he'd asked the question and cringed internally. She'd warned him that this was a sore point for Jared. He hated feeling judged for his choice to live close to humans and treat them as equals.

"Yeah. I guess most gods would choose the penthouse, right? I don't know what to say. I tried to live there once but it felt too big and too cold up there. I live by myself so there's no point having all that extra space. I mean, it's got four bedrooms. I rent it out for a low price to a nurse and schoolteacher and their kids. They deserve it." Jared looked uncomfortable and embarrassed. Quinn's heart went out to him. This whole thing probably wasn't easy for him, either, having to explain his decisions to a virtual stranger.

"That's actually really cool, you know," Quinn said thoughtfully. "Regular hard-working people never get the chance to live in penthouses in fancy buildings, in what is clearly the most expensive part of the city. And people who have money tend not to think the way you do. As someone who grew up with nothing, I respect what you're doing here."

"Thank you." Jared flashed him a genuine smile as the elevator doors dinged open and they exited to the thirteenth floor and approached his apartment. "Not all the other gods get that. Some gods, like Zeus, think we ought to rule over humanity and live in palaces. Oh, I forgot to ask—you're not allergic to dogs, are you?"

"Not that I know of," Quinn replied.

"Good."

The front door lock clicked, and Jared pushed the door open. Almost instantly, deep excited barks came from the back of the apartment. A large, dog-like creature bounded across the dark walnut floors, the tips of its claws clattering on the herringbone hardwood. Jared crouched down to greet his beloved pet.

"Hey, there's my good boy!" Jared laughed, scratching and stroking its three frantic heads, while three rough pink tongues lapped at his face. "How's my buddy? Did you miss me?"

Quinn stared, rooted to the spot, almost as if he hoped the dog—*dogs?*—operated like the T-Rex from *Jurassic Park*.

Maybe it won't see me if I don't move.

The creature looked like a normal dog—a Rottweiler crossed with a black Labrador Retriever, if he wasn't mistaken. Yet Quinn was quite certain that no pet shop or breeder supplied dogs with three heads. It took another second before Quinn realized that he recognized the animal.

"Cerberus?" Quinn's whispered acknowledgement was enough encouragement for the pup. It left its owner and wandered over to the stranger, its tail wagging, curious about the bags Quinn held.

"Yup, that's my boy."

"He's uh…a little intimidating," Quinn replied, speaking soft and slow, trying not to agitate the curious creature that sniffed at him.

"Don't worry—he won't hurt you. If he was going to attack, he would have done it already," Jared replied jokingly, leading both Quinn and Cerberus back into the exquisitely furnished condo. "Besides, I think he likes you." Here, the dark-haired Death God's tone turned sincere and he motioned to his pet as one of its exuberant heads tried to nuzzle into the side of Quinn's leg.

"Uh-huh." Quinn tried not to sound skeptical but he couldn't stop staring at the sinister teeth in the three separate mouths that were far too close to him for comfort.

"Are you scared of dogs?" Jared seemed surprised but also slightly saddened. "Usually the incarnations of Athena get along with Cerberus really well."

Ever since he could remember, he had been wary of dogs. Well, at least any that were bigger than a toaster. Quinn credited his apprehension to some experience in his forgotten childhood, or perhaps the recurring, half-remembered dreams that plagued his subconscious. Only, the tone of disappointment in Jared's voice made Quinn keep

G.E. White

this fact to himself.

"No, just never had a dog myself—at least, not that I remember. I don't know the right...protocol for how to act around them. But something strikes me. Shouldn't Cerberus be much bigger? And shouldn't he be in the Underworld?"

"This is just an alternate form he can take. And while you're right, he should be down there, guarding the gates of the Underworld, he's not really needed at the moment. That is, people don't try to break in as much as they used to. So, with time he got bored and started causing havoc: digging up Justine's gardens, ripping the furniture apart, using ghouls as chew toys. Eventually Joe and Justine got sick of it and gave him to me to look after. And something about being in the Second Realm makes him a lot calmer. He doesn't wreck my stuff. Maybe it's because here he has to stay in this smaller form? I don't know. But his collar does allow any of the Underworld gods to summon him back to his post if something goes wrong."

"Makes sense, I guess," Quinn conceded, still clutching the bags of donations. "So, now what?"

Jared's eyes widened for a second. "Oh my God, I'm such an ass. You'll have to forgive me. I haven't had to host houseguests in...well, ever. Or at least, not people who weren't related to me or in relationships with people I'm related to."

"S'okay," Quinn replied, his own nervousness amplified as he absorbed Jared's anxiety. "But maybe if I could trouble you for some water? I haven't had anything to drink since one, and I could really use it."

"Dammit, yes, of course!" Jared practically dashed to his sleek, open-concept kitchen and seconds later, he'd thrust a glass of ice-cold water at Quinn. He suddenly realized that Quinn was still holding the bags and didn't have a free hand. "Okay, let's trade. I'll take the duffle bag, you take the water. Then let me show you where you'll be staying tonight."

He's just as shy and nervous as me. Quinn immediately felt more at ease. *Maybe he's not so intimidating after all?*

Jared and Cerberus led the young man into the guest bedroom. "Here, let me get you some clean towels. Why don't you take some time to get cleaned up? It's been a long day. I'll order us some pizza. After all, you're in Chi-town, you need to have deep dish pizza."

"Sounds amazing." Quinn gave the man his most genuine smile, starting to feel a bit more at ease with him.

Jared smiled back and nodded, pointing out the direction to the bathroom and turning to leave.

"Hey, Jared?" Quinn interrupted, plucking up his courage. "Thanks for rescuing me from those ghouls and trying to be nice to me. It's been a really long, really messed up day. And you've been really generous. I appreciate it."

"Yeah, it's nothing." Jared didn't look directly at him, but from this angle, Quinn could see his smile. "Gonna go feed the dog and order us that pizza. Have a good shower!"

With that, the God of Death whirled around and shut the door behind him.

Taking a second to breathe, Quinn looked around. The bedroom was decorated in the same dark tone as the rest of the condo, or at least the parts that Quinn had seen. There was a painting on the wall that Quinn recognized. Around the age of sixteen he'd been really into art, and his photographic memory helped him recall the name now. It was *Hypnos & Thanatos, Sleep and his Half-Brother Death* by John William Waterhouse. It made Quinn smile to imagine the two seated figures in the painting as Jared and his twin James. The thought brought back that same rush of heat that Quinn felt when he'd tripped while exiting Charon's boat. He pushed the sensation away, trying to forget all about it.

I have much bigger things to deal with. I don't have time to develop a crush. No matter how hot he is...

G.E. White

Taking a seat on the softest bed he'd ever encountered, Quinn emptied out the contents of the two bags and gaped at the goodies he'd been so generously given: brand-new packets of underwear and socks, a stack of designer jeans and cool graphic t-shirts, toiletries, and even a gift pack of various cologne samplers.

This is too much! And it's all new! I thought these were supposed to be hand-me-downs?!

It took a minute of gawking and wondering before Joe's words echoed back in Quinn's head. The current incarnation of Hades had told Quinn that Justine had purchased these things for the men in her life while on her latest spring break girls' trip in the Second Realm.

Apparently, she'd gotten their sizes wrong and hadn't yet had a chance to return the mistakes. As for the toiletries, Joe's job as Hades took up so much of his time, he barely ever left his palace. Justine always bought him stacks of everything he could need. After all, it's not as though delivery companies serviced the Underworld.

It's like they knew today's my birthday.

Only Quinn had never been gifted anything close to even one of the items laid out on the bed before him. He decided he'd have to repay them somehow, but that thought just led him down a rabbit hole.

Am I truly free now? And if I'm a god, what's my job? Do I get paid? Are there health benefits? What have I gotten myself into?

There were no answers. And the persistent churn in his stomach made Quinn push the existential crisis to the back of his mind. The last meal he'd had was his Spartan breakfast of plain oatmeal at Cedar Hills, and it was well past dinner time now. He had to deal with this mess, one thing at a time.

Okay, I need to be strategic here. That means answers later. First shower and then food…then I'll figure the rest out as I go.

∾

As Cerberus' three heads all dove into their separate bowls of kibbles and began to chow down, Jared leaned back against his kitchen counter and exhaled slowly.

I am really cocking this up.

Realizing he was still covered in dried dog slobber, he quickly washed his face with the hand soap he kept by his kitchen sink and instantly regretted it. He was a stickler for his elaborate twelve-step skincare routine, and he'd just broken a cardinal rule by using this harsh soap on his face.

Come on, get it together!

He poured himself a double serving of sixteen-year-old scotch and downed half of it in a single swig that burned like hellfire as it slid down his throat. Behind him, the sound of the shower indicated that Quinn was taking his advice. Pushing aside his disappointment in himself and the weight of the moment, he dialed the number of his favourite pizzeria and placed an order.

He hadn't anticipated that he'd be having company today, so with Quinn in the shower, he took the chance to tidy up the few things he needed to, to return the place to its typically immaculate condition. As he picked up magazines and straightened cushions, he glanced into his den and noticed an item on his bookshelf that drained all the colour from his face.

Rushing over, he pushed past his massive teak desk and leather office chair and almost tripped over Cerberus' dog bed. There, on the shelf with all his most cherished personal effects, was the duck.

The stuffed toy duck sat propped up against the back of the shelf, its head lolling forward due to the meagre cotton batting in its neck. The fuzzy white terry cloth of the duck's body was worn thin in places, yet it remained soft to the touch. The feet and beak, constructed of yellow felt, had fared better than the rest of the toy. The beady black eyes still shone, despite the scuff marks. Overall, it hadn't changed a bit since he'd first acquired it fourteen years ago. In his mind, he

G.E. White

could still see it strewn on the wet asphalt, where its previous owner had accidentally dropped it.

He'd already broken so many rules in his time as Thanatos. It couldn't have possibly mattered to anyone at that point if he kept the damn thing. It wasn't as though its owner would be collecting it anytime soon. At least that's what he reasoned back then.

Do I tell him? Jared tossed the thought around in his head for a good minute. *Suppose I did tell him what I did that night, what would he do? He'd probably not trust any of us. Or he'd want something from me. Revenge. Answers. I probably can't give him either. Maybe he'd have some sympathy. He'd understand—I was just eleven years old. I didn't know better. I guess I thought I was doing him a favour...only question is, would he see it that way?*

The possibility that Quinn would hate him forever drove Jared to shove the stuffed toy into the bottom drawer of his desk, behind all the filing folders. He locked the drawer for good measure and returned to his tidying.

The shower turned off just as the buzzer by the front door rang. Jared paid for the food and laid out a couple of place settings at the black granite breakfast bar. He'd just picked out a good red wine when Quinn emerged from the guest bedroom in a simple sapphire-blue v-neck and a pair of matching navy-blue silk pyjama pants. It was all Jared could do to keep himself from staring at the adorable man in front of him.

Quinn stood a couple inches shy of six feet tall, only a few inches shorter than Jared himself. His slender runner's physique suited his delicately featured face. He had keenly observant silver-grey eyes that enhanced his inquisitive nature and sharp wit. Jared found himself bewitched by that shy smile that lit Quinn's whole face up. Not to mention the endearing way his wild mop of ash-blond hair fell into his face, and how he played with it when he was nervous or lost in thought.

He couldn't tell if fate was being kind or cruel to him. This incarnation of his former beloved was stunning, in his own sweet way. Yet, he knew that nothing was set in stone. They barely knew each other; it was quite possible that the two young men were incompatible. It wasn't fair to assume just because their connection happened before it would happen again. Still, Jared couldn't shake this growing feeling.

How is it that we've only just met again and already I feel as though we were meant to be together?

"Hey, food's here!" Quinn flashed Jared that heart-melting smile. "Smells delicious! I've never had deep dish before."

Jared shook the thoughts from his head and acted like a proper host. He invited Quinn to take a seat and served him a couple slices.

"Well, even if you had, if you've never actually had it in Chicago, then you've never *actually* had deep dish. Oh, and I hope you like red wine?"

Quinn raised his eyebrows at the bottle. "I don't know? I've only ever had the occasional beer at a couple high school parties. But today *is* my twentieth birthday, and in Canada, where I'm from, I'm legally allowed to drink after my nineteenth birthday, so why not indulge."

"Oh, happy birthday! I didn't know!" Jared poured the wine and then went to his freezer and pulled out a box of chocolate cheesecake. "Lucky for us, James and Sofia left a bunch of snacks here last time they visited."

Quinn's eyes lit up at the sight of the boxed dessert. "This day has been so crazy. Between finding out I'm Athena, being attacked by those Danaids and Ghouls, and now this? The stuff your family gave me and the fact that you're letting me stay here. And you even have my favourite dessert. I don't know what to say."

The gratitude evident in Quinn's words tugged at Jared's heartstrings. "How about we put on some music, drink this wine, eat this pizza, and forget for a moment that your whole world just got turned upside down, then? I can tell you're reeling from everything today, and tomorrow you'll be taking your first steps to setting up a whole new life. You might as well enjoy this peaceful evening."

"That's very thoughtful of you, Jared. Thanks."

"A toast then," Jared proposed, lifting his glass. Quinn mirrored his gesture with his own drink and smiled at him.

"And what are we toasting?"

"You. Happy Birthday, Quinn. May you have many more!"

Their glasses clinked together and their eyes locked for a second. Jared breathed in. They were sitting right next to each other, almost touching. The unintentional romantic atmosphere made Jared aware that it would be nothing for him to take Quinn's head in his hands and kiss the man in front of him. Silently chastising himself, he quickly banished the bold thought. Quinn blushed a deep crimson, as if he'd read Jared's mind, and diverted his gaze in shyness. Jared took the cue to clear his throat, and they both sipped at their respective drinks instead, before resuming dinner.

After a few bites, Jared got up to put some music on.

"You have any preferences?" Jared asked, "It's your birthday. You can choose."

"I like everything. And yes, I do mean everything. I like the details of how music is composed. Sometimes, I just like the expression of emotion. But how about we go with jazz? It seems fitting, being in Chicago and all."

Soon, Quinn directed Jared to assemble a playlist of Muddy Waters, Willie Dixon, Sam Cooke, Herbie Hancock, and Mavis Staples. "They're all actually from Chicago too!" Quinn exclaimed.

"That's really cool how you do that, you know, remember all those facts and details. In all the lifetimes I can remember, you're always like that, and it never ceases to amaze me." Jared didn't mean to confess that, but it just came out.

"Can you remember more of our past? I mean, not *our* past, but your past and my past. But I guess also our, like, shared history…"

Quinn trailed off awkwardly, seeming to hunch in on himself.

"Bits. Not all of it. However, unlike a lot of other gods, my brothers and I tend to have long memories. Every time we're reborn, we awaken really quickly and get started on handling our duties young," Jared noted. "Joe was found using the Soul Calendria, shortly before it disappeared, and when James and I were born, he knew immediately who we were. Our parents had already been made aware of all this god stuff when Joe was found, so having two more kids being part of the club wasn't as big of a shock. They've got a beautiful property on Lake Michigan, and we all still visit them when we can. But I've been collecting souls with the help of my reapers since I could walk and talk."

"That seems like a lot to handle. Given the very sombre stuff you guys are responsible for. Especially at a young age."

"I sometimes wonder if it's not better to wait. Like you did. You get to grow up normal. Without all that god crap messing you up as a kid." Here, the memory that asserted itself in the forefront of his mind made his heart race.

Should I just tell him what happened?

"Seeing you and your family together makes it seem like it might be nice to grow up knowing exactly who you are and where you belong in the world," Quinn replied with a tone of thoughtful melancholy.

Nope. I can't tell him. He grew up all alone. In foster care. And he ended up in an institution. All because of what I did. But what if he could understand why I did it?

"Or it could stifle you and make you feel like you're limited to whatever fate you've been assigned. It might make you resent your life," Jared replied, his heart heavy with the recollection of the countless souls he'd reaped and the various ways in which they died. The things he'd seen in his short life made it feel like he'd been alive for a million years. It was a burden he had hoped to spare Quinn.

"Fate you've been assigned, eh?" Quinn echoed back, a slightly troubled look on his porcelain features. "Like the soulmate you might be stuck with?"

"Ah," Jared's eyebrows arched as he understood his guest's meaning. "Well, that's not what I meant. Sure, for an eternal fuckboy like Zeus, or a player like Hermes, or Aphrodite, the whole being bound to a specific spouse over the millennia could be the proverbial ball and chain for them. But that's not the case for us Underworld gods."

"Right. Long memories."

"And we're committed. Loyal." Jared had a feeling he knew where Quinn was leading the conversation. "You never hear stories of us cheating. Or hurting the ones we love. Never on purpose anyway."

"So does that mean that Underworld gods and their respective spouses always meet up?" Quinn twisted his hair nervously. "In every lifetime?"

"For the most part. I'm not saying that our individual lives don't have any bearing on our fates, but far more often than not, we all end up finding each other. Pasithea and Hypnos, Persephone and Hades..."

"And Athena and Thanatos," Quinn finished, gesturing toward himself and Jared as he spoke. "So, what happens if someone comes back...different."

"What do you mean *different?*"

"I mean, Athena was a woman and, well, I'm not."

"Does that bother you?" Jared hadn't considered that possibility. Then again, he retained some memories of Thanatos being a woman at various times in history and it hadn't upset him in the least. He assumed other gods would be the same way.

"I'm not sure." Quinn shrugged, but he didn't look relieved. "I don't exactly understand how any of this works."

"Our souls are malleable—they have to be, or there would be no point to our reincarnation. True, many core things stay the same, most of what we value or hold dear, or aspects of our personalities. As Athena, no matter which incarnation you are, you will always thirst for knowledge. That's the essence of your nature. But things like sex, gender, sexual orientation—those are all different things, and while they're important, they aren't the be-all and end-all of who we are. Therefore, they aren't carried forward from iteration to iteration."

"That makes a lot of sense."

"As for the whole question about what happens if someone comes back in a different gender than the one they had when they were originally recognized..." Jared started. "Let's just say we have our roots in ancient Greece. A little homosexuality never bothered us. I think you'll find that most, if not all, gods would be considered pansexual. We love who we love and that's about it."

"A progressive way to be. I like it." Quinn smiled.

"Glad you think so," Jared replied. "I'm also glad you're not one of those asshole homophobes!" The idea that Quinn might possibly hate Jared for his sexual orientation had worried him before this conversation.

"It's a *little* hard to be a homophobe when your first crush is Prince Eric from *The Little Mermaid*."

"Oh, so you're... ?" Jared let the question hang in the air, half unspoken, hope rising in his chest.

Quinn wiped his mouth with his napkin before continuing. "Oh, yeah, I'm gay. Knew since I was a little kid. Never questioned it."

"Me too," Jared replied. "But you probably caught that when James was teasing me."

"Yeah, and now that I know all about our shared past, I gotta say I'm relieved. It would have been so awkward if one of us was straight...you know...because of...everything...or at least the potential. Not that anything is going to happen, or has to happen... I'm not saying this properly." Quinn's jovial expression darkened. Then he tensed up again. It took a few painful seconds of silence before he asked the question both of them had been dancing around since the truth of their past lives was revealed: "So, if we, as vessels of these reincarnating gods, are destined to always be together, and we have compatible sexual orientations in this lifetime, then, where does that leave us? As in, you, Jared, and me, Quinn?"

"Athena and Thanatos or not, you are Quinn and I am Jared. Just like everyone else in this world, we either fall in love with each other or we don't." Jared rushed to get the words out, emboldened by Quinn's direct line of questioning. "All we can do is get to know one another in this incarnation. And we let the chips fall where they may. But if I'm not being too bold, I hope that we could be friends for now. I'd like to be your friend, Quinn."

"I would like that. I mean, it sounds more than reasonable." Quinn relaxed and shot him a satisfied smile. "That takes a lot of the pressure off, actually. We'll just focus on being friends. And we'll see what the future holds when we get there."

"Good." Jared picked up their polished off plates and loaded them into the dishwasher. "So, Prince Eric, huh?"

"Are you about to tease me for liking a cartoon character?" Quinn washed his hands as he spoke. "As if you didn't!"

"Nope. I was more of a Luke Skywalker guy myself. Much cooler. Had that whole badass fighter pilot and laser sword-wielding Jedi thing going. Not to mention he was played by a *real* person."

"Wow, so judgmental!" Quinn said in mock indignation. "And we only just met!"

Jared laughed. "What can I say? I'm a monster. A monster who happens to have cake…" With that, Jared opened the now-thawed box of cheesecake and served up two slices.

"I would offer to put a candle in it, but the only candles I have are those big decorative scented ones in the glass jars. Plus, if we start singing 'Happy Birthday,' Cerberus will try to join us, and the howling of a hell-hound is bound to piss off the neighbours," he explained as he returned the remaining dessert to the freezer.

Quinn laughed and waved it off. "Don't worry about candles and songs. So long as it's chocolate, I'm good!"

Pouring a couple of snifters of cognac, Jared was about to take his seat at the countertop when Quinn interrupted.

"Can we sit on your balcony instead?" That shy smile was back, and he was blushing again. "I could use the fresh air."

Jared agreed and the two young men carried their cake and liquor outside.

Settling down on the ornate wrought-iron patio set, Jared looked out over Lake Michigan. The city lights sparkled all around them, just beyond the park. The trees below had begun to change from a sea of lush greens to a patchwork of little flames of reds, oranges, and yellows. Even in the darkness, he could see their colours, lit by the lampposts that marked the lakeside trail. Somewhere out there, he could hear the haunting nocturnal cries of hooting owls, who nested in the parkland that surrounded the water. Above, a full silver moon hung in an indigo canopy of twinkling stars and reflected back in the shimmering waves of the lake.

"It's so beautiful." Quinn breathed beside him, the cool autumn breeze ruffling his hair. "I get why you choose to live here."

"It's really special to me." Jared turned to him and once again raised his glass. "I'm glad I got to share it with you."

"I know it has been the most bizarre day of my life. But this might actually be the best birthday I've ever had." Quinn returned the unspoken toast and looked him deep in the eyes, his sincerity radiating out. "Thanks for this, Jared. It really means a lot."

"You're very welcome, Quinn. It's my pleasure. Also, that was a very sad thing to admit." Jared tried not to get caught up in the deep swell of emotion he felt at Quinn's sentiment. So he tried to revert back to his typical sarcastic sense of humour to lighten the mood. "This? This is your best birthday? Didn't you get attacked by Danaids and Ghouls today?"

Quinn chuckled. "I admit it was…a bit of a misadventure, but it turned out pretty nice at the end, don't you think?" He smiled at Jared before polishing off his slice of cheesecake with relish.

"Still, next year, we have to have an actual party. The whole family would kill me if we didn't celebrate you properly next time." Jared picked up their now-empty dishes and led them back indoors.

"Your family seems really nice." Quinn helped him clean up, seeming to have relaxed and opened up quite a bit since their initial meeting. "You're lucky to have them."

"I am." Jared wiped his hands dry on a tea towel and leaned against the bar. "I really hope that you get a chance to spend more time with them. I want for us to all be in each other's lives. Regardless of whether or not you and I mean anything to each other beyond just being friends, I want you to be part of the family the way you always have been. You matter to us."

Quinn stared at Jared for a good long minute. A slow tear wound its way down his cheek, which Quinn was quick to whip away. "You know the crazy part is that I kind of believe you. I've...never had—"

Just at that moment, Cerberus started barking. One of his heads nuzzled at Jared's leg, another held the leash in its mouth, and the last one held the plastic container Jared used for poop baggies.

You've got to be kidding me! Really?!

"I'm sorry!" Jared exclaimed.

Quinn shook his head and cleared his throat. "The joys of dog ownership, right?"

"He needs to be taken out for his nightly constitutional," Jared explained diplomatically, trying not to say anything gross.

"Hey, I get it. Dogs gotta dog. Even when they're hell-hounds." Quinn shrugged. "It's honestly okay. If you're cool with me just sitting around while you take him out?"

"Of course, and help yourself to any drinks or anything." Jared put his coat on as he spoke.

"Actually, you wouldn't happen to have any chamomile tea or

anything like that?"

"Maybe. I'm not really a tea person myself. But my brother and his girlfriend are. Check the upper cabinet over where the coffee maker and electric kettle are. There might be a tea sampler that Sofia left behind."

"Thanks." Quinn moved toward the kitchen as he spoke. "I feel like I'm still too wired to sleep and it's already getting pretty late. Plus, I don't drink alcohol very often so I'm just gonna stop for tonight. While I still feel relatively normal."

"Wise idea," Jared conceded, wrangling the ever-exuberant Cerberus so he could attach the leash to his magical collar. "Then again, given you are who you are, that makes sense."

Quinn grinned, but it seemed as though the gesture was more at himself than at Jared. "Yeah, I guess I am Athena, aren't I?"

Cerberus' whining continued to pull Jared from the slight haze of inadvertent romance that had settled around the pair over the course of the evening. Quinn noticed it too and flashed him a sweet, understanding smile. "Go! It's okay! I think I can handle making myself a cup of tea!"

"Right, see you soon!" Jared exited the building with a speed that would make Carter proud. Luckily, Cerberus was no ordinary dog and relished the opportunity to exercise his own formidable speed. Once they reached the dog park near their building, both pet and owner finally stopped to breathe.

"All right buddy, talk about shitty timing." Cerberus whined, cocking all three of his heads to the side in a gesture that always made Jared laugh. "Okay, okay, I still love you, you big mutt, even if you are a mood killer. But hurry it up!"

Minutes later Jared was back in his apartment and washing his hands. He'd found Quinn curled up on the leather sectional, wrapped in a blanket that used to be draped over the foot of the guest bed, a mug of tea steaming in his hands. He was watching a true-crime documentary, clearly riveted to the television screen.

"These dramatic reenactments always crack me up." Jared leaned against the entertainment unit and grinned at the hacky acting.

"I'm trying to figure out if this man actually killed his parents or not."

"I could just tell you. One of my Reapers would know. I could ask them."

"Please don't! No spoilers! I'm trying to suss it out on my own."

Jared laughed. One day in and they were already behaving like an old married couple. Still, he supposed that could be expected given they'd spent countless lifetimes together before now.

"If you don't want to watch this, we can change the channel. It's your house after all." Quinn shot him a sweet smile he couldn't help but return.

"Nah, it's okay. Enjoy your show."

"Come watch with me."

"So bossy." Jared chuckled as he attempted to sit on the corner opposite Quinn.

Once again, Cerberus interfered with his plans. The giant doofus jumped up onto the couch and settled in. "Okay, buddy, that's cute, but it's time to get off," he said as he tried to shove the massive beast from the couch.

One of the heads turned toward Jared and growled, giving a clear message that the dog would not move unless he wanted to. He doubted the beast would actually bite him but had learned over time that Cerberus would not be persuaded. Defeated, Jared had no choice but to sit right next to Quinn. Their thighs touched as Jared settled in and he tried not to think about it.

For the next half hour, they sat and watched together in relative silence.

"This tea is really good. Don't know what it is, though—didn't have a label," Quinn murmured. The show had just ended and he was bathed in a soft blue glow from the television screen. "Smelled like chammie—chamo—no, ugh. Chamomile, but mixed with...huh. I dunno."

Jared frowned. Quinn sounded so odd. Like he was a wind-up doll slowly running out of power. "What tea did you take?"

"The one from the tin. You know, the tin with the little flower stickers on it?" Quinn's voice was slurring slightly. And that's when Jared realized what had happened.

"Oh shit."

"Whaaa?" Quinn flashed Jared an increasingly dopey smile.

"Crap, you drank James' tea!" Jared didn't know whether to panic or to laugh at Quinn's delayed reaction and spaced out expression.

"James... ?"

"He's an insomniac. Justine and Sofia make this special tea for him so he can actually sleep. He stores some here for when he comes to visit!"

It took a good few moments before Quinn seemed to understand his words.

"Oh...shit..."

"Indeed."

"Nah, nah... S'okay." Quinn yawned and handed his now-empty mug to Jared. "I pro'lly should get some sleep."

The tea-addled young man attempted to move, but clearly struggled. "Uh-oh..."

"I got you." Jared helped Quinn extricate himself from the blanket and stand up. "Come on."

The pair tried to shuffle over to the bedroom, but Quinn had been drinking the hypnotic tea for almost an hour and it had really begun to impact his motor functions.

"Jus' lemme sleep on the floor...is fine..." Quinn made to face plant into the hardwood, but Jared caught him. Using his supernatural strength, he swept the smaller man up into his arms with one graceful motion and proceeded to carry him to the guest bedroom.

Almost as soon as he'd curled up against the hard planes of Jared's chest, Quinn passed out. Jared tried not to disturb him as he gingerly placed him down on the queen-sized bed. With a sigh of disapproval, he noted that all of the things his family had given Quinn were still strewn about the bed in disarray.

Another lifetime, another messy, absent-minded Athena.

Jared took the time to clean it up, neatly arranging everything in orderly little piles on the dresser. Before he left the room, he pulled the down comforter up from the foot of the bed and gently draped it over the sleeping young man. He exited and shut the door behind him but leaned against it for a moment, listening to Quinn snoring lightly on the other side of the wood panel. The burden of his guilt over what happened fourteen years prior suddenly engulfed him, a suffocating shroud of shame.

What am I doing? I only just met this guy and I'm already so out of my depth. On top of everything, there's a very good chance that I may have utterly ruined his life. No matter the excuses I've made over the years, it was my decision that left him all alone, stuck in foster care, and without the love and support that we could have provided him. I wish I could change what happened. But I've ruined everything. Maybe... Maybe I don't deserve to be with Athena in this incarnation. Maybe all I can do for Quinn is be a good friend. He's gonna need one now that his whole life has changed.

CHAPTER THIRTEEN

Q<small>UINN CAME TO</small> in the early morning hours as a warm and gentle ray of sunlight cast itself across his face. Blinking in the new light, Quinn turned his gaze to the side, once again taking in the painting depicting the original versions of Hypnos and Thanatos. The sight brought the world into stark focus. Visions of rainbow-hued flames, feral mad women, sinister ghouls, and a cadre of Greek gods and demigods swirled about in his mind. He remembered the feeling of invigoration as he stood in front of the Olympian fire, feeling more like himself, yet completely foreign at the same time. But most of all, he remembered the kindness of the people he met, Surina, Leo, Carter, Joseph, Justine, James… Jared.

So, it wasn't a dream.

A persistent headache also reminded him of his ungraceful descent into the Underworld. He felt around his head and sure enough, the bump from his fall was still there, even if it had reduced significantly.

Okay, so the headache is probably a result of this head injury, coupled with last night's alcohol consumption, not to mention that weird tea that made me pass out. I didn't drink much water yesterday, so I'm probably dealing with inflammation and dehydration. I can fix this.

Sneaking out of his room and trying to keep as quiet as possible, Quinn rifled through Jared's sleek bathroom until he found some ibuprofen and a bottle of multivitamins. Next, he grabbed one of the sports drinks by Jared's gym bag to replenish his electrolytes. Finally, he just needed some protein and caffeine.

"Breakfast and coffee," Quinn said, recognizing how hungry he truly was. It struck him that making breakfast for himself and Jared might be a nice way to show his gratitude to the gorgeous god. Cerberus watched him lazily, still sprawled out on the couch where he'd been the night before. "What do you think, boy? Should we make breakfast for Jared? Do you think he likes pancakes?"

Cerberus whined, all three of his heads alternately yawning or chewing on his paws. Meanwhile, Quinn flew through the cabinets of Jared's spotless kitchen. Pretty soon he had coffee brewing and pancake batter whisked. Golden hash brown patties, slices of bacon, and links of breakfast sausage sizzled in a couple pans on the stove as he chopped onions and bell peppers for omelettes. Using mathematical precision and his supernatural memory recall for the recipes, Quinn crafted a gourmet meal that was timed out perfectly so everything would be completed at the same time for maximum warmth and freshness.

He was so hyper focused on his task that he didn't hear Jared wake up.

"Wow." Jared wore a pair of black designer boxer briefs and a black silk robe that still hung open as the bleary-eyed man wandered into the main living area of his apartment.

Wow is right…holy shit. He's so hot. Quinn tried not to accidentally cut himself as he stealthily checked Jared out. Seeing him shirtless was a little exciting. He thanked whatever luck he possessed that he had cooking to distract him from ogling Jared like a crazy person.

For a second, the God of Death said nothing. He just stared, his dismayed eyes roaming back and forth over the piles of dirty dishes, empty food containers, and spilled ingredients that coated every surface in his kitchen. "This…is a lot…"

"Oh no. You're mad." Quinn cringed as he took in the mess he'd made and the somewhat horrified look on Jared's face. "Aren't you?"

"No. No, sorry. Not mad. Just…surprised. That's all. And still waking up." Jared began to gingerly pick up the already cracked egg shells. "I usually just have a smoothie for breakfast. And a fistful of supplements. I mean, I typically work out first thing in the morning."

"I'm sorry. I thought I was doing something nice for you by making you breakfast. And don't worry about the mess—I promise I'll clean it up after!"

It took a second before Jared stopped fussing around, threw his hand up, and shot him a conciliatory smile. "Fine, actually it would be nice. I haven't slept in or had a sit-down breakfast in years. Besides, it all smells delicious!"

"Good!" Quinn brightened as Jared started to relax. "It seems like you have a hefty responsibility, with your job and all. I think it's awesome that you're taking some time for yourself today."

Minutes later, the pair had taken their steaming plates of food out to the balcony as Jared explained he couldn't relax and enjoy the meal if he had to stare at his filthy kitchen. By this point however, the dark-haired man had managed to get some coffee into his system and seemed to be in a lighter mood. Something about seeing his host smiling and savouring his rare time off made Quinn really happy. A feeling of quiet contentedness settled over them as morning dawned over the Windy City.

184   G.E. White

They passed the repast in pleasant, if shallow, conversation. They discussed favourite books and movies, what kinds of cuisine they both enjoyed, and some of their hobbies. As it turned out, despite his ultra sleek apartment and his designer-label fashion sense, Jared was actually a bit of a science fiction nerd. It had started when he was a kid and only as a way to appease James. Now he apparently had a deep appreciation for the genre all on his own. And he loved art, architecture, and design. He was even a fan of poetry.

"So, you're telling me that the current incarnation of the God of Death is really into postmodern poetry?" Quinn's question sounded a touch incredulous, but Jared always seemed to surprise him. It's true that they'd only known each other less than twenty-four hours, and sure it was awkward at the beginning, but they'd already started getting used to each other.

"Sure, I love Ginsberg. But also, transcendentalists like Whitman. And surrealists like Neruda. That's actually something I picked up from you. You taught me to appreciate art and poetry. Or, the last you and the last me."

"Do you know much about the last Athena and Thanatos?" Quinn sipped at his coffee. Yesterday, the topic of their past lives felt like so much pressure. A pressure he couldn't possibly live up to. But after their talk and their decision to just remain friends for now, that weight was lifted. Now, the topic of their history was one that made him curious. "Were they one of the iterations of ourselves that were together?"

Jared smiled. "Yes. They were married. Mathias Bettencourt and Gloria Hoffman Bettencourt. Thanatos and Athena."

"Why does that name sound familiar?" Quinn closed his eyes and let his mind wander to a number of buildings and plaques they'd passed on the cab ride last night. "I've seen the names before. All over the city. They must have been rich and important. If I'm not mistaken, the Bettencourt family ancestors include titans of industry, politicians, military leaders, and even a few famous artists. Right?"

Jared's eyebrows raised. "You noticed all that last night? From the cab?"

The question gave Quinn a bit of a start. How *had* he known all that? Yes, he had been paying attention to the various parks and memorial plaques scattered throughout the city but never stopped to think that he would be able to read them while in a moving vehicle. He was also aware that some of the information had come from guidebooks he had read years ago when his school planned a weekend trip to the Windy City.

So this is what it's like to be Athena, huh?

He ducked his head, almost bashful as he answered. "Yeah, well and stuff I'd read years ago about Chicago. That's how I recognized where we were yesterday. Is that weird?"

"No, of course not," Jared assured. "Just, still getting used to the whole Athena deductive reasoning and keen observation thing."

"I'd love to learn more about them—the Bettencourts. Or at least the ones that were our former selves."

"Gonna run off on a research bender?" Jared laughed. "I thought you said you'd take care of the kitchen?"

"Oh, shit! Sorry!" Quinn's cheeks reddened. He wasn't a disgusting slob, but he'd always been a little messy. And judging by Jared's home, he was the exact opposite. Jared clearly liked things "just so" and would be irked by the slightest deviation. "Let me get started on that cleaning now that we're finished eating!"

Jared grabbed his hand as he reached for the empty plates. "Hey. Thanks for making me slow down and enjoy the morning." Then he let him go and got up. "I'm gonna hit the shower and get dressed."

Blushing more furiously, Quinn mumbled something back before rushing off to the chaotic kitchen. The friendly ease with which they'd been interacting had suddenly evaporated as a wave of butterflies and flush of heat made Quinn's heart flutter. He needed to focus on anything that didn't directly involve Jared. So, true to his word, he got down to business cleaning the kitchen.

All he has to do is touch me and I start developing feelings. I need to get it together. I don't even know what I'm supposed to be doing. Maybe once I figure out this Athena stuff, I can revisit the possibility of some kind of relationship with Jared? I mean, I haven't felt this way about anyone before. And given our history, it feels inevitable. But I need to be smart about this. I only just met him.

It took Quinn half an hour to get the kitchen squared away and just about as long for Jared to get dressed. The blond man marvelled at the amount of time it took for his host to preen. When he finally emerged from his bedroom, Jared was dressed in dark-washed skinny jeans, a pair of designer combat boots, and a long-sleeved, leather-trimmed, form-fitting t-shirt that showed off his enviable physique. His face was freshly shaven and his hair was perfectly coiffed. Quinn smelled the delicate scent of sandalwood and vetiver as Jared passed him to feed Cerberus.

"Is this your idea of casual clothing?" Quinn joked but suddenly felt inadequate in his donated pyjamas.

"I guess. Kind of." Jared shrugged as he watched the dog eat. "Surina said she was coming to pick you up, but I think she actually meant me. She asked me to take a few days off to help her deal with something. I didn't know she'd be bringing you into the fold, so to speak. But I was under the impression there was more to this than finding Athena. The outfit is in case she drags me into some kind of mess. I'm not going to ruin a designer suit mucking around in the First Realm."

"Oh, so this is not casualwear. It's like, survival gear." Quinn raised his eyebrows and smiled like a Cheshire Cat with a secret.

"What? Do you hate the outfit?" The look on Jared's face gave Quinn the distinct impression that people tended not to tease the God of Death.

"It's just—I didn't realize Prada made combat boots. You look like you're about to go to fashion week in an active warzone. Are...are there utility pouches on your boots?"

"Umm, yeah? So?" Jared still didn't get the joke, which was even more endearing to Quinn. He didn't know much about the realms, but the thought of Jared getting stuck in some muddy swamp somewhere, fighting some mythical beast while trying not to dirty himself or damage his shoes, made Quinn smile even wider.

"I'm just teasing about the whole militant-chic look," Quinn relented. "You do look nice. You have a great sense of style. I kinda envy that."

"Thanks." Jared's own cheeks actually seemed to redden. "Okay, why don't you go take a shower and get dressed? I'll go walk Cerberus and call Carter and Surina. She and I will go out and handle whatever Sebastien needs us to do, and you and Carter can track down all the information that Gloria Bettencourt left after her death."

"Why do we need to do that today? Shouldn't I go with you and Surina?"

"Because you just 'woke up' as a god. And your first day on the job was a bit of a rough one. I think you probably need to rest, recuperate, figure some stuff out, and then you can join us on assignments. Besides—"

"Surina made me agree to help her when she signed me out of Cedar Hills," Quinn interrupted, worry starting to rise in his gut. "What if she sends me back for not doing whatever she wanted me to do?"

"No one will ever take you away, Quinn." Jared's face darkened and his voice was thick with sudden emotion. "I promise."

The two men stared at one another for a long second, the words seemed to have cast a spell upon the two of them. Heat rose up Quinn's body as he gazed into the pale flames of Jared's eyes. It was the dark-haired Death God who broke the intense silence. "Now that you've awakened, it would be unethical to leave you institutionalized when there's nothing wrong with your mental faculties."

Right, Quinn thought, embarrassed that he'd misread the emotions between them. *Jared and the others all have jobs to do, and Athena does too. They need me to do my job. That's all.*

"So, where do I start with this whole learning to be Athena thing?"

If Quinn wasn't mistaken, Jared looked slightly relieved. "Well, I didn't know when I'd meet you, but when I inherited this building seven years ago, I got this package with a USB key that is alleged to be from the estate of Gloria Bettencourt. The instructions that came with it said that I was to keep it secret and only give this to the next Athena, that only you'd be able to unlock it."

"What is it?"

"No idea. I've privately had it tested with every kind of decryption tool I could get my hands on, but the password is some kind of puzzle or game or something. I was thinking that maybe you could try your hand at unlocking it? You know, apply that Athena brain of yours to the challenge?"

Earlier Quinn might have shied away from the puzzle, figuring it was beyond his capabilities. But as more and more information seemed to come easily to him, Quinn found himself nodding in agreement. "And what about Carter? Is he my babysitter or something?"

"No, but the last Hermes, a man by the name of Percival Carruthers, was a close friend of Gloria's. Maybe Carter can remember something from his past life, or maybe old Percy left him something that could help solve the puzzle?"

Quinn was torn. On one hand, what Jared proposed was logical and wise. Not to mention the very tantalizing possibility that he might have some secret inheritance waiting for him made this option appealing to him. After all, the last Thanatos had left his successor Jared an entire apartment building. Gloria was his wife. She might have left something to Quinn as well.

On the other hand, now that he was in this world of gods and monsters, he felt this growing sense of curiosity. He wanted to know anything and everything about all of it. Being left behind by Surina and Jared felt like being sidelined. And after the year he'd spent in Cedar Hills, he was eager for something to challenge his brain. Something to engage him and invigorate his intellect.

Hmmm, cracking the mystery behind this USB key could be rewarding. I should stay here and work on this and let Jared and Surina handle the big stuff for now.

"Okay. No, you're right. That's the smart move," Quinn conceded, noting the relief and satisfaction on Jared's face.

"I'll get the computer set up in my office and let you take that shower then."

"Perfect, see you later!" Quinn waved Jared and Cerberus off for their morning walk, then he went to get dressed.

☙

By the time he'd finished showering, Jared was just returning home. He was on his phone, having some kind of heated conversation. Quinn didn't want to interrupt even to say hello, so he just slipped back into the guest bedroom and pulled on his new clothes. Once dressed, Quinn gave himself a once-over in the full-length mirror that hung on the back of the door.

Being a foster kid meant he'd spent most of his life wearing out-of-date clothes that weren't even the right size. The man looking back at him in the mirror was not someone he recognized. He wore the same kind of stylish skinny jeans as Jared, with a periwinkle-blue, loose-fitting, long-sleeved t-shirt that set off his silver-grey eyes.

Quinn picked up a pair of cerulean socks in a funky, comic book print that reminded him of a Roy Lichtenstein painting. He wondered which of the Doyle brothers Justine had intended to gift these socks to? They didn't exactly scream sombre Joe, punk James, or metro fashionista Jared. But they were perfect for him.

He exited the room with his white shell-toe running shoes in hand and came across Jared and Surina arguing tersely in the living room.

"Surina!" Quinn went over and stopped abruptly, letting his shoes fall to the floor.

Do I shake her hand or hug her?

Instead, he just waved awkwardly and then internally cringed at his actions. "So, umm, I heard about the miasma..." he started, trying to take the focus off his embarrassing entrance. "Hope you're feeling better!"

"I survived. So—" Surina began to reply but Jared cut her off abruptly.

"So, she and I are going to call Sebastien and smooth out a few wrinkles in his so-called plan. Why don't you get started in the office? When we've figured things out, I'll call Carter to come help you."

Quinn looked between Jared and Surina. They were keeping something from him, though neither of them seemed like they were going to divulge what exactly that something was. But the tension between them was thick as raw honey.

"Sounds good. I'll just be in there." Quinn motioned to Jared's study as he moved toward it, picking up his shoes on the way, not wanting to further exacerbate the situation. "You guys can come get me if you need me for anything, okay?"

He didn't even wait for them to respond. Instead, he spun around and booked it to the study. Out of respect for Jared's privacy, he closed the door most of the way. The sliver he left open was for his own curiosity. He wanted to know what the two of them were arguing about, even if he understood it probably wasn't any of his business. Still, he couldn't help himself as he strained his ears, hoping to catch what they were saying.

"...did you stop to consider..."

"Oh, so now you're the..."

"...just...call him...settle...all."

Unfortunately, being Athena didn't seem to come with supernatural hearing. He could only catch snippets of the argument, and nothing he could string together that would explain anything.

Fine, eavesdropping is a rude habit anyway. And I have a puzzle to solve that might end up making me rich. So, I better get on it.

Quinn seated himself at Jared's desk and logged into the guest account of the computer's operating system. He'd taken computer science in high school, and like most subjects, he'd excelled at it. Still, he doubted he could succeed where decryption programs had failed. He was a gifted programmer but only knew a small handful of languages in which to code. *Still,* he reasoned, *it couldn't hurt to try.*

Navigating to the USB key's explorer window, Quinn's eyebrows arched as a DOS program initiated by itself, and a pop-up dialogue box appeared on the otherwise empty screen.

*Never argue with the square root of two because it is...*the cursor flashed in the first of ten empty boxes, waiting for his input.

Nodding his head, Quinn realized how to respond to the question. The solution had to be ten digits long. Instead of trying to write out a ten-digit number, as if he were some kind of human calculator, Quinn knew this was a bit of a trick question. The answer was a single word: *irrational.*

Upon typing it in, a new question popped up. He took that as a sign that his previous answer had been correct.

After all, why would the program allow me to continue if I got the questions wrong?

This time, he was given a mouse cursor and two nearly identical images. Here, the program commanded Quinn to click on all the differences between the two images, indicating that he could only continue once all the incongruities had been uncovered.

It took him a minute to resolve this problem, but he systematically scanned both images until the job was done. Immediately after his answer was accepted and the images faded to black, a new problem presented itself. This time, the dialogue box contained a small clip of music and asked him to identify the piece it came from.

A truly glorious snippet of an operatic aria poured from the speakers but lasted for only three seconds. Quinn gasped, suddenly recognizing the piece as *Tristes Apprets, Pales Flambeaux* by Rameau from his opera *Castor et Pollux*. After he keyed in his response, a new question appeared.

This time he was asked the formula to calculate the volume of a donut-shaped torus of unknown dimension. There were little buttons for him to click on that featured mathematical symbols, like pi and the equal sign. Clicking on any of them would cause that figure to appear in the field that was meant to contain the final equation.

"V equals bracket pi times minor radius squared, close bracket, times bracket two times pi times major radius, close bracket..." Quinn mumbled the answer to himself as he clicked the buttons to input it into the program. The problem disappeared, indicating he'd correctly solved it.

Another question popped up after that, so he answered that too. And the next. And the next.

With a slowly spreading smile, Quinn was starting to understand why this program had so confounded the decryption software. If the game had just been to solve math problems, a single computer program would easily have been able to solve all the presented problems and thus unlock whatever was hidden in the flash drive. But this password program was a tricky beast.

Sure, it asked math questions. But it also asked for image comparisons. And music identification. And word puzzles that required knowledge of colloquial terms from several different places and times. There were just straight up trivia questions in here, too, like, *What are the names of Santa's reindeer?* and *What is the capital of the state of New York?*

There was no single decryption program capable of answering or solving all those different kinds of questions and puzzles. By his estimation, it would take about a dozen different types of decryption programs to unlock the USB key, which would likely slow any standard computer down to a snail's pace. What's more, it required the user input of a single someone who knew or could figure out the answer to these questions by themselves. There would be no tricks or hacks here. After another few minutes of playing along with the program, a new prompt appeared.

Ready for a real challenge, Athena?

With a quirk of his eyebrows, Quinn bit his lip and smiled.

"Sure, why not?" he spoke aloud, as if the program could hear him, then he clicked on the *Okay* button.

Another question popped up, but this time there was a little timer in the bottom corner of the screen. It had begun to count down the moment the dialogue box appeared on the screen.

"Gloria Bettencourt, you wily old witch." Quinn breathed in at the sight of the added layer of challenge to this password game.

Without realizing it, Quinn began to tap into his god powers. His brain processed the information presented on the screen quicker than any human possibly could. And so he continued, answering questions, solving puzzles, analyzing, and identifying. With every hundred questions, Quinn would be left with less and less time to answer. His slender fingers flew over the keyboard and mouse. Quicker and quicker, the problems came at him like waves of attackers.

His brain fairly hummed with the challenge. Somewhere in the back of his mind it felt like he'd answered millions of questions and that he'd been at it for hours. But he was too focused to notice the time. Only twenty or so minutes had passed since he'd started. He might have also noticed that his eyes had begun to glow a copper sulphate blue.

Finally, a dialogue box appeared with an icon at the top of it in the face of a cackling devil, replete with signature red horns.

The ominous message within made Quinn's stomach drop.

Answer correctly, or all the data contained on this device will be erased forever. What is the devil's own prime?

Quinn knew the answer wasn't 666 because that wasn't prime and whatever the answer was, it had to be thirty-one characters or digits long.

And he only had two seconds left to answer.

I know this! It's 1000000000000000066600000000000000001... Belphegor's Prime!

Supernatural speed aided him in completing the final puzzle. For a second the screen went blank. Quinn almost screamed.

Did I screw up?! Did everything get deleted?!

A little pop-up box appeared. A pixelated red balloon icon bounced over the words *Congratulations, Athena! Are you ready to learn everything?*

Below that were two simple buttons: *Yes* and *No*.

With a suddenly dry mouth, Quinn wondered if he should call the others into the room to discover the secrets contained in the USB key with him, but he remembered something Jared had said. When he inherited the apartment building and the little thumb drive, he'd been told to keep the device secret.

This is for my eyes only, as the new Athena.

Either way, Jared and Surina's voices echoed into the den. They were still angry, or so it seemed.

Nah, I'm not gonna bother them. They have other things to worry about. Plus, my curiosity won't let me wait!

Quinn maneuvered the cursor and clicked on the *Yes* button.

For a second, the screen went blank again. Quinn could hear the fans and hard drive whirring away at top speed. A faint odour of burning electronics began to fill the room.

Then, the real program began. Images flashed at lightning speed. Screenfuls of text in several different languages burned into his retinas. And on top of all that, a wall of sound, created by layering countless clips of spoken word overlaid with several different musical pieces, attacked his ear drums.

To the casual observer, the screen would have appeared to be nothing more than strobing blasts of painful light. The sound ratcheted louder and louder, soon blasting from the straining computer speakers. Somewhere in the distance Quinn heard three barking dog heads and someone bursting into the room. He couldn't see his eyes glowing that same electric blue once more.

As if in a dream, Quinn noticed vaguely that the burning smell was so much stronger now.

Suddenly, an explosion on screen triggered a real-life explosion as the computer burnt out, the case blackening as acrid smoke poured from the vents.

As the small explosion rocked the desk, it was as if Quinn, too, had been hooked up to the computer, only to have his plug yanked from the socket. The eerie blue light faded from Quinn's eyes as he fell headfirst into unconscious darkness.

☙

Jared had just given up the fight when Cerberus had begun to bark. He and Surina had taken their argument to the balcony as they phoned Sebastien. After twenty or so minutes of arguing with both of them, Jared had had enough. He'd passed off the phone to Surina for the two to hash out their argument and opened the glass sliding door, just as the barking started.

Curious and alarmed, Jared followed the dog's increasingly frantic howling to where he sat outside the den. Pushing the door open, Jared witnessed the rapid-fire flashes of coloured light dance across Quinn's entranced face. The blond man sat there, open-mouthed, staring at the screen, his eyes glowing a bright blue.

G.E. White

For a second, Jared had no idea how to react. Then, the computer exploded, causing the Death God to yell and shield his eyes. He lowered his hand a second later to look for his companion.

To his horror, Quinn began to seize. He slipped from the chair and slumped to the floor, twitching violently, his back arching and limbs contorting into uncomfortable positions.

Falling to his knees beside the young man, Jared tried to soothe him or stop his erratic movements, smoke still pouring from the smouldering electronics.

"Hey!" he yelled, holding Quinn's face in his hands. "Come on, wake up!"

Quinn's only response to his prompting was to fall into a catatonic state.

He's not breathing!

"Oh fuck!" With a groan of agony, Jared realized that fate might have played a cruel trick on him. He might lose Quinn right now, even though they'd only just met. "Please be okay. Please."

Tears threatened to pour down his angular cheeks as the whites of Jared's eyes went black. Wisps of smoky black flame wreathed them now. Tapping into the power of Thanatos, the dark-haired man thrust his hand into Quinn's chest. It passed through the solid flesh and bone, as if it were made of aether.

Jared's heart was beating wildly. He held his breath as he reached for the Threads of Quinn's soul and pulled them to the surface. Silver and blue glowing wires of shimmering light emerged from within the blond man's body.

With a sigh of relief, Jared tossed his head back and let the tears fall from the edge of his face for a good second before he did anything else.

They're all still glowing! And not one of them has been snipped! It's not his time to die right now. He'll make it. I just have to stabilize him.

The God of Death placed his right hand on Quinn's chest,

squarely over top of where his heart ought to be. Using his left hand to cradle Quinn's head, he leaned down and gently let his lips form a seal over Quinn's mouth.

Drawing from his own life force, Jared exhaled into Quinn. He could feel the breath of life pulling at his own Threads to pass the healing from one man to the other. This was one of Thanatos' many gifts. If the person's Threads were not cut by the Fates, then he could return them to the land of the living, turning them away at Death's door, so to speak.

The life force within Quinn began to stabilize. His heart rate was still a bit thready, but at least Jared could feel the blood pulsing through the prone man's body. Suddenly, the lips underneath his felt warm, insistent. Almost as if they were kissing him.

Quinn's hand weakly flopped onto his own chest to hold the hand Jared had placed over his heart. For a second, time stood still. Their lips remained locked. The world fell away.

"Umm, this isn't *Sleeping Beauty.*" Surina's voice cut through the intensity of the moment.

Jared pulled away from Quinn and turned his head to cast a withering glare at the demigod.

"I swear to God, Surina…" Jared's voice was thick with emotion. She must have felt it, too, because she actually backed off, refraining from her typical snark with a whispered apology.

"Whoa. I didn't realize… Is he okay? Did he just, like, pass out or something?"

"I don't know." Jared bit out through gritted teeth. "I just—"

Quinn coughed and sputtered. With a low groan, he tried to prop himself up on his elbows but couldn't manage to keep his upper body off the floor.

"Quinn!" Both Jared and Surina exclaimed simultaneously.

"Guys…" His voice was weak and hoarse.

"What happened? I saw lights flashing and then all of a sudden, you collapsed and started seizing up. I—I gave you my life force to wake you up. That's what I was doing," Jared rushed the words out, still embarrassed by Surina's interjection.

Quinn looked like he was trying to think but the grimace on his face indicated how painful that was. "When I try to remember it, my brain aches."

"It's okay. Don't worry about it for now. We're gonna—"

But Quinn didn't let him finish. His face strained as he pooled every last ounce of strength to force himself off the ground and attempted to push past Jared. His body revolted against him and he began to fall once more.

"What are you doing?!"

"Need to puke!"

Quinn's croaked words kicked both Jared and Surina into action. With gentle encouragement and supernatural speed, they flanked him and helped him to stand. Once they'd led him to the bathroom and got him situated, they stepped outside. A second later, his violent gagging was followed by the unmistakable sound of Quinn's breakfast ejecting from his mouth and splattering into the toilet.

Having seen people in the worst throws of illness, on their actual deathbeds, this sound, while still disgusting, was nothing new to Jared. Surina on the other hand, looked a little green herself, and judging by the horrified frown on her face, it seemed clear that she was well outside of her comfort zone.

"I'm calling Robin." Surina's voice was uncharacteristically serious. To Jared's surprise, she sounded a little scared. "This doesn't seem right."

Surina stepped away from the bathroom door and pulled her phone from her pocket as she went. An anxious, whining Cerberus followed her as she paced back and forth across the living room and talked to the current incarnation of Asclepius, the God of Medicine. Jared leaned against the wall and let his back slide down until he found himself sitting on the floor, staring into his own hands.

Minutes ticked by. The toilet flushed. The sink began to run. Soon, Quinn emerged from the bathroom, shaky but otherwise cleaned up. Jared got to his feet and offered him a hand, but the blond man shook his head.

"It's okay. Whatever that was has passed. I'm all right."

"I don't know, you don't seem all right to me. You're still looking really pale. And you clearly can't stand on your own just yet."

"Just gimme a minute and I'll be okay," the younger man insisted. "I just need some water and to sit for a minute. Don't trouble yourselves. Please. You've already done so much to help me."

"Too late," Surina marched back to the pair, an authoritative look on her face. "Robin's on their way over."

"Robin?" Quinn asked, inquisitive to the core, despite his weakened state. "Who's that?"

Surina explained as Jared dashed to the kitchen and brought Quinn some water. Soon the dark-haired pair had Quinn comfortably laid up on the sofa and fairly burrito-wrapped in blankets. Cerberus, eager to help, jumped up on the chaise part of the leather sectional, all three heads gazing intently at Quinn, as if staring at the young man would keep him from falling ill again.

CHAPTER FOURTEEN

"THAT OUGHT TO do it," Robin commented in a staccatoed German accent, as they put their stethoscope away in their chic black leather medical bag. "You're a little on the weak side, a bit of fatigue, some dehydration, and you got banged up pretty bad on the fall into the Underworld. Though, I do commend your efforts to alleviate your headache."

Quinn had just put his shirt back on following his examination by the gods' very own doctor. Once Robin arrived, they quickly ushered Quinn back into the bedroom he had been borrowing. The current incarnation of Asclepius was a tall, rather muscular physician, topped with a very short, stylish cut of brown hair. They also happened to be one of the world's most preeminent cancer research scientists. The broad smile that brightened their kind face perfectly matched the sympathy in their warm yet mischievous hazel eyes.

"Thanks." He shook their offered hand. "So, what do you recommend?"

"Ice pack for your head. At least eight glasses of water, if not more. A good bowl or two of soup. There's an awesome bone broth place here in Chicago I can recommend. Oh, and most important, sleep. Tons of rest."

"Got it." With a deep sigh, Quinn nodded. "But what about that whole seizure thing? What caused it?"

"If I were to guess? You haven't used your powers as a god that much before. Sure, you read fast and you have good memory recall. But that's just you, Quinn. Being an awakened Athena is like being you, but on speed. You, times a million. You on your own is the trial version, while you as Athena is the premium that comes with all the bells and whistles—durability, faster reflexes, supernatural levels of cognition, deduction, observation, and photographic memory. Whatever Gloria was attempting to tell you in that computer program is most likely rattling around in your skull. You're just gonna need to figure out how to use your powers to tap into it."

To hear all that he should be capable of, so cleanly laid out before him, was a bit jarring. "That's all, eh?" Quinn chuckled nervously. "Just learn how to be a god, no big deal."

"This is all a lot. I get it. Well, I mean, not really." Robin's dry sense of humour made Quinn smile. Others might find them a touch cynical and abrasive, but Robin was hilarious in their own way. "I'm way older than you kids. I was found back when we still had the Soul Calendria. I always knew what I was."

Quinn's eyebrows arched. "Yeah, that's super helpful to me, doc," he couldn't help the tone of sarcasm that snuck in.

"Sorry. Point is, you're tired. You need a proper day off. Get a massage. Take a nap. Read a book. No, actually, don't," Robin joked. "We don't want you to go through another one of those information

G.E. White

overloads, okay?"

Nodding and assuring the doctor that he'd heed their advice, Quinn got off the bed on shaky legs. Robin helped to maneuver him through the living room to the den where Jared and Surina huddled together, arguing in hushed tones, but he could hear them much more clearly than he'd been able to before.

Are my powers as Athena getting sharper? I couldn't hear their argument well enough to make out what they were saying before. Now, it's crystal clear.

"Come on, Surina, you know he could use the rest. His whole world has been completely turned upside down since you got him out of that institution yesterday morning. And then this happens. The least you can do is cut him some slack!" That was Jared's frustrated voice.

Surina scoffed. "I'd love to, but Sebastien says this can't wait, and I agree. We need to get moving."

"Moving where?" Quinn asked, he and Robin choosing to interrupt at that moment.

Beating Jared to the punch, Surina was the first to speak. "Before Jared stupidly handed you some kind of computer thingy that messed up your brain, I'd actually come here to take you to meet Sebastien. He has something he wants to talk to us—well, you—about. A job, of sorts."

"And he needs you. He won't settle for anyone else." Jared snorted and rolled his eyes. "And it needs to be right now, because apparently Sebastien can't wait a day. Even though we already waited twenty years to get Athena back and one single day cannot possibly hurt his agenda."

Surina whipped around to face her aggravator. Though Quinn couldn't actually see her eyes behind her ever-present shades, he was certain that they were brimming with frustration.

"No, this can't wait," she ground out. "As much as you disapprove, Quinn has a responsibility to all the realms. He's already lagging behind; he needs to get back in the chariot, and that won't happen if you keep coddling him. And frankly, we don't have the time to do this your way."

"Could you please not talk about me like I'm not here!" Quinn barely recognized himself as the words came flying, unbidden, from his lips.

His companions pulled up from their tense standoff to gape at him, having the grace to look embarrassed.

"Sorry for yelling. I'm just getting a little frustrated. It's been a bit of a day, or a couple days even. Listen, Surina's right." Quinn took a deep breath before he continued. "I learned a long time ago that there is no such thing as a free meal. I need to earn my keep, and I'm okay with that."

"Quinn, that doesn't mean—" Jared started.

"You don't need to shelter me, either, Jared. I'm an adult. I'm capable of making a decision about what I should and shouldn't do on my own," Quinn interrupted. "You've had most of your life to get used to your role. So I'm a bit amateur-hour, and I have a lot to learn. Okay. Fine. I own that. But I do want to help. If I have to hit the ground running because the others need me to start pulling my weight, then sure. I'll do what I need to do. I'm a quick study. I'm sure I can handle it."

"Umm, hi." Robin cleared their throat and took in the bickering group with a raised eyebrow. "Remember me? The doctor? Yeah. I'm saying no."

"No?" Surina looked like she wanted to fight, but Robin just sighed and gave the young woman a coldly analytical glance, not unlike a school principal disciplining a teenage delinquent.

"Are we gonna have trouble, Surina?"

"You don't understand, we have a mission and the stakes are unbelievably high. We need Athena. We have to go. Now. Sebastien's waiting for us."

G.E. White

"Whoa, slow your roll, cowboy! I could just call Sebastien and tell him. Quinn needs rest today. He's not going anywhere. The Moirai might have a lot of clout with the gods, but we're all still human, and doctor's orders override everything else."

"Yeah, Surina!" Jared jabbed, jumping on the bandwagon. "I told you! Thank you, Robin."

"Don't thank me just yet," Robin said, holding up a well-manicured hand, stopping Jared. "Quinn's right, too, he can go do missions once he's healed. The world does need Athena. His god powers should speed up the healing process. If there's no bump on his head tomorrow, then he's good to go."

"See? Nothing to worry about!" Quinn started up, relieved that Robin had stood up for him against Surina and Jared.

"Not so fast, kid. That whole earn-your-keep nonsense..." Robin rested a steady, reassuring hand on the young man's shoulder. "You're where you belong now. There's no earning your way into a family. You're just in it."

Quinn was shaken. This was the third time in only two days that he'd been treated like he was family by a group of strangers. First the Doyles, then Jared, now Robin. Leo and Carter seemed excited to have him around and even the ever-sarcastic Surina genuinely seemed to want and need his help.

But he couldn't let them see how much their casual acceptance affected him. How it shot an arrow into the broken core of his heart and instead of hurting him, it filled him with a sense of purpose and belonging he'd never felt in his whole life.

Clearing his throat and pushing the feelings down, Quinn nodded. "Okay, no. You're right. I'll rest for today, and tomorrow, first thing in the morning, we'll get going. Besides, you're coming, too, right, Jared?"

"Yeah, I am." Jared sighed as he got up from the leather office chair. "You're right. I might have my concerns, but it's your life and your choices. Surina and I will be there, and I'll make sure that you don't get used or pushed. You're still new to this."

Nodding once more, Quinn was overcome by Jared's implied care. He was only coming to make sure that nothing bad happened to the newly awakened deity. "Thanks, Jared, I'm sorry to impose on your hospitality another night. I'll stay out of your hair, and sorry again for ruining your computer. I keep saying I'll pay you back, and I really need to be writing this all down somewhere so I can actually do that one day."

"Think nothing of it," Jared smiled at him. "After all, Surina made me take some days off, anyway. And you don't have to stay out of my hair. We can hang out as much as you want, or feel up to."

"This is nice, kids, but I gotta go. I've got appointments to get to." Robin sounded bored, but the smirk on their playful face suggested they weren't as annoyed as they were pretending to be.

"Ugh, take me with you," Surina scoffed, rolling her eyes behind her sunglasses. "I don't wanna be a third wheel to these two."

"Come on, let's just hope this portable Gate Leo gave me actually works. Bless his daft heart, but 50 percent of the time he gets these wrong. Ever since Erica went on vacation, I spend half my days calling Carter to come get me from wherever the hell Leo has stranded me."

With a wink and a wave, Quinn watched in awe as the God of Medicine retrieved a small scalpel from their bag and pricked the tip of their finger, drawing blood. Stooping to the floor, Robin drew a line along the wood floor, before standing and drawing the scalpel upward. The blood continued to flow from the blade and hung in midair as Robin's movements created the outline of an arched entryway. Once complete, the outline flooded with white light, which glittered and glistened like the sun's rays falling on the sea.

Quinn was starting to get the hang of just how Gates worked but to see one formed out of thin air was a sight to behold.

Robin stuck their head into the portal for a moment, before pulling back to motion the young demigod over to join them. "Okay, yeah. It's good!" Robin called out. "You coming?"

"Yeah, be right there!" Surina called over. "Hey, lovebirds, be ready by eight a.m., sharp. No bullshit this time, okay?"

Jared looked as though he were about to lob a grenade at Surina, but Quinn, ignoring the jab, intervened, not wanting there to be further tension between the other two.

"That's great, Surina, we'll be ready! Bye!" Quinn called out and motioned for her to join Robin. Surina nodded, somewhat satisfied, and left.

Neither Quinn nor Jared spoke for a solid thirty seconds once the magical sparks had dissipated. Then, they were alone once more.

"Are you sure you're up for whatever they have planned for tomorrow?" Jared sounded skeptical, but Quinn could tell his doubt was directed more toward Surina and Sebastien than toward him.

"Yes. And no. But I'll have you with me." Quinn cast him a smile he hoped would reassure the dark-haired man. "There's also something else. Something I didn't want to say in front of anyone else."

"Oh?" Jared was about to leave the den when Quinn put his hand up to stop him.

"It's that USB key. I swear something about it looks familiar. Like… I don't know. But it's like, I know there's something important about it." Quinn moved to the burned husk of the computer as he spoke.

"What do you mean familiar?" Jared's eyebrows arched. "You saw it before, it never struck you as familiar then. What changed?"

"I can't explain it. I just know it's important." Quinn shrugged but gingerly grabbed the little plastic flash drive and attempted to pull it out of the singed port but something on the surface gave way. "Wait…"

"What?" Jared's tone of concern had turned into one of genuine curiosity. "What is it?"

Furrowing his brows, Quinn followed his hunch, squeezed down on the plastic, and pushed it to the side. He found it gave way and he gasped as a small arrowhead fell out of the destroyed shell.

"What the hell?"

"Oh my god!"

The two young men spoke at the same time. Quinn held the two inch-long little metal piece up and turned it slowly between his thumb and forefinger. Upon further inspection, it was clear this wasn't an actual arrowhead, but some kind of pendant. The shining gold metal was dotted with four separate facets in which a gemstone might be fitted. The cage that made up the majority of the pendant was empty and looked like a large prism could be fit into it, while the filigree at the base held three smaller openings. One on the tang and one on each of the barbs to either side of the stem.

Two out of three small divots were empty, with the one in the centre containing a small, sparkling stone. The prismatic crystal caught the noon sun and peppered their faces in freckles made of reflected rainbows. It was cut in such a way that it shimmered no matter what angle he tilted it.

"But what is it?" Jared whispered, a look of awe and surprise on his handsome face.

"I have no idea. But I know it's meant for me. Or else, why would the last Athena go through all that trouble of testing me?" Quinn could feel in his gut that the little piece of jewellery was meant to be his. He handed it to Jared for the other man to inspect.

"I don't feel anything. But let's just remember that Gloria specifically said to keep this whole USB thing a secret. Let's assume that applies to any hidden treasures you happen to find inside that USB key."

"So, we keep it to ourselves?" Quinn liked the idea of a secret that only he and Jared shared, but it felt a little weird to keep it from Surina.

"If you're looking for my opinion, then yes, we keep it a secret. Or at least, we pretend it's nothing for now. We don't tell Surina. Because you know she'll tell Sebastien and who knows who he'll tell. And we already told Surina and Robin about the USB. Haven't we given away enough of Gloria's secrets?"

"I don't know about that..." Quinn started as Jared handed the pendant back to him. "This *Sebastien* might know something about the pendant. Shouldn't we ask him?"

"Maybe we should learn more about it, or at least figure out why Gloria thought it should be kept a secret."

A thought occurred to Quinn as Jared spoke.

"Hey, what if she was trying to tell me about the pendant when the program fried my brain? What if all those images and that text and those sounds, what if that info dump was mentally encoded to keep something secret?"

"Something only that Athena brain of yours can decipher?" The dark-haired man's eyebrows arched as he considered the possibility. "All right, so tap into that. Figure out what it is."

Quinn leaned against the edge of the desk and closed his eyes, the golden arrowhead pendant clutched tightly in his hand as he tried to remember the rush of audiovisual data.

The exercise hit him with a wave of nausea and vertigo that had him sliding off the desk. Jared caught him by the shoulders before he fell too far.

"Whoa!" The dark-haired Death God's voice was laced with worry.

"Yeah," Quinn said with a groan as he pressed his palms to his forehead. A sudden stab of a headache had just struck like lightning between his eyes. "So, not gonna try that again anytime soon."

For a few seconds, neither of the two gods said a word.

"Okay," Quinn conceded, "we keep the pendant a secret for now. Tomorrow we meet Sebastien and as we do this mission, I'll work on honing my god powers. After all, Robin did say that if I were to use the full extent of my Athena abilities, I'd be able to process Gloria's message."

"Sounds good." Jared smiled. "Now, how about we take it easy the rest of the day?"

☙

The next morning, Quinn stepped out of Jared's building, dressed in a pair of beige hiking pants and a fitted light-blue hooded sweatshirt. The newly discovered pendant now hung from a chain around his neck and tucked inside his shirt. He also carried a small cross-body bag with a change of clothes and a couple toiletries, as Jared had warned him this task may take a couple of days. His gaze was focused on the stairs as his feet guided him down the accessibility ramp, Jared following after him.

Reaching the bottom, he looked up, suddenly dazzled by the majestic vehicle parked on the curb in front of them. Surina stood by the flashy car, a key fob dangling from her fingers.

"Glad you two could make it," she said, swinging the key-fob around her finger.

The design of the car was sleek: a two-door coupe, matte slate grey. It was a thing of beauty. Quinn had never considered himself a gearhead by any stretch, but he *had* gone through a phase in his early teens where cars were a fixation.

Taking a moment to inspect the vehicle, Quinn came to the conclusion that the car wasn't a model he recognized. "Is this a new Tesla model?" he asked.

"Hardly. Take a look," Surina said, gesturing to the grille of the machine with her chin.

Quinn bent down to inspect the front of the car. There, in the centre of the grille, was the letter *H*. The image of a hammer crossed over an anvil behind it dissuaded Quinn of the notion that the insignia was from Honda or Hyundai.

"That symbol. It's Hephaestus', isn't it?"

"There's our know-it-all," Jared chimed in. "Incarnations of Hephaestus have always been at the forefront of engineering, so he's made all of our vehicles in the past century. Tyrell, the current incarnation, designed this one about four years ago." He opened the passenger door, waving Quinn into the back seat.

The young god almost argued his way into the front seat, but taking in Jared's long legs, he decided he could suck it up and let him have the much-needed legroom. He slid into the back seat, noting that the interior was just as posh as the exterior, with smooth, white faux-leather and grey panelling.

Jared adjusted the seat back into an upright position and climbed into the passenger seat, while Surina walked around the car to take the driver's seat.

"Seat belts," she reminded, prompting the two men to strap themselves in. She slipped the key into the ignition, giving it a turn, and practically cooing with pleasure as the engine rumbled to life. "Hear that?" she said. "Listen, it's purring. That is the sound of a happy car."

"You know, I've heard that purring in cats can also be the sound of irritation or nervousness," Jared commented.

"I was under the impression that whoever sits shotgun is supposed to keep their trap shut," she shot back.

"Only when it comes to the radio."

Surina gave a huff of irritation but ignored Jared as she flicked on her signal before pulling out into traffic. Quinn hoped that the use of the signal and her adherence to the speed limit meant she was a safe driver, yet as they slowly made their way onto more congested streets, he could see Surina's shoulders shift and tense with frustration.

"Oh, come on! The light is green!" she shouted to the driver in front of them, even though the man couldn't hear her. The minivan ahead began to move forward at a snail's pace, forcing them to poke along after it.

Seeing the tension mounting into what could be full-blown road rage, Quinn sought to engage Surina in a conversation. "So, is this your car?" he asked.

"Actually, all the cars belong to Hephaestus. He loans them out to whichever god or goddess needs them. Sebastien doesn't drive, so I end up using it mostly, but if someone else needs it, he'll recall it. Still, it's a nice car."

"I can tell."

Once again, the minivan in front of them slowed, though no signs or lights dictated the action. *Perhaps they're lost,* Quinn thought to himself, amused.

Surina sighed in exasperation. "Okay, that's it," she said, moving her hand from the wheel to the gearshift on her right.

Quinn watched as she slid the stick shift from third gear to a position between the two extra gears, labelled *R1* and *R2*. At first, all he felt was a tingling sensation. As if the air was electrified, the fine hairs on his arms stood on end. But then he saw a shift in the scenery outside the vehicle—the streets, buildings, and cars before them were still visible, but appeared to be less substantial, like they were simply an image of the outside world and not a reality. Overlapped with the faded views of the city were images of a large meadow set against a forest.

Quinn was reminded of when his childhood television would occasionally cross two-channel signals, resulting in the faded image of a *Batman* cartoon laid on top of the local news.

Once the change in gears was complete, Surina, apparently operating without concern for the slow driver ahead, stepped on the gas.

Quinn's arms flew up to protect his face from the impending crash, but when no collision occurred, he hesitantly peered through the gap his arms created. The minivan in front of them was now behind them. They continued forward, passing straight through another car. The passengers in the other vehicle flitted by like ghosts projected onto a dimly lit movie screen.

Quinn expected to feel something, anything: a chill, a rush of air, the tingle of electricity as the spectres brushed by, but not even the lightest breeze disturbed his hair. "What just happened? Where are we?" he asked.

Jared gave a snort of amusement, shifting around in the passenger seat to face him. "Technically, we're not *anywhere*—yet we are everywhere."

"Don't say stuff like that, you're going to freak him out." Surina tilted her head toward the middle of the car, addressing Quinn in the back seat. "What he says is not *exactly* true. There's some truth to it, but overall, he's just being poetic."

"So, what's going on?"

"As we told you, Hephaestus designed and built this car. We call it the Phantasm. We may be invisible, but we aren't entirely free of the rules of the corporeal world. We aren't hitting anything because we are occupying the space *between* spaces. Right now, we're in between both the First and Second Realms. We can travel through both realms, but in this state, we can't interact with either of them."

"So, in the car, we can shift between all the realms?"

Surina shook her head. "Not all of them. Aetherum, that's the material that was used to build this car, can only travel between the First and Second Realms. Access to the Third Realm is pretty much forbidden; only a few gods even know how to get there, let alone access it."

Quinn slumped back in his seat, getting used to the ethereal scenery. "Why only a few?"

"To be honest, we don't really remember. Our best guess is that some of us have been known to get a bit...cantankerous in our old age," Jared said wryly.

Quinn narrowed his eyes, staring the other man down. "Which means...what, in plain English?"

"Which means that we don't want to risk one of you getting pissed off and destroying a whole country. But that would only be a minor inconvenience, compared to what else you could do with access to Olympia, or so I hear," Surina explained, taking a right down one of the phantom streets.

"So, there's like a giant panic button in the Third Realm?" Quinn guessed.

"Once again, not completely sure. There are a few things we know that are locked away there, namely the Golden Fleece and Ambrosia. Robin would love to get their hands on the former, but currently that's not in the cards," Jared groused. "There's an understanding that something dangerous is being kept there, and some gods' responsibilities are less—well, not less *important.*"

"That's a good term for it," Surina argued.

Jared sighed. "Okay, so some gods have more powerful impacts on the realms than others. So, we're not going to give the keys to the castle where a potential weapon is stored to someone in charge of music, if you're picking up what I'm throwing down," Jared continued.

Quinn nodded. "Who *does* have the keys, so to speak?"

"No one really knows, though, there is a rumour that the Moirai may have access, as well as a couple of other Underworld gods. Most likely Mister Popular over here," Surina said with a toss of her head toward Jared.

"You?!"

"Yeah, I mean, it would make sense," Jared replied. "Being the one who actually feels the weight of taking lives gives me some credit... when making tough decisions."

"Wow, anyone else rumoured to have access?"

"Actually, there is: you," Jared answered.

"Oh," Quinn said, his tone betraying his mask-like expression.

The rest of the ride passed in a blur, though this was not only due to the spectral plane they travelled through: Quinn's mind spun with the implications of this new information. Not only was he part of his companion's little god club now, but he was also one of their elites. The thought made him queasy.

As Surina pulled onto the highway, Quinn realized he had no idea just where this Sebastien lived. Was this going to be a long drive? Yet, before he could voice his question, they passed through a strange-looking arch, which seemed more substantial than the rest of the scenery.

Suddenly, they were passing a battered sign reading *Gardiner Expressway.* The name of the road jogged Quinn's memory.

"We're back in Toronto. How did we get here?" As far as he knew, they had just been in Chicago moments ago. Then, he gasped. "We went through another Gate, didn't we?"

"Fastest, most reliable method of god travel," Surina replied.

As they pulled off the highway and into the downtown core, Surina made another turn onto a mostly empty street and switched the gearshift back to the Second Realm, easily driving down the now-solid city street. Spotting a vacant parking space outside a towering condominium complex, she parked the car on a sharp turn, bringing the Phantasm to a jerking halt.

Quinn blinked owlishly, motionless, even as the other two unbuckled their seat belts.

"Quinn?" Jared queried. "Time to go, we're here."

CHAPTER FIFTEEN

THE ELEVATOR RIDE to the elite condo suites, where Sebastien awaited them, was oddly quiet. Neither Surina nor Jared had spoken a word since exiting the car, and they all silently watched the floor display light rise.

Quinn's mind spun with everything that had happened in the last two days. He had surprised himself with how well he was handling the whole situation. There were only a couple of times when he thought he had gone completely off the deep end, and this was all a figment of his broken psyche.

He felt too much in control of the situation for it to be a hallucination. So, until he could prove otherwise, it was probably best to just run with what he was given. He glanced over at the faces of his other companions and smiled. Hallucinations or not, their company was infinitely better than what he was used to.

His thoughts brought Quinn back to the man they were to meet: Sebastien Azeri, Surina's so-called employer. He had to be quite the employer if Surina took orders from him, as her sarcasm and snark appeared to be her preferred method of communication. From what she had said so far, Quinn had deduced that Sebastien was some sort of psychic or oracle, while Jared referred to him as the Moirai—a title he was unfamiliar with. His mind continued to conjure up an image of a sage old man with a scraggly white beard, caterpillar eyebrows, and circle spectacles. Quinn shook his head to clear it of the cliché. Evidently, he had spent too much time marathoning the *Lord of the Rings* films back in high school.

The elevator chimed, and the doors slid open to reveal a long corridor with doors lining the walls. Quinn followed Jared and Surina to the last entrance on the left. Surina pulled out what appeared to be a simple set of house keys and unlocked the single deadbolt. As she turned the key, Quinn heard several other heavy locks snap open.

Surina turned the knob and eased the door open, ushering the others in.

"Take off your shoes," she instructed, before proceeding to do so herself.

Quinn toed off his new sneakers and took a moment to glance around the condo penthouse. His eyes widened as they roamed the sprawling room and its floor-to-ceiling windows curling around the corners of the apartment.

The place was the epitome of chic, with stainless steel appliances, black granite countertops, hardwood floors, and a matching black, cream, and taupe colour scheme. It should have been impersonal and cold, but it felt like a home.

At the kitchen island stood a man with stubble and wavy brown hair that fell to his chin. He wore a pair of grey slacks and a white sweater. His back was still facing toward them as he placed six glasses on a tray alongside a white bowl holding sticks of cinnamon.

"Surina, there you are. Just in time for *horchata,*" he greeted, turning to them with a tray in his hands. *"Hola* Quinn, I'm Sebastien."

"Pleased to meet you," Quinn answered with a bow of his head.

The Seer standing before them was definitely not who Quinn had been expecting. His young, lithe figure and slow, musical drawl, coupled with his quiet, gentle demeanour, made Sebastien appear more like a bookworm than a source of power. But then, Quinn guessed that any book the man read would have to be in Braille, if Sebastien's cloudy golden-brown eyes, focused on nothing in particular, confirmed his suspicions.

Surina snorted. "Don't act like you didn't know when we'd be here."

Sebastien smirked indulgently as he maneuvered around the furniture with practiced ease and placed his tray on the coffee table.

"You hate it when I act like a know-it-all and you hate when I try to play dumb. There really is no pleasing you, is there, Surina?" he asked, a smile softening his words.

"You're just trying to get on Quinn's good side before he gets to know you," she teased.

"Well, unlike some people, *I* like to try to make a good impression," the blind man quipped back. "Quinn, Jared, please come take a seat."

Quinn flopped down onto one of the couches, with Jared joining him soon after. Sebastian and Surina took a seat on the loveseat opposite them.

When everyone was settled, Sebastien began to serve the exotic, creamy drink. Quinn took the offered cup and graciously agreed to Sebastien's offer to grate some cinnamon on top. Taking a sip of the concoction, Quinn was surprised to taste that it was not only sweeter than normal milk but was also ice cold.

He also couldn't help but notice that two extra glasses sat on the tray untouched.

"You expecting more company?" Quinn asked.

"I have some business with Carter and Leo. They should be here shortly," Sebastian answered.

Quinn nodded and the four of them fell into a moment of silence as they all took sips of the horchata.

"So, you're Surina's boss?" Quinn asked suddenly, unsure of how to start the conversation.

"Is that what she calls me?" Sebastien asked. "Well I guess that's better than calling herself my babysitter."

"Bratsitter is more like it," Surina said, nose buried in her cup.

"Despite what she says, she likes me." Sebastien winked in Quinn's direction. "As you can see, I'm not running at 100 percent," he said, gesturing to his sightless eyes. "So, I have Surina do some of my legwork for me, as well as some minor errands I don't feel like doing. You see, my responsibility among the gods demands much more attention than most."

"And that would be?" Quinn prodded.

"Surina didn't tell you?"

Quinn began to shake his head before he remembered the man couldn't see the gesture. "No, sir."

"No need for *sirs,*" Sebastien replied, obviously amused. "We're all equals here."

Quinn noticed that Surina turned her head away at her employer's words, almost as if she were ashamed. If Sebastien was aware of her gesture, he showed no indication of it as he continued. "I am this generation's incarnation of the Moirai—the Fates."

Quinn furrowed his brow. *The Fates? That couldn't be right.* "Wait, weren't the Fates three separate people?"

"You're speaking of the three sisters: Clotho, who spins the Thread of Life; Lachesis, who measures the Thread; and Atropos, who cuts it," Sebastien said grimly. "There was a time when I was known as those three separate beings. I'm better now, though."

"Better?" Quinn echoed.

Jared placed his hand on Quinn's shoulder, drawing his attention. "The Fates were originally recognized as one person—an oracle that told the past, present, and future. But the strain of that depth of information became too much for her. It ended in one of the incarnations killing herself, her mind and soul so fractured that she was split into three separate bodies when she was reborn. That was the generation in which we earned our names from the Greek Pantheon, and that's why the Fates are generally thought of as being three people and not one."

"But as I said, I'm better now," Sebastien assured Quinn. "I figure that everyone is allowed a little mental breakdown once in a while, especially with a job as stressful as mine. Luckily, over the years the other gods, namely Thanatos, Hermes, and Hera, have helped to make my job easier. It has allowed me to focus more on the day-to-day weaving of the Threads—bringing people together and pointing them down the paths they are destined for. My abilities also allow me to see future conflicts—to a degree. And though it might not seem like it, I'm a very busy man."

"So, you need me to do something for you," Quinn concluded.

Sebastien smiled. "Originally, I had planned for just Surina and Jared to deal with this matter, but I think that both you and my investigation would benefit from your participation. Think of it as... on-the-job training."

Quinn shifted awkwardly in his seat. "I don't really know what I could do to help, but I'll try, if you want. I do want to step up to whatever responsibilities I have as Athena."

The truth of the matter was that Quinn had no clue what this man wanted from him. For all he knew, he wanted him to go slay a dragon or something. The idea was far-fetched, but between three-headed dogs and dimension-shifting cars, dragons were probably a step toward normalcy. Hopefully, the task Sebastien had in mind wouldn't be too difficult.

"It would probably be better if we explained the situation first,"

Jared scolded, taking in Quinn's worried expression.

"You're right," agreed Sebastien, setting his glass back on the tray. "So, let's start with the basics. At one time, many of the gods had temples dedicated to them, where their followers would gather and worship them. All that remains here in the Second Realm are ruins, but they continue to thrive in the First Realm. Now, when you think of the followers of a temple, you're probably picturing priests and priestesses. While that's partly true, our worshippers are also soldiers, doctors, explorers, and many other workers dedicated to their patron god or goddess. Almost every temple trains their followers in some form of combat."

"So, you're worried about these soldiers?" Quinn asked, confused.

"*Si y no,*" replied the blind man, slipping between languages. "At the moment, I'm communicating with three different temples, each of which held an artifact of great importance. So far, two of these temples have been broken into and their primary artifact was stolen."

"And what are these artifacts?"

"Stars," Jared answered. "Well, pieces of a star—the North Star to be precise."

Quinn twisted around to gape at Jared, unsure of what he had just heard.

"Tell me, Quinn. What do you know about astronomy?" Sebastien asked.

"Offhand, not much," Quinn replied. "But I know what the North Star is. I just don't understand how pieces of it could be housed anywhere, let alone stolen."

"That's because what you know about the North Star isn't exactly true," Surina said. "There isn't just one North Star, but three. Scientists have been able to figure out that much so far."

"What do you mean?" he asked, leaning forward to place his glass on the tray before him, intrigued by Surina's tale.

The woman picked up a spoon from the drink tray, manipulating it to demonstrate her words. "Well, at any given time the Earth is moving three different ways. First, it orbits the sun," she moved the spoon in a circle around one of the glasses on the table. "Second, it spins while on an incline," she tilted the spoon on an angle and spun it between her fingers. "These first two motions are what create our perception of days and seasons. However, the Earth is also moving in another way that is so gradual we can't see the change in our own lifespans. The axis of the Earth is changing. Kind of like a spinning top that's losing speed." As she spoke she tilted the angled spoon making it arc ninety degrees to the right. "When this axis changes, the star closest to us, that we know as the North Star, Polaris, will be further away, making Vega the new North Star. This movement will continue, eventually making Thuban, the North Star. But these movements take thousands and thousands of years," she explained.

"What scientists don't know is that these three stars were once all part of the same star and that that one North Star had a metaphysical counterpart here on Earth," Sebastien continued.

"Metaphysical counterpart?" Quinn asked, confused.

"Yeah, it generally looks like an enormous diamond, but, like, magic. Hence the name metaphysical," Surina jumped in. "It's a very powerful and highly sought-after artifact."

Quinn sat back, taking all this in. "Powerful, how?"

Surina appeared suddenly bashful as she awkwardly hummed a couple lines of a well-known tune from a children's movie, causing Quinn's face to twist with confusion. "It's the Wishing Star," she clarified.

"You're kidding!" Quinn gasped.

She shrugged. "Where do you think they got the idea in the first place?"

"So, it really grants wishes?"

"Well, it used to," Jared interjected. "A long time ago, the Temples of Apollo, Artemis, and Demeter—also known as the Solar, Lunar, and Earthen Temples—went to war over the Star. All of them were frightened about the possibility of another temple acquiring the Star to use it against them. But after a great battle between the temples, the Star was broken into three pieces. Now, with the threat of misused power out of the way, the three temples made a truce. Each took a piece of the Star as a sign of their pact, comforted in knowing that the other two temples couldn't use the Star against them."

"But now two of those pieces have been stolen?" Quinn was increasingly becoming alarmed. What did that mean for him—or the world?

"Unfortunately, yes." Surina sighed, obviously frustrated. "The bigger problem is that both the Temple of Demeter and the Temple of Apollo claimed that a magi from one of the other temples stole it."

"Magi," Quinn muttered to himself. "You've mentioned them before. What are they?"

Surina scowled. *"Magi* is a term for temple acolytes who have been trained in the magical art of their temple god or goddess," she said. "Not all followers are official magi, but all of them train to be one. When I said there aren't humans in the First Realm, I was only partly truthful. You see, the humans who are descended from various incarnations of gods and goddesses can train at one of these temples as well, if they want to."

"You mean, these temples are a demigods only club?" Quinn asked.

"I didn't say that. The other four races are allowed to study, too, as long as they don't cause any trouble. Though, the latter could be said for the demigods as well. There's a reason the gods mostly operate in the Second Realm—the First Realm is fairly peaceful. Granted, there are often issues that spring up from discontented Wrathborn, but the magi of the various temples keep things pretty much well in hand. The gods have rarely had to step in with them, but with this being a dispute between temples, it's gotten kind of messy."

Quinn nodded. "So the temples each think that magi from different temples are stealing from them now?"

"Apparently. Which could be really dangerous," Jared replied. "Before the thefts, these three temples have worked closely together. Every few years, they'd bring their best and brightest magi apprentices together for a tournament, and the top twelve from each Temple Order would be awarded a place in one of the Twelve Houses."

"Houses?" Quinn asked, his mind soaking up every bit of information given to him.

Jared seemed not to notice. "Teams of three, and one magi from each temple. Each house reflects one of the Houses of the Zodiac and performs a slightly different function. The Houses act as law keepers, detectives, explorers, search and rescue and other emergency services—both here, and in the First Realm."

Sebastien cleared his throat, bringing the attention of the three back toward their host. "Regardless, the issue is that while usually these temples work together, the theft of two pieces of the North Star has made each of them suspicious of one another."

Surina wore a grim expression. She leaned farther back in her seat as Sebastien spoke. "This whole situation might just give the First Realm something it hasn't seen in over two millennia: a war between gods and their temples," she said, worry edging into her voice as she turned to glance out the window.

Quinn watched her intently as he turned his newly acquired information over in his mind. He began to open his mouth, dozens of questions on the tip of his tongue, but was instantly halted by the sound of muffled cursing coming from behind the apartment door.

"Goddammit," a familiar male voice boomed from behind the heavy metal. "Sebastien, how the hell am I supposed to get in again?" Leo called.

"Let me do this," came another voice from behind the door, and a moment later the various locks clicked open. The door swung to

G.E. White

reveal an embarrassed Leo, whose hand was still wrapped around the doorknob, and a slightly annoyed Carter.

"Sorry about that," Carter said, stepping inside and closing the door behind Leo and himself. "Apparently Leo lacks my finesse when it comes to locks."

The God of War grunted, "Not really used to unlocking doors, I usually just break 'em down."

"And you guys still let him sub in for Erica?" Jared asked the seer, a note of disbelief in his tone.

"I like to consider it a lesson in patience for him," Sebastien replied. "It may prevent him from acting rashly in the future—"

"But that's part of my charm," the God of War interjected as he sauntered into the room, dropping down on the couch beside Quinn. "Hey, man. Seems you passed initiation."

"I guess you could put it that way. Hopefully I'll make a half-decent Athena," Quinn answered, a slow smile spreading across his face.

Carter took a seat on the ottoman, shooting Quinn a satisfied smile before focusing on Leo. "That reminds me, it's time to pay up, Leo."

Leo sneered, a low growl emitting from deep in his throat. Still, he retrieved his wallet and counted out three hundred dollars in large bills, before reluctantly handing them to the Messenger God. "It was a lucky guess," he grumbled.

Putting the words and actions together, Quinn narrowed his eyes, switching his gaze between the two new arrivals in suspicion. "Did— did you guys place a bet on me?"

The annoyed look on Leo's face melted away and he had the decency to look a bit contrite as he explained. "After you left yesterday, Carter was so certain that you were Athena he called back to make a little wager. And I was fool enough to take it."

Quinn turned his attention to the man in question. Carter just shrugged his shoulders, unrepentant. "Hey, I saw an opportunity for some quick, easy cash so I took it."

Quinn's analytical mind found no fault in Carter's words. In fact he was kind of impressed, but he figured he should get used to this type of wheeling and dealing when it came to the Patron God of Thieves.

"Don't suppose I'd get a cut of your winnings," Quinn gently teased. "You know, what with being the subject of your wager."

"Not this time, but I'll be sure to let you in on my next easy score."

Surina chuckled good-naturedly. "Yes, gods forbid you actually have to do some hard work."

Carter snorted dramatically, "More like 'gods forbid' I get to sit down. Do you have any idea what it's like to have Lady Poseidon, Lord Zeus and all the other Olympians breathing down your neck? 'Where's my package? Did you read my memo? Hera kicked me out of the group chat!' I swear it's like wrangling satyrs."

Quinn put a hand to his mouth attempting to stifle the laughter that bubbled in his chest.

"Yes, well; speaking of hard work, Leo, did you bring what I asked for?" Sebastien interjected, clearing his throat.

"Right here," Leo replied, digging into his pocket and pulling out what appeared to be a black feather quill.

"And that is?" Quinn asked.

"A portable Gate. Once activated, this baby should open up a door that will drop you right in front of the Temple of Apollo," Leo explained.

Thinking back to the magical scalpel that Robin had used to create a portal, Quinn figured that it made sense.

"Mind setting that up, Leo? Quinn, Carter, and I have some things to discuss," Sebastien said as he stood. His head dipping, he motioned for Quinn and Carter to stand as well.

Leo furrowed his brow. "There's not really anything to set up. It's already keyed to Jared, like you asked."

"Well then, perhaps you could have some horchata. There are extra glasses on the tray. Surina knows where everything else is."

Surina crossed her arms stubbornly. "Don't expect me to wait on him. There is nowhere in our contract that says I have to play host."

"Spoilsport," Leo pouted.

The Seer shook his head and sighed. "Please behave. Jared, watch them, will you?"

"Will do," Jared replied as Sebastien beckoned Quinn to follow him. Carter was already walking down the hall of the condo, obviously knowing where to go.

"Come on, Quinn. It won't take long; just a little chat in my workshop," Sebastien assured.

The young man glanced warily over at Jared, who gave him a gentle smile. "Go ahead, he doesn't bite."

Quinn stood and followed Sebastien, who led him farther into the apartment and down a narrow hallway. To Quinn's amazement, the Moirai and Carter turned, stepped through, and disappeared into a full-length mirror mounted on the wall.

Quinn came to a halt in front of the mirror, seeing only his own reflection with the mirrored view of the hall behind him. He inspected the mirror's golden border. From what he could see, only a wall lay behind it.

Sebastien poked his head out of the mirror, the surface rippling around him like water. "Coming?"

Startled, Quinn jumped back a step, "Yeah, I—I—"

"Well, hurry up, then. Just walk right through, it doesn't hurt."

Watching Sebastien disappear back into the mirror, Quinn took a calming breath before stepping through after him.

Crossing from the hallway to Sebastien's workshop was like entering another dimension. At first one might describe the area as a vast cavern system, but the beautiful luminescent crystals that jutted out from both the ceiling and floor, bathing the cavern walls in rainbow hues, were unlike anything Quinn had seen. Attached to the thousands of crystals were bright, colourful Threads that wove above their heads.

Each strand appeared to glow with an ethereal and eerie light, and many criss-crossed over one another in the world's biggest game of Cat's Cradle. Some strands became so entangled that it was impossible to see where each one ended and another began. The cavern split off in several directions, each tunnel leading to yet another cavern filled with even more Threads.

"It's a lot, isn't it?" The words, spoken uncomfortably close to his ear, startled Quinn. He whipped about to see Carter standing at his shoulder. Sebastien stood several metres ahead of them, seeming to be inspecting a particular cluster of Threads, running the tips of his fingers over them with infinite care.

Quinn looked up at the strands above them. "That's one way to put it," he said in response to Carter's question. "I don't know how Sebastien doesn't find it overwhelming—I mean, obviously he did. But I can't see how just Jared and your help can make a dent in all this."

"Well if it was just Jared and myself helping him, I would agree with you, but a Thanatos of the past offered a more stable solution. Look again," Carter's words were accompanied by his left hand pointing out into the cavern.

Quinn gazed ahead into the rainbow-hued glow of the large cave. At first, he saw nothing different, but then, there! Dozens of little lights congregated around the Threads at various places throughout the area. As Quinn focused further on these lights, ghostly figures started to appear, seemingly made up of the little luminosities. The more he looked, the more lights appeared, filling out gaps and making the figures more discernible. Some were human, others merfolk and centaurs. Quinn was certain he could even make out a couple of fae flittering about the Threads, like the ones who teased him at Cedar Hills.

"What are they?" he asked, though he had a distinct feeling he already knew the answer, that is, if Thanatos had been the one to offer this solution to the Moirai's workload.

"They're souls of the dead," Carter said, confirming Quinn's suspicions. "Don't worry they're not forced to do this. In fact, most souls would beg for the opportunity to work here. Here, they may get to see their loved ones or even great-great-great-great-grandchildren. Sebastien has to cycle the souls out every couple of months in order to be fair."

With his eyes now adjusted to better see the souls, Quinn could make out the smiles on several of their faces. This was indeed a wonderful place for the dead to visit.

"His helpers keep track of many of the Threads, write reports on those that need to be entwined, you know, all that good stuff. As long as the other gods keep their domains in order, Sebastien can keep this whole operation well in hand."

Quinn, noticing that Sebastien was now quietly conversing with one of the spirits, took this opportunity to get more answers. "So which gods are actually active? Surina mentioned that a lot of the gods are unaccounted for, so who is around?"

"Luckily, there are still quite a few of us," Carter replied. "From what I remember, Anna and Tyrell, or Aphrodite and Hephaestus, are in Jamaica, while Del—Zeus—is in New York, acting as CEO for Spark Electric."

"Del? As in Del Specht, the billionaire?" Quinn had heard the name many times, usually accompanied by the word *asshole*. The man had been on the cover of *Forbes* magazine over a dozen times. Known as a cutthroat businessman, Del's company provided power for over 80 percent of the continental USA, while his new tech division was starting to give other electronic giants a run for their money. He was also known to price gouge when he could and outsource jobs to cut costs. The man had no loyalty, not to his customers, employees, or even his wife, Nina, who divorced him last year, taking a decent chunk of his wealth along with her. Stories of his philandering often splashed onto the main pages of gossip websites.

Carter nodded in affirmation. "Makes a lot of sense doesn't it?" he said. "At least Nina, that is, Hera, got out of their marriage with a decent ruling on the alimony. Though between you and me, I hear she's been drinking through her payments on a regular basis," the Messenger God continued with a conspiratorial wink. "Apparently she's been offered a spot on the next season of *The Real Housewives of New York.*"

As Carter further described the dysfunctional former couple, Quinn could easily see how the roles of the former King and Queen of Olympus now fit and nodded in agreement. "Sounds like they're both pieces of work."

"I don't really have beef with Nina, but Del—usually any incarnation of Zeus, really—is a real asshole. I'm kind of surprised that Jared didn't already tell you."

"I'm taking it that he's not a fan. Not that I really blame him," Quinn commented.

"Let's just say that when it comes to wrongs that Zeus has heaped on the Underworld gods, it gets kind of personal. Supposedly there's some really messed-up, dark shit there. I don't know all the details. But you didn't hear that from me."

Curiosity tickled at the back of Quinn's mind but, not wanting to start gossiping about the man who had been his soulmate in so many other lives, he decided to let Carter continue his roll call.

Carter absently scratched at his chin as he recalled the other gods. "Okay, so you already met or at least heard about Leo, the Doyles, Sofia, Erica, and Robin. As for the others, Hestia, currently known as Maribelle, is pretty busy with her new Lifestyle Network."

"Wait, do you mean *Baker's Hearth and Home,* Maribelle Baker? The celebrity lifestyle guru and chef who's on all those morning shows? That's Hestia?" Quinn asked. Though, as he described the silver-haired matron he had seen countless times on television and on the covers of lifestyle magazines, the image fell into place. "Yeah, I guess that checks out," he conceded.

"You'll notice a lot of gods find their way into positions of power and influence," Carter explained. "Take Mei-Lin, she's the current incarnation of Poseidon and heads up the biggest nautical shipping company worldwide, Triton Enterprises. Granted, she also has her pet projects, namely fundraisers for clean water initiatives and other sea-based environmental causes. There are a bunch of lesser-known gods still around, mostly the Charities and the Muses and the like, but I kind of doubt you'll have much need to call on them, or they you. The only other heavy hitters that come to mind are Miranda— Themis, Goddess of Law and Order—who is somewhere in the UK heading up several INTERPOL teams. She's got her hands full, what with our constant black sheep of the family, Eris, Goddess of Discord. She's currently known as Lana, and as far as we can tell, she's some-where in Russia, hacking countries and corporations alike, spreading propaganda and misinformation online, destabilizing governments, polarizing people. You know, her usual bag," the Messenger God finished with a snort of disgust.

As Quinn ticked off of each god listed, he came to a disturbing thought. "So of the Olympian gods we're missing Apollo, Artemis, and Demeter—the three gods of the Celestial Temples."

"Hence you can see why this whole theft issue has gotten so messy," Carter continued giving voice to his own thoughts. "To be honest, I'm thrilled you're here. With you missing, along with the three Celestial Gods, things had been getting pretty hairy. Not to say that things weren't shitty to begin with."

"What do you mean?"

"Well, let's break it down. In the last twenty-plus years, there has been a growing amount of chaos in the world. Because Artemis is MIA, more and more animals are finding themselves on the endangered species list. Demeter on the other hand has been having a hard time of it ever since the Industrial Revolution. After Gaia was destroyed during Zeus' revolution against the Titans and primordial gods, Demeter had to step up her game, not just being the Goddess of Agriculture, but nature itself. It was a lot, and the advent of the Industrial Age really messed her shit up. It seems that every incarnation has a shorter and shorter lifespan. The last few decades have been the worst—climate change, colony collapse, forest fires. I wouldn't be surprised to find out that the last incarnation of Demeter has already passed and we're onto a second we have yet to meet."

"As for Apollo, luckily, while he has a major connection to the arts, and even a bit of medicine, Robin and his Muses have kept things afloat in his absence. Yet, they can't take his role as the God of Prophecy. He usually has a hand in guiding people, but without him around a lot of it falls to Sebastien and it's hard to keep up, on top of everything else. Between his absence and yours, for a long time there were no heroes, just lots of misinformation, a rise in conspiracy theories, radicalization, and ignorant people gaining power. Of course, there were some people fighting for justice, as Themis is still around, but people generally back down more than step up when you guys aren't there."

Listening to Carter's words, Quinn was finally getting a clearer picture of just what role the gods played in the grand scheme of things. It was kind of interesting as he noted that not only did the gods have an impact on the world at large, but the world at large could also have an impact on them.

"Well I'm here now," Quinn assured him. "And I'm ready to do what it takes. You know, it's kind of strange. Like, I always wanted to do good, leave a mark on the world, but now I might actually have the chance to do so."

Carter snickered to himself. "Trust me, your former self has already made quite the mark."

"What's that supposed to mean?"

G.E. White

"You mean, you can't guess? Think about it, when it comes to the pursuit of wisdom, what is the greatest leap forward in human progress and communication in the last century?"

It only took a moment for the answer to come to Quinn's mind. His eyes widened in realization. "No, that can't be."

That smug grin of Carter's was once again back in place. "Well, it's not like Gloria did it all herself. My former self, Percy, also had a pretty big hand in its conception."

That made perfect sense, the greatest tool in communication and the sharing of information.

"We helped create the internet," Quinn said in awe. Now that he thought back on it, Gloria and Percy more inspired the concept and, through their investments as silent partners, helped bring the internet to the masses. If he remembered correctly, one of Gloria's grandchildren had started a website that was now known as *Freepedia*, the world's largest free encyclopedia. The recollection gave him a start. He didn't know what disturbed him more, the fact that ever since his run-in with Gloria's program he was slowly starting to access some of her memories, or the fact that his previous self had children, and grandchildren, ones that she shared with the former Thanatos.

Quinn shook his head, banishing the thought and the tangent it may take from his mind, focusing again on Gloria's non-biological contributions to the world. "We helped give the world the internet—that's amazing."

Carter gave a small sneer as he scrunched his nose. "Well, it was supposed to be. Don't get me wrong, the internet is great, and has been super useful, but after Percy died, and then Gloria a few years later, the essence of the internet began to change. It still shares information and brings people together, but it's also become an echo chamber and tool for misinformation. The dark web, hate sites, human trafficking, conspiracy theories—they've all thrived on the internet. It's not what you and I meant for it to be."

This was probably the first time that Carter sounded melancholic. He may not have known the other man for long, but the serious look on his face appeared somewhat out of place for the normally energetic and chatty Messenger God.

However, before Quinn could comment on Carter's last observation, Sebastien turned from the spirit he had been conversing with to wave the two of them over.

"Sorry about the delay," Sebastien said. "Just had to check in on a couple of projects," he explained. "I've got the instructions for your next deliveries right here, Carter. Come along, I'll explain the details." He patted a stack of papers now clutched in his arms. "Once that's out of the way, Quinn, we'll have our chat."

Quinn nodded and followed after them as they moved farther into the cavern. The two men walked a couple paces ahead of him, discussing the importance of a particular idea being planted in a mortal's brain and how a simple choice of what summer camp to go to would set him on the right path. Or something like that, Quinn wasn't trying to eavesdrop.

He instead took to examining every detail of the strange crystal caverns, smiling at the various spirits as they worked away. Yet, as he glanced down a tunnel, a flash of gold caught his attention. The colourful object was too large to be a spirit or Thread, but *something* had definitely passed by the opening down that tunnel.

The other two gods were preoccupied with their conversation and didn't seem to be deviating from their path, so a quick look wouldn't be a huge issue, Quinn reasoned to himself. He ducked into the tunnel and exited the other side. Once again, he only caught a glimpse of the being as the tail end of it disappeared down another corridor.

Quinn blinked; had the large appendage he saw been a tail? "Hey guys!" he called back down the tunnel he just travelled, hoping to gain either Carter or Sebastien's attention. Neither of the two gods returned his shout, but Quinn's curiosity would not allow him to give up his pursuit. He just needed to get a good look that this thing and then he would head back.

Jogging over to the tunnel the creature had entered, Quinn turned to see that the path was empty. The ceiling of the tunnel was high, like the rest of the caverns, but no spirits could be seen tending the strands along this section. In fact, Quinn couldn't help but notice that unlike the other filaments, these ones were dull. No light pulsed out from them, making the only points of illumination the various coloured crystals.

He crouched down to inspect several Threads that lay on the floor, their severed ends visible. Were these the Threads of those who had already passed? It would explain why no spirits lingered here.

A tremor rumbled through the tunnel, making Quinn jump to his feet. An earthquake? He had been under the impression that this particular place was well beyond the reach of the human Realm, perhaps even in the fabled First Realm. But as the rumbling appeared to move across the tunnel from one end to the other, he distinctly became aware that this was likely not an earthquake. Dust rained down on him from the vaulted ceiling, and as Quinn looked up, he saw a distinctive hole at one end.

Out of the hole slithered a golden-scaled creature. Reptilian in nature, the head of the giant snake appeared to be that of an African bush viper with marble silver eyes, while its iridescent scales stuck out about it like spikes. The creature was huge, it's head the size of a double bed, while the length of its body continued to slither out of the hole.

Quinn froze in fright. While he had encountered some magical creatures, nothing he had come across had been this massive. He stayed still, hoping the creature wouldn't notice him and would be on its way.

It appeared the creature was going to enter the cavern Quinn had just exited—hopefully to continue on its way in the opposite direction of Quinn's exit. However, as the giant serpent flicked it's tongue out to taste the air, it became stock-still. Suddenly the creature whipped its head around, its molten mercury eyes pinning Quinn with a wild look.

Intimidated, Quinn stepped back, which appeared to be all the invitation the creature needed. Rearing its head back, the viper hissed, before lunging at him with bared fangs.

CHAPTER SIXTEEN

LEAPING OUT OF the way of the snapping fangs, Quinn took off in the opposite direction. It took a moment for the giant snake to turn about and continue the chase. Catching sight of the full length of the creature, Quinn would guess it was about twenty-five metres long. He was also acutely aware that he was being herded away from the path back to Sebastien and Carter.

While Quinn had never been hugely involved in sports, he at least fancied himself a half-decent runner. His aptitude in track and brief head start were probably the only things that were keeping him out of reach of the giant viper. As he exited the tunnel into one of the larger caverns he turned sharply, heading to the left.

"Carter!" he called out, hoping that somewhere the God of Communication could hear him.

The viper was fast on his heels, barrelling out of the tunnel moments later, continuing the chase.

Quinn noticed with dismay that this cavern, like the tunnel they just left, housed only broken Threads and therefore no ghostly spirits who might help him, or at the very least alert Sebastien to his predicament. As he continued to run, the slight burn in his chest reminded him that he wouldn't be able to keep up this pace indefinitely. He currently held no weapon to fend off the beast, though he was sure if he tried to face the viper, armed or not, it would be a mistake.

He glanced about the cavern, hoping to find something to help him escape, but only saw the long line of now lifeless strings. Glancing at the rocky outcroppings that jutted out from the floor, he supposed it was better than nothing. Snatching up a handful of strands, he noted that one end was secured to a set of crystals. Perfect. He still had a bit of a lead against the viper and used the valuable seconds to twine the dozens of Threads in hand around two large outcroppings as he ran past, creating a high tripwire in the serpent's path.

As Quinn continued to run, he pulled the strings taut before letting them go. He glanced back, and while the Threads had managed to slow the creature down, the serpent was able to power through the barrier, snapping the strands. As the two continued their chase, Quinn was relieved to see up ahead a more populated area. Living Threads were woven about in this place, and a couple of spirits could be seen working away.

"Hey! Get help!" he called out to the spirits who looked up from their work to see Quinn rushing toward them. The spirits appeared as shocked as he felt, freezing as he and the giant serpent approached. Here it appeared that the strands they were tending were fairly new, as they were short and still being woven as they were latticed closer to the ground, almost creating little dressing screens.

Quinn ducked under the makeshift screens in an attempt to keep moving in a straight line. Horror struck him as he realized his error;

G.E. White

he had led the viper to rip through the newly formed Threads. He glanced back, but to his surprise saw that the serpent wove itself around the suspended strings, careful to not damage either them or the spirits tending them.

Having not been looking ahead, Quinn tripped, falling to his knees. He scrambled to his feet, this new information already churning in his brain. The detour the serpent was forced to make allowed Quinn to remain ahead, though just by a moment. What had started as a slight burning sensation in his chest now spread up to his throat, choking him as he gasped for air. Quinn knew his time was up.

That's when he saw it: another tunnel. However, unlike the others, this one had some Threads spread across the opening, almost like a loose web. Embracing the adrenaline coursing through his veins, Quinn expended one last burst of energy, diving to the side and through one of the small openings created by the criss-crossing strands. He cleared the opening and tumbled across the tunnel floor, cradling his head for protection.

As he came to a stop, he looked up to see the golden viper just outside the tunnel, hissing and spitting in anger. Just like Quinn had deduced, this creature was some sort of guardian. It would never damage the Threads, not even to catch an intruder.

"Quinn! Where the hell have you been?!" came the shouted question.

From his position seated on the ground, his upper body propped up by his arms, Quinn craned his head around to see both Carter and Sebastien standing a few paces behind him.

Carter looked furious, though Quinn could swear there was a note of concern in his words, while Sebastien stood at Carter's shoulder, a bemused smile gracing his features.

Ignoring Carter's question, Quinn pointed at the viper that sat on the other side of the Threaded web. "How come neither of you told me there was a big-ass snake roaming around?"

"Python isn't a snake, he's a wurm—a wingless and limbless

dragon," Sebastien explained patiently. "As you probably figured out, he is the guardian of this domain. I had planned to introduce you to him, so we might avoid him mistaking you for an intruder, but it looks like no harm was done."

The Seer approached Quinn and helped him off the tunnel floor. As Quinn regained his breath, Sebastien led him back over to Python, who appeared to have calmed in Sebastien's presence. Taking Quinn's arm, Sebastien guided it up and through an opening in the suspended strings toward the nose of the giant wurm. Instinctively, Quinn wanted to pull his arm away, but allowed Sebastien to offer it up to the dragon.

"Don't worry, old friend," he addressed Python. "Quinn's one of us."

Python flicked out his tongue, tasting the air and getting a better whiff of Quinn's scent. It then moved forward, allowing Quinn's palm to touch the tip of its snout. When Quinn realized his hand wasn't going to be ripped from his arm, he gave himself permission to appreciate the beauty of this majestic creature.

The iridescent gold scales gave off a prismatic shine in the light of the glowing crystals. On closer inspection, Quinn could now make out flecks of emerald green in the wurm's silver eyes. Petting the snout of the wingless dragon caused the beast to close its eyes in contentment. The absolute magic of the moment hit Quinn full in the chest, stealing his breath once again. "He's incredible," he whispered in awe.

"That he is," Sebastien agreed. "And from now on you needn't worry about him chasing you, unless you feel like playing some games with him. We rarely, if ever, have to worry about intruders, so I fear that he gets a bit bored at times."

Just minutes ago, the wurm was trying to devour him, yet now Quinn felt a fondness for this creature. "Yeah, maybe we could go on a run sometime, now that I know he won't eat me."

"Ugh! I can't believe you," Carter grumbled in frustration. "You know you nearly gave Sebastien and I a heart attack, disappearing like that."

"I knew where he was the whole time," Sebastien assured.

"Fine, whatever—nearly gave *me* a heart attack. Jared and the Doyles would have my head in a vise if anything happened to you. You got anything to say?" The Messenger God punctuated his irritation by placing his hands on his hips.

Moving away from Python, who now turned to continue his patrol, Quinn ducked his head, having the good sense to look sheepish. "Yeah, I'm sorry about that. I caught a glimpse of Python and wanted to check him out, didn't think I'd be gone long, or that what I was looking at might try to kill me."

The other man's eyes narrowed as he scrutinized Quinn's face for sincerity. Apparently finding it there, Carter rolled his eyes. "Whatever. I guess I shouldn't be surprised. Athena has never let a good mystery go uninvestigated. Guess I should get used to it once again."

Sebastien turned to face Quinn. "Speaking of investigations, I believe it's time for you and I to have that chat. I trust you can find your way out on your own?" The last question was directed to Carter.

"Shouldn't be a problem," Carter replied. "I'll see you around, Quinn—try to keep your nose outta trouble."

"I'll try."

Carter's trademark smirk returned to his face, and with a curt nod and a now familiar gust of wind, he was gone.

☙

Soon after Carter's departure, Sebastien led Quinn to yet another cavern covered in glowing Threads. This particular area seemed smaller than the others, though perhaps it was due to the disproportionately large number of glowing strands. Sebastien continued into the cave with Quinn trailing after him—the latter curiously inspecting an unusually clustered amount of Threads that led to a giant tangle in the centre of the room. The newly awakened god peered even more closely as the strands began to vibrate violently. Suddenly, and with a collective human-like screech that rose into the air and hung over them, the tangle exploded, leaving only frayed, limp strings behind.

Quinn jumped back, eyes wide. "What just happened?"

Sebastien turned back toward the tattered, hanging remains of the Threads.

"Those would be the passengers of Sunrail Airways, Flight 436 to Dubai."

Quinn cradled one of the frayed strands. "That plane just crashed, didn't it?" he whispered.

Sebastien nodded. "Engine failure."

"And you orchestrated all of this?" Quinn tried to bite back his accusatory tone. He wasn't naïve. He knew that tragedies like this happened—whether it be due to neglect, human error, or as people often put it, an Act of God. The last phrase had often been used to describe a freak accident that no one could have predicted, but perhaps the phrase should be taken more literally.

Sebastien turned toward him as a pained yet resigned expression moved across his features. "I did what needed to be done. It's not always a fun job. People's lives have to end, and sometimes they end abruptly."

"Were there children on board?" Quinn asked.

"A few."

"And that doesn't bother you?" Quinn asked incredulously.

"I never said that," Sebastien replied, stepping closer to the now-dull strings, hanging limply about them. "I know these people better than you. I know the circumstances of their birth, the people they loved, the plans they made, and the dreams they had. I know just what it is that they are leaving behind. I mourn for the missed opportunities, but this was their fate. You'll notice that some Threads still hold the broken ones up. They continue to exist because they are remembered, and to be honest, it's not really the end for them."

Quinn wrinkled his nose in a soft sneer. "No offence, but I've seen

G.E. White

the Underworld. Spending an eternity floating down a river doesn't seem like a great reward. I guess some get to see their loved ones again by working for you, but it's not the same."

"That's just the first part of the journey. The transition from life to death is jarring, to say the least—especially for those who die suddenly. The rivers give them time to come to terms with what has happened, before they move on."

Quinn supposed that made sense, but if the rivers of the Underworld weren't the final destination, what was? "Where to?"

"Most of them end up at the Elysian Fields. A heaven, of sorts—to put it in layman's terms."

"And the others?" Quinn asked with a tilt of his head.

"A very select few are relegated to Tartarus."

"You mean Hell."

"I guess you could call it that. But, only a select few end up there. Usually people whose crimes were perpetrated with violence, malice, and joy. It is one thing to hurt or kill another for survival, or in battle; it is another to do so for sport. You have to be a true monster to receive such punishment, but that's not to say there is no chance of redemption for them. As for the rest, they are the ones who cannot move on. Not without help, anyway. They usually end up returning to the land of the living, becoming the shades that haunt the places and people they can't let go of," Sebastien tilted his head back, as if admiring the Threads of Life around them.

Quinn's brow furrowed as he examined the man. "You can see them, can't you? The Threads? I mean, not just here, but in us." He pointed at one of the crystals where a strand appeared to emerge. "That's not an origin point is it? We are."

A bashful smile crept across Sebastien's face. "Most people—or gods—don't figure that out," he admitted. "There was a time I could see the corporeal world, but that was a long time ago. Now, all I have are the Threads."

Quinn's gaze drifted down to the fibre he now held in his hands. "The people left behind—the shades—do they ever get help? Learn to let go?" he asked, his thumb gently running over the Thread's short, frayed ends.

"Jared and his brother Joseph have been known to round up some of the wayward souls, but some are very resistant. Sometimes, being on Earth is what they want."

Sebastien turned away and continued to stroll along the path under a bower of woven Threads.

Quinn jogged behind him to keep Sebastien's pace. "So, what did you want to talk about?"

"A couple things, if I'm being honest," Sebastien replied. He walked over to a large group of strings, kept away from the others. Quinn noticed that there appeared to be nothing different from these Threads compared to the others, so why separate them? The new tangle of Threads criss-crossed and wove over one another, but where one strand ended, frayed, a new one would be tied on and continued.

As Quinn stepped forward, a strange sensation of familiarity washed over him, as if he were looking at a piece of art he had seen before.

Zeroing in on one fine, blue Thread among the countless others before him, Quinn reached out to touch it. As his fingers closed in on it, Quinn suddenly disappeared. Or at least, his mind did.

☙

Quinn came-to on a hard, uncomfortable bench. Sarah Elizabeth Wyland was his name—or the one he, *she*, had once gone by. A gifted fabrics dyer, weaver, and merchant, Sarah had been an anomaly in her small, patriarchal village of Salem, Massachusetts. She had taken over the family business after her father had died and had grown her business far beyond her father's success.

G.E. White

Before his death, her father had warned her that she was far too clever for her own good, and others wouldn't find her wit humorous or her success inspiring. Sarah knew that she should have listened to him.

She had noticed that unrest had arisen recently between the many families who had settled in Salem. Fueled by unexplained illnesses, and due to a hearty fear of the unknown, several women had already been tried and hung for witchcraft. These women had been outsiders—a beggar, a slave, a nonbeliever—and so their deaths meant little to the Christian churchgoers who assumed they had nothing to fear. Until they did. In the small town, villagers' claims of being possessed continued to spread. No man, child, or especially women were safe from accusation.

Sitting on the accused's bench in the town hall, and listening to the magistrates and people she had once thought of as friends testify against her, Sarah knew she had been a fool to think that she could escape the hysteria.

Though she knew her true position within the realms, Sarah had become a churchgoer in order to better fit in with her community, so she might be able to continue to educate them and spread her wisdom. She had assumed that her mask of devotion would shield her peculiar ways, and her long nights spent working closely with Annabeth Graves, from the prying eyes of her neighbours. Her plan might have even worked, had she not underestimated the fragile nature of a powerful man's ego.

Magistrate Eldenbrook's air of superiority had always raised her hackles, so when the man had very publicly announced his desire to court her, Sarah instinctively did the only thing that came to mind: she laughed. She had realized her mistake instantly and quickly tried to soften the blow, claiming that she wasn't suitable for a man of his station. And yet, the insult in her voice had been obvious, and the damage had been done.

Three weeks had passed since her rejection of Eldenbrook, and now she sat in front of the same man who sought to destroy her for her slight. And as her former lover Annabeth Graves took the witness stand, her face marred with the dark, bruised signature of her father's fists, Sarah knew her fate was sealed.

Annabeth met Sarah's eyes for only a fleeting moment, but in it, Sarah tried to convey her love and her forgiveness for what Annabeth now had to do. Sarah only hoped that Annabeth's betrayal would at least spare her from Sarah's own fate.

Though Sarah knew that her soul would be reborn, it did not alleviate her fear of death. Worse still, she might not even have the comfort of having Thanatos himself present when she passed to claim her soul. Death would hurt, it would be humiliating, and it would be the end of Sarah Wyland's generous and empathetic reputation in the annals of history.

ↄ

Ripping his hand from the Thread, Quinn came back into himself with a jolt. The tumultuous emotions of Sarah Wyland still raged through him as he turned accusing eyes toward Sebastien.

"Why didn't you stop me?" he demanded, but quickly shook his head as he realized, ashamed, what he was saying. "You couldn't see me; of course, you couldn't have stopped me."

"Of course, I saw you, and I could have stopped you," Sebastien countered. "I knew you would be drawn to the Threads of your past lives, just like the others before you. Every Athena does this; your curiosity is unending. Though I must say, I had hoped you would choose a less disturbing moment to relive, but Sarah's life was enlightening, at least."

"So, it's true. That was another version of me, just like when I was Kim Si-Min and Gloria Bettencourt."

G.E. White

Sebastien nodded. "And there are countless other iterations of your past lives as well. They are all you, and yet, at the same time, not."

"I still don't completely understand," Quinn said, shaking his head.

"That's one of the things I wanted to discuss. The concept of reincarnation is not often an easy pill to swallow. I have found that having a more hands-on approach makes the transition easier. I'm sure all of this has been weighing on your mind."

"A little," Quinn admitted sheepishly. "Though Jared helped me to understand some of it." He assumed that Sebastien was aware of Thanatos and Athena's connection, but not wanting to wrestle with the emotions that thought stirred, he left it at that.

"I just want to make sure you're not overwhelmed."

"I'm all right," Quinn assured him, trying to inject confidence into his voice that he didn't entirely feel. "So, what's the other thing you wanted to talk to me about?"

"The North Star."

"And we couldn't have this conversation in front of the others?" Quinn asked skeptically.

"While the Star is capable of granting a wish when all of its pieces are brought together, that is not its main function. The Star's true purpose has only ever been known by myself and Athena, and that is why we are not having this conversation with the others. But technically, I'm not telling you anything new—simply reminding you.

"Since its birth, the Star has acted as something we call *Ojos del Eterno*—Eyes of the Eternal. It is a satellite, of sorts, seeing and recording everything it comes across. It predates the gods, and even the first races. The wealth of information and knowledge it contains is priceless. It's the world's memory. But this information can only be accessed when the Star is whole, so you can understand how serious things would become should it fall into the wrong hands," Sebastien explained.

"But you said no one else knows this information," Quinn said, digging his hands into his pockets.

Sebastien shrugged. "True, but people throughout history have stumbled upon many things they hadn't been looking for, and I'm not willing to risk that."

Quinn suddenly stood still, the ceasing of his footsteps causing Sebastien to turn toward him. "So why tell me all of this?"

"If the three of you should retrieve the Star, but it has somehow been made whole, I need you to handle the situation."

"Me? Don't you trust Surina and Jared?"

Sebastien couldn't hide the conflicted expression that flickered across his features. "I do. But if I can leave them unaware of the Star's true power, I will. Knowledge of any kind can be a heavy burden, as I'm sure you're learning, what with your little episode yesterday."

Quinn buried his chin against his chest, still slightly embarrassed by the fuss he had created in the wake of Gloria's program. "Yeah, I still don't completely understand what happened, but I can't shake the feeling that she was trying to tell me something important." As he spoke, Quinn unconsciously gripped the pendant that lay hidden under his shirt.

"I wouldn't worry about it. The answers will come to you when you need them," Sebastien assured. Quinn wished he felt the same confidence that the older man projected. "Come, the others are waiting for us." Having changed the subject, he quickly turned around and headed back through the mirrored entrance, leaving Quinn with no choice but to follow.

❧

Entering Sebastien's living room once more, they found Surina mopping up a puddle of spilt horchata, though she didn't appear too unhappy about the chore. After glancing at Leo, Quinn realized the reason behind her good temperament as the God of War dabbed at the soaked crotch of his pants with a paper towel, a grimace etched on his face. "So sticky," he grumbled. It appeared that Carter had already made his exit.

"I thought you said you'd watch them?" Quinn said to Jared with a chuckle.

"I did watch them," the Death God rebutted. "No one said anything about intervening."

"Touché."

Surina stood, tossing the soiled dish rag into the sink.

"Well, I'm about ready to go," she declared, her boots already laced. "You two done with your little meeting?"

"For now," Sebastien replied as Quinn and Jared slipped their shoes back on, picking up the bags they had left at the door. "Everything ready, Leo?"

"Yeah, yeah," Leo groused. He gestured to the quill he had brought, now sitting on the coffee table.

"*Bueno,*" the Seer said, turning to Quinn. "Well, I guess this is good-bye for now, but I'm sure I'll be seeing you again soon, so to speak."

"I'll take your word for it."

Hearing a slight hiss, Quinn turned his head in time to see Jared lift the jagged edge of the quill from the palm of his hand, which was now coated in his blood. Mirroring the actions he had seen Robin perform the day before, Jared drew an outline of a doorway in the air. Again, the outline burst inward, creating the glittering portal of liquid mercury.

"Cool," Quinn breathed, still impressed with the ritual.

"Yeah, damn things sting, though," Jared commented. "Just a couple steps, and we'll be on the Greek isle of Delos."

"Just a couple of steps," Quinn echoed as he walked forward in wonder. Surina's hand fell into the crook of his elbow, and she gave him a reassuring squeeze before pulling him through the Gate.

CHAPTER SEVENTEEN

A WAVE OF sudden dizziness swept over Quinn as they stepped across the threshold of the Gate. For a moment, he felt weightless, unsure what direction was up or down. The disorienting sensation left as quickly as it had come as a ray of blinding sunlight fell upon him.

A hand on his shoulder steadied the young man. Quinn shielded his eyes against the bright sun and looked up to see Jared beaming down at him.

"What a rush, huh?" he asked the other man.

Surina stood on the other side of him, unflinching in the harsh rays thanks to her dark glasses.

Quinn nodded dazedly and was about to step forward when an irritated honk startled him. He turned toward the sound, before stumbling backward into his companions. "Whoa!"

There, sitting on the flagstone walkway and flapping its wings in agitation, was a giant pelican. The animal had apparently been sleeping when the three of them landed in the narrow alleyway.

Backing away seemed to calm the bird, though Surina hissed at the sight of the creature. "Petros, I'd know that bill anywhere."

"Huh?"

"The pelican. It's sort of like a mascot for the island of Mykonos. That idiot Leo sent us to the wrong island," she growled.

Jared patted her on the shoulder as they exited the alleyway, with Quinn following behind them. "Relax. Delos is just off the coast. No big deal."

The narrow streets were lined with white plaster buildings leading downward toward the idyllic coastline. Many eclectic storefronts featured knick-knacks engraved with the name of the island or small statues of the ancient Greek gods. Others displayed postcards and local handmade jewellery. Quinn even saw ancient and medieval weapons, such as swords, shields, and daggers, carefully laid out next to their tourist counterparts.

"But the Gate should have dropped us right on Delos." Quinn could tell by Surina's tone that she was in the mood for an argument.

Jared shrugged, strolling down the sloping streets toward the harbour. "Hey, this isn't Leo's normal gig. He was probably just following the instructions Erica left behind, made a small mistake, and was a little off in his calculations."

"I'd say he was a *lot* off," Surina mumbled grumpily.

Quinn glanced down at the sunlit streets. "I don't mean to interrupt, but shouldn't it be later? We left sometime after noon, right? So shouldn't it be nighttime here?"

"See!" Surina hissed at Jared, while gesturing to Quinn. "Leo couldn't even get the switchover right, and now we're over twelve hours behind schedule. You know it's going to be a royal pain getting into the First Realm unnoticed."

Jared dismissed her concerns with a wave of his hand. "Whatever, we'll just catch a ferry over to Delos. It's like a half-hour ride at most. We'll just have to make sure that no one is watching when we make our exit."

Surina stopped short, causing Jared and Quinn to pause and turn around.

"Something wrong?" Quinn asked.

"Maybe she's worried she'll get wet, and the water will melt her," Jared joked.

Surina glared at him. "It's fine, we'll take a ferry," she said, rushing past the two men and down the street.

Both Jared and Quinn shared a look but said nothing as they hurried to catch up to her.

છ

After speaking to one of the local ferry men, Jared ushered his two companions onto the boat. Soon they were moving across the choppy water to the island. Ten minutes into the trip, the two men realized what had caused Surina's strange behaviour.

Surina sat on one of the ferry's small benches, her head and arms sprawled awkwardly over the side of the boat. A pained groan escaped her lips as the boat hit another rough wave. Her naturally tanned skin had turned a greenish shade, but her glasses had miraculously managed to remain on her face despite the choppy waters.

Quinn couldn't say he was in the most comfortable position either. The weather was, as could be expected, hot, so Quinn had removed his sweatshirt to reveal the v-neck t-shirt beneath. However, this allowed the gritty salt from the sea spray to cling to his now-exposed arms. But then, that was a minor inconvenience compared to Surina's suffering. He looked down at her with sympathy and gave her a light pat on the back. "You could have just told us you get seasick. I'm sure we could have found another way to get there."

"Like what?"

"A helicopter or something, I don't know. You said the gods have money, why not use it?"

Surina gave a belch and moaned. "No, it would have taken too long. Ugh."

Jared snickered in the background, prompting a scathing look.

"Besides, Jared here has a horrible fear of flying," Surina sneered, causing the Death God to choke on his laughter.

"Really?" Quinn asked, amused. The two were still working on forming a friendship, but Quinn still occasionally found the older man a tad intimidating, so it was nice to see that he wasn't as perfect as his exterior would let you believe.

Jared turned away, pretending to no longer be interested in their conversation.

"Oh yeah," Surina replied, swallowing heavily. She continued, now loudly enough for Jared to hear, "I heard that when his older brother tried to take him on a trip, he had a freak-out on the plane, and they were forced to sedate him."

"You're kidding."

"No, I'm serious," she replied, with a low chuckle that tapered off into an agonized moan as the boat dropped down a wave.

Jared shook his head and wandered toward the back of the boat, where the captain stood. Quinn followed him with his eyes, but couldn't see any trace of actual anger—just annoyance.

Quinn turned back to the seasick Surina and presented her with a bottle of water and a blister pack of Gravol. "Here."

"Where did you get that?"

"Picked it up at the kiosk while you and Jared talked to the captain," he said with a shrug. "I used to get nauseous while on the bus to school; figured I might need them, but I'm actually feeling okay. So here, take them."

"Thanks," she replied, popping one of the pills into her mouth and chasing it with a swig from the bottle.

Surina gave a sigh of relief as she laid back and waited for the medicine to kick in. Quinn sat down beside her, studying her profile, a soft smile gracing his lips.

"I know I shouldn't tease him," Surina admitted.

"Maybe not. But hey, who among us can say they teased Death and lived?" Quinn joked.

"What did you think he would have done to me? Kill me, over a little good-natured ribbing?" she scoffed. "I'll admit the gods have a reputation in the past for being petty, but they've grown. Besides, if Jared ever wanted me dead, he would have to do his own dirty work."

Quinn folded his hands in his lap, unsure of what Surina meant. "I thought he could just kill someone with a touch." Not that he thought the considerate Death God would ever stoop to such an action.

"Only if it's their time. If it's not, he has to kill someone the old-fashioned way. But it's not really in his nature."

Quinn smiled at the words, he may have only known Jared for a few days, but he was certain of his kind nature and was glad he wasn't the only one to notice.

He was about to ask Surina just how well she knew Jared when the subject of their conversation sauntered over to them, looking far too cheery for his own good.

"We're going to be docking soon," Jared said.

"Already?"

"See for yourself." Jared gestured behind Quinn, who turned around in his seat to follow his hand.

The island appeared to be mostly made of jagged, greying rock, with only three modern-era buildings visible from the port.

"That's it?" Quinn asked.

"It's not a huge island. No one actually lives on it, save for the caretaker and his family."

"How come?"

"Delos is a holy island. Technically, no one is allowed to be born or die here. People come in to work at the museum, or come with the visitors to give tours, but that's it," Jared explained.

Quinn inspected the landscape, assuming that one of the buildings had to be the groundskeeper's house. The closest building to the port appeared to be some sort of ticket booth, while the one farther up the hill was probably the museum.

The remnants of what appeared to have once been a city wound up the steep, beige-coloured landscape, while white columns in various states of erosion poked out from the island's rocky terrain. Most of the stone walls Quinn could see with the naked eye were in some sort of state of collapse, with only one temple high on the mountainside seeming to be intact.

"Is that the Temple of Apollo?" Quinn asked, pointing at the structure.

"Actually, it's the Temple of Isis," Jared replied.

Surina moved to stand near the boat's ramp. Quinn knew she was anxious to be the first one off the craft. The captain waved to the groundskeeper and his son as he moved the boat into a docking position.

"Isis? Isn't that an Egyptian god?" Quinn said.

"Yes, and one of the other names Aphrodite went by—at least in one incarnation," Jared explained. "Delos is kind of special that way. It was considered one of the first multicultural and theological hubs of the ancient world."

Once the boat had come to a complete stop, the three travellers quickly disembarked, Surina moving faster than the others. She took a moment to collect herself and settle her stomach, before waving the other two ahead of her.

Jared stopped by the small building, flashing his ID to the middle-aged man behind the glass. *"Yia soo,* Belen," he greeted.

"Yia sas, Mr. Doyle. Haven't seen you in a while, you've gotten taller," the tanned man replied, the Greek greeting rolling off his native tongue.

"Work's been keeping me busy. You know how it is."

"Right. I see you've brought a new face with you this time," Belen said, tilting his head to get a better look at Quinn, who stood partially to the side of the booth.

"Belen, this is Quinn."

The young god gave a small wave. "Hi."

"You'll probably be seeing Quinn again," Jared continued, after noting that his companion seemed unsure of what else to say.

"It's always nice to have more visitors. I assume that Miss Malik will be joining you as well?"

Jared glanced back at the woman in question, who now hung her head as she braced her arms against her knees.

"Yeah, once she regains her dignity."

"Ha!" Surina barked, unamused.

Quinn shook his head as he plucked one of the visitor pamphlets from a plastic display case and began to examine the map inside. Jared turned to the seasick woman. "You gonna be okay?"

Surina straightened and stood up, inhaling a deep breath before trudging over to the three men. "I'll be fine. We should really get going." Turning to Belen, she dipped her head in apology. "Sorry we can't stay for a chat."

"I understand," the Greek man assured her. "Another time, perhaps. Anyway, have a good trip."

Jared gave a farewell nod, before ushering Quinn and Surina past the entrance and onto the island.

Once out of Belen's earshot, Quinn turned to Jared. "Won't he notice that we haven't left by closing time?"

"Relax, man. Belen and the other caretakers of Delos are on the gods' payroll. They're the descendants of demigods, and they make sure that no one accidentally stumbles upon something they shouldn't. Not that it's very likely, but it's good to have someone running the place who will turn the other way when you don't make it to the final ferry."

Quinn bobbed his head in understanding, absently taking note that they had moved from the dirt road toward a weathered stone pathway. They were now trailing behind a small tour group that occasionally stopped at each ruin site.

The tour guide paused at what had once apparently been a circular storeroom or well dug deep into the earth. Quinn chuckled as the man kicked his leg out toward the pit, giving a cry of "This is Sparta!" as he jokingly reenacted the famous scene from the *300* movie.

The tour group soon moved on, leaving the three of them lingering at the storeroom. Quinn looked about the ruins, trying to picture how the city had once looked, but he couldn't put the pieces together. What had once been a multicultural metropolis had been reduced to stone and dust. Only partial walls and statues remained, though many were so degraded that only the illustrated guides posted in front of the city's sites showed how the rocks had once been built.

The small tour group, now far ahead of them, gazed up at the famous Lions of Delos. From the spacing of the statues' bases, it was obvious that at one point there had been six of them, but now only five stood facing the terrace.

A couple of island caretakers sat on a large rock, watching the tourists. One blew his whistle angrily at a young tourist who attempted to step over the safety guardrail while trying to get a better picture.

Using the distraction, Surina motioned for the others to join her in standing at the edge of the circular pit. "Jared, if you could do the honours," she said, gesturing to the yawning darkness at their feet.

Jared brought the tip of his finger to his mouth, giving it a sharp bite. Blood welled on his finger, which he moved to hold over the pit. A drop fell inside the crevasse but hit some invisible barrier, making it ripple like water.

"All right, time to go," Surina said, before vaulting over the edge of the stone barrier and into the storeroom. Quinn watched in awe as she appeared to fall through the ground and disappear.

"Okay, your turn," Jared said.

"What? Just jump?" Quinn asked incredulously.

"Yep."

"Uh, okay," he replied shakily and climbed up to perch on the edge, swinging his legs over the stone. "So, all I have to do is jump?"

"That's the idea."

"But what's below?"

Jared smirked. "You're about to find out." With that, he gave Quinn a light shove.

CHAPTER EIGHTEEN

As Quinn fell, he clenched his eyes shut to ward off the sense of vertigo overcoming him, but only a moment passed before he came to an abrupt stop. The sensation was not unlike the suddenness of a faulty elevator as it shifted between levels.

He opened his eyes and was greeted with bright and colourful light filtering through the stained-glass roof over his head. Quinn blinked a couple of times as he took in his surroundings, seeing that they were not in the pit of the ancient storehouse, but at the centre of some sort of gazebo.

Though he had barely fallen through the portal, he knew that where he now stood was foreign ground. While the rocky terrain was similar to what he had just left, none of the trappings of modern society were visible. What remained in its stead were structures reminiscent of an ancient and holy world.

The gazebo where the three of them now stood was made of the same carved stone they had stepped upon. It towered over them, resplendent in its architecture. A stone pathway cut through light green grass and led toward the Terrace of the Lions in the distance.

Quinn's eyes widened as he took in the grand structures of all six lions, pristine and majestic in their beauty, as they looked over a lake. He dug into his back pocket and pulled out the small pamphlet he had received at the Delos entrance. He unfolded the map, curious as to where the wonders of the ancient world had been in the place—and time?—they had left behind.

According to his map, the lake they were looking at was known as the Sacred Lake. In the Second Realm, all the water had dried up hundreds of years ago, leaving only barren and rocky plains, contrasting the beautiful waterfront Quinn now saw before him. But what was even more impressive was the structure that sat in the middle of the lake. The massive temple jutting out of the water was clearly the Temple of Apollo, immaculate as the day it was built.

Yet Quinn knew somehow that this wasn't the original temple—or at least, how it had looked standing in the Second Realm. First of all, it was in the wrong place. Secondly, it was much larger than it had been in the realm he had just left behind.

The young man continued to gape at the temple's majesty as Jared and Surina stepped down from the gazebo. Before Jared could make his way over to the terrace, Surina stopped him by placing a hand on his shoulder.

"Surina?" the Death God questioned.

"I want you to take the lead when we get inside," she said.

Jared pulled back, confused. "What? But you know temple politics better than I do."

Quinn, overhearing their conversation, stepped closer to the pair.

"That might be," Surina replied, "but it would be unwise for two gods to be seen taking their cues from me."

"I don't understand," Quinn jumped in.

"I might have more knowledge in this situation, but you two still outrank me. I doubt they'd appreciate someone like me ordering you guys around. Besides, they'll be more likely to help us if orders come from one of you."

"Even though we don't have any real authority here?" Jared persisted.

Surina snorted. "You're a god. What other authority could you possibly need?"

"But we're not their god."

"Apollo has been missing for decades. So, unless you know where he or she has been hiding out, we have to make do with you. On the bright side, if they don't listen to you, they will listen to him," she said, gesturing toward Quinn.

"Me? Why would they listen to me?"

Surina adjusted her sunglasses as she turned to face him. "Athena has always been a well-respected god, even among the followers of other gods. Athena's considered the peacemaker of the gods, so to disregard you could be taken as an insult."

"But I'm not educated enough to lead this investigation," Quinn protested.

"You probably won't have to," she assured him. "Even if the Solar magi aren't happy following Jared's lead, they'll be scared to death of what could happen if they didn't try to cooperate, if you'll pardon the pun."

Jared rolled his eyes. "Fine, whatever, though you know they'll only cooperate with me to a degree. Now, can we please get moving already? It's getting cold."

Indeed, the sun had almost completely set, while a cool wind blew in from the sea.

Surina nodded, and the three companions picked up their bags to trudge across the terrace to the water's edge.

Quinn approached the shoreline, his lips set in a perplexed frown. "So how do we get across? Do we have to swim, or do we wait for a boat or something?"

"Or something," Jared replied. "You're gonna love this." The dark-haired man's eyes seemed to sparkle as he addressed Quinn.

Facing the temple across the water, he called out, "Jared Thanatos Doyle."

The sound of massive rock formations grinding together caused Quinn to fix his attention upon the lion statues lined up behind them. The lion's eyes, which had originally been closed, opened slowly. A bright light emanated from them to the water below, creating a pathway between the statues across the lake's surface.

"Now, here's the fun part," Jared said gleefully, walking forward and putting his foot down onto the edge of the lit path. Quinn marvelled at how Jared effortlessly strode across the water without getting wet.

Surina gave him a nudge. Quinn stumbled, but soon fell in step behind Jared as Surina took up the rear.

The three mounted the stairs to the temple entrance, which was barred by two massive stone doors that swung open as they approached. Jared entered the temple first, his head held high with confidence, while Quinn quietly shuffled in behind him. Surina stood at his back, a silent sentinel taking in their surroundings.

They now stood in the vast, brightly lit main hall of the temple. Large columns stood to either side of the hall, revealing small corridors that led to other rooms of the temple—most likely the magi's quarters or mess hall, Quinn guessed.

In the centre of the temple was an impressive, golden model of the solar system. Each planet appeared to be made of blown glass, supported by metal bars attached to the base and orbiting around a wire sphere where a model of the Sun should have been. But at the centre of the mobile's galaxy, there was only a gaping hole and an empty stand.

Quinn noted, with a grin, that Pluto was still part of the planetary lineup. He had hated the planet's formal removal from the galaxy's main planets.

Several individuals milled about the temple hall, all dressed in a tan uniform of pants and a tank top with a jacket or cloak over top.

The dulcet tones of a harp floated across the room. Quinn turned to see a young girl with what appeared to be flowered vines growing from her head in place of hair. She was playing the instrument to the side of the main hall as a couple of magi listened intently.

Farther down the hall, a man and a centaur sparred with broadswords. Quinn's eyes widened in wonder as he gawked at the quadruped. He figured after his run-in with Cerberus and Python, nothing could phase him, but this First Realm inhabitant was incredible to behold.

The sound of hooves against the marble floor pulled Quinn's attention from the two sparring partners toward a man in blood-red robes approaching the three. The man pulled back the hood of his robe, causing Quinn to reassess his earlier judgment of the man's humanity—that is, if the curved horns emerging from the magi's brown curls were any indicator.

Surina leaned in toward his ear. "Try not to stare," she whispered.

"He's..."

"A satyr," she supplied.

"Explains the hoofbeats," Quinn whispered back.

"Lord Thanatos," the satyr greeted, giving a slight bow. "We're honoured by your presence here. I am Arthur Malin, one of the head instructors at the temple."

"Instructor Malin, there's no need for formalities. Jared is fine." The Death God smirked.

"Jared it is then, but only if you call me Arthur. And who is this?" the satyr questioned, tipping his chin toward Quinn.

"This is Quinn, the latest incarnation of Athena."

"Lord Athena," Arthur gasped. "Bless my stars, they've finally found you." He clasped Quinn's hand between his own and bowed his head in a gesture of reverence.

The young man stood awkwardly, unsure of how he was expected to respond. "Yeah, you can just call me Quinn. I'm kind of new to this whole thing," he admitted.

"No need to worry," Arthur assured, patting his hand. "You always were a quick learner."

Quinn tried to hide a wince. The satyr wasn't wrong, but the young man still felt himself struggling with how his role as Athena seemed to make people believe they knew him.

Arthur finally turned to acknowledge Surina, his kindly expression becoming guarded as he took in her presence.

"Miss Malik, you seem well," he said stiffly.

"As well as can be expected," she returned.

"We're here in regards to the theft you just had," Jared said, cutting into the terse exchange.

Instructor Malin's smile returned as he turned to face the God of Death. "Of course. You probably want to speak to the high priest."

Jared nodded. "If we could."

"That shouldn't be a problem," Arthur responded. "I believe he just finished his dinner and should be in his study. I'll take you there."

Quinn watched the exchange with increasing interest. Two things were obvious from his observations thus far: First, Arthur and Surina were familiar with one another, though how that came to be and under what circumstances was a question for another time. Second, it was clear that the terms on which the two had parted were not the friendliest, if Jared acting as a buffer between the two was any indication.

Perhaps that was why Surina wanted Jared to act as their leader, despite Surina supposedly knowing the community better.

Arthur beckoned the three to follow behind him as he trotted deeper into the temple, his cloven feet resonating against the floor. Several of the temple initiates stopped their training and watched them with a veiled curiosity as they passed by.

At the back of the temple stood a broad set of stairs leading to an observation deck. The four ascended, before being ushered through a door at the top of the staircase platform.

Inside was a circular room, appearing to be a library or study of some kind. Floor-to-ceiling bookshelves ran the length of the room. A lute lay against a chair with sheet music haphazardly strewn across the floor at the chair's feet. A large, wooden desk sat at the study's far wall where the high priest was hunched over a journal, writing intently. Quinn was surprised to note that the man appeared younger than Instructor Malin, with a shock of blond hair that was only just beginning to grey at the temples.

The high priest wore a finely pressed white dress shirt, although a blood-red robe with gold embroidery along the collar and edges was draped over the back of his chair. His demeanour seemed to be that of unrest, and as Quinn looked on, the man closed his book with a sigh of frustration.

Arthur bowed his head respectfully as he approached the desk. "High Priest Reeves, Lords Thanatos and Athena are here to speak to you about the Star." Reeves lifted his head to reveal steely-blue eyes, which narrowed slightly as he took in his visitors.

Quinn bristled as he noted that Surina was once again overlooked, though she did not appear to be irritated by the purposeful dismissal. Then again, he supposed, her ever-present sunglasses made her expression hard to read on a good day.

The high priest stood, revealing himself to be a man of impressive height and stature. He seemed more like a soldier than a man in the priesthood. Considering the training the initiates were conducting downstairs, this temple composed itself quite differently from any church, synagogue, or mosque back home in the Second Realm.

Reeves bowed respectfully to the two men.

"My lords," he greeted. "First may I say, I'm honoured to meet the new Lord Athena. The world sorely needs the God of Wisdom, and I hope your return is a good omen for the return of our own Lord Apollo. I just wish we could have met and conversed under better circumstances."

As he spoke, Arthur pulled out a couple of chairs from their resting place against the wall. Reeves motioned for them to sit, and Quinn was surprised that Arthur offered Surina a chair, despite their earlier tension. The three visitors took their seats as the high priest slumped back into his own.

"We'd like to hear exactly what transpired on the night of the theft," Jared said.

The older man nodded. "I wasn't actually present during the time of the theft, but the accounts I've collected from the guards on duty seem quite accurate."

Jared dipped his head, gesturing for the high priest to continue.

"It happened after curfew—almost everyone was in their dorms or asleep. As for Vega, well, I'm guessing you've seen the statue in the main hall."

"The one of the solar system? It's beautiful!" Quinn blurted excitedly, before quickly shrinking back in his seat, embarrassed by his outburst.

The high priest smiled indulgently at Quinn's enthusiasm. "That would be the one. As you probably noticed, the Sun was missing."

"That's where you keep your piece of the North Star, right?" Quinn asked, quickly putting the pieces of what he had seen and heard together.

"Exactly. So, as you can imagine, it would be a feat to climb up there unnoticed. But considering the perpetrator, I guess I shouldn't be too surprised."

"Perpetrator?" Jared echoed, confused.

"Lunar magi," Reeves explained.

"What makes you so sure it was Lunar Magi?" Surina joined in, her face a mask of composed curiosity.

The high priest's forehead became lined with irritation as he turned to face her. "As you know, we work very closely with both the Lunar and Earthen Temples and are very familiar with their wardrobe and weapons. The thief was dressed in the cloak of a Lunar initiate and carried their standard silver bow and quiver."

"Isn't that a little too convenient?" Surina challenged.

"What do you mean by that?"

"Well, think about it. You said yourself that it didn't surprise you that a Lunar magi was able to climb onto the statue unnoticed. Why is that? Because you know a great deal of their training focuses on stealth. So, if the thief knew there was even the slightest chance that they would be seen, why would they dress in something that would proclaim to everyone who they were?"

"Maybe they were overconfident," Reeves sneered. "Or it could have been a deliberate, open act of war."

"That's not the way of the Artemis temple," Surina replied defensively.

The high priest frowned. "Aren't you being a little biased, Miss Malik, considering your connection with your grandmother's temple?"

Surina stiffened in her seat. "I'm merely pointing out the irregularities in this case. I'm sure you're aware of the accusations laid upon your people by the Earthen Temple High Priest."

"Are you accusing me of something?" Reeves said quietly, but in a way that made Quinn shiver as he heard it.

"No. I'm just saying that things aren't adding up."

"How did the thief escape?" Jared cut in, attempting to defuse the mounting tension.

Reeves focused once more upon the Death God. "To be honest, we're not entirely sure. One minute they were there, the next they were gone. We believe they used illusionary tactics. Lunar magi are often well versed in such arts."

The last remark was almost spat toward Surina. Though she was not fully a god by blood, Quinn was surprised that the man would be so openly hostile to a demigod. But considering that she was a descendant of the goddess whose temple supposedly stole from them, his disrespect became more understandable.

"So, the thieves literally just disappeared?" Quinn asked.

"At least from sight. We kept the temple locked down for as long as we could, thinking that the thief still might be hiding inside, but we never found them," concluded Reeves.

"Is that all the information you can give us?" Jared prodded.

"I'm not familiar with all the details. Perhaps the guards who were on duty that night can give you more information."

The large grandfather clock behind Reeves chimed nine, pulling the high priest's attention from his inquisitors.

"Unfortunately, your questions will have to wait until tomorrow. Vinewall and Kalling, who were on duty that night, are about to retire for the evening. You are welcome to stay the night. I'll have Instructor Malin escort you to the guest chambers."

The three stood, Jared reaching to shake the high priest's hand.

"Thank you, Priest Reeves, for your help. We'll do our best to get to the bottom of this."

Reeves shook hands fervently. "I pray that you do."

Arthur gestured for the three travellers to follow him just as the high priest spoke once more.

"I feel as if you have a right to this knowledge; if Vega is not retrieved before the sun sets on the fifth day after this meeting, the Apollo magi will have no choice but to declare war on the Temple of Artemis."

Jared and Surina paused, but to Quinn's surprise, nodded.

"We understand," said Jared. "We will do everything in our power to keep that from happening."

"I'm sure you will," Reeves agreed somberly.

After a tense moment in which Quinn was sure that Surina and the high priest would tie in a staring contest, Malin led them out of the room. Despite the calm way both of his companions had accepted Reeve's threat, Quinn could not quell the unease that rose in him.

CHAPTER NINETEEN

THE DOOR TO the guest room had barely closed behind them when Quinn rounded on Jared and Surina. He pursed his lips as he tried to make sense of what he had just witnessed. "Um, can someone explain to me just what happened there? I get that we're trying to be respectful while in another god's temple, but Reeves just said he's going to start a war in five days if we don't find their piece of the Star, and the two of you barely batted an eyelash." He turned to stare Surina down. "And this was *after* you seemed so determined to pick a fight with him. So, will one of you please tell me what's going on?" While he was irritated at his companion's seeming lack of response to the threat, he attempted to keep his tone civil.

"Quinn, you know that we will do everything we can to get the Star back before the Apollytes declare war," Surina said firmly.

"But why don't we just tell them they can't go to war?" he reasoned.

Jared furrowed his brow at Quinn's skepticism. "What makes you think that I have any right to do so?"

The words took Quinn aback. He was still trying to figure out his role and influence as a new god. "You're a god," he answered awkwardly, unsure of his reasoning. "Shouldn't that mean they have to listen to you?"

"Well I could argue the same to you," Jared challenged, not unkindly as he moved to invade Quinn's space. "Why didn't *you* say something?"

Quinn backed up, his legs folding as they hit the foot of the bed. He sat on the plush covers, floundering as he grasped for a reply.

Jared's expression softened. "I'll tell you why, because you knew it wasn't your place. For us, being called a god or goddess is like being called a king or a queen. Yes, they understand that we have powers that they don't and that they should respect us, but let me ask you this: Would the people of France obey an order given to them by the Queen of England?"

"No."

"Why not?"

"Because they're not her people," Quinn replied, understanding dawning upon him. "Only Apollo can tell the Solar magi what to do."

"Exactly," Jared confirmed.

"And so far, you haven't been able to locate this generation's incarnation of Apollo, Artemis, or Demeter. So, how do the temples continue to operate normally?" Quinn asked.

"They're very well organized among themselves," Jared assured him.

"I think it's time you had a crash course in how these temples work," Surina commented.

"That sounds like a great idea," Jared said, standing. "You give him the rundown while I head down to the kitchens and have them rustle us up some food."

"Good plan," Surina conceded. "I'd offer to go myself, but it's close to their curfew. They won't go out of their way to help me when they're about to head off for the night."

"And even if they don't take orders from me, they're far more likely to show me respect and hospitality this late. Or, maybe they'll make an exception for me based on my dashing good looks and impeccable sense of style." Jared smirked, shooting a wink toward Quinn, before slipping out the door.

Quinn cursed his fair complexion as the flirtatious gesture caused heat to once again flood his cheeks. They were just supposed to be working on being friends, but Jared's teasing was making it difficult for Quinn to keep that thought in his head.

Luckily, Surina decided not to mention Quinn's beet-red blush and simply pulled her chair closer to where he sat, their knees almost touching.

Quinn's thoughts were fixated on Jared's charming nature and comments from before. The other god had been nothing but kind to him so far. There had even been a couple of times when it seemed that perhaps Jared might also feel the attraction. But he had yet to make any comment or action to confirm it. Still, Quinn couldn't help wondering if this was just Jared's nature and he could easily turn his charm onto someone else. *Perhaps someone less of a mess than me,* he thought bitterly.

"Jared might seem like a flirt at times, but it's mostly an act," Surina said, as if reading Quinn's thoughts. "In all the time I've known him, I've never seen him dating anyone."

"How long have you known him?"

"Personally? About four years, ever since I started working with Sebastien. But that's not important right now. What *is* important is making sure that you understand the way these temples work, especially as we'll be heading to the Lunar Temple sometime tomorrow."

"How different can they be from one another, really?" he asked her.

"Very. There are temples dedicated to almost every god, though some are more active than others. Some just revere what ideals the god or goddess embodied in their first life, while others adopt their god's practices and even work for them, should they have some agenda to fulfill."

"Agenda?" Quinn asked skeptically.

"I didn't mean it like that," Surina said tersely. "Take Artemis, for example. Generally known as the Goddess of the Hunt and the Moon, she also protected youth and animals. Lunar magi who follow Artemis act as an extension of her hand by guarding against poachers and helping young children and teens who are abused or exploited in both realms. Or at least, they do their best. Without Artemis, the innocents of the world are suffering."

"You mentioned that these temples work together, though too."

"Yes, and no. Of the temples that exist today, those of Apollo, Artemis, and Demeter are the most active in the First Realm. But all of them have very different practices and skills they impart to their followers."

"Such as?" Quinn prodded.

"The skills of a magi usually reflect those of their patron god or goddess," Surina elaborated. "In the main hall, we saw a pair of acolytes sparring with swords—and Apollo was known as the bearer of the golden sword."

"So, everyone in here knows how to use a sword?" Quinn asked.

"Not everyone," Surina sighed as she sunk back into her seat. "Apollo was also associated with the arts, music in particular."

"The girl we saw playing the harp," Quinn replied, realizing how her words all fit together. "So, not everyone here is being trained as a warrior?"

"On the contrary, that girl was probably just as dangerous as anyone wielding a sword. Music performed by a Solar magi can cause a lot of damage if they want it to. Sometimes, it will distort their enemies' perceptions; other times, the sound the acolytes produce can vibrate so intensely that it can cause aneurysms in the listeners' brains. Though, the worst one I've seen has been the ability to control the actions of the Apollytes' enemies, making them turn on one another."

Quinn straightened his posture. "You mean, like mind control?"

"Not in so many words—more like hypnosis. Those under the influence of their song are completely aware of their actions, but are unable to stop themselves from following through."

Quinn pulled his legs up to his chest and wrapped his arms around them. "If a Solar magi can control someone's actions, and they had contact with a Lunar Magi, would it be possible for the Solar magi to force a Lunar magi to steal their temple's piece of the Star in order to frame them?"

Surina pursed her lips in thought. "The thought crossed my mind, but I'll admit it's highly unlikely. A Solar magi who uses an instrument has to keep playing to keep control of their subject, and the target subject must be able to hear the music. Otherwise, it has no effect."

"Still, people here could have staged the whole thing."

"And I'm not ruling that out," the dark-haired woman agreed. "But I also have to consider the other temples and their opportunities for treachery."

"Such as?" Quinn pressed, eager to hear more of Surina's theories.

"The Earthen magi at the Temple of Demeter aren't usually considered warriors, and that's a mistake. Earthen magi are typically chemists, botanists, and alchemists, but that doesn't make them any less dangerous. With their combined knowledge, they can concoct hundreds of powerful potions and poisons."

"Like?"

"They've got one that turns the user invisible. Other potions can make them fly, or breathe fire—I remember they had this one they called Bull's Blood. It could grant a ninety-eight-pound weakling the ability to rip a grown man in half."

Quinn leaned forward, cradling his head in the palm of his hand. "Anything there that could help them in a heist?"

Surina frowned but nodded. "Their invisibility potion would make the most sense, but since the thief was seen, I'd have to rule out that one. Plus, I think it would be more likely that they would just tamper with the whole temple's food supply to put them out of commission. Potions that give the drinker special skills only work for a limited time, but poisons, those are permanent, unless you get an antidote."

"I see. And the Lunar magi?"

"They are hunters for the most part," she said. "Archery and other weapon skills are a big part of their training, though both illusionary and protective magics are also taught. Overall, the Lunar Temple's main focus is on tracking and stealth, so the fact that they would blatantly wear their own training uniform during a theft doesn't make much sense to me. Still..."

"Do you think they're capable of doing this?" Quinn asked.

"The Lunar magi are capable of both wonderful and horrendous things, so as much as I hate to say it, yeah, they could have done it," Surina admitted.

"I guess we'll have a better chance to really get to the bottom of things when we visit the Lunar Temple tomorrow," Quinn sighed, lying back on the bed.

Surina stood and crossed toward the small divan, situated by a long, low dining table, typical of an ancient Greek villa. "Speaking of which, when we head over, there are a few things you should be aware of."

"What do you mean?"

"Well, you're a god. The Lunar magi will obviously treat you as someone befitting your status," she said, the formal words awkwardly hanging from her tongue. "But I'll be honest, Artemis has rarely taken lovers, so her number of descendants is fairly small. Her followers are usually similarly minded. That being said, they'll expect you not to engage in certain behaviours. If you catch my meaning..."

"What do you mean by that?"

"I was trying not to make this awkward, but I guess you need me to spell it out," Surina groaned.

"Listen, we all know there's that whole Thanatos and Athena thing. And it seems like you and Jared have hit it off in this lifetime. I mean, I can tell you two are into each other."

"Whoa, Surina!" Quinn couldn't help the furious blush at her insinuations. "Way off base!"

"I know it's none of my business, but I'm only saying it because you should know that it would be a mistake to give in to any carnal temptations that might come your way when we go question the Lunar magi. Although it's not exactly written down anywhere, it's understood that sexually-charged PDA is a no go in the Temple of Artemis."

Quinn scowled at the older woman. "So, what you're saying is, to keep my hands to myself? Gross, Surina, what kind of person do you take me for?"

Jared and I are just friends, he insisted in his mind. *Nothing more!*

He couldn't deny that he found the man attractive, but he was entirely capable of being professional.

"I take you for a twenty-year-old man with hormones and an obvious attraction," she deadpanned. "And I know that Jared has his charms. Plus, you were alone together, shacked up in his condo for two nights..."

"First of all, nothing happened between us. We ate food. We talked. We watched TV. Don't worry, me and my hormones didn't besmirch his virtue or anything. Jared and I actually talked about this, like grown adults. Because that's what we are. We both know the history between our past selves but we're just gonna be friends for now. That's it."

Surina looked surprised but shrugged. "I think it's smart. I'm not saying that you shouldn't pursue something should feelings arise down the line, but you have bigger things to deal with right now. Though, to be honest, I should probably be more worried about *your* virtue than Jared's," she continued, her neutral demeanour giving way to a gentle ribbing.

Quinn's face burned at Surina's words, though he couldn't come up with anything to say in his defence.

"Is it really obvious that I think he's attractive? I mean, do you think Jared knows?"

"I'm only teasing. Don't worry," she assured, "I won't mention any of this to Jared."

A moment later, Jared returned to the room, his arms overflowing with platters containing mountains of food. The plates were piled high with small dinner rolls, fresh fruits, various cheeses, and slices of roasted meats.

"My charm and dashing good looks were victorious once again," he proclaimed, proudly displaying his spoils, before placing the food on the dining table and pulling up one of the armchairs.

Quinn hastily joined his companions at the table and began to help himself without saying another word. In seconds, he'd gotten himself a dinner roll piled high with smoked turkey and Havarti cheese. He was about to take a bite but noticed that the other two hadn't yet moved to touch the food. Jared and Surina watched with thinly veiled amusement as he enthusiastically put his sandwich together.

"*Someone* is hungry," Jared observed.

"Aren't you?" Quinn countered. "We haven't eaten anything since we left Sebastien's."

Surina approached the food and grabbed several slices of cheese. "He's got a point," she said, popping some brie into her mouth. "I'm starving."

"I'm glad that your appetite has returned," Jared said with a smirk.

Surina's lips quirked to the side in what Quinn recognized as her version of a scowl. "Was that supposed to be a jibe about my seasickness?" she sniffed.

Jared raised his hand in a placating manner. "Not at all. Honestly, I'm glad you're feeling better."

The woman huffed, any aggression she had had was now released from her body. "Thanks."

Quinn smiled. He found that he sincerely enjoyed being in both Surina and Jared's company, and to see that the two genuinely got along, despite their occasional combativeness, warmed his heart. "Well, if you kids are finished kissing and making up, I suggest we finish eating and head to bed.".

Jared checked his watch. It was getting late, and some rest was in order. "Fine by me," he agreed, before shoving a couple apple slices into his mouth.

Surina nodded as well, stealing a dinner roll before lying down on the divan.

"What are you doing?" Quinn asked.

"Getting settled, what does it look like?" she replied.

"We have two big beds; we can easily share."

She gave a soft chuckle. "That's a cute offer, but you're a little young for me."

If Quinn's face had been red before, he was flushed positively scarlet now.

"That's not what I meant," he protested. "I just meant, you could have one, and that us guys could share. You know, completely platonic; if that's all right with you," he finished lamely, turning to Jared.

Jared scratched at the back of his head. "Yeah, I guess that's fine. I mean, it's not a big deal or whatever." The words came out in a rush as the dark-haired man attempted to keep the mood casual.

"Well that settles it." Quinn moved to claim the right side of the

G.E. White

other bed as Jared began to take off his shoes. He undressed, leaving only his boxers and undershirt on, and Quinn did the same, actively making a point not to check Jared out as they stripped down.

Surina was now on the other bed, unzipping her boots. She had already shrugged out of her bomber jacket and removed her bra. Both were now draped across one of the room's chairs, though her tank top remained on. She took a pair of pyjama pants from her bag and began stepping out of her undone jeans, completely unbothered about being seen in her bikini cut underwear.

Quinn averted his eyes, but then turned to watch her intently as Surina pulled a long, black scarf out of her discarded pants' pocket. She leaned against the pillows and removed her ever-present sunglasses.

To Quinn's disappointment, her eyes remained closed as she replaced her glasses with the dark blindfold. From what he could see, there was nothing wrong with her eyes: no scarring, discolouration, or burns on her surrounding skin. So what exactly was the problem?

"What's the blindfold for?"

"My eyes are sensitive to light," she replied simply.

Her tone indicated to Quinn that there would be no further explanations, and when he turned to Jared for some sort of clue, he found that the other man was already under the covers with his back to him, seemingly asleep.

By the time he had looked back over at Surina, she too had snuggled down under her covers.

Quinn blew out the remaining lantern and crawled underneath the heavy blankets.

He lay awake for some time. It was difficult trying to ignore the form of the Death God beside him. He really hoped he didn't do anything in his sleep to embarrass himself. He shot a quick glance over at his bedmate, but could only see the back of the other man's head.

Quinn rolled onto his side, facing away from Jared, and tried to focus on Surina's words and actions—there was a puzzle here.

However, as Quinn pondered Surina's situation in the now-darkened room, he knew in his heart that there was more to her actions than a simple aversion to light. *Just what was it, exactly?* Before he could contemplate an answer to his own question, Quinn found himself slipping under waves of the past few day's exhaustion and soon slept soundly without dreaming.

G.E. White

CHAPTER TWENTY

SURINA WOKE TO the sensation of her blindfold shifting across her face. "Do you have a death wish?" she growled. She heard Jared snort as he playfully began to tug at the fabric again, much like a dog with a toy rope.

"No, I'm just messing with you," he laughed.

She batted his hand away and sat up, pulling the sash from her closed eyes.

"I should have known it was you," she grumbled, placing her sunglasses back into position.

"Why's that?" Jared asked, now sitting on the floor in between the two beds.

"Because Quinn isn't that stupid," she teased. Looking down at the seated Jared, Surina couldn't help but smile. She had been introduced to the current God of Death over four years ago, and though the two occasionally butted heads, she considered him a friend. The two could laugh, joke, fight, and tease, and she never had to worry that Jared would ever seek more than the almost sibling-like relationship they had been slowly crafting.

Looking over at the windows, Surina guessed it was about nine in the morning, if the position of the sun was any indication.

"Just so you know, I already contacted Leo. He said he'd send Carter over later today to give us the next Gate," the Death God said as he traced the grooves in the wood floor.

"Hopefully it'll be more accurate than the last one," she replied.

Looking about the room, Surina noted that someone had come in that morning, as the platter from the night before had been replaced with one bearing three bowls of porridge. One bowl had already been scraped clean.

"Where's Quinn?" she asked.

"After finishing his porridge, he hightailed it into the bathroom to wash up." The sound of the other god sloshing around in the bathtub confirmed Jared's story.

Surina rose from the bed, stretching her arms as she attempted to work out the kinks in her back.

"You should have seen the way he just inhaled that porridge," Jared chuckled. "You would think he was raised by wolves."

Surina frowned. "Or, the poor kid grew up in foster care with no one to care enough to teach him to be better. I've seen his files. I know what most of those foster homes were like. He would have had to be quick and scrappy just to get a bite to eat."

"I didn't think of that..." Jared's face burned an uncharacteristic red. "He wasn't that way at my house. He was much more laid back and well mannered."

"Well, you're you. You intimidate people. You're so posh and bougie, and you act too cool for the rest of the world. He was trying to impress you."

G.E. White

"You think so?"

"I know so."

During the last two months of Quinn's stay at the Cedar Hills Mental Health Facility, Surina had spent her time tracking him down and working on the cover that would grant her access to him. Her work had required hours of research into Quinn's case, as well as his life in general.

As each new aspect of his life was revealed to her, Surina couldn't help but feel for Quinn. With no memories of his life before, his story had been one of abandonment, hardships, and disappointment. Not once had the young man been permanently adopted by the countless couples he went to stay with. It hadn't mattered how bright he was or how well behaved, he had always been passed over due to his age or god-related health scares. No one seemed to want a kid or a teen, they wanted a baby. And even worse, Surina had noted from her case files, Quinn didn't even seem to blame them for that.

The reports had continued to concern her as she had read about his half-baked teenage plan to stay on the streets with his foster sister Andi. Learning of the young woman's fate was heartbreaking, but Surina just found herself grateful that Quinn was smart enough to know when to come in from the cold.

Things apparently hadn't gotten much better for Quinn after leaving his foster homes. Despite his high scholastic average and the university scholarships he was offered, Quinn had been forced to turn them down, as they didn't even begin to pay for all of the associated costs of his living arrangements. It was only through his work at a local community college that he had any hope of enrolling himself.

When Surina made the journey to Cedar Hills, she had expected to find a jaded and defeated young man. Yes, he was skeptical of the story she told him, but then, who wouldn't be? Quinn still had a spark of curiosity, and it was something that Surina suspected had kept him going all this time: the idea that if he gave up now, he would never find out just what else was out there and what he was capable of.

"Did you know that he was homeless for a time?" Surina asked Jared with an even tone that belied her inner thoughts.

Jared looked up from his bowl of porridge, which was now almost as empty as Quinn's.

"Really?" he replied, the honest curiosity in his voice tinged with sorrow.

Surina collected her own breakfast and sat back down on the bed. "Yeah. He'd been in foster care since he was six and was constantly shuffled around. When he was fourteen, the foster family he was placed with turned out to be pretty shitty. He and another girl took to the streets. They were able to avoid the police and Youth Services for almost a whole year, but when his foster sister got hooked on drugs and overdosed, he ended up going back. But at least he was put with a different family," she said between mouthfuls, shaking her head.

Jared stood and placed his empty bowl on the dining table, before crossing over to the window. Surina couldn't help but notice a strange tension in the way he moved. "And before that?" he asked.

"Who knows," Surina shrugged. "No last name, no memory of what happened. And with no family to claim him, he just ended up in the system. It's not that uncommon."

Jared's expression darkened. "And no one has any idea what happened to his parents? Grandparents? Aunts, uncles...anyone?"

If Surina had been speaking to Carter, she would have thought nothing of the rapid-fire questions, but Jared valued and respected privacy so the questions were oddly prying. "Nothing. And obviously, there were never any missing person reports matching his description. It's likely that any family he has is dead."

Surina moved to stand in front of the mirror above the small desk, smoothing down her hair.

"You think so?" Jared prodded, his back still turned to her. She detected a strange tone to his words. Was it guilt?

"It's just a guess, but then you would know better than me. Do you remember them? His parents?"

Jared crossed his arms and shook his head. "I'm not present for everyone's death; you know that. It's physically impossible."

Surina became alert, hearing his undercurrent of self-recrimination. "But you're aware of them," she argued.

"To a degree," he shrugged, strangely nonchalant about the whole thing. "My job is to harvest the grain, so to speak. I try not to get involved."

"You mean, after you got into trouble for making deals."

⁂

Jared rounded on Surina, his eyes boring into hers. There was no way she could know, he assured himself, not about that particular incident. But what about the one before it? He gazed at her face, relieved to find no judgment in her expression, only a thinly veiled curiosity. Jared quelled the urge to ask just what she was referring to as Quinn stepped out.

He was dressed in a brand new outfit; another gift from Justine. With his hair still damp, he practically glowed in his new acid-washed jeans and raglan-style t-shirt. The sight caused Jared's heart to skip a beat, but Surina's last words sank like a lead balloon in his stomach.

"I really need to thank Justine for all these clothes, they're great!"

"Hey, looking sharp," Surina agreed.

"Yeah, they look good on you," Jared commented offhandedly, brushing past the other man and into the bathroom, quickly shutting the door behind him.

Leaning against the now-closed door, Jared attempted to slow the beat of his frantic heart. He had foolishly allowed himself to entertain the idea of slowly moving toward a stronger connection with Quinn, but Surina's statement reiterated why that was a bad idea. The closer

Quinn got to him, the more likely he would discover Jared's secret. Then any chance of salvaging even a friendship with the current Athena would be lost.

He closed his eyes, his mind drifting back to this morning when he had first woken up. It had been a moment of both bliss and horror. Somehow during his sleep, Jared's traitorous body had moved to spoon up behind Quinn and had slung a proprietary arm over his waist. For a moment he had basked in the warmth and comfort the position had given him, before catching himself and practically flinging himself out of the bed.

Luckily Quinn had slept through the movement and had been unaware of the compromising position they had found themselves in. His rebellious mind kept insisting that sleeping curled behind the other man had felt right on some level. Still, Surina's reminder of his past transgressions made it clear that he needed to put some emotional distance between them.

℘

Quinn glanced back at the closed door. Jared had barely even looked at him before shutting him out. He couldn't help but feel a bit snubbed. He had figured if anyone would have something to say about the new clothes, it would be the image-conscious Death God. "What's his problem?"

Surina gave a noncommittal shrug. "When you gotta go, you gotta go." She picked up the small duffle bag and pulled out a pair of pants and a button-up blouse she planned to change into. She paused as something else in her bag caught her eye.

Quinn rubbed roughly at his scalp, towel drying his hair, when he noticed Surina pull out a clunky-looking bracelet with a large dial on it.

"What's with the bracelet?" he asked.

"I found it on the body of one of the Danaids," she said, placing it on the bedside table. "It's obviously more than just a piece of bling, but until we know what it does, I've been told not to activate it. Unfortunately, we know that the Danaids couldn't have made it, nor could they have gotten into the Second Realm on their own."

As she spoke, Quinn picked up the cuff, looking closely at the dial before flipping it over and inspecting the inside of the band.

"I was going to show it around to the temple leaders, see if they recognized it, but after last night—"

"Wait!" Quinn interrupted. "Do you see that?"

He tilted the band toward her, pointing at the inside track just below the dial. Surina's eyes squinted as she tried to make out what Quinn was gesturing at.

There, lightly etched into the metal, was a small symbol, or at least part of a symbol: a hammer crossed over an anvil. If the light hadn't caught the engraving at just the right angle, it was likely Quinn never would have noticed it.

Or maybe this is part of being Athena?

"That's Hephaestus' symbol, isn't it?" Quinn asked, recalling that he had seen the same symbol on the grill of the Phantasm.

"Yes, but I've never heard about him working on anything like this," Surina replied.

"Is it possible that he kept this to himself? That he gave this to the Danaids?"

Surina twisted her features into a scowl. "Anything's possible. For all we know, this might be an experimental device, made with the purpose of trying to bring the Danaids under control. The only way we'll find out for sure is by getting answers from Tyrell himself. I'll take some pictures and send them to him, see if he can explain." Peering over at Quinn, Surina smiled.

"You've got a good eye. I had that for a day and I never caught that," she complimented. "Nice work."

Quinn shrugged as if it were nothing, but he practically glowed under the praise.

For the next little while, the two of them sat in comfortable silence as Quinn put his clothes from the day before into his small pack while Surina finished her porridge. The young man turned away respectfully as Surina changed from her sleepwear into a clean top and underwear, though she put on the jeans she had worn the day before.

Finally, Jared emerged from the bathroom in a cloud of steam, impeccably dressed as ever, with not a single hair out of place.

Quinn brushed his messy hair out of his face at the sight, wishing he could look half as well put together instead of like a scarecrow whose head was stuffed with too much straw.

Surina sat by the window; she was now emailing pictures of the cuff to Tyrell back in the Second Realm, while Quinn caught Jared up on their discovery. Once everything was sent, there was nothing to do but continue on with their investigation until Tyrell got back to them.

"So, who's ready to make some friends?" Jared joked lightly.

☙

Tracking down Magi Vinewall and Kalling took the better part of an hour, going from one person to the next before they finally found the two sparring in the back courtyard.

Vinewall was a lithe man with angular features and intense green eyes. His pointed ears betrayed his fae ancestry, though his slender arms did nothing to hinder swinging the gigantic claymore he held at his partner. Kalling, on the other hand, was a much stockier specimen, most likely human, and on the hairy side. The latter clenched his teeth as he blocked the heavy blade with a broad shield.

"I don't know what you want us to say," Vinewall ground out, between blows.

"Well, what exactly happened that night?" Jared asked, from where the group stood on the sidelines, out of the path of attack.

"It's hard to explain," the thin man huffed.

"What's to explain?" snorted Kalling. "Guy bloody disappeared is what happened."

Quinn turned to Surina, his expression questioning if that was even possible.

The woman pursed her lips but ignored Quinn's silent question. "You can't mean that literally," she challenged.

"The hell I don't," Kalling boomed, stepping away from Vinewall to speak directly to the three travellers, "I know what I saw."

"But it's impossible to Gate into a temple through anything but the temple arch; the wards won't allow it," Surina argued.

"That's what I thought, until that night." Kalling scratched his bearded chin, sounding perplexed by what he said next. "When we were on patrol, I felt this crackle in the air while passing by Vega. We both did."

Vinewall nodded in agreement.

"You heard a crack?" Quinn asked.

"Not a crack, a crackle. And it's not so much that we heard it, but felt it. Like the air was electric. I looked up at Vega, and in a blink, someone was there dressed in the robes of a Lunar Magi, reaching for it."

"Did you see his face?" Jared prodded.

"No. I called out to him, her, whomever they were, but they didn't even look at me. Just grabbed the Star and vanished."

"And that was it?"

"That was it," Kalling confirmed. "After we sounded the alarm, the whole temple searched for hours, but there was no sign of them."

Jared sighed, disappointed. "Well, thanks anyway."

The two magi bowed their heads in acknowledgement to the three, before turning back to their match.

The Death God shook his head as he walked away from the

courtyard, Quinn and Surina trailing behind him. "That just doesn't make any sense."

"You're telling me," she said. "Each temple only has one Gate inside, but it's a permanent fixture, usually somewhere secure, like the basement or a vault. But our thief didn't come in that way."

"I'm assuming that teleportation is just a myth, then? I mean, no one can do it here, right?" Quinn butted in. "Or you wouldn't use Gates, right? But maybe Carter, I mean, Hermes? How else does he get around so quickly?"

"Hermes is fast, but he can't make himself incorporeal; walls stop him just like anyone else, so he uses a ton of portals. Jared's reapers or Sebastien's tenders on the other hand can pass through solid matter, but they're invisible—Kalling and Vinewall wouldn't have been able to see them."

Suddenly, a crack of bright light appeared several metres to their right. The light continued to grow, as if someone was carving a line in thin air, and travelled up and around in a half circle, creating a doorway. Once the outline was complete, the door filled with light, and a familiar, yellow-clad figure rushed through the Gate a moment later.

The luminescent door flickered out behind Carter, who surveyed the area, giving himself a self-satisfied nod.

"I see that Leo is starting to get the hang of creating Gates," Surina called, gaining the man's attention.

Carter whipped his head around. Catching sight of the three travellers, he zipped over to them. "Actually, it's been a bit of trial and error. This was the third Gate he gave me."

"Wish I could say I'm surprised," she sneered, but by now Quinn could tell that there was no malice behind her expression. "When you see him next, let Leo know that Mykonos is lovely this time of year."

The God of Communication barked out a laugh. "Mykonos, huh? Well, at least he got you in the right country. I've already visited the Eiffel Tower and a mascot amusement park in Japan today." Digging into his messenger bag, he pulled out another black quill, similar to the one they had used in Sebastien's apartment. "Hopefully you'll have more luck than me with this one. It should take you right to the Lunar Temple, or at least Ephesus—in the First Realm, that is."

"Here's hoping," Jared said, taking the feather from him and beginning the blood ritual once more.

"What? No chit-chat? No updates?" Carter whined, disappointed. "Quinn, buddy, help me out here."

"Oh, so he's your buddy now?" Surina said, amused.

Carter swung his arm to rest across the back of Quinn's shoulders. "Absolutely. We may not know each other super well at the moment, but I can tell Quinn and I are gonna be best friends, ain't that right?" he said, posing this question to the god beside him.

Quinn flushed a bit under the attention, but couldn't help but feel pleased at Carter's proclamation. The other man was fun and quick-witted; he could think of much worse people to call a friend. "For sure," he said somewhat awkwardly.

"That's the spirit," Carter crowed, giving Quinn a friendly pat on the shoulder. "Besides, this is inevitable. You and I are always best friends. In every lifetime."

"Yes, well, unfortunately, we don't have time to spill the tea. Kinda busy here, trying to stop a war," Surina said.

Carter huffed, pulling himself away from Quinn. "No, I get it. Work comes first. Okay, well, I guess I'll just talk to you all later, then. I might want to take a look around here—size up what kind of force Reeves and his magi might be able to whip up."

"Knowing Reeves, that's probably not a bad idea," Surina replied as Jared finished drawing the archway in the air before them. Once again, light exploded from the outline, creating the doorway that would lead them to their next destination. "Let us know if you find anything."

"Don't I always?" Surina nodded, before stepping into the light and out of sight.

"We'll contact you soon," Jared assured the Messenger God, before following her.

"Would a *thank you* be too much to ask?" Carter muttered to himself. As Quinn approached, the other man surrendered his sour look to give the God of Wisdom an encouraging smile. "Well it was good to see you again, even if it was just for a moment. Good luck out there, and be careful." He stuck his hand out for Quinn to take.

Taking Carter's hand, he was a bit surprised when the brown-haired man pulled him in for a single-armed hug, patting Quinn on the back. "Thanks, Carter," Quinn mumbled shyly. "You be careful too. I've never had a best friend before. Looking forward to seeing what that's like once all this mess is done."

And with those words, Quinn stepped away from his new friend and through the portal into the unknown.

CHAPTER TWENTY-ONE

Blinking furiously and struggling to overcome the ringing noise within his ears, Quinn noticed several changes in the terrain.

A dense forest stood where the lake they had just left had once been, its shaded floor now covered with a blanket of mist. Quinn noticed a palpable shift in how Surina and Jared held themselves; their muscles coiled tightly under their clothes.

"Okay, Surina, this is your show. What do you want to do?" asked Jared.

"Well, thanks to our genius Leo, we are once again not where we're supposed to be. The scenery's familiar, but Ephesus and the actual temple are still a couple of kilometres due west. It shouldn't be too long a walk, but we're gonna have to stay sharp," she replied, putting away her phone and the map she had opened when they arrived.

Swinging her pack down from her shoulder, Surina crouched and began to dig through its contents. After a moment of searching, she pulled out a small dagger and sheath, handing both to Quinn.

"Here, take this," she said briskly. "Attach it to your belt. It's my old training knife. It might not look like much, but it's good for protection."

Quinn furrowed his brow, puzzled. "Protection? From what? I thought the Temple of Artemis was in league with you guys—you especially, Surina, being one of her descendants and all."

"It's not the temple I'm worried about. I'm more concerned with the local wildlife."

"You mean, like bears and wolves?"

Surina let out an exasperated snort. "Yeah, something like that." She shifted her pack onto her shoulder, before gesturing with her chin toward the forest. "We better get a move on. We don't want to be stuck out here when it gets dark. We'll travel single file; I'll take point, Quinn in the middle, Jared at the rear."

Jared moved behind Quinn without a sound, while the young man shuffled awkwardly after Surina.

The forest had grown fairly dense, causing Quinn to look more often at where he stepped than at Surina's back in front of him. Even though he monitored the path ahead carefully, he kept tripping on the various roots and stones that sprung from the shrouded underbrush.

Quinn couldn't help the pout maring his features as he stumbled along clumsily. But Jared and Surina somehow managed to travel with graceful strides; their footsteps so silent and smooth one might have believed they were floating. It was enough to make the younger man green with envy.

Thirty minutes into their journey, Quinn tripped over a hidden root and went down with a muffled curse. A twig snapped loudly under his knee as he landed, causing several birds above him to take flight.

Jared was beside him in a second, giving him a hand up. "You okay?"

Quinn flushed with embarrassment, but he took the other man's hand. "I'm fine," he muttered, climbing to his feet.

"Shh!" Surina hissed, her eyes keenly focused on the surrounding woods.

Both Quinn and Jared gazed out into the thick trees, searching for what had spooked her.

Standing perfectly still, Quinn could also hear the rustling of nearby leaves—something was definitely out there. He tensed as he saw a large figure dart between the trees, not twenty metres from where they stood. Unconsciously reaching for the knife hanging from his belt, Quinn's mind went back to his first encounter with Python, which had almost turned deadly. His imagination ran wild as he tried to picture just what sort of creatures called this forest home.

Surina's frown deepened, her hand sneaking into her coat to retrieve her watch. She, too, had seen the creatures, which were now circling them, if Quinn's ears were accurate. "Neadian wolves," she whispered.

Quinn's eyes widened in fright. She couldn't be serious. The animals he had seen briefly were too large to be wolves, but then the same could be said about Python. Plus, the low growl that echoed through the trees argued otherwise. The earth beneath his feet shook with fervour as small fissures appeared in the tightly packed dirt.

Quinn's hand trembled on the hilt of the knife. He had never dealt well with large dogs, in any form. Cerberus was the only exception to date. Quinn assumed that his aversion had something to do with the dream that had plagued him where, just like now, the snarling of a wild dog in the mist terrified him.

Could the whole thing have been some sort of memory?

"What do we do?" he whispered, internally chastising his brain for bringing up a thought it had no time to unpack.

"Don't panic, and don't run. We'll keep on moving, but slowly. Jared, switch places with me and keep heading along this path, but be ready, just in case. Move!" she ordered.

Quinn continued to stand stock-still after Jared stepped forward, but forced himself to fall in step behind the Death God. His eyes no longer watched his footing, but darted about, attempting to track the creatures that followed at a distance.

As they moved along, it soon became apparent that there were more than one of the creatures out there—two or three, from the sounds of it.

Quinn attempted to quicken his pace as he noticed the shifting figures move closer. In his haste, he stumbled, sprawling once again across the forest floor. Seizing his moment of weakness, one of the creatures leapt from the woods toward him.

Eyes wide in horror, Quinn finally got a clear look at the beasts that pursued them. Surina had been right; they were wolves—that is, if wolves grew to be the size of horses. They were covered with dark-grey fur, and their yellow eyes were devoid of pupils, yet Quinn felt their gaze pierce him as the wolf in front of him snarled, baring its massive fangs.

Quinn reached for the knife, but by the time he grabbed the handle, the wolf was practically on top of him. He threw his arm up, shutting his eyes tightly as he anticipated the excruciating sting of claws or the wolf's jaws clamping down on him, but neither came. He opened his eyes, only to see Jared standing between him and the beast.

The older man was holding off the creature with a long black scythe that Quinn had never seen before. The wolf had its teeth around the staff Jared held, while it used its paws, bracing against the dirt, to try to pull the weapon out of Jared's hands.

Quinn heard a sharp yelp and turned his attention to Surina, though he quickly discovered that the sound didn't originate from her.

One of the other wolves decided to join its packmate in the attack and charge Quinn's companion. However, Surina was prepared, as the bow in her hands attested. Quinn saw an arrow jutting from

G.E. White

the wolf's flank as the creature limped back into the surrounding mist.

A growl to his left pulled his focus away toward the wolves' last pack member. Quinn had yet to release his grip on the knife, so when the beast lunged at him, he moved on pure instinct. He jumped out of the way with lightning-fast reflexes, sharply swinging the blade downward and catching the wolf across its shoulder. The creature whined in pain as it quickly backed away from the knife and its wielder, into the undergrowth.

Jared kicked the wolf attached to his scythe in the chest, forcing it to let go. Swinging his weapon in fluid arcs across the creature's muzzle, he drove the beast farther and farther back until it turned tail and ran.

Quinn stood shaking as the adrenaline from the encounter continued to work its way through his system. He stared after the retreating creatures, unsure of what surprised him more: seeing the beasts close up or realizing he had helped successfully fend them off. "Did you see the size of those things?!" he gasped in awe.

"Yeah, we were lucky. Probably just pups," Surina commented as she slung the bow over her free shoulder.

"Pups?" Quinn echoed hoarsely.

"Yeah, Neadian animals are all monstrous sizes. When the wolves become fully grown, their howls can split the ground apart. I say we hightail it out of here before they bring back Mom and Dad."

Quinn paled further as his imagination conjured images of two-story-high, fanged monstrosities.

He was woken from his imagination by a firm hand on his shoulder. He glanced up to see Jared standing at his side, the god's expression a reassuring one. The scythe that he held in his other hand seemed to disintegrate before his eyes, turning into black smoke that soon dispersed.

Explains why I never saw the thing before.

"Come on, we don't have much farther to go," Jared assured, giving him a friendly clap on the back. Quinn tried not to revel too much in the comfort the other man's presence gave him.

The small group moved forward, though Quinn still kept a watchful eye on the woods surrounding them. His heart rate gradually slowed to a less frantic pace. Sanctuary for a goddess or not, Quinn could not wait to be free of the forest and its oversized inhabitants.

∽

Despite Quinn's paranoia, the rest of their journey to the city of Ephesus was uneventful. They entered the city from the south, and Quinn was once more impressed by the newness of the so-called ancient city. The design was thousands of years old, yet the smooth marble columns and polished flagstone streets appeared as if they had been laid yesterday.

It was already late afternoon, and the streets were filled with the city's inhabitants. Almost every person they encountered was a member of one of the first four races. A centaur with a long dark mane of braided hair shaped hot steel over an anvil, safety goggles protecting her eyes from the flying sparks. Small faeries, similar to the ones who had visited Quinn in Cedar Hills, flittered about tailed by multicoloured streaks of light. Their larger fae brethren walked about, the size of humans, their pointed features and luminescent eyes designating their lineage.

The nymphs strolling about, while humanoid in shape, could never pass for human; their eyes and skin displayed a variety of unique skin colours and textures, and their hair appeared composed of either flowers, ice, fire, rock, or thick metal ropes.

The three travelled westward along the main street, where a satyr wearing a comedy mask beckoned the crowd to come and see an evening play. Slightly to the north, the streets sloped downward, lined on the left side by intricate floor mosaics. At the bottom stood a large building built in the Greek style with Corinthian columns lining the entrance of what Jared identified as the Celsus Library.

"Oh, check this out," the dark-haired man said, pointing to a solitary tile on the path where the outline of a foot and an etching of a woman's face stood in sharp relief.

"And?" Quinn asked, unimpressed.

"It's a special marking. Like on a map," Jared said.

"Does it lead to the temple?"

Surina snorted, overhearing her companions. "Hardly."

"Then what?"

"A bordello," Jared answered.

"You mean, like a brothel?"

"Yep. You see, people would tell their spouses that they were going to the library," Jared explained. "Which technically was true, it's just that very few people knew there was an underground passage that travelled under the road and into the basement of the brothel across the street."

"Are you saying that this is also in the Second Realm?"

Jared nodded. "Well, at least it used to be. The equivalent of where we're standing in the Second Realm is still the site of Ancient Ephesus in Turkey. Though as you probably guessed, all that's left are ruins, though they're still in pretty good shape."

"I see."

"All right you two, let's pick up the pace," Surina called from ahead of them. "The temple is just a little farther. Once we pass the other theatre on the right, we'll hit a small patch of forest, and the temple is just beyond that."

"More forest?" Quinn practically croaked.

"Don't worry," Jared said. "It's too small to house any more monsters."

True to his word, as the two followed Surina out of the small city and into the forest, nothing unusual stirred in the bushes and trees they passed.

They soon reached the clearing where the Temple of Artemis stood erect, proudly displaying the same familiar stone columns and arches Quinn had seen at the Temple of Apollo. But while the Apollo temple kept unwanted visitors out with a moat, the path to the Artemis temple appeared unhindered by any obstacles.

Flagstones were embedded in the ground, creating a straight line across the clearing leading to the temple steps. Lined up on either side of the path were four daunting statues. To their right perched a statue of an eagle, its wings wide open, looking as if it was about to snatch up its next meal. Behind it was the figure of a female archer, her bow and arrow poised ready to fire. To their left, a stone stag reared up on its hind legs as if attempting to fend off an attacker, while the statue of the bear behind it also stood on its hind legs with its claw poised to strike.

Jared walked toward the temple, unperturbed by the threatening sculptures around them. Quinn wandered in behind him, his pace much slower as he turned back to Surina.

"So, what gives?" he asked.

"What do you mean?" she replied.

"Most places that we've been to have needed a password or identification to get in, but not this place. Do they not have any safeguards?"

"You're looking at them," the dark-haired woman said, pointing to the stone sculptures. "They can see us."

"The Magi?"

"No, the statues."

"The statues?" Quinn said, some skepticism sneaking into his tone. *Well I suppose I've seen stranger.*

Surina grinned as they walked along the path. "Artemis is one of the most suspicious gods, being a protector goddess and all. She wasn't just worried about her own safety but also for those under her care."

"Her followers," Quinn supplied.

Surina nodded. "The statues don't just *see* us, they see *into* us. Anyone with malicious intentions toward the occupants of the temple will have to deal with them before they even think of getting inside."

"You mean, they come to life?"

"Just like *Night at the Museum*," Jared chimed in.

Gazing up at the towering statues that seemed to leer down at them, Quinn suppressed a shudder at the thought of being trampled under stone. As the group passed underneath them, the eyes of the stone figures appeared to follow their movements.

As Surina led Jared and Quinn toward the temple's large doors, the doors dragged open, as if pushed by invisible servants. Quinn noted that their arrival had been anticipated, if the temple initiates who lined the great hall as they entered were any indication. Every acolyte—whether human, centaur, faun, or nymph—wore indigo blue cloaks. No one approached Surina's group, however, even as their hosts whispered to one another in small groups.

While the layout of the Artemis temple was similar in terms of infrastructure to the Solar Temple, the large display of the solar system was absent, as were the inclined steps that led to the Apollytes' observation deck. Instead, the Lunar Temple had a wraparound second level that could be reached by a pair of winding staircases at the back corners of the hall. Initiates leaned over the railing of the second floor to catch a glimpse of their visitors.

The back wall beneath the railing that drew Quinn's attention. Jutting out from the wall was a semicircular pond, encased by a three-foot-tall wall. But it was the engraved image on the stone above it that was striking.

The carving was set in the image of a beautiful and fierce-looking woman holding a bow and arrow. Surrounding her were animals of all species, along with two children. Farther above this tableau, shapes depicting the stages of the waxing and waning moon had been carved in an arch across a painted sky. And at the centre, where the full moon was placed, shone a crystal like stone, unlike anything Quinn had ever seen, yet something was oddly familiar about it.

Polaris.

Quinn gazed up at the Star in wonder as the sea of onlookers parted. The high priestess, an elderly woman in grey robes, approached the trio. Everything about the woman radiated serenity, from her warm brown eyes to her silver hair that fell braided over her shoulder. As she looked upon Jared, Surina, and Quinn, her thinned lips turned up into a gentle smile.

"My lords," she greeted Jared and Quinn with a slight bow. "Surina," she said, her fondness for the woman standing in front of her evident to everyone in the entrance hall.

"High Priestess Edelias," Surina replied with a bow of her own.

Behind Edelias stood another woman, also clad in grey robes. Her black hair was closely cropped to her head in a pixie cut, accentuating her pointed, fae features. She watched the exchange between the high priestess and visitors with a knowing grin.

"It's good to see you all," the elder woman said sincerely. "You remember Sylvia," she said, facing Surina and gesturing to the short-haired woman behind her.

"Of course," Surina nodded, before turning to the woman in question. "A priestess already?"

"Instructor, actually," Sylvia corrected.

"You always did have to be the best," Surina said, more cheerfully than Quinn would have believed possible, coming from her.

"It really is good to see you, Surina," the instructor said as she bowed once more to the three visitors. "I'm glad you all could come, though I had hoped that it would be under better circumstances."

"Then you know why we're here?" Jared asked.

"Because that imbecile Reeves couldn't protect Vega, and so has pointed the finger at us," Edelias jumped in, irritation shot throughout her tone. "And to think, just over two months ago, they were accused of the same crime by the Temple of Demeter," she huffed. "Yes, I'm well aware of the situation. Lord Moirai has been kind enough to keep us in the loop since the first robbery. We were told that the three of you would arrive soon. You have our permission to search the grounds. I guarantee the only Star you find here will be Polaris."

"Thank you, but I want you to know we are not here to judge. While we need to do a routine search, we are also here to help protect Polaris," Surina assured.

The high priestess tilted her head in thanks. "Of course. I'll show you the grounds, and from there, you can continue your search."

"Sounds like a good idea, but I doubt the place has changed a lot since I was last here. I'll just begin my search on the lower east wing, if that's okay," Surina replied.

"Of course, you go ahead. We'll meet back in my study in time for supper."

Surina nodded in agreement. "See you guys later," she said with a small wave of her hand.

She slipped away into one of the passageways, the eyes of almost every initiate and magi on her.

"Don't you all have something better to do?" Sylvia called sternly to the onlookers.

Hearing their instructor, the temple followers were quick to disperse, rushing off to train, study, or just avoid milling around. Quinn watched in amusement as Sylvia went about wrangling up stragglers, practically frog-marching them out of the main hall.

⚗

Jared and Quinn followed the priestess all over the west wing of the temple, though Edelias allowed them to peruse each area to their hearts' content.

Quinn found that he was both relieved and disappointed when neither he nor Jared could find anything indicating that the Lunar magi had taken Vega. He briefly wondered if Surina had found anything of note in the east wing, where the archives, armoury, and gymnasium were.

Finally being able to jump headfirst into this investigation seemed to light a fire underneath Quinn. Getting to look about the temple satisfied his curiosity in the best way. It was like scratching an itch that had bothered him for ages. Quinn couldn't help but smile as he searched, yet he could sense curious eyes boring into his back. Whenever he looked up from the object he was inspecting, he would see the flutter of indigo cloaks as his audience would rush out of sight.

"You'll have to excuse them," the high priestess said, each time Quinn's onlookers turned tail and fled. "We haven't had a god visit our temple since Lord Ares came to give a battle demonstration several years ago."

Despite Edelias' assurances of her temple's general curiosity, Quinn really couldn't fathom how the temple initiates and magi justified spying on them so relentlessly.

Actually, that was only half true. He figured that the female followers, along with a few of the male ones, were enchanted by the handsome Death God. He couldn't blame them for whispering excitedly to one another whenever Jared passed by, as he found himself also shooting glances over at the other man. In some ways, Jared was like gravity, his charisma and good looks just naturally drew others to him.

Quinn, in comparison, saw himself as fairly ordinary. While at an above average height, he'd never had an impressive build, having always been on the wiry side. He was also in need of a haircut, he noted, as his floppy blond hair fell once more into his face. Annoyed, he blew it upward and away from his eyes. What exactly did these people find so fascinating about him?

He understood that to them he was considered royalty, but he still wasn't much to look at when put next to a looker like Jared. And perhaps that was it; that was his magnetic effect upon the temple's acolytes—the fact that someone ordinary-looking had a hidden power that people rallied around.

He wondered, not for the first time, if there was still a temple dedicated to Athena. He knew that the Parthenon had been dedicated to Athena, but he doubted that the structure remained in the First Realm. Quinn found that he still distanced himself from his previous incarnations. No matter how he tried to look at it, he could not reconcile that he and the goddess' soul that garnered him such respect from strangers were one and the same.

Now, if someone had told Quinn that Surina was actually the reincarnation of Athena, that would have been a different story. She had an aura around her that demanded respect, which was probably why High Priest Reeves' behaviour toward her had irked Quinn so much.

Surina's reception here at the Lunar Temple had been very different from their welcome at the Apollyte temple, and while there was still some wariness toward their little group of travellers from the initiates and Magi, a sense of awe was evident in their keen interest toward Surina. Quinn had a nagging feeling that it was more than just her being a descendant of Artemis, especially if Surina's interactions with Edelias and Sylvia were anything to go by.

"So, what gives with Surina?" he suddenly asked Jared as the two of them searched through the second level of the temple library.

Jared poked his head out from under a desk he was checking for hidden panels. "What do you mean?"

"I'm talking about that little scene back there with her and the high priestess."

"They know each other," the Death God said with a shrug.

"Yeah, I got that. But how?"

"She's a descendant of Artemis—her dad probably brought her here once."

Quinn gave Jared an unamused glare. "It's more than that. Don't treat me like I'm an idiot. She's a magi here, isn't she?"

"It's really not my place to say." The Death God sighed.

Quinn propped his hands on his hips in a childish display of frustration. "What's the big deal? Why can't you tell me? Is there some sort of rule that while you're a magi for one temple, you can't help another? She's a Lunar magi or she's not, it's that simple."

"Well, she's not. Not anymore."

Quinn's irritated features softened as he realized that he had struck upon a sensitive topic. "What happened?"

Jared sighed, "I don't really know all the details, and I've said too much already. If you want to ask her, that's your business, but keep me out of it."

The weary tone with which the other man addressed him made Quinn feel a little sheepish for being so nosy, but once presented with a mystery, he knew he always had to follow his instincts to the bitter end.

Despite his burning curiosity, Quinn let the subject drop, turning his attention back to the bookcase he was inspecting.

He skimmed over the books on the shelf, some in English, but many more were in Latin, Greek, and a couple in Hindi. Of the ones he could read, all of them displayed interesting titles that made Quinn's fingers itch to turn their pages, such as, *One with the Bow: An Archer's Practical Guide; Daimon Lore: The Undefined Race; The High Priests and Priestesses of the Temple of Artemis, 1723–1837;* and *Masks of the Hunter: The Early Incarnations of Artemis.*

Yet one title caused him to halt in his tracks: *Lunar Tracking, Spellworks, and Charms.*

Quinn plucked the book from the ledge and flipped through the pages, stopping on a few passages that caught his attention.

Mark of the Moon: When placed on an object, creature, or person, this mark acts as a homing device, allowing the caster to follow the marked

G.E. White

object or individual wherever they go within the same realm.

Quinn gasped. *Perhaps one of the magi could mark Polaris and trace it back to whoever had taken the other pieces!* However, the following notation dissuaded him of that idea:

Please note that this spell has no effect on magical artifacts or enchanted individuals due to the Magical Interference Principle (MIP). More clarity on MIP can be found in Priest Byron's work, God Magic: Principles and Limitations.

Quinn curled his lip. *Okay, scratch that.* He scanned further down the page, to where an outline of a wolf was scribbled beside another passage:

Lupine Familiar: This magically created Familiar is specially designed to assist in detecting and tracking other creatures. A successfully engineered Lupine Familiar should possess a keen sense of smell that will allow it to follow a particular scent. However, this is the extent of use for the Familiar, as it holds no solid form with which to be used as a weapon.

The next paragraph detailed the creation of the spectral blood-hound, and though the information was interesting, it was not very useful to Quinn. Though he knew he should be focused on finding Polaris, it was his curiosity concerning Surina's place within the Lunar Temple that continued to nag at him.

It was possible that her time here was documented among these shelves, but as he glanced about at the packed, ceiling-high book-shelves lining every wall, Quinn knew he would not have the time to indulge his interest. If he wanted to learn more about Surina's life as a Magi, the only person he could ask was the demigod herself.

CHAPTER TWENTY-TWO

AFTER LONG HOURS of searching for any clue that might lead them to the other pieces of the North Star, all three investigators came up empty-handed. The only thing of any interest they had come across was an escape tunnel, accessible from the kitchen. Quinn and Jared had followed it, only to discover it led to the woods behind the temple. Furthermore, it was apparent that no one had used the tunnel in years, as Quinn discovered when he'd had to rip up some old roots in order to open the trap door.

Quinn, Jared, and Surina, along with High Priestess Edelias, took their dinner in the elderly woman's study, where she regaled them with stories of Surina's youth.

"You should have seen her the first time she came here—all sharp elbows and knobby knees. Braces, too, if I remember correctly."

"I was twelve," Surina said defensively.

"But then, most of the other initiates were more preoccupied with the blindfold she wore," Edelias continued, as if she hadn't heard the younger woman. "They all thought she was blind, but they soon learned that blindfolded or not, she was easily the best of our new initiates."

"So, she did actually train here," Quinn confirmed. "To be a Lunar Magi, I mean."

Surina cleared her throat awkwardly at Edelias' praise. "Yes, I was a Lunar Magi. It's really not that interesting," she said, turning to the high priestess. "They don't want to be bored with my childhood stories."

"Actually, I'd be very interested in hearing more about you. Jared only mentioned she'd been a Magi, but not much else," Quinn said brightly.

Jared smirked into his glass of wine, pointedly ignoring the scowl Surina shot him from across the table.

"Yes, she was a Magi. One of the best, as I recall. But it took her a while to learn how to work well with others. Almost cost her a spot in the House of Gemini," the high priestess said, a kind smile lighting up her face.

"She still has trouble with that," Jared quipped.

"Hey, if I can work with a peacock like you, I can work with anyone," Surina replied.

"That might be true now, Surina, but I distinctly remember a gangly young initiate who quite enjoyed terrorizing her schoolmates," Edelias commented.

Surina paused the slicing of her potato, wagging her knife toward the priestess as she spoke. "They *let* themselves be terrorized. Half of the things they feared me for were things they had made up themselves. They started the rumour that I was a *lamiae,* so you can bet that I was going to run with that and make them believe it."

"Lamiae?" Quinn asked.

"A vampire, of sorts," Jared explained.

"Cool." Quinn turned to Surina. "So how did you pull that one off? You didn't bite anyone, did you?"

"Just Orpheon and Cybella, but they had it coming," Surina replied with a smirk.

"As I recall, they refused to leave the temple for two weeks, thinking they had been turned," the older woman said with a disapproving look toward her former initiate.

"Oh yeah," Surina said, her voice radiating with malicious glee. "Well, they should have thought of that before they hacked off most of my hair. Also, if they'd paid attention in your lectures on dark creatures, they would have known you can't be turned into a lamiae—you have to be born one."

Edelias shook her head. "I should have known that adding that human fiction to the library was a mistake."

"I don't know about that. I mean, it was in the fiction section. They should have realized the human interpretations of lamiae are based on half-remembered truths or just complete fantasy. Besides, I happen to like some human fiction. I thought that *The Count of Monte Cristo* was a very compelling story."

Quinn almost jumped in to ask how Surina's time as a Lunar magi came to an end, but a glance from Jared told him that now was not the time. The young man quashed his curiosity, shoving another spoonful of peas into his mouth, pleased that they weren't cold for once.

As the meal continued, it was Jared who brought the discussion back to the situation at hand.

"Though I'm pretty certain you and your Lunar magi are not responsible for the theft at the Temple of Apollo, the fact of the matter is, there is still a thief out there. And if we don't catch them and retrieve Thuban and Vega, we're going to have a very bloody situation on our hands."

Edelias' eyes narrowed in confusion. "What do you mean?"

Surina sighed. "If we can't find the culprit and the stolen pieces of the Star, the Solar magi are going to march on the Temple of Artemis, declaring war in order to get it back."

"War? I knew Reeves blamed us for the theft, but I thought he had more sense than to attack us—especially with the charges being laid against his own temple. You must know we don't have it," the elder urged Surina.

"I know," the younger woman assured.

Jared steepled his fingers in thought. "By themselves, the pieces of the Star aren't of much use."

Brought back to the private conversation he'd had with Sebastien, Quinn bit the inside of his cheek, determined not to say anything. As far as he knew, there was no point in mentioning the Star's other role.

"Only when the three pieces are forged back together can a person make a wish. The break-ins at the Temples of Demeter and Apollo were a couple of months apart, but I don't think our thief is going to wait too long this time to strike again," Jared said heavily.

"Why do you think that?" Quinn had a hunch, but he needed to hear it from Jared himself.

"Because he knows we know about him, or at least know about the burglary. Whoever he is, he's done a good job of covering his tracks and creating confusion by using various clothing from the different temples. But now that we're aware of the thefts, he doesn't want to give us the time to improve the security around the last piece, or for us to hide it. He'll strike soon, probably in the next day or two."

Surina smiled softly behind her napkin. "You think we can catch him in the act."

"That's the idea," Jared confirmed. "As long as we have at least one of us on guard for the next few nights, we're bound to see him—if not outright catch him."

"Sounds like a half-decent plan," Surina agreed. "And to be honest, at this point, I don't know what else we can do. I would suggest swapping Polaris for a replica, but we don't have time to make one."

Quinn was already starting to slide down in his chair from exhaustion. How much longer would these conversations take? Only half aware from sleepiness, he agreed to take the second watch alongside Surina.

The four continued to eat, the calm silence broken only by the polite chatter between Surina and Edelias as the two women tried to fit four years' worth of catching up into hours. Quinn found his gaze once again drawn to Jared, who had been oddly quiet since the plan for the night had been formed. He was puzzled to see a sad expression on Jared's face as he looked intently at the high priestess. Quinn watched as the latter gestured wildly with her hands, describing a prank one of the initiates had pulled during dinner one night. It pained Quinn to see such a look on the other man's face. *What was it that made Jared look so morose?*

୧୭

As night fell, the three of them camped out in front of Polaris while several magi stood guard on the walkways above.

Although they had been given bedding to lessen the chill of the stone floor they had to sleep on, Surina grumbled about her frozen hands, rubbing them together vigorously to remove some of the redness they had accumulated in the cold. Growing up in cramped houses for most of his life, and being used to his fair share of uncomfortable beds, Quinn quickly slipped into an uneasy sleep.

୧୭

Dragged through the dark and unrecognizable streets of his dream, Quinn felt himself watch the strange scene in vivid detail, almost as if from above. The face and figure of the man who tugged his child self through the streets of the city were clear as day, and the fingers curling around Quinn's small hand were long and thin, almost skeletal. His guide wasn't terribly tall. A couple of inches short of six feet maybe, but his face, like the rest of his body, was gaunt and pale, as if ill or half starved. The man's mousy blond hair fell lankly against his skull, but his slightly sunken blue eyes, hidden behind his rectangular-framed glasses, were kind and determined.

Quinn's heart swelled as he felt the absolute trust his child self directed toward this man, but he still had no idea who he was.

As the dream always unfolded, the sound of dogs barking in the distance spurred Quinn and his guide onto the bridge. As their dream selves always were, they quickly found themselves cornered by their pursuer and his dog. While the features of the man in front of him were still murky in the dim light, one thing was painfully clear to Quinn: their hunter was no adult. Lanky and awkward, the boy must have just hit puberty.

But the most striking change in Quinn's dream this time was the presence of another being. While his sickly looking guardian conversed with the silent boy, Quinn's eyes were drawn to a woman, neither young nor old, who stood just over the boy's shoulder.

Quinn took in her features, still surprised that he had not noticed her before. Wispy white-blonde hair fell in long curtains about her face. She stood about a foot taller than the young man in front of her. However, it was her eyes that truly captured Quinn's attention, both sad and empty, yet containing the most vibrant colours of orange and purple—a sunset, perhaps, before the day falls into darkness.

He peered up at her as she stared back at him, silent and unmoving. His attention was soon drawn elsewhere as his guardian knelt down in front of him and placed a loving kiss on his brow.

Quinn clenched his hands, becoming aware once again of the plush stuffed animal held in his left hand. He briefly glanced down at the creature and, though it was hard to tell in the dark, he could see that it was a bird of some sort—white and yellow. A goose, perhaps?

The child Quinn had once been was looking up at the man, whose eyes swam with tears of relief and sadness as a question entered his mind: *Had this man been my father?*

He opened his mouth to ask but suddenly found himself lifted over the rails of the bridge, plummeting toward the cold waters below.

☙

Quinn's eyes snapped open as he felt a hand on his shoulder, gently shaking him into consciousness.

Glancing upward, he saw the smooth, dark lenses of Surina's glasses staring back at him—so different from the eyes of the woman in his dream.

Though he had never seen Surina's eyes, Quinn knew that she couldn't have been the one in his dream; her hair was the wrong colour and texture. Quinn shook his head free from his lingering theories just in time to see Jared hunker down into his own bedding for the remainder of the night.

"Our turn?" Quinn yawned.

"Unfortunately," Surina replied, completely alert.

She sat on the edge of the fountain, fiddling with her protean watch, transforming it one moment into a sword, the next a mace, before finally stopping on a bow. She tested the strength of the weapon as she drew the string back toward her chest, and an arrow materialized out of thin air.

"Obviously, nothing happened," Quinn mused aloud, as if to reassure himself.

"Jared said his shift was painfully dull." Surina rolled her eyes, obviously displeased with Jared's report.

Her comment was punctuated by a soft snore from the Death God.

"I hate people who can do that," she grumbled, relaxing the string of the bow and causing the arrow to disappear. "Fall asleep at the drop of a hat."

"Did you not sleep well?" Quinn asked.

Surina laid her bow across her lap. "I slept okay, I guess. What about you? You were mumbling in your sleep."

Quinn stood and slowly meandered over to sit a few feet away from Surina at the pool's edge. "I keep having this dream," he explained. "It's always the same, but I'm pretty sure that the events in it actually happened."

"And?" she prodded.

"I don't know anyone there. There's a sickly-looking man, who I think I might be related to, and the two of us are being chased by a shrouded figure and dogs. I think the person chasing us has a pack of dogs."

Surina pursed her lips in thought. "What do they look like?"

"I don't know, the hooded person's features are always fuzzy. As for the dogs, I only ever see one, but I can never make out what kind. But there is definitely more than one as I can hear them. Every time, we all end up on a bridge, but tonight, there was someone else there, a woman. Her hair was so blonde it was almost white, and her eyes were orange and purple. I've never seen eyes like that."

Surina frowned. "I have."

"You have?" Quinn asked in disbelief.

She nodded. "You're right, orange and purple are very peculiar colours for eyes. And only one person has ever been known to have them."

"Who?"

"Mnemosyne. In this incarnation, she goes by the name Seraphina.

Human mythology says she's a Titan, but she's actually a lesser god. Her realm of dominion is memory."

"Memory," Quinn breathed, horror dawning in his eyes. "So she's the reason I have no memories before that time?"

"Yes, and no," Surina said, almost reluctantly, Quinn thought.

"What do you mean?"

"Well, first of all, we don't know for sure if that's exactly what happened. Mnemosyne doesn't just take someone's memory away for shits and giggles. If anyone truly understands the importance of memories, it would be her. She wouldn't take them unless she had a very good reason—or if someone above her rank asked her to."

Quinn hung his head and absently picked at the microscopic lint on his jeans. "So you think someone put her up to it?"

"Most likely," Surina said, glumly. "But perhaps she had a good reason."

"A good reason?" he hissed. "What reason could possibly give her the right to take away my past?"

"Some things are better left forgotten," Surina reasoned, the sorrowful tone of her voice not escaping Quinn's notice. In that moment, he felt his theories surrounding Surina's connection to the Temple of Artemis click into place: the way the initiates and magi would stop and stare; her familiarity with the other two temples; everyone's reluctance to mention something painfully obvious—a proverbial elephant in the room.

Something bad had happened when Surina had been a Lunar Magi. Something that left Surina an outcast among her peers. The High Priestess Edelias and Sylvia seemed to be the only people who weren't whispering behind the young woman's back.

Putting aside his own questions about Mnemosyne and whoever might have ordered his memories erased, Quinn focused on the woman in front of him—the one who had pulled him into this world in the first place. Glancing at her face, which was still partly obscured by her glasses, he realized he didn't really know anything about her. In fact, he really didn't know *any* of the people he had been spending the past few days with. The linear life plan he had tentatively laid out before she had entered his life was a distant memory. And any thoughts of him trying to lead a quiet life inside the walls of the Cedar Hills Mental Health Facility were now long gone.

Surina, Carter, Sebastien, Leo, Jared, and his family—all of these people—they were what his life would be from now on. They would become his friends, perhaps even his family, and the least he could do was get to know them.

"You said that some things are best left forgotten. You're talking about your time here?" he asked Surina, surprised at his boldness.

"What do you mean?" she returned defensively.

Keeping his voice low so that the guards above wouldn't hear them, he pressed on, "You're a Lunar Magi."

Surina fiddled with the bow in her hands and shook her head. "Not anymore."

"But you were at one point, so what happened?"

She turned her head toward Polaris, glittering above them, and sighed.

"There was never a time that I didn't know about the gods and their role in the universe. My father was the Afghani son of an incarnation of Artemis, he died early in my childhood under questionable circumstances. He inherited some of her abilities and talents, which in turn, were passed on to me. But I never met my grandmother; she died before I was born."

"What about your mom?"

"My mother was…a difficult woman. Emotionally distant and constantly disappointed in me it seemed. I tried my best to make her proud of me, to be a good daughter, well behaved, listened to my tutors, worked hard, but it was never enough." Surina sniffed, surprising Quinn. He had thought her to be the best of them when it came to hiding her emotions. "I also had a sister of sorts. My mom had adopted her a long time before she met my dad. She was a lot older than me and had zero interest in me. Shortly after I hit puberty my mom shipped me off here. No hug or kiss goodbye, just a frigid note saying I was better suited here. I never saw her after that. So, for the next six years I lived and trained here. I didn't have many friends, so I focused on my studies and training: hunting, tracking, laying traps, Lunar magics, archery, swordplay, the languages of animals, the power of the moon—I learned it all. I thought that if I became a successful Lunar Magi, my mom would have to be proud of me. At first, I wrote to her every week, occasionally she wrote back. She didn't say much other than that she was glad things were going well for me. The sad thing was most of my letters were about how much I hated it here. It was obvious she wasn't reading the letters so I stopped writing. As I said, I didn't have any friends, really, but I grew to love the work."

She looked down at the bow in her lap before continuing. "By the time I was eighteen, I achieved the rank of magi. And even luckier for me, the Temples of Artemis, Apollo, and Demeter needed to fill the roles of the three houses' residents who had just retired. They held a tournament for magi from all three temples to compete for a spot in the Houses of Virgo, Leo, or Gemini. Over two hundred magi participated, only nine were chosen. I was one of them."

"I was so proud," Surina said softly, although her tone showed nothing of that emotion. "I was the new Lunar representative for the House of Gemini. I couldn't wait to tell my mother, but I should have realized it meant nothing to her."

Quinn leaned in, listening intently.

"Neither she nor my so-called sister came to my swearing-in ceremony. Nor did they answer any of my letters or calls. At this point I was an amazing tracker, and the House of Gemini specialized in investigating missing persons. So I took my knowledge and resources and did what I do best—I found them."

Her listener waited with bated breath. "And?"

"My sister immediately brushed me off and was gone. As for my mom, it was like she was looking right through me. She said I had done as well as I could, and though she had wanted more for me, she was starting to think that was out of my grasp. Like rising to the position I had was some sort of participant ribbon, instead of the honour that it was. I could see it in her eyes, she'd already washed her hands of me, so I returned the favour, turning my back on her and devoting myself to the House of Gemini. Haven't seen her since."

Surina's words hit Quinn like a blow to the gut. "I'm so sorry."

"Why? That woman has always been a terrible excuse for a mother, you had nothing to do with it."

"I know," Quinn said helplessly. "It's just…"

"It's what people say," she filled in.

Quinn bobbed his head in agreement, ashamed. "So, if you were so set on working in the House of Gemini, why did you leave?"

"That's a bit more complicated. I was a member of that house for over four years and had two of our best magi as my teammates. They were probably my best friends."

"What were they like?"

"Well, all of us were human, which some people found a bit odd. But then, all of us were descendants of our patron gods. First there was Victor Kurosawa, an Earthen magi from the Temple of Demeter. He was as smart as they come, always thought through everything he said and did and had this almost fanatical sense of justice. Out of the three of us, he was the most level-headed. I had some unresolved anger issues at the time, but he always kept me in line. As for our Solar Magi, he was something else. I don't think I've met anyone as perpetually happy and pleasant as Lear Reeves."

Quinn felt a thread of unease coil in his chest. "Reeves? You can't mean…"

"High Priest Reeves' younger brother," Surina filled in.

"Lear's pleasant demeanour evidently isn't a family trait," Quinn observed dryly.

Surina chuckled darkly. "While I'll admit that Orion has a rod up his butt, he wasn't always that hostile toward me. He never really liked me, but at least he respected me back then."

Quinn blinked in confusion but said nothing more, silently urging his companion to elaborate upon her story.

"During a job in the First Realm, Lear was hurt badly. We were cut off from any support, and Victor didn't have the ingredients needed to treat him. He couldn't save him, but I could. Too bad I screwed up."

"What do you mean?" Quinn pressed.

"I made a mistake in attempting to heal Lear, and I killed him."

"You mean, you couldn't save him."

Surina shook her head. "He would have died if we had done nothing, but what I did killed him faster."

Quinn sat in stunned silence.

It had been a mistake; she had said so herself. She hadn't meant to kill Lear; she was trying to help him. The whole thing had been an accident, he told himself. But then, why did Surina look so guilty?

"After that, I left the House of Gemini and resigned as a Lunar Magi. Victor returned to the Temple of Demeter and became an instructor there. He said he never blamed me for what happened, but after a few months, he stopped contacting me. Since then, the House of Gemini has been unrepresented. Some people think it's cursed."

Quinn tucked a stray strand of hair away from his face as he mulled over Surina's story. He knew something of the pain that could come from a single mistake. The incident at the library had suddenly robbed him of his freedom and the future he had planned for himself. Yet in the end, it had led him to the life that he lived now—a life where he got to see and experience things that most people could only imagine, a life where he may even get the family

G.E. White

he so desperately wanted.

Looking back at Surina's story, he supposed that he didn't have a right to compare his misfortune to her tragedy. His situation had turned out all right in the end, while Surina's had ended with one friend dead, another no longer speaking to her, and her own belief that she was responsible for the whole thing.

His thoughts brought Quinn back to the question he had had before: *What exactly was this mistake that had led to Lear's death?*

He opened his mouth to ask, when Surina suddenly threw her hand up, gesturing for silence. "Do you feel that?" she whispered.

Quinn paused, his eyes drifting down to his arm, where the fine blond hairs prickled as they began to stand on end.

CHAPTER TWENTY-THREE

THE ARRIVAL OF the intruder was neither flashy, nor abrasive. They were just suddenly *there,* dressed in the traditional green cloak of an Earthen Magi. The thief clung, spider-like, to the side of the relief overhang above the pool, using a crowbar-like instrument to pry Polaris out of its fixture.

Their viper-quick movements left little time for Surina to react. By the time she was able to conjure, draw, and release an arrow, the Star was already in the thief's hands.

But the burglar was not quick enough to dodge Surina's arrow. A sharp cry came from the thief's mouth as the projectile tore through the edge of their left bicep and the crowbar slipped from their fingers.

"Drop it!" Surina commanded as the thief leapt to the floor with Polaris tucked under their injured arm. The commotion roused Jared from his slumber, and in what seemed like a fraction of a second, he scrambled to his feet and summoned his scythe.

The thief shrunk backward as both Jared and Surina directed their weapons toward them. Though he still wielded Surina's old dagger, Quinn stood back from the confrontation, not wanting to get in the way of his highly skilled companions. He noted with disappointment that, despite the fact the thief stood directly in front of him, their identity remained a mystery—the large cloak they wore to conceal their body hid both their stature and gender, while their hood and scarf-like mask shielded the majority of their face.

During the standoff, the high priestess, accompanied by several guards, rushed into the hall and blocked all visible exits. Edelias stepped past Quinn and the others to address the trapped criminal.

"Stand down. There is nowhere for you to go."

The thief glanced about, seeing for themselves how precarious their situation was. Still clutching the Star under their left arm, the shrouded figure slowly raised their right hand in a gesture of surrender.

"Lower your weapons," Edelias said sharply to Jared and Surina.

"You can't be serious," Surina protested.

"I will *not* have unnecessary bloodshed in this temple," the high priestess hissed. Turning a pleading look toward Jared, she entreated him firmly. "Please, Lord Thanatos? I'm sure you'll get more information out of a live body than a dead one."

"That's your opinion," Jared sniped, even as he began to lower his scythe.

Surina followed the priestess' instruction as well, though the jutting line of her chin and the tightness of her lips betrayed her reluctance to do so.

Once the threat of the thief's previously imminent death was defused, Edelias turned to the crouching burglar, commanding their attention. "Now, who are you?"

For a moment, in which neither Edelias nor the cornered figure attempted to move, there was no answer. Then the thief held up a single finger, in a gesture used when asking for time. Slowly opening one side of their cloak, they displayed a rolled-up parchment, motioning as if they were in the process of removing it from their pocket.

The high priestess nodded her consent and stepped closer to receive the document.

Quinn scrutinized the scene but found his eyes drawn to the sight of metal encircling the thief's left wrist—a bracelet, maybe, or perhaps a watch. Either way, there was something about it that aroused his suspicion.

The thief held out the scroll toward Edelias, the way a professor might present a student with a diploma, with the curled end of the paper offered first.

As the glint of sharpened metal flashed, Quinn watched in horror as the thief's hand suddenly surged forward, thrusting the rolled parchment and the small slim dagger it concealed into Edelias' chest.

Quinn opened his mouth in anguish, but it was too late. Edelias tumbled backward from the thief, the blade protruding between her ribs.

"No!" cried Surina, dragging most of the attention away from the thief toward the temple's fallen leader. While the other initiates focused on the wounded woman, Quinn turned his head toward the attacker and was able to catch a glimpse of the thief fiddling with the cuff on their left arm. A second later, they and the Polaris Star snapped out of sight, disappearing as silently as they had arrived.

Quinn stood stock-still, his mind unable to process what was happening before him as his gaze moved to the crumpled high priestess, lying as if she was a rag doll a child had tossed to the ground. Edelias was limp, her life's blood staining her silver robes and hair a vibrant red. Her brown eyes seemingly pleaded for some understanding as to how this had happened.

Surina rushed to the high priestess' side, her bow lying forgotten on the floor where she dropped it. Her hands trembled as they hovered over her mentor's body, whose breath came to a sudden shuddering halt.

The magi who had been on patrol duty were frozen in shock and made no move to rush to the priestess' side. Instead, it was Jared who broke the stillness, his feet nearly silent on the marble floor as he approached Edelias' body.

Quinn felt a quiver of hope as his companion crouched down beside Edelias. Jared was the God of Death—Quinn was positive that if anyone could recall the high priestess' soul, it would be him. He watched in anticipation as Jared placed his hand on the woman's face, the former's eyes closed in concentration. Quinn waited breathlessly to see the woman's fingers twitch, or for her eyes to clear and blink back into life. But there was no sound, save for the young man's sudden choked exhalation of the breath he had been holding as Jared closed Edelias' eyes forever. The God of Death reached into his pocket and pulled out two golden coins, placing one on each of the corpse's eyelids.

Jared suddenly stood, facing the onlookers, but his expression did not betray any sadness: resignation, perhaps, or a bone-deep weariness. It was then that Sylvia, followed by several other magi, rushed into the hall from one of the side corridors, skidding to a stop as they took in the scene before them. Sylvia's mouth gaped open in shock and disbelief at the sight of her fallen mentor as she locked her eyes upon Jared, who simply shook his head.

"I'm sorry," he said, turning and walking briskly from the hall into one of the corridors, the other magi parting for him as if he were Moses and they were the Red Sea. Jared's words awoke the crowd from their stupor as they scrambled into motion, crowding around the fallen high priestess.

Quinn knew that there was nothing he could do to alleviate the temple's grief, but anger and confusion coursed through him—he was certain that Jared could have saved her, and he had done nothing! Making a split-second decision, Quinn fled the scene, chasing after the Death God.

Jared hadn't gone very far—just far enough to be alone, having escaped the corridor and up a flight of stairs leading to a balcony overlooking the surrounding forest. Quinn marched up to his friend, fists clenched in the anger he barely held at bay.

Sensing his presence, the God of Death turned to him, his face a mask of icy irritation. "Out with it. Say what you're here to say."

The note of accusation in Jared's words only helped flame the hurt and sadness welling up inside him. "What is *wrong* with you?" Quinn hissed. "Why didn't you help her?"

"There was nothing I could do."

"The hell there wasn't! You're the Grim Reaper—the God of Death! If anyone could have saved her, it was you! You stabilized me after Gloria's program, you saved me. I'm sure they could have healed her if you had just given her the chance."

Jared looked away from Quinn, his expression grim. "It's not the same."

"How?! How is it not the same? Is it because I'm a god and she's not? As if her life means less than mine?" Quinn couldn't keep the hurt out of his words. Quinn felt that he knew Jared to be better than that. *Could I have misjudged him?*

The older man gritted his teeth, as if he was trying to hold something back. "It has nothing to do with her status or yours. It's not the same because it wasn't your time, but it was hers."

Quinn recoiled, as if he had been struck by a fist, his observations from earlier that evening finally making sense. "You knew. Tonight, at dinner, you kept staring at her. You knew, and you didn't warn her?"

Whipping around to face Quinn, Jared's expression was clouded

G.E. White

with a heart-wrenching despair. "Warn her? What good would that have done? For all I knew at the time, she was to die in her sleep. Who was I to tell her that her time was up? To let her last few hours be spent agonizing about how little time she had left and all the things she would leave unfinished?"

Quinn's expression softened slightly as the older man poured out his grief. "You could have changed it," he said weakly.

"No, I couldn't have. I can't just reverse death when I feel like it," Jared replied sternly. "These powers we have are not here for our own convenience. They're a responsibility. The sooner you learn that, the better."

Quinn lowered his head in contrition as Jared swept past him and back down the stairs. The second the other man had exited, the strength in Quinn's legs gave out and he collapsed to a seated position on the floor. Quinn's eyes began to burn, but he refused to let his tears fall as he sat on the cold stone floor, cradling his head in his hands.

C/Ɔ

For the rest of the night, sleep eluded Quinn. He spent the next hour on the ground, but when his thoughts began to overwhelm him, he rose and used the remaining hours before dawn to roam the halls. The few magi and initiates he stumbled across in his wanderings gave him plenty of space, as if they sensed his desire for solitude. Guilt clouded his thoughts as he tried to distance himself from Jared's words.

During the short time he had known about his role as a god, Quinn had believed that this was his chance to truly make a difference in the world. But witnessing Jared's inability to change something he supposedly had control of shook his confidence. If Jared was powerless in that situation, what hope did Quinn have of being any help to people who needed him?

Worse still for Quinn was the sinking feeling that he had personally wounded Jared, and there seemed to be no way he could rectify the situation. While he had been resolute in his plans to just remain friends with Jared, he couldn't deny that he was warming to the idea of getting to know the man on a more intimate level. But then he had to go and be a self-righteous idiot, spewing bullshit about things he knew nothing about. His heart ached thinking that he had sabotaged any possibility of the two getting closer.

On the other hand, he also had Surina to consider. The woman had been candid with him tonight, something that he was sure was a rarity. Her tale about her abandonment from her own mother and sister struck a chord with Quinn. She, like him, had been alone. Yet her bond with Edelias was genuine—probably the closest thing Surina had to a loving maternal figure. But now she was gone, he couldn't begin to know how to offer comfort to Surina.

Quinn's frantic wandering led him back to the library and toward the books that had always soothed his troubled mind. Walking his fingers along their spines, he was about to give up on finding a story to bury himself in when the words on a leather-bound tome jumped out at him: *The Gods: Their Symbols, Signs, and Realms of Power.*

Pulling the book from the shelf, Quinn turned his back to the bookcase and slid down to the floor. He carefully pulled back the book's heavy cover and flipped past the table of contents to the first chapter, skimming over the introductory paragraph but pausing to look at a table listing the gods and their symbols.

According to the text, most gods had more than one animal they were associated with. While his powerful brain absorbed all of the information before him, Quinn took a moment to note some of the key gods he knew about.

Apollo was most often associated with a swan, but also had connections with the raven, mouse, and wolf. As he already knew, Artemis' chief animal was the stag, while her other symbols were also part of the hunt—animals such as the bear, wild boar, and quail.

Quinn was surprised to note that he himself only had two animal symbols associated with Athena: the first being the owl; the second, the crow. Thanatos also had a winged creature for his symbol: the butterfly. The delicate insect's role as a sigil of the God of Death seemed appropriate to Quinn. Not only were butterflies a symbol of beauty, which Jared had in spades, they were also associated with transformation. In the philosophy texts he had read over the years, death and transformation were often grouped together. Many held onto the idea that death was not the end, but like a caterpillar's metamorphosis, a transformation into something else. Farther down the table, Demeter was listed as having a gecko, pig, and a garden snake as her icons.

The mention of Demeter's snake icon piqued Quinn's curiosity. As he recalled, the second shadow that had emerged from behind Surina in Erebus had been a snake. Was it possible that she, too, had a connection to Demeter? But Quinn distinctly remembered that the shadow behind Surina had a hood, similar to a cobra rather than a garden snake.

Moving from the table of animal symbols to the section discussing the gods' realms of influence, Quinn quickly turned the page over. Part of him wished to read further to find out just how much influence he himself had, but a stronger impulse suggested that he avoid the responsibility. He considered reading over a paragraph discussing Thanatos, to discover just what kind of power Jared had, but with the argument they had just had fresh in his mind, Quinn felt that skimming over Jared's gifts might be construed as an act of distrust. The sound of the breakfast bell tolling made the choice for him. Closing the book and placing it back on the shelf, Quinn trudged through the corridors to the mess hall.

The temple initiates and magi sat like shadows in their seats, picking away at their food. Sylvia—perhaps now High Priestess—sat at the head of the table, attempting to put on a brave face. Her expression, though calm, did not reach her eyes, which brimmed with worry and grief.

Surina's face was set in her ever-present mask of composure, though a trained eye might have noted the small quiver across her lips. Edelias' chair stood vacant at the centre of the head table, a testament to the treasured life lost only hours earlier.

Quinn briefly wondered what the temple had done with Edelias' body. There couldn't have been enough time for her to have been cremated or buried. Most likely, the high priestess would be given a plot in the cemetery behind the temple, but he doubted that he, Jared, and Surina would be able to stay around for the funeral.

Quinn slowed his pace as he approached the table, his eyes focused on the hunched, solemn figure mindlessly pushing his porridge around his bowl. He had been lucky enough to not run into Jared during the rest of the night, and at this point, he *still* could not for the life of him discern what to say to the Death God.

"Quinn! I was starting to worry," Surina called.

Her concerned tone only reminded Quinn that Jared wasn't the only one he didn't know what to say to. Even though he had only seen Surina and Edelias together for a day, he could tell they had been close.

"I didn't mean to worry you, I just..." his eyes travelled over Jared's form, noticing for the first time the other man's less-than-immaculate appearance. It seemed that he wasn't the only one who wasn't able to get some rest.

"I know, I was shocked too," Surina finished for him.

"So, what happens now?" Quinn asked.

"Well, there's not much point in sticking around here," Jared said from his end of the table, finally joining the conversation.

"What do you mean?"

The Death God refused to meet Quinn's gaze. "What I *mean* is that so far our presence hasn't helped much in this case." Jared stood, pushing the half-eaten bowl of porridge away from his body. "It's time to move on and maybe be of some use to other temples." With those words, Jared shouldered his way past Quinn, anger and defeat colouring his cheeks.

Quinn turned to follow him, but Surina's hand on his shoulder stopped him.

"Let him go. He won't go far without us, he's just frustrated."

Quinn nodded, knowing that it was more than simple frustration that had angered the other man. Just as he opened his mouth to tell Surina about their argument, a shrill sound, emanating from Surina's hip, warbled through the air. Sure enough, the demigod fished her ringing phone from her jacket.

"Hello? One second, Tyrell."

She pulled the device away from her ear and pressed the speakerphone button as Quinn huddled closer. "Okay, go ahead."

"Who else is listening?" Tyrell's deep, accented voice came through the speaker.

"Just myself and Quinn—uh, Lord Athena, that is."

"Really?" Tyrell replied.

"Yes. In fact, he was the one to notice your symbol on the bracelet I showed you," Surina said. "So, do you have any information for us?"

"Well, I'm not 100 percent sure. I would have to actually hold the cuff to be certain, but it appears that the materials used to make it were mine, although the cuff itself is not of my design."

"Do you know what the specific materials are?" Quinn asked.

"As a matter of fact, I do, Lord Athena."

"Quinn is fine," the young god assured Tyrell.

"All right, then, Quinn. Apparently, someone raided one of my storehouses, but they were very specific in what they took. The only things missing were some spare parts for the Phantasm."

At Tyrell's words, Quinn's mind flew back to the night before. Moments before the thief had appeared, both he and Surina had experienced the electric crackle that the guards at the Solar Temple had described. At the time, the sensation was oddly familiar, but he had dismissed the thought as the theft had escalated into murder.

Quinn suddenly realized where he had experienced that feeling before.

"Surina, give me the cuff."

Surina's brows rose above the frames of her glasses, but she complied, fishing the device from the bag at her feet. "What do you need that for?"

"I want to try something," Quinn answered, grabbing the cuff from her hand.

"Tyrell, I'll have to call you back," Surina said into the receiver. Without waiting for an answer, she pressed a button, ending the call.

Clutching the metal bracelet, Quinn jogged out of the dining hall, back to the scene of Edelias' murder, Surina following close behind him. Standing on the ledge, near the display where Polaris had once stood, Quinn slipped the cuff on his own wrist.

"What are you doing? Take that off!" Surina commanded.

"Sorry, you're just going to have to trust me on this one."

Surina leapt forward to pull him from the perch but found herself grasping thin air.

Quinn was gone.

CHAPTER TWENTY-FOUR

Quinn went from staring at Surina's concerned face to suddenly gazing at the ruins of ancient Ephesus. When he had turned the cuff's dial, he had felt the tingle of electricity in the air he associated with the Phantasm, followed by a momentary sensation of weightlessness, a feeling which soon dispersed as he landed in his new location.

In the distance, he could hear the low murmur of tourist voices as groups meandered along the stone walkways.

Only a single column remained from the temple he had been standing in only moments before. The ruins he now looked upon appeared to be somewhat off the tour's normal path, which gave Quinn the time to thoroughly inspect his surroundings. Already he could see that the dust below his feet had been disturbed by someone else's footprints, but what really confirmed Quinn's suspicion of his location being the thief's escape route was a splatter of recently dried blood accompanying the footprints disturbing the undergrowth.

"And right over this hill, we'll see the Temple of Artemis' remains," came the thickly accented voice of one of the tour guides.

Jolted from his investigation, Quinn scrambled to push his sleeve up to reveal the cuff. Turning the dial back to its original position, he again felt the now familiar sensation of electric voltage, followed by a moment of weightlessness as he suddenly found himself back in the First Realm temple.

Surina stood a few feet away, the tension in her body dissolving as she noticed him. Her relieved expression quickly gave way to anger as she stalked toward him, giving him a harsh shove. "Don't you ever do that again! What the hell were you thinking? You could've been killed," she shouted.

"I seriously doubt that," Quinn responded.

"Did you even have any idea what that thing could do?"

"I had a pretty good idea," he replied with a shrug. He really hadn't meant to worry her, but after seeing the thief work the device, he had assumed the cuff was used for transportation. However, the more he thought about it, he realized that his actions were hasty. The cuff could have delivered him straight into the thief's clutches.

"I swear, if you weren't under my protection, I'd kill you myself for pulling a stunt like that," Surina threatened him, though, from the worried tone in her voice, Quinn knew that she didn't truly mean it. "So what happened?" she asked, notably calming herself to better learn what information he had to convey.

"I figured out how our thief has been getting around. They've been using this," Quinn explained, holding up his arm to display the cuff.

"You're saying that whoever made *that* was able to use Tyrell's materials to create a teleporter?"

"Not exactly. I mean, technically, I didn't go anywhere."

"So, what happened?" she asked, impatience now evident in her tone.

"I switched realms. I figured it out when Tyrell mentioned the materials came from the Phantasm's spare parts," Quinn said. "You said it yourself, that the car was crafted from aetherum, in order to allow travel between the first two realms. So, all the thief had to do was get into the geographical position in the Second Realm where the Star would be in the First Realm, switch into the First Realm, grab the thing, and switch realms again to the Second."

As Quinn fleshed out his theory of the thief's escape, excitement and pride visibly radiated from him. He turned to Surina, hoping for some sort of praise or acknowledgement of his thoughts, but found that her expression was still troubled.

"What's wrong?" he asked.

"Hmm? Oh, it's not that I doubt you're right, it's just, at the moment, that information doesn't do us any good. By now, the thief could be halfway around the world—and in either of the two realms."

Quinn wilted slightly under Surina's reasoning before his face lit up with an idea. "But the Star won't do the thief any good either."

"What do you mean?"

"The Star's main purpose is to grant a wish, right? But it can only do that when it's whole."

"They need to put it back together," Surina finished, understanding slowly dawning on her features.

"And I'm guessing that's not an easy thing to do."

"Next to impossible, actually. I think I know who we're up against." She paused for a moment, calculating the next course of action. "Go get something to eat, then get Jared. We're going to be leaving soon."

Surina made a quick exit as she typed a number into her phone, leaving Quinn with the awkward task of collecting Jared. It was odd. Other than the first time they met, Quinn had never seen the Death God angry. Irritated, sure, but not angry. And of course, it didn't help that Jared's anger was directed at him.

But then, Surina *had* instructed him to eat first. Perhaps while he filled his belly, Quinn would figure out just how he could clear up the unpleasantness between Jared and himself.

☙

Jared stood in the doorway, looking into a room the setting sun had painted with an orange glow. His chest ached as he recognized its lone occupant, who was lying in a simple bed by the open window.

He prayed that he might wake and not have to witness this scene again, yet his mind rebelled, trapping him in the memories of his former self.

His feet moved him, unbidden, into the room, his mouth moving silently as the scene played out. Perhaps if he prayed enough, he might never have to witness this scene again.

The year was 1915. At the time, he had been a British boy of just eighteen: Elliot Fisher, with fiery-red hair and a face full of freckles. He would never forget the room where he now stood; even two reincarnations later, the memories lingered, and maybe it always would.

"You really shouldn't keep the windows open all the time; the night air isn't good for you," Jared/Elliot scolded, moving swiftly across the room to shut the aged and battered window frames.

"I think I'm a touch beyond the need to worry about what a cold might do to me," the figure on the bed replied.

Elliot turned toward the bedridden woman, drinking in her appearance as her story bloomed inside his memory.

Alice Rydell was a forty-year-old woman with a waterfall of dark brown hair and a pair of grey eyes that haunted him still. This incarnation of Athena, unlike the one—Quill? No. Quinn—he knew now, was deathly pale with hollow cheeks and dark circles under her eyes—weary eyes that were now fixed upon him. "I didn't think you'd come," she said, almost too softly for him to hear.

"Of course I came. Did you think I'd leave without saying goodbye?"

"So, you're actually going?" Alice attempted to lift her head from her pillow but fell back after raising her head only a few inches, panting softly with the effort.

Elliot shrugged. "It's not like the war is going to end soon. I go where the work is."

"Marcus is already on the front lines, I hear," she commented.

Elliot nodded, his thoughts flashing to the current incarnation of Ares. "The guy is having a ball, if his last letter is anything to go by. I don't really get it."

"Despite your job, you've never been a horribly violent individual."

"I know I've been on the battlefield before, but I don't remember..."

"You're scared," Alice stated.

"Terrified. I'm the only one who never sees me coming," he said, a slight quiver in his voice.

"Some might consider that a blessing."

Elliot lowered his head, shame creeping into his heart as he gazed upon the woman reclining in the hospital bed. Each breath she took was an act of terrible strength as illness wracked her lungs.

He had known Alice since he was a child and still found it difficult reconciling the frail figure before him with the beautiful young woman he had once looked to for guidance and comfort. He knew that the two had shared an intimate bond in many incarnations. Elliot was even willing to admit that he found Alice attractive. Yet, while the bond and love they held for each other were strong, in this incarnation it wasn't romantic.

"Before you go, I have a favour to ask of you," she said, a cough abruptly choking off her voice.

Elliot sat on the side of her bed, clasping her hands between his own. He waited for the coughing spell to pass, noticing with a heavy heart the almost transparent skin covering her bony fingers. "Yes, of course," he said. "What is it?"

Alice stared directly into his eyes, her gaze unwavering. "I want you to end this."

Elliot's face creased in confusion. "End the war?" he asked. Watching his past self's anguished confusion, Jared already knew Alice's answer and wished fervently that he might not have to hear it again now. Still, the vision marched grimly onward, granting him no reprieve.

"No, me. I want you to end me." Alice's gaze trapped Elliot's own. He had never been able to refuse her anything.

"You mean, kill you?" he asked as he stood, his hands slipping free from hers. He had half turned away from her when Alice's voice drifted back to him. "I wouldn't ask this of you if there was any hope for me."

"It's not your time, though," he argued.

"I'll decide when it's my time, damn it!" she snapped, the anger draining out from her as quickly as it had come. "Look at me, Elliot. I'm dying; you and I both know it. Yes, I might have another month or two left, but is it worth it? Do you remember what I always told you?"

Elliot hung his head but nodded. "Death is necessary, but not always the end."

"That's right. I will die here—whether it is today, tomorrow, or weeks from now, it is not far off. You're going to have your hands full on the battlefield looking after the dead while trying to stay alive yourself. I don't expect you to come back for me when I pass, but I want you to be the one to ferry me on."

Elliot's eyes burned at her words, while the back of his throat tightened painfully. "I can't," he croaked, shaking his head and fighting back the tears threatening to fall down his cheeks.

"Please," Alice choked out as tears of her own began to gather in her eyes. "You think I don't know what's happening to me? I'm weaker every day. It gets harder to speak, harder to move, or eat—or even breathe. Soon I'll only be able to lie here and shit myself, hoping that one of those damn nurses will check in on me. I don't want to die like that. I'm a god, damn it! I just want a little dignity."

Elliot's eyes met Alice's as Jared felt his former self consider her plea. He cringed as he heard Elliot say, "How do you want to do it?"

The lines on Alice's face smoothed, revealing a shadow of her former youth. "Morphine. About two-hundred millilitres should do it. Dr. Taggart keeps several vials along with a syringe in a blue cabinet down the hall."

"You're really sure about this? If we go through with this, it will be the end."

"I'll see you again," she assured herself.

"But it won't be you. You know how it works; Alice Rydell will never be brought back."

"As it should be. I've had a decent run, perhaps not as long of one as I would have liked, but I have no complaints where the company is concerned."

The next few minutes of Jared's memory passed in a blur, though he was well aware of the actions that would take place. How Elliot did as Alice bade him, moving along the hospital corridors unseen after retrieving the morphine and syringe she asked for. Elliot returned to the room and gently laid the glass vials on Alice's bed.

Alice took his hand in hers and gave it a reassuring squeeze.

Elliot filled the fifty-millilitre syringe with the clear liquid. He knew he would need to administer four syringes of morphine, one by one, but one look into the older woman's eyes told him that he would not hesitate to do this for her.

Once the syringe was filled, Elliot took the arm Alice offered him, the veins in the crook of her elbow clearly visible through her paper-thin skin. Jared remembered the next few minutes with horrific clarity: how easily the needle slid into her arm and the contented look she gave him as he pushed down the plunger on each of the four syringes.

Worse still was the smile Alice graced him with as she wheezed out her last words.

"Thank you."

CHAPTER TWENTY-FIVE

Jared stirred as he awakened, the memory of his former self still haunting him. His chest felt tight and heavy as he remembered what he allowed himself to do to his fellow god—no, his friend.

In a way, her death had also marked the end of his own time as Elliot. He had left to help the war efforts a day later and had somehow managed to survive the next three weeks on the front lines of battle. As he struggled to collect the souls of each life snuffed out on both sides of the conflict, the guilt from Alice's death weighed more heavily on him each day.

Finally, the day came when he couldn't bring himself to care anymore. He, and what was left of his company, had been holed up in a damp trench for the past four days. Elliot had moved farther down the line to relieve himself—a small amount of privacy in a communal, tightly packed space. After finishing his business, he slowly made his way back to the others.

He had heard the enemy soldier long before he saw him, but he was so tired. Elliot could practically feel the boy's—for that was all the soldier was—heavy breathing on the back of his neck as the young man lifted his hunting knife above his chest. It wasn't until his last moments that Elliot turned about to face his attacker, but he still made no move to protect himself. As the knife plunged deep into the crevice where Elliot's neck and left shoulder met, the attacking soldier's eyes grew wide, expecting his enemy to fight back, or call out for help. But the soft gurgle of blood that pushed past his lips was the last sound Elliot ever made before the Death God's spirit flew toward its new reincarnation.

This wasn't the first time this memory had haunted Jared's sleep. He had pleaded with his twin many times to help him guard his sleeping mind, but James offered no solution.

"You and I both know that it's a memory, not a dream. I have no control over those."

Jared had then tried to contact Seraphina. If anyone could destroy the mirage of the past, it would be her. Yet every time he got close to finding her, she would disappear, as if she and the wind were one and the same.

His relationship with the current incarnation of Mnemosyne had been complicated for a long while. Seraphina had been fourteen years older than his eight-year-old self when she first approached him. The request she had levelled at him had changed their lives forever. Not knowing any better, he had given in to the request and later used it to leverage her help when the time arrived. Too bad neither favour brought them any comfort. They had both been wrong, both made mistakes.

Jared sat on the bed and hung his head, his thoughts circling back to Quinn as they often had as of late. He knew that it had been not only Quinn's words, but the other man's very presence that had irritated his old scars. But Jared could no more blame Quinn for his memories' resurgence than he could his brother for being unable to help him. Guilt gnawed away at him for how he had handled the situation last night, allowing his emotions to get the better of him and snapping at the younger god.

A hesitant rap came at his door. Jared heard the movement of lightly clad feet shuffle as the person on the other side of the door shifted back and forth anxiously.

Jared rubbed at his eyes and tamed the sleep-mussed locks of his hair. He knew who stood behind the door but was still reluctant to answer the visitor. The anger he had felt toward Quinn had long since left him. He knew that Quinn was not Alice and did not yet understand the weight that the Death God's job pressed upon him.

The knock came again, followed by Quinn's wary voice. "Jared? You awake?"

The concern and contrition that bled through Quinn's words melted the remaining ice around Jared's heart. No, Quinn wasn't Alice, but Jared wasn't Elliot anymore either.

Jared stood, banishing the memories of his former self as he went to let Quinn in.

☙

Quinn didn't have to wait long before Jared pulled open the door.

While Jared no longer radiated anger, he looked weary. Running an almost self-conscious hand through his hair, the Death God moved aside and, with a jerk of his head, motioned for Quinn to enter.

Quinn hurried into the room, lest Jared change his mind. Now freshly groomed, Jared appeared more like his usual self as he moved to lounge on one of the small beds.

"So?" Jared asked expectantly.

G.E. White

"Oh, um, Surina told me to tell you to pack up your things; we're going to be leaving soon."

"Is that so?"

"Yeah. She thinks she knows who the thief is…" Quinn trailed off, noticing Jared's intense gaze upon him.

"How did she figure that out?"

"I found out how they were getting in and out of the temples. They were using this to switch between the First and Second Realms, at the exact location of the Stars," Quinn said, gesturing to the cuff, still attached to his wrist. "Surina took it from there."

Jared nodded. "That was pretty clever of you."

Quinn gave a snort of derision. "To be honest, that was probably the cleverest thing I've ever done. For the so-called God of Wisdom, I don't feel very smart. It feels as if I'm always doing or saying something stupid…" He left the statement open-ended, finally making eye contact with Jared as he looked up.

Jared's stern demeanour melted away as a soft chuckle escaped his lips. "I take it that this is you trying to apologize?"

"Trying, yes—though your laughter isn't making it very easy." The gentle smile Jared blessed Quinn with instantly relieved the tight feeling that had gripped his heart. It appeared that any anger Jared had felt toward him had been forgiven, but Quinn felt Jared deserved to hear his apology. "I'm sorry about what I said last night. It wasn't right of me to make judgments like that," Quinn continued, flopping down on the bed opposite Jared.

"No, it's okay. I mean, what you said was wrong, but with us having the powers that we do, and being the way we are, I know where you're coming from. Going from the regular world to what you're living in now, it's easy to expect that there should be some magical fix for everything." Jared stood, his expression troubled. "To be honest, there *was* a way for me to save Edelias."

"Then why didn't you?" Neither anger nor betrayal coloured

Quinn's question, only concern and honest curiosity.

"It's as they say: there has to be balance in the universe. If I had chosen to save her life, I would be condemning someone else to a premature death. So, can you understand why I did nothing?"

Quinn contemplated Jared's request for a moment. "I do. I hate the fact that we're supposed to be gods, but don't seem to have the power to change things when we need it. At least not without major strings attached. It sucks, but I can tell you don't like it either." But then, who possibly could? Faced with overwhelming power and temptation, Quinn doubted he would be able to do the right thing. "So, are we okay?" he prodded Jared once more.

"Yeah, we're good. Besides, I doubt I could stay mad at you for very long, especially with Surina breathing down my neck once she caught wind of the situation."

"Oh, I see, that's how it is. You're just accepting my apology to avoid an ass-kicking," Quinn grinned, warmth flooding through him at the thought of his renewed banter with Jared.

"No! And who said anything about an ass-kicking? I merely implied that there would be nagging—and lots of it."

The return of the easygoing man he'd gotten to know at the beautiful lakeside apartment caused the corners of Quinn's lips to pull up into a full smile. "Speaking of nagging, we should probably get going before Surina has to come after us."

"Agreed."

Quinn couldn't stop himself from beaming. He had warned himself not to put too much stock in his and Jared's friendship as it was so new. Still, his connection with Jared, and by extension, his connection with the rest of the Doyle clan, had already become essential to his new life among the gods. He couldn't picture his future in this strange new world without them. The argument last night could have imploded any friendship or bond the two might have had, so he was truly thankful that the two of them could talk through their problems like rational adults.

Putting any further thoughts of his and Jared's connection away, Quinn helped Jared round up the few belongings he had unpacked, returned them to his bag, and headed to the door.

☙

Upon entering the main hall once again, the two men caught sight of Surina and Instructor Sylvia conversing in hushed tones. Sylvia clasped the bespectacled woman's hand, the gesture showing both gratitude and reassurance.

"Thank you for being here," Quinn heard her say as he and Jared caught the tail end of the conversation.

Surina nodded. "I know the temple is in good hands and I promise, once this is over, I'll be sure to come back."

"I know you will."

Sylvia's smile dwindled as a small group of Lunar magi jogged by, gripping bows in their hands and full quivers on their backs.

"What's going on?" Quinn asked, approaching the two women.

"Just taking some precautions," Sylvia replied.

"I've already sent word to the Solar Temple about the theft and the murder of the high priestess. But whether Reeves will take it as truth, or simply believe that the whole thing was staged by the Temple of Artemis, is anyone's guess," Surina added.

"Well, with any luck, we won't have to worry about him. You still have a couple of days," Sylvia said.

Surina nodded. "I promise that we will do everything we can to retrieve the Star fragments in time."

Sylvia bowed her head slightly in gratitude. "Your word is good enough for me, Surina."

Turning to her companions, Surina gestured for them to follow her. "Let's go."

Jared gave a slight bow to the priestess, which Quinn copied hastily.

"Goodbye, Priestess Sylvia," he said, attempting to read the emotions in her fae features.

"Goodbye, Quinn."

Sylvia's use of his first name triggered a swell of warmth in Quinn's chest. His face broke out in a genuine smile, with the knowledge that there were people who saw *him,* and not just him as Lord Athena.

"Come on!" Jared shouted back, snapping Quinn from his reverie. He turned from the main hall to follow the Death God and was surprised to find that they were not leaving the temple, but going deeper into its depths, down a dimly lit staircase.

"Where exactly are we going?" Quinn asked, jogging to catch up to the others.

"The temple has its own entrance into the Gate system," Surina explained. "I've already contacted Leo and let him know to expect us."

"That doesn't really answer my question," Quinn persisted. "You said before that you might know who's behind this, and now we're suddenly on the move. Care to elaborate?"

"You're the one who actually made me realize what was right in front of us. We've already figured out that the thief's been using this cuff to switch between realms in order to steal the Star fragments. The cuffs are pretty peculiar on their own. As you know, they're made from Tyrell's materials, but they weren't built by his hands."

"Is it possible that he built them during a previous life?" Quinn asked.

"No," Jared cut in. "While Hephaestus may not be able to list all the creations he's made, he recognizes them when he sees them."

"So who else could build something like this?" Quinn asked, taking the cuff off his wrist.

"I know of only three: Brontes, Steropes, and Arges, the Cyclopes. They are daimons descended from Gaia, and at one point, they worked under Hephaestus as apprentices."

The use of the word *daimon* sent up a red flag in Quinn's brain. He had encountered the word before—but when, and where? *"The Undefined Race,"* he said, the image of the book's spine coming to the forefront of his mind.

Both Jared and Surina turned to Quinn at his statement. "There was another race, wasn't there?" he continued, now addressing the other two. "A sixth race."

"Seventh, no wait, eighth, technically," Jared admitted with a sigh. "The Titans and the gods came before them. Though I don't know if you can truly call the daimons a race." His tone was resigned, as if he was stating facts without discrimination.

"What exactly do you mean?"

Jared paused on the step he was standing on, scratching his chin. "Well, the term *daimon,* or *demon,* has been thrown about a bit liberally in mythology. The Christians use it to describe an evil spirit or fallen angel, while in the classical sense, it referred to nature spirits or gods that they classified as representing states of being—like sleep, love, hate, death. You get the idea."

"And I'm taking it, that's *not* what you're referring to."

"No," Surina interrupted, standing on the steps below them. "You remember how I said before that the gods made mistakes that cost them their immortality?"

Quinn nodded.

"Well, it wasn't just due to taking sides during the wars. Turns out, most gods couldn't keep it in their pants, and it didn't seem to matter which race they hooked up with. When they coupled with humans, their offspring were demigods, but when it came to other races, the results were daimons, though some daimons were created through magic and experimentation."

"But what are daimons, exactly? Why are they not considered a race?" Quinn pressed.

Surina shook her head and continued to head down the stairs, forcing Quinn and Jared to follow her. "Daimons range in size, shape and genetic makeup. Most daimons would be listed under a bestiary class of species; their ranks include giants, dragons, sirens, Gorgons, and the Cyclopes, just to name a few."

"But unlike us, they are eternal," Jared jumped in. Quinn shot the man a puzzled look. "It means they never grow old or sick, though they can be killed."

"So, I'm guessing that they're in the First Realm?"

"Not exactly. You see, even though many of them have…monstrous forms," Jared said, struggling to find the correct words, "having a god for a parent means that almost all of them inherited some form of magic. And almost all of them are capable of taking on human forms or disguises. Because of that, and the fact that they generally keep to themselves, they've been allowed to stay in the Second Realm."

"But they somehow have access to the First Realm?" Quinn prodded.

"They can't remain in their human formsat all times," Jared said with a shrug. "You think *they're* our thieves?" he asked Surina skeptically. "There was only one thief that I saw, and they were far too small to be one of the Cyclopes. Besides, do you think they could even come up with this plan, let alone pull it off?"

"I'm taking it that these guys aren't very smart," Quinn said as his eyes darted between his companions.

"I wouldn't necessarily say that; they do have a sort of cunning," Surina answered. "But I agree with you, Jared. I don't think they could've come up with this plan, or pulled it off. Not on their own. But they may have played a major role in it, not just by making the cuffs but in reforging the Star."

"And you know where they're going to do this?" Quinn asked.

"There's only one place they *can* do this. The fact that I didn't realize it earlier pisses me off." Surina punctuated her statement by aggressively batting an abandoned cobweb from her path.

"Care to let the rest of us in on your revelation?" Jared huffed impatiently.

"Quinn, do you remember where I found that cuff?"

"On a Danaid, in Erebus," he answered.

"Exactly. Now, since then, I've been asking myself: What were they doing there? We know now how they got there, but as for the why, who better to make sure a place remains empty than a bunch of bloodthirsty Danaids?"

"They need the Olympian fire, don't they?" Quinn reasoned, coming to a halt at the bottom of the staircase.

The basement where they now stood was dusty and laden with dirt. At one point, it had been used as a storage room, if the old-fashioned trunks and crates were any indication. The room had obviously been abandoned for something more functional. Standing among the forgotten boxes of old uniforms was a freestanding door set in a stone archway. Several of the stones had strange symbols carved into them.

"Makes sense," Jared agreed. "It's the only fire hot enough to reforge something as powerful as the Star. But we're still missing something. Neither the Danaids nor the Cyclopes could figure this all out, so who is the third party?"

"Who says there are only three parties?" Quinn countered.

Surina let out a disappointed sigh. "Whoever they are, they have an insight into the temples. In order to map out where they would switch in and out, they would have needed to have been in each location once already, at least."

"You mean, they needed to have been a magi." Quinn blanched at the thought.

"Yes," she said. "A fully trained and licensed magi can travel between the three temples. It could be a magi from any of the three Celestial Temples."

"Didn't you check in with the other temples to see if anyone was missing?" Jared asked.

"Yeah, I did. And according to them, everyone is accounted for."

"But that doesn't make any sense," Quinn protested.

"I know, but we'll figure it out later. We've already wasted enough time as it is."

Jared approached the door in front of them and, after smearing a drop of his blood on the archway, he tapped several of the marked stones within it. As he touched each stone, they gave off a faint blue glow, accompanied by a musical chime. Quinn recognized the chime as a code. The door swung open to reveal a familiar lounge and an even more familiar face.

Leo Russo was as big and burly as the young god remembered him. His red hair appeared flame-like in the lamplight behind him as he waved the three inside. "About time you showed up."

CHAPTER TWENTY-SIX

Stepping through the Gate this time was different from the others. It was unnerving for Quinn to be able to see his destination while being transported over a long distance. Disoriented, he stumbled across the threshold, even as he was steadied by the large hands of the red-haired giant standing next to him.

"Careful there," Leo boomed. "Switching realms while using a Gate makes you dizzier than most trips."

"We're in the Second Realm?"

"We have to be," Surina cut in, walking farther into the lounge. Quinn glowered at her easy steps, whereas he had to hold still to make sure his breakfast from earlier didn't make an unwelcome reappearance. "Erebus only exists in the Second Realm," she continued. "And seeing as we only have one of the Cyclopes' devices, entering the realm from this point is our only option if we want to catch them in time."

"Ooo, we gonna do some brawlin'?" Leo said excitedly. "You know I love it when you get violent."

"You love when *anyone* gets violent," Jared quipped, moving to lie on one of the comfy brown couches.

"I know what I like." Leo shrugged, unbothered.

"Most likely," Surina said, answering Leo's question, though refusing to be baited by his teasing. "That's why I would like you to come with us, Leo. I took out about a dozen Danaids, but there's likely thirty-seven more waiting in the wings."

"It's going to take some time to reforge that thing," Jared supplied, his voice muffled from his sprawled position, facedown, on the couch.

"True, but they already have at least a twelve hour head start. So here's how it will go: Quinn, I want you to stay here while the three of us head down to Erebus. We'll contact Carter and the two of you can let everyone else know what's going on."

"Whoa, hold on," Quinn protested. "What do you mean I have to stay here?"

"Quinn, this is not an investigation anymore, it's a bust. Most likely, we'll be dealing with about thirty Danaids on top of three Cyclopes, who are going to be a handful on their own," she explained.

"You think it's going to be violent?" Jared butted in.

"You think it *won't* be? Either way, I don't want to take any chances."

"And what about me? Don't I get a say in this?" Quinn persisted.

"No," both Jared and Surina chimed together.

"Wait a minute." Quinn's cheeks flushed as he grew more agitated. "*I* was the one who figured out how they were getting around, and I want to see this through to the end. I mean, I'm a part of this, right? What happened to this whole on-the-job-training thing?"

"Quinn, this is dangerous. If things go wrong, you could be killed," Surina reasoned.

"So could you," he countered. "So could any of you; are you guys somehow more expendable than I am? Jared and Leo are gods, but I don't see *them* standing on the sidelines."

"He's got a point," Jared supplied, speaking directly to Surina. "You've been handling this investigation thus far not only because of your insight into the inner workings of the three temples but also because Sebastien and I trust you. But I also trust him," he continued, gesturing to Quinn. "We're going to be running in there half blind as it is, and we both know that Quinn's smart, maybe he'll see something we won't."

Surina's shoulders slumped in defeat. "You *cannot* honestly be considering this."

"He's just gonna follow us anyway," Jared reasoned.

She shook her head. "I don't like this."

"I don't think any of us do. But it'll be okay in the end, we'll watch each other's backs," Leo encouraged. And, as if a light bulb switched on in his head, Leo held a finger up in sudden remembrance. "One sec."

The burly man ran into the back room. The three others could hear him banging around, obviously hunting for something. Some muffled curses spilled from the adjacent room before Leo let out a triumphant *Ah-ha!*

The War God's face was aglow as he exited the storage room, hefting what appeared to be a waist-high claymore on his hip. "Quinn can borrow this. Always brought me good luck."

Quinn took hold of the sword and almost toppled over as Leo relinquished his hold on the weapon. With some effort, the shorter man was able to heft the blade upward to lay against his side.

"I think I might be better off with something I can actually lift," he said.

"Fine," Leo sniffed, taking back the weapon with ease. "I guess I could take old Sheila here out myself. It's been a while since we've bonded."

Quinn raised a curious brow at Leo's moniker for the weapon, but Surina pulled his attention away from the sword soon enough.

"Don't mind him, you can keep using my dagger," she reassured him. "But you're going to listen to *everything* we say. If we tell you to run, hide, or stay put, I don't want to hear any arguing."

"Yes, ma'am. Listen, I'm not really keen on weapons, but I've got to ask, what's with the swords? Haven't you guys heard of guns?" Quinn asked.

"Swords don't require bullets," Surina said with a tight-lipped smile. Pulling the small dagger from her bag, she handed it to Quinn once more. "Besides, it's a much more elegant weapon. For a more civilized age."

"I suppose. Wait, did you just quote *Star Wars* to me?"

ℰℐ

Surina shot another message to Carter, entrusting him to alert the other gods of what was going down. Then after taking a couple more minutes to get geared up and rehydrated, the four of them set off.

The hallway they entered felt familiar and foreign all at once. Even with the aid of Jared's scythe, which now emitted a dim light, Quinn still stumbled against the walls of the cramped corridor. He knew he had travelled down this path before, but he couldn't shrug off the feeling that this air seemed different—closer, *heavier,* as if they were struggling through a jungle's undergrowth. He noted that evening was falling as they approached the cavernous hall ahead, but it still seemed darker than it should be.

Exiting the narrow corridor, Quinn's eyes widened at the tangled web greeting them. Gnarled wooden branches twisted tightly around one another to create a wall that blocked their entry. The wooden bower did, however, have one small opening just wide enough for a single person to squeeze through.

"Shit," Surina muttered. "This was the reason I wanted to hurry."

"You knew this was going to happen?" Leo asked, taking Sheila and slashing at the wood. He looked triumphant, an expression replaced by irritation as the blade bounced off, having dealt barely any damage to the bark.

"Not this *exactly*, but I figured they'd want to slow down anyone who came after them."

"I don't understand. What's the problem? We can just go through here, right? It's big enough for each of us to get in," Quinn reasoned.

"Yeah, and then we walk straight into a maze, with dozens of different pathways and only one correct exit," Surina groused.

"You've seen this before," Jared said, matter-of-factly.

"It's an Earthen magi spell; they call it Woven Wanderings and use it to confuse, trap, and slow down their opponents. As Leo just demonstrated, you can't cut it down. If we try to go over it, the walls will just grow taller. There's no choice but to go through it, which is the last thing we want to do." Surina sighed in frustration. "It could take us days to get through this thing. Fuck!" she cursed, slamming her fist against the wooden barrier.

In the dim light of Jared's torch, Quinn could make out the worried faces of his fellow gods. *There had to be some way to get through the maze relatively quickly!*

"How do the Earthen magi get through it?"

"They walk through it like anyone else, but they know the path. Something about an odour that only they can detect while they mark the correct turns," Surina explained.

"So shouldn't we be able to just track them?" he asked her.

"Normally I would, but we're standing on concrete—no disturbed dirt or grass to follow."

"What about tracking them by smell?" Quinn persisted.

"Do any of us look like a bloodhound to you?" Leo snorted.

"Tracking like that is a little beyond us."

Quinn pursed his lips as he considered the problem before them.

"What about a Lupine Familiar?" he suggested, causing Surina's eyebrows to shoot up toward her hairline as she turned to him with an incredulous look. "I read about them at the Lunar Temple. They're used for tracking, right?"

"That's right," Surina breathed. "I had completely forgotten about them. I guess we could try. To be honest, I haven't conjured one in years. I might not be able to anymore."

"It's worth a shot," Jared argued.

Surina nodded in agreement. "Okay, here goes."

Taking a deep breath, she held out her hands, palms down, and though Quinn couldn't see them, he was certain her eyes were closed tightly in concentration.

As she muttered the Latin words, a light glow appeared to pulse outward from her palms. As the light grew in size, it began to form into a vaguely animalistic shape, thinning in some areas and thickening in others, as if it were moonlight sculpted on a potter's wheel.

With one final burst of light, which caused the four companions to glance away instinctively, the spell was complete. Looking at the spot where Surina had directed her hands downward, they were greeted by the sight of a spectral wolf cub. The pup thumped its tail against the ground playfully.

"Cool," Quinn breathed in awe, crouching down to pet the Familiar. The wolf cub yipped its pleasure, attempting to lick Quinn's hand. The young man laughed at the gesture, noting how the sensation wasn't at all similar to when Cerberus had greeted him. Petting the Familiar pup felt more like putting his hand through a heavy fog.

Surina snorted. "That's nothing. Just wait until you meet one of Jared's reapers. First time I saw one, I nearly pissed myself."

"To be honest, I hope I never have to," Quinn replied.

"Hey, they're good guys. A little on the bony and rotten side, but all and all, good guys," Jared protested, indignant.

"Can we get this show on the road?" Leo interjected. "I came on this trek to break some skulls, and this chit-chat's getting boring."

"Right," Surina knelt beside the wolf Familiar and held out the Danaid cuff. The wolf scented the cuff and pulled back with a sneeze. Surina stood and jerked her chin upward. "All right, you know what to do."

The apparition gave an excited bark, darting into the maze. Surina trailed after it, followed by Quinn and Jared, with Leo and his massive sword bringing up the rear.

The walls of the maze were high enough to touch the ceiling, only enhancing the darkness of the paths they followed. Evening was approaching in the city above, if the minimal light streaming in from the skylight window was to be trusted. Dusk or not, Quinn had to admit that the low light made it reasonably easy to keep track of the spectral wolf.

Whenever the four encountered a fork in the path, the cub would lift its head, its nose twitching as it tracked the scent. Sometimes it took the cub a minute or two to sniff around before choosing a path. They were now moving slowly but surely across the cavern hall, although Quinn noticed that they would often have to move great lengths to the left or right before they could progress farther forward.

"Whoever made this wants it to really slow us down," Surina observed.

"I'm guessing this is *slightly* more complicated than other wooden mazes you've encountered?" Jared stated.

"I suppose. But then, I was usually working with the creators of the maze, not against them."

Gradually, the skylight at the centre of the hall appeared closer. Though he didn't carry a watch, Quinn's newly enhanced awareness allowed him to calculate that they had been travelling for a couple of hours at least. He couldn't shake his feeling of irritation, knowing they still weren't even halfway through the maze. Just then, the pup paused at one of the entrances, its hair rising as it growled. Suddenly, it stiffened, ears flattening against its head before giving a yelp and dispersing into mist.

Turning the corner, the four found themselves in a bright clearing. They had reached the centre of the maze.

There, at the centre of the clearing, lay the source of the Lupine Familiar's unease: a cloaked figure, lying eerily still.

G.E. White

CHAPTER TWENTY-SEVEN

FOR A MOMENT, no one moved as they fixed their gaze on the prone form in front of them. Suddenly the body lurched upward as it fought for air between heaving gasps. Quinn sprang into action, pushing past the others as he ran to the stranger's side.

"Quinn!" Surina barked, her warning unheeded as Quinn knelt by the figure and pulled the hood of their dark-green cloak away to reveal the bruised and worn face of a red-haired woman in her late thirties. The woman gave a groan and attempted to roll onto her side, before hissing in pain.

"Hey, take it easy," Quinn said reassuringly, placing a steady hand on the woman's shoulder.

Surina approached the pair, her face guarded as she crouched beside the other woman. "You okay?"

The woman weakly nodded, struggling to sit up, even with Quinn's assistance. "Yeah," she croaked. "Just sore. And a little disoriented."

"What's your name?" Jared asked.

"Pyra. Pyra Rhysman."

"You're an Earthen Magi," Surina observed, gesturing to the cloak draped over the other woman's shoulders.

Her companions looked on in suspicion as they contemplated this new development.

"I am."

"And I'm guessing you know what's been going on and how you got here?"

Warily looking up at the demigod, Pyra nodded. "Well enough to have an inkling of why you're here."

"So what happened?" the Death God inquired. Leo stood off behind the others as Jared, Quinn, and Surina circled around the injured woman. "Did your partners decide you won't get a stake in the big wish?"

"It's not like that," Pyra protested.

"Then what is it like?" Jared challenged.

"The people who left me here, they weren't my partners, but my abductors," Pyra explained. "The Cyclopes brothers needed access to the temples, so they took me."

Quinn turned to Surina. "I thought you said that everyone in the Earthen Temple was accounted for?"

"I did," Surina replied, suspicion colouring her words.

"Wait," Pyra pleaded. "I was posted on a six-week botanical survey mission; I'm not due back for at least another week, so they wouldn't have reported me missing."

"So, you're saying that Arges and his brothers are behind this? And that you were taken to give them information on the layout of the temples?" Surina pressed.

"That's right."

"Who else was involved?" Quinn watched Surina's jaw clench as she contemplated Pyra's story.

"What? No one. At least no one that I know of," Pyra replied. "They kept me in a cave, and I never saw anyone else."

Jared frowned, turning to Surina. "Even if she didn't see anyone else, there had to be another party. The person we saw at the Lunar Temple was too small to be a Cyclops—unless that was you?" he asked, directing his question toward Pyra.

"No! It wasn't me!" she said frantically. "I'll admit I gave them the information on the temples..."

"And the uniforms?" Surina interrupted.

The other woman hung her head. "That too. And *this,*" she said, gesturing to the maze around them. "But they said they'd kill me if I didn't help them. Hell, they almost did that anyway."

"I'd say they worked you over pretty good," Surina said, her gaze drifting over the bruises marring Pyra's exposed skin. "My question is, if you built this, how did they get through the rest of it without you?"

"They didn't, I took them through to the other side. Once there, they said I was free to go, and all I had to do was go back the way I had come. Seemed simple enough," Pyra said with a shrug. "That is, until they beat me and made retracing my steps next to impossible. I think they expected me to die here."

"Can't you just deconstruct this thing?" Jared questioned, looking at the hellish maze around them.

Pyra shook her head. "I would if I could, but I just don't have the energy."

Surina winced, hissing as she clutched at the edge of her jacket.

"You okay?" asked Quinn.

The demigod tilted her head back, looking at the sky above her. Night had fallen, and the chamber had dimmed. "I'm fine. I just didn't realize how late it is, I..." Surina trailed off as she reached into her pocket, only to come up empty-handed. "Shit! It's gone!"

"What's gone?" Leo asked.

Surina gave a shake of her head. "My protean watch. I must have dropped it back in the maze. I need to get it back. You guys rest up here, I'll backtrack and be here again before sunrise."

"What? You gotta be kidding me. I thought you were the one who wanted to move quickly?" Leo argued.

"I know, but moving forward while it's dark is dangerous. And there's no way I'm facing any Danaids or Cyclopes unarmed. Besides, I need a couple of hours to get my energy back to make another Familiar," she reasoned.

Jared pointed to the woman Quinn was helping to prop against one of the maze walls. "What about Pyra? Couldn't she guide us?"

"Not in her condition, and we can't leave her here like this. A few hours shouldn't make too much of a difference. Perhaps by then, Pyra will be able to guide us herself."

"If you say so," the Death God conceded.

"So we agree, finally. Okay, you three should rest here with Pyra. I'll be back as soon as I can."

Concerned, Quinn lifted his attention from Pyra's wounds. "What if you get lost?"

"I won't. I marked the trail along the way." Surina's confidence was contrasted by the worry in her voice.

"I could go with ya," Leo offered.

Surina levelled her gaze toward the God of War. "Thanks, but I'll move a lot faster on my own."

"You sure?" he prodded.

"I'm sure. I also have some private matters to attend to," she said, shooting him a meaningful look.

"Gotcha."

Surina turned to Quinn. "I want you to look after Pyra the best you can." Reaching into a pouch attached to the tactical belt about her waist, she retrieved a small first aid kit and tossed it toward him.

"Me?" Quinn echoed, catching the small box with ease.

"Yeah, you." With that, Surina turned back the way they had come, disappearing into the maze.

"She seems high-strung. Well, more high-strung than usual," Jared corrected himself, smirking.

"She's probably just worried about the Star." Quinn tried to reason out Surina's actions, but he, too, was confused. What exactly was so dangerous about travelling at night? It wasn't like the chamber they were in was much darker than it had been a few hours ago. In fact, the full moon rising in the sky was starting to illuminate some of the maze through the skylight. But Quinn trusted Surina enough to know that whatever reason she had to make them stop, it was a good one.

Turning to the task that Surina had assigned to him, Quinn had to admit he felt for Pyra. Whether she was being honest about her involvement in the theft was debatable, but either way, she hadn't deserved the beating she'd received.

Quinn crouched down to Pyra's level as she sat with her back against one of the maze's wooden walls. Setting the kit down beside him and retrieving a water bottle from his own bag, he twisted open the lid.

"Here, have some water," he offered, holding the bottle to the Magi's lips.

Pyra sipped at the water as Quinn tilted the canister, giving a wave of her hand when she was satiated.

Bruises were visible on Pyra's face, yet the swelling was minimal, although dried blood caked the shoulder of her cloak. Quinn took some gauze from the kit and fashioned it into a tourniquet for Pyra's upper arm. Pushing the material away from her shoulder, Quinn noted that a tattoo of a horn graced Pyra's back.

"That's an interesting design. What is it?" He asked.

"Huh? Oh, right, ah, it's part of a goat head."

"On your back?"

"Demeter's symbol," Pyra explained. "I've had it so long, I sometimes forget about it. You know what I mean?"

"I guess," Quinn said hesitantly. Something about what Pyra said did not quite ring true.

The words he was about to say were interrupted by a massive crash coming from somewhere in the maze behind them. Jared and Leo turned toward the sound, wide eyed.

"Surina?" Jared called.

The only answer he received was the echo of another crash in the distance.

Quinn stood, already making his way toward the sound when Leo's hand landed on his shoulder. "Wait," the God of War ordered.

"What? She could be hurt," Quinn protested.

"Surina can take care of herself," Jared assured the younger man. "We stay here; we don't know what's out there yet. She'll be back, don't worry."

Quinn's frown deepened. There was something hidden here, something that the other two weren't saying. He was starting to get really sick of this whole cloak-and-dagger routine. Wasn't he part of the team? But picking a fight right now didn't seem like the right move. Surina had asked him to look after Pyra, so instead, Quinn focused on ensuring his charge was cared for to the best of his capacity.

It was times like these that Quinn was thankful for his impressive memory, as he used the skills he recalled from the first aid pamphlet he read back in the fifth grade to gently wash the caked blood away from the gash on Pyra's arm. He stopped abruptly, noting that the bruised skin around the wound was yellowing.

"Does it hurt?"

"It's not too bad."

Quinn nodded, but said nothing else.

An hour crept by with little said among the group. Leo and Jared took turns pacing the clearing, alert on the first watch. The crashes they had heard earlier in the night occasionally repeated, with Quinn protesting each time that Surina had been gone too long and that they should go look for her, to which the two older men would reiterate their reassurances.

"If she was in trouble, she would have called for us, trust me," Jared said, and even though Quinn couldn't find a shred of insecurity or doubt in his words, he couldn't shake the feeling that something sinister was going on in the maze.

Rounding quickly on the injured woman behind him, Quinn propelled a series of rapid-fire questions at her, his thoughts turning into action.

"Did they tell you to put anything else in the maze?"

"What? No! J—Just the maze," Pyra stammered.

"Yet you don't have any of your Earthen magi potions left. Are you sure you didn't use one of them in the maze?"

Leo and Jared turned their attention from the maze to Quinn's interrogation of the magi.

"No, the Cyclopes took them from me when they grabbed me," she replied testily, running a hand through her thick mane of hair.

Quinn appeared to deflate after hearing Pyra's information, both disappointed and relieved. Standing and pacing away from the woman, he sighed. "That's too bad. I'm sure you could have used that Bull's Blood. The superspeed would have come in handy while getting away."

Pyra gave a snort. "Don't I know it, but those damn daimons got the drop on me."

Jared and Leo exchanged a look. What exactly was Quinn trying to prove here?

"But then, you didn't actually need to run from them anyway, right?"

The Earthen magi sneered in indignation. "What do you mean? They almost killed me, can't you see it?!" Oddly enough, her excessive gesturing toward her visible bruises and cuts did not appear to slow Quinn's tirade.

"You say that this just happened to you, but most of those bruises are yellowing and old. Older than a day for sure, more like a week. And while I *will* admit that the cut on your arm is fairly recent, it perfectly matches the wound Surina inflicted on the person who stole Polaris and murdered Artemis' high priestess."

"I…"

"Furthermore," Quinn persisted. "I don't think for a second that you're an Earthen Magi. Not one of Demeter's symbols is a goat, and Bull's Blood gives you strength, not speed. If you were an Earthen Temple Magi, you would know that. So, if you're not an Earthen Magi, you're an accomplice."

As each word left Quinn's mouth, Pyra's face drained of colour. Then the blood started to rush back into her head, painting her glowering features an unsightly scarlet. She suddenly pushed off the wall with more strength and dexterity than her injuries should have allowed. Quinn stepped back, while Leo and Jared gripped the handles of their weapons.

"I was just supposed to keep you busy for a while, point you the wrong way," Pyra muttered, almost as if to herself. "I had really hoped it wouldn't come to this."

The three gods tensed, readying themselves for the woman to attack them or reach for a weapon. Instead, a far more gruesome sight awaited them.

Pyra's body began to writhe, her limbs breaking and reforming anew. From under her cloak, two sharp points extended from the back of her tattooed shoulder, revealing two prongs attached to a goat head.

Her once-elegant features became elongated and contorted as her skin grew coarse and covered with fur, and her face became surrounded by a lion's mane. Looking upward, frozen in place, Quinn watched as the beast that had once been Pyra grew two stories in height.

The clothes she had once worn lay in tatters at her clawed feet. Her cloak was thrown from her shoulders, even as she stood on all fours. The goat head that emerged from her back twisted and turned to face Quinn and his companions.

The spine of the four-legged creature extended beyond her body. The creature's tail was covered in scales, ending in a serpent's head that hissed a warning to the immobile men.

The three heads of the beast gave simultaneous roars, as Leo, Jared, and Quinn staggered backward, Quinn's eyes fearfully wide. "What *is* that?" he cried, turning to Jared, whose mouth was set in a grim line.

"The daimon Chimera."

CHAPTER TWENTY-EIGHT

Quinn barely had time to grip the dagger attached to his belt before Chimera's lion head opened her mouth, spewing a column of fire. Leo tackled him to the ground, the two barely escaping being incinerated by the inferno raging overhead.

"It breathes fire?!" Quinn gasped.

"That surprises you?" the War God replied as he pulled Quinn to his feet.

Jared had his scythe ready as the chimera's tail attempted to strike him. Quinn stood frozen, watching the two gods dodge Pyra's sharp claws, scorching flames, and gnashing teeth as each of her three heads lashed out. He would have assumed that these men—these gods—would be able to dispatch this creature with ease, but the blows of their blades seemed only to irritate her instead of wound.

G.E. White

Pyra's tail whipped suddenly to the right, catching Leo in the side and sending him flying into the wall, where he slumped to the floor, dazed. Hissing her victory, the creature turned to her next threat, lunging at Jared.

A massive paw crashed into the Death God's chest, pinning him to the ground. The strangled cry that escaped his lips jolted Quinn from his fear-induced stillness. The world seemed to come into crystal clear focus, and before he was even aware of what he was doing, Quinn was moving.

Clasping his dagger in his right hand, Quinn charged the chimera's far side, sinking the blade deep into the daimon's left thigh. Pyra reared back, releasing Jared as she roared in pain. Her loud reaction shocked Quinn, who recoiled and dragged the blade, now covered in black ichor, out from the wound it had created.

Pyra wheeled on the God of Wisdom, spitting out a stream of fire. It was coming at Quinn too quickly! Knowing he had no time to dodge, Quinn threw his arms up in a vain attempt to shield his face. He closed his eyes, expecting to feel the flames eating away at his clothes and skin at any moment.

The blast never came.

Instead, he heard a loud crash and felt a gust of wind on his face as something massive broke through one of the maze walls and into the path of the flames.

Quinn lowered his arms to see what had shielded him from the blast. He raised his eyes in wonder, taking in the scaled beast in front of him.

Python?

However, he noticed that the scales of the giant serpent were not a rainbow-hued gold but a pearlescent silvery-white. Although the creature before him was still massive, it wasn't as long as Python, being perhaps only ten to fifteen metres long.

The hood of the serpent flared as it hissed at the daimon, the former coiling its tail and poised to strike.

Jared pulled Leo back to his feet, and the two tugged Quinn away from the two beasts, sizing one another up.

"What *is* that?" Quinn asked, in both fear and awe. The god strained his neck as he watched Chimera try to gouge the serpent with her horns.

Jared gripped the back of Quinn's head, turning him away from the battle and tucking his face into his chest in a protective embrace. "Do *not* look directly at its face," he snapped.

While at any other time Quinn may have relished in the strange hug, his mind wouldn't relinquish his question. "What's going on?"

"Just...stay out of their way," Jared instructed, dragging Quinn behind one of the maze walls, giving the duelling creatures plenty of space.

Once again, Quinn realized that Jared and Leo knew something he did not. The whole situation had gone from strange to downright unbelievable. He had assumed the serpent was the cause of the noises they had heard earlier that night, but that didn't explain Surina's disappearance. And why was this creature protecting them, unless, perhaps, it had been conjured up by Surina?

It was an unlikely explanation, but Quinn would rather believe that the snake was protecting them than assume the serpent was just fighting off another predator.

Another crash from behind the wall caused Quinn to poke his head around, curious to see what was happening, while making sure not to focus on the serpent's head.

Pyra leapt onto the snake, latching onto its scales with the lion head's massive jaws. The serpent, now partially wrapped around its opponent, hissed in pain. Looking once more at the chimera, Quinn noticed that all of her heads avoided gazing upon the serpent's face. Obviously, Pyra knew there was danger in meeting its gaze. Unfortunately for Chimera, it was her caution that blinded her to the serpent's retaliation.

Rearing backward, the serpent bared its fangs before sinking them deep into Pyra's left side. The cry of the daimon was cut short as the serpent's venom raced through her body, quickly turning it to stone.

Now coiled around the statue of Pyra, still frozen in mid roar, the silver snake tightened its grasp, crushing its defeated opponent until the latter exploded into broken pieces of rubble.

Quinn was suddenly yanked back by his shirt collar and spun around to face the other two gods.

"What did I just say about looking at its head?" Jared fumed, worry colouring his words.

"I wasn't," Quinn retaliated defensively.

"Shh!" Jared hissed.

The two others fell silent as they listened to the slide of scales along the cement. Hearing the giant serpent slither over the remains of Chimera, the three men behind the tangled wall stiffened in fear. The creature moved toward them, pushing its snout through the wall's entryway.

Quinn gripped his dagger, tensed to strike, yet Leo's hand on his shoulder stilled his attack. The snake flicked its tongue once, twice—tasting and smelling the air.

Suddenly, it gave a snort before slithering away, back across the clearing and out into the other half of the maze. Once the creature was out of range, Jared and Leo gave a sigh of relief and slowly moved back into the clearing, Quinn trailing behind them.

"Again—what was that? Another wurm, like Python?" Quinn asked.

"A basilisk. Making eye contact with it, or being infected with its venom, will turn any living thing in its path to stone," Leo said.

Quinn nodded at the War God's explanation. "Like Medusa?"

"Medusa was a Gorgon and a daimon, however, she was mortal—unlike her sisters—and never received the gift they had."

"What do you mean? What gift?"

"The basilisk was another monstrous form for the Gorgons. Just as Pyra here went from a human form to a chimera's, the Gorgons were able to change from a human body to a basilisk."

Quinn bit his lower lip in thought as he surveyed the wreckage. "So why did it leave?"

"*She* came to her senses."

Rounding on Jared, Quinn scowled. "I thought we were done with keeping things from me. What is going on? You obviously know something I don't..." just then, the faint memory of his time in Erebus came to the surface. "You said basilisks take on human forms, Jared."

"All daimons do. Gorgons and basilisks are basically one and the same. Daimons have at least one human parent, in the form of a god's incarnation. It's what allows them to stay hidden here in the Second Realm," the Death God explained, his voice faltering in anticipation of Quinn figuring out the meaning behind his words.

Quinn's gaze glanced over Pyra's remains, now just shards of rock and dust. "You two weren't concerned about Surina, even after we heard those noises, because you knew she was the one making them. That was her, wasn't it?"

Jared glanced at Leo frantically, looking for any direction on how to proceed. The large man just gave a wave of his hand, as if to say *the cat's out of the bag anyway.*

"It's not really something she's proud of—her daimon ancestry, that is," Jared sighed.

Quinn's eyes narrowed. "Her glasses, her unwillingness to look at anyone directly in the eye, I figured there was more to it than just a sensitivity to light. I remember reading the myth of Medusa, and thought perhaps she had some connection with it."

"Medusa's dead. Has been for centuries," Leo reminded him. "Surina's mother was Stheno, one of the eternal Gorgons."

Stheno. It may have been strange, but it felt good to Quinn, to put a name to the woman who had so damaged Surina's self-worth.

"Obviously, Surina's not fully Gorgon herself, which has left her impaired," Jared continued.

"Impaired? How?"

"She lacks control over her daimon abilities. Only the most ancient of the mythological texts mentioned that the immortal Gorgon sisters could 'turn off' their deadly sight. Medusa and Surina never could. And it's the same with the basilisk transformation. Surina's the grand-daughter of an incarnation of Artemis, and she not only inherited some of her magic but also has some of her power dictated by the cycles of the moon."

As Jared explained Surina's Gorgon abilities, the bits of information Surina had offered up the night before started to fall into place. Stheno obviously was disappointed in Surina's lack of control over her powers, as if Surina was at fault for her genetic makeup and the disadvantages it put her at. "So every full moon she transforms, whether she wants to or not?" Quinn asked, his question sounding more like a statement.

"Just like a werewolf," Leo quipped. "Though we think she keeps a certain amount of control over her actions—an awareness of some sort."

"And she didn't want me to know?" Quinn asked, somewhat hurt by the fact that Surina didn't trust him with that information, or that she believed he would think less of her.

"I don't think she wanted anyone to know, if possible. Surina sees it as a weakness," Jared said.

Quinn's eyes widened at the statement as he turned again to see the rubble that was once the fire-breathing Chimera. "She just crushed Pyra! I wouldn't call that a weakness."

"And if she thought you were a threat, she woulda done the same to you," Leo said simply, but not unkindly.

Quinn shuddered at the thought of being trapped in Surina's coils, his life slowly squeezed from him. Surina was his friend. Well, sort of. He was certain that she would be able to restrain herself from attacking him.

Mentally shaking himself free of that troubling image, Quinn turned to the others. "So, what do we do now?"

Jared looked up through the skylight, observing the sky's lighter hues. "It'll be sunrise in a few hours. Surina will go back to her usual self then."

"And we'll still be lost in this goddamn maze." Leo snorted.

Gazing at the maze entrance that the basilisk had left through, Quinn couldn't help but let out a chortle. "I don't think the maze is going to be much of a problem."

Jared and Leo gathered around him, puzzled at his amusement. Where once there had been a thick tangle of magical thorns and branches, in their place lay piles of stone rubble, which neatly cleared a wide path to the other side of the cavernous hall.

Jared sucked in his breath, astonished. "Huh, would you look at that."

CHAPTER TWENTY-NINE

WITH ONLY A few hours of darkness remaining, Leo told Quinn and Jared to get some rest, assuring them he had already slept most of the day and was fit to stand watch. The concrete floor offered little comfort, and Quinn couldn't actually sleep. Lying on the floor, his mind raced with the events of the past forty-eight hours.

He wondered what he should do when they met up with Surina. Would it be best to say nothing at all? Perhaps the best course of action would be to act as if he didn't know and discretely pretend that the other two had not spilled her secret. For the most part, he had unravelled the secret for himself. Jared and Leo had just been kind enough to fill in the blanks. Of course, Quinn couldn't act completely naïve; something had obviously happened, and Surina was more than aware of her monthly transformation.

Quinn figured that if he laid down, he would be out in a matter of minutes, yet his brain refused to be quiet. So instead, he sat gazing at the inside of his eyelids, attempting to block everything else out.

In what seemed like a second's time, Leo shook him into consciousness. Jared was already standing at the ready, scythe in hand. While both gods appeared not completely rested, they at least seemed alert.

Turning his head to the right, Quinn saw Surina. If it weren't for the slight tangles in her hair and the weary slope of her shoulders, he would have assumed she had been with them the whole time.

"Hey," he said.

"Hey," she echoed, somewhat awkwardly.

"So, when did you get back?"

Surina exchanged glances with the other two gods before answering. "Not long ago. Twenty minutes, maybe."

"I see," Quinn replied.

"It's okay," she assured. "I know you know." Her posture, along with her tone, seemed almost a challenge, as if she were daring him to say something. Quinn, seeing through her façade, offered a reassuring smile. "I know you might not think so, but I thought you were pretty cool last night."

Surina allowed her lips to turn up in a half smile. "Might seem cool to you, but let me tell you, it's hell on the teeth sometimes." She ran her tongue across her gleaming canines, emphasizing her point.

Leo clapped a friendly hand onto Surina's shoulder. "And we appreciated it. Certainly made short work of the maze for us."

"I wish I could say that I did it consciously, but I think the beast in me was just getting pissed off."

The others snickered at the comment, Quinn gladly. He was grateful to have a moment free of the tension saturating the last few days.

Surina turned toward the far side of the hall and began to pick her way through the crumbled remains of the once high wall. "Come on, let's get this over with. I don't know about you guys, but I am seriously looking forward to a day off and a long bath."

Quinn eagerly climbed after her; Jared and Leo followed. He stepped up and over the scattered rocks, picking up his pace to walk in step with Surina. Keeping a light smile on his face, he wondered if it was enough to prove to her that her transformation didn't scare him, nor did it change his opinion of her.

Surina occasionally turned her gaze toward him, appraising him silently. After a few minutes of travel, she cleared her throat softly to gain Quinn's attention without alerting the two men behind them.

"I hear it was you who figured out that Pyra wasn't what she seemed."

Quinn nodded solemnly. "Yeah. You know, there was a time when I always took people at their word."

"And now?"

"I can't say I'm hypervigilant. I'm just more aware. Aware that people who lie about the little things will eventually lie about the big things too. I guess I should say that I'm just more aware of *everything*. I'd often notice when little things didn't seem to add up, but I never paid it much mind, and now I do. It kind of makes my head heavy."

Surina tilted her head in a sign of understanding, offering Quinn no empty platitudes. Instead, she leapt down from the last bit of rubble to the exit hall below, offering her hand to steady the others as they descended.

Leaving the hall, they were greeted with the now familiar alcove and staircase leading into Erebus. Right away, Quinn noticed two distinct differences from the last time he had looked over the halls: Firstly, the hole Surina had used for her impromptu elevator was gone, as if it had never existed. Secondly, the god issued police tape that usually hung across the bottom of the staircase was missing.

"Good to see they finally fixed the staircase," Leo commented. "Too bad we can't use it."

Quinn turned to him, a questioning look in his eyes.

"They'll be expecting us to come through this stairway, and they'll be watching," Leo explained. "The path gets narrower as it descends, creating a bottleneck."

"Another successful defence tactic," Jared added.

Quinn's eyes wandered over to Surina's jacket and the watch chain that spilled out over the edge of her pocket. "I guess we could take the elevator."

The others turned to him, Surina's eyebrows raised at Quinn's suggestion.

"Last time, we were able to enter Erebus from a different path by using it. The tunnel it leads to was technically a dead end. So they wouldn't be keeping an eye on it, right?"

Surina bobbed her head in agreement. "It makes the most sense, if we want to take them by surprise."

"Let's do it, then," Jared concurred, though his expression gave way to confusion as Surina corralled them together. She pulled out the protean watch, turning it into a sword before beginning to draw a circle around them.

Jared had just begun to open his mouth when Quinn beat him to the punch.

"I'm really sorry if I throw up on you," he told his friend. He really hoped it wouldn't come to that.

"What?!"

But before Quinn could expand on his statement, Surina finished the ritual, stabbing the centre of the circle with her sword.

Suddenly, they were falling, Jared's hand clenching Quinn's arm tightly enough to cut off the younger man's circulation.

༄

The sudden stop didn't jar Quinn as it had before, although his companions weren't as certain on their feet after they landed. Regaining their balance, the three gods and the demigod stepped out of the shaft and into the dank tunnel.

"Why doesn't the floor keep going?" Jared asked, glancing back toward where they had just exited.

"It's better not to think about it," Quinn assured him.

Suddenly throwing her finger to her lips, Surina gestured for silence. To their right, a faint light flickered against the wall of the tunnel entrance, and the sound of clanging metal echoed along the corridor.

Surina stepped softly, motioning for the others to do the same. Jared followed her, agile as a cat, as Leo directed Quinn to walk in front of him. The young god attempted to follow silently, slowly placing each of his sneakers in front of the other.

The group paused as they approached the entryway.

Peering into the hall, Quinn's jaw dropped as he gazed upon gigantic men-like shapes with intimidating auras. When Surina had speculated that the Cyclopes were involved, Quinn had envisioned one-eyed creatures from his childhood lore. Nothing could have prepared him for the giants who stood illuminated by the Olympian fire.

Two of the hulking figures were gathered around the iridescent flame, one clad in jean overalls, the other dressed in what looked like a mechanic's jumpsuit. Sitting directly in the centre of the Olympian flame were the three pieces of the North Star. The seams of the Star were almost nonexistent as the two giants used oversized sledge-hammers to pound it into submission. Each man wore protective visors to shield their singular eyes from the sparks that flew with each strike of their hammers.

A third hulking figure—the last Cyclops brother—stood off to the side of the hall beside the main entrance, a massive axe clasped in his meaty hands.

"Okay, so we have Arges watching the door, while Brontes and Steropes work on the Star," Surina informed them, pointing to each of the Cyclopes with a jut of her chin.

For a moment, Quinn could only hear the Cyclopes' hammer blows against the Star meshing with the grunts of the labouring daimons, but then he became aware of a soft rustling above him. He tilted his head upward, glimpsing the glittering eyes of the remaining Danaids as they scuttled about the tops of the columns like spiders, fearful of the light.

Jared followed Quinn's line of vision toward the women nesting near the ceiling. Despite their bloodlust, the sheer size of the Cyclopes kept the Danaids from attacking the daimons working below.

"And they're still keeping the Danaids on call," Jared whispered in disgust.

"I was afraid of that," Surina replied.

Quinn swallowed thickly, realizing that their opponents now clearly outnumbered them. He had faith in his new friends, but as for himself, he wasn't too sure. When he had insisted he come along with the others, he knew that there could be danger. Staring out at the numerous foes who awaited them in the next room, Quinn felt his bravado start to waver. His eyes trailed over the blade in Arges' hand as he envisioned himself cleaved in two, or even worse, crushed by the monstrous hammers Brontes and Steropes easily swung behind their heads.

"Maybe we should get some backup? There's got to be someone else we can call, Carter, James, anybody," Quinn said urgently.

"No time," Surina hissed.

"No time, for most people," Jared said, shifting the scythe he held in his right hand before tapping its base on the floor three times. He then reached into his pocket and pulled out a small whistle. Quinn stiffened as Jared brought it to his mouth, fearful of the inevitable shriek that would reveal their position. Yet, as Jared blew on the whistle's mouthpiece, he heard no sound.

A moment passed, and nothing happened. Quinn looked up at Jared expectantly.

"They'll be along shortly," he assured him.

"We have to act now. The Star is only a few hits away from becoming whole," Leo insisted.

"A room full of Danaids and three, armed Cyclopes sounds like fun," Surina snorted. "So what, we just rush the place?"

"Do you have a better idea?" Leo countered.

Quinn again took a look about the cavern, his eyes assessing every enemy, before turning to take stock of their own team. Quinn already had an inkling of what Jared had just done, and combining that with the tools they had on hand, a plan started to solidify in his brain. "What about a diversion?"

Surina's brows furrowed underneath her glasses. "What did you have in mind?"

CHAPTER THIRTY

Arges sneered as he watched his two brothers toil over the Olympian fire, trying to reforge the Star. His siblings seemed more than happy to do the grunt work for their employer, despite the fact that the use of the Star's one wish was already planned out in advance. Still, Arges didn't fully trust the woman who had set their task.

Scarlet had contacted him two months after their initial meeting, bringing with her another one of their daimon siblings. Chimera, or Pyra as she was calling herself now, wouldn't have been his first choice for an accomplice—at least, not in the role she was currently playing.

Arges was willing to concede that Pyra was strong and agile, but she was not the stealthiest of their kind. He had assumed that Arachne would be the one daimon to pull off the actual thefts, but according

G.E. White

to Scarlet, the woman was preoccupied with another task, whatever that meant.

Yet, Pyra had proven herself time and again as she returned from each temple, a Star fragment in tow.

The Cyclops supposed he should also be grateful to Scarlet's stooge, Victor, who Arges first met at the Fox and Fife. The deceitful Earthen magi might have provided both the temple disguises and a map of the three temple floor plans, but Arges trusted the man even less than he did his mistress.

Yes, everything was coming together, just as Scarlet had planned, but it did not quell the unease Arges felt. The deed was almost complete, the Star almost reforged, but Scarlet and Victor had yet to arrive, or even contact them since they had retrieved Vega.

You would think that Scarlet would want to be here when the Star was completed, Arges thought to himself, perturbed. He knew what the wish was going to be and had little desire to take the wish for himself. Arges may not like Scarlet, but he and his brothers believed in her cause.

Scarlet had already talked others into joining her quiet revolution: Arachne, Chimera, Minotaur, and the Graeae, to name a few. Even Echidna was on board, and she had been essential in bringing the Danaids to heel. There was even a rumour that Scarlet had convinced some of the lesser gods to side with her. Once the Star was restored, the wish would rectify the mistakes made by the Creator Itself as well as the foolish beings It had left in Its wake.

Arges admitted he had no love for the gods—fickle creatures with too much power and not enough sense. But then, could he really blame them? Their mortality left them shallow—the lessons they had learned in lives before not always carrying over to the next.

The whole thing seemed a bit backward to Arges: that the ones who lived—the ones who remembered—had little power compared to the gods, while the ones who forgot guided the realms.

Glancing up into the inky-black heights of Erebus Hall, Arges could make out the miasma-cursed women at its peak, and snorted. The fact that these creatures—little better than wild dogs—had not yet rebelled was impressive, though Arges knew they would turn on his brothers and himself with no hesitation if threatened.

The eldest of the Cyclopes brothers turned back to his job at hand, pleased to note that soon their part in the scheme would be over and done with.

The sudden sound of a barking dog interrupted Arges' thoughts and stilled his brothers' work. Steropes and Brontes paused midswing when an animal's cry echoed throughout the chamber.

Arges spun around to see a canine dart out from one of the collapsed tunnels, its fur seemingly composed of both mist and moonlight. Brontes lowered his large hammer as the creature approached. With some difficulty, the hulking Cyclops bent down to the dog's level and attempted to pick it up clumsily with his sausage-like fingers. His hand fell through the creature as it vanished in a cloud of smoke, but before he was able to retrieve it, a skeletal limb burst from the ground, gripping tightly onto Brontes' forearm. The Cyclops pulled back, only to bring the body attached to the arm with it.

What had once appeared to be a human form was now a skeleton, draped in rags. Its lack of muscle belied its strength, and the scythe clasped in the creature's boney hand made it all the more intimidating. The living skull almost grinned at the Cyclops. Brontes' eye widened in alarm behind his protective visor.

Suddenly, a dozen other skeletal figures, some human, others once belonging to the other four races, burst from the walls and ground, each armed with a blade—broadswords, rapiers, sickles, katanas, scythes, even scimitars.

Arges hefted his axe up to his shoulder, ready to swing. "Reapers!" He called to his brothers, turning to cut down one of the creatures. The skeleton made a horrifying yowl as Arges took off its left arm and

G.E. White

knocked it backward, but the reaper seemed unphased by the blow, simply taking the fallen arm with his other hand and reattaching it before springing back up for another attack.

The appearance of the reapers had roused the Danaids from their uneasy stillness, and the feral women began leaping down from the rafters where they had been lurking.

Out of the same tunnel from which the fog-like dog had sprung from came four other figures, quickly drawing Arges' attention. He identified three of the four as the Lords Ares and Thanatos, along with the mutt Cerberus, who seemed to grow with every step it took until the three-headed canine stood over a story tall. It took Arges a moment to recognize the woman as the half-breed Surina Malik.

With an angry roar, he slammed the reaper he was fighting into one of the pillars, crushing countless bones into dust. *It won't be getting up from that,* the eldest Cyclops thought grimly.

Arges growled as he took in the scene around him; they were supposed to have more time. Even with the help of the Danaids, his brothers still struggled to fend off their attackers.

Steropes now swung his hammer back and forth, attempting to hit Surina and deflect the arrows she sent his way. Lord Thanatos, along with his reapers and Cerberus, kept the Danaids at bay, slowly whittling down their numbers, while Ares grappled hand to hand with Brontes, both men having discarded their weapons in hopes of overpowering the other.

It dawned on Arges that it was only a matter of time before they were defeated; before all their work would be for nothing. He dropped his axe and snatched up Brontes' fallen hammer. Rounding on the North Star, still sitting within the Olympian fire, he swung downward.

Almost there.

The wish was on his lips, and in only a few more hits, it would manifest. Soon, the humans would be no more.

⟢

Quinn watched the battle from his appointed spot, crouching just inside the tunnel. Despite his contribution to the "shock-and-awe" attack, as he put it, having Surina send out a Lupine Familiar as a distraction before sending in a wave of Jared's reapers and Cerberus, Surina still insisted he sit out the actual fight. But after seeing his friends spar with both the Danaids and Cyclopes, and viewing their obvious knowledge of battle, he reluctantly understood their decision.

Quinn pulled the dagger Surina had lent him closer to his chest as he witnessed two Danaids tackle Jared from behind. He scrambled to his feet, breathing a sigh of relief when Jared, with the help of Cerberus, threw the madwomen off his body. The God of Death looked none the worse for wear.

While Quinn wasn't overly surprised by the appearance of Cerberus, who had been magically summoned by Jared's dog whistle, he had to admit that when the first of Jared's reapers had sprung from the ground, he had been petrified. He had even taken a swing at a reaper, unaware it was an ally and not a foe.

Luckily, Jared had intervened.

Relax, she works for me, he had assured Quinn.

Now watching the skeletal figures defending his friends, Quinn was truly grateful for their presence, especially as they kept the miasma-frenzied Danaids occupied.

Surina, Quinn observed, baited Steropes tauntingly, staying out of range from his long hammer to fire arrows from her transformed protean watch. Leo appeared positively gleeful as he wrestled and traded blows with Brontes. The fight had probably been the most action he had seen in weeks.

While he was relieved that his friends were safe, Quinn had one question creep up, unbidden, in his mind: *Where was the third Cyclops brother?*

His question was soon answered as Arges appeared from behind one of the columns, hammer held high as he swung it down onto the Star.

Quinn's stomach clenched in dread. It was evident that with only a few more swings, the Star would be whole. He glanced back at his friends, each still thoroughly engaged in their own battles. Any warning he could shout to them would only be a distraction for them, which at this point, could be deadly.

Which meant...

Clutching his dagger in his hand, Quinn darted from the tunnel as quickly as his legs could carry him.

Arges brought the hammer down again. The sound was deafening.

Yet as Quinn moved forward, the rest of his friends and the enemies they combated seemed to move in slow motion. It was a peculiar feeling—all of Quinn's senses were acute, taking in every movement and noise around him. He could see where his enemies were going to move and could plot just where and how he needed to evade them. Weaving through friends and enemies alike, Quinn only had eyes for the Star.

Bang! The hammer's weight as it struck the Star caused the entire chamber to reverberate with solemnity.

Quinn leapt over the fallen bodies of two Danaids.

Crash! The Star's crystal practically sang with the final blow of Arges' hammer. The North Star glowed and pulsed with energy, once again whole.

Arges dropped his weapon, the wish on his tongue as he reached for it.

Racing to the pyre, heedless of the scorching flames, Quinn dove at the Star with outstretched arms.

Pain as he had never experienced before shot up his right side as fire engulfed his shoulder. Despite the agony, Quinn's only thought was to keep his friends safe as his arms closed around the Star and brought it out of the Cyclops' reach.

As soon as Quinn grasped the Star, its shape and texture changed—*shifted* from large and smooth to something long and sharp. But the Star's transformation was lost on the young man as he tumbled down the steps on the other side of the fire.

The pain overwhelmed Quinn as he gratefully fell into unconsciousness.

CHAPTER THIRTY-ONE

Jared had just cut down the last group of Danaids, making sure to keep clear of any spilt blood, when Arges let out a rage-fueled roar of defeat. The Death God whipped his head around just in time to see Quinn tumble from the flaming pedestal. The sight caused his heart to leap into his throat.

The Star was gone. Something smaller lay clasped in the fallen man's arms as he rolled to a stop at the base of the Olympian dais. Any thought of their opponents quickly fled Jared's mind. He felt strangely numb as he hoarsely cried out Quinn's name.

With the Danaids now defeated, the battle ground to a halt as all beings in the hall turned toward the flickering Olympian fire.

Jared ran over to his friend, Surina at his heels. He knelt beside Quinn's body, gasping at the damage clearly visible along his side. The fire had easily eaten through Quinn's jacket and shirt and now left trails of charred skin and angry blisters in its wake. Only the slight rise and fall of the young man's chest betrayed the fact that he was still alive.

Leo stepped closer, trying to assess how dire Quinn's situation was, only to be fended off by Jared.

"We've got this. Get Cerberus and help the reapers secure the prisoners," the Death God choked out.

"But—"

"Just do it!" Jared snapped.

The rough, almost hysterical note in Jared's voice was what finally persuaded the War God to follow the directive. Turning to the Cyclopes brothers, Leo was pleased to see that the remaining reapers and Cerberus already had the giant daimons surrounded. None of the three brothers had any motivation to fight. Not with the Star's wish torn from their grasp. Arges sported some burns of his own on his hands and the side of his face, where the fire had flared up during Quinn's dive.

The Star had disappeared and was no longer a threat. A wish had been made. The question was now, what had it been?

Surina's face was grim as she and Jared gently rolled Quinn onto his back, an action that would have likely been excruciatingly painful if the young man had been awake.

With a shaking hand, Jared gathered in his power, black oily smoke seeping from his eyes. He reached forward, his hand passing through Quinn's chest to once again grasp the blue Threads that had come to mean so much to him in such a short time. His heart sank as he pulled the Threads to the surface. While not severed, they were starting to fray, and their internal light was dimming as Quinn's soul moved closer and closer to death.

Silent tears began to pour down Jared's face. Why would fate be this cruel? To let them reunite just to break them apart?

"It's bad, isn't it?" Surina hissed.

Jared nodded his head dumbly, his face set in a mask of grief as he gently let go of Quinn's Threads, the black smoke of his eyes retreating.

"He's dying." Surina's flat statement wasn't a question.

"Yes. Being unconscious is a blessing for him right now." His words rang hollow as an empty feeling gnawed away at him.

"Can't you do something? You've got to do something!" she shouted, her normally strong composure cracking.

Flashes of Quinn's then unmarred face as he demanded the same miracle only a day before passed through Jared's mind. He wanted to help. Every nerve in his body practically screamed at him to save Quinn—do something, anything—but he couldn't.

He knew what the consequences would be should he break the laws of nature to snatch Quinn from the Underworld's grasp. He and Seraphina had witnessed it first hand, the grief they would pass down to another. Their own hubris had not only caused suffering for another but, in truth, only briefly delayed what was written in the stars.

Alice's worn, but kindly face came to the forefront of his mind. Throughout Jared's life as Elliot, he had struggled with the responsibilities weighing on his young shoulders. The guilt he felt for being able, but not willing, to release the dying from his own deathly grip had almost overcome him. Yet Alice had sometimes been able to ease his pain and tortured thoughts with the simple logic she was so adept at.

You know that there are times when a life can go either way, she had said to Elliot gently, after a particularly traumatic death he had assisted with. *But if you can't save their life without using your powers, then they weren't meant to be saved. Balance has to be maintained, and you have to be fair to everyone—not just the people you know. Their lives are not yours to toy with.*

So, what could he do now for Quinn? His friend, his potential soulmate.

Surina could easily read the conflict etched in Jared's eyes as he assessed the broken and burned body of their charge. The sound of Quinn's breath grew choked as blood bubbled from his lips. His extensive burns, combined with his hard fall onto the concrete dais, had obviously broken several bones and caused internal bleeding.

Quinn was going to die in a matter of minutes; anyone could see that. Surina cursed her fate, once again finding herself in the same position that she had been in many years ago with Lear.

The dagger she had armed Quinn with lay a foot from the boy's prone form. With a shaking hand, she picked it up. It hadn't protected him earlier, but perhaps it could now.

"What are you doing?" Jared asked, lifting his head to follow her actions.

"Trust me," was the only reply Surina gave as she took the blade in her unsteady left hand and dragged its sharp edge along her right palm.

Blood welled to the surface of the wound, which she raised to the dying man's lips. She rolled her hand into a fist and squeezed her blood from the cut, allowing it to dribble into Quinn's slack mouth. The young man choked slightly on the thick liquid as it hit his tongue, but Jared gently stroked his throat and Quinn swallowed it all.

Surina gave a nod of thanks, despite the wary look Jared threw her way.

"You're sure this is going to work?"

She shook her head slowly. "No. I screwed up once before, but this should be the right way to do it."

"But there's a chance it might not be?"

"I'm only half Gorgon. But, unless you've got some miracle you can pull out of your ass, it's the best I can do," she growled.

Jared hung his head, unable to face her scorn. As he looked down, his eye was caught by a wondrous series of events.

Quinn's remaining healthy skin appeared to be fluidly rolling away from the edge of his wound toward the worst of the blackened flesh, leaving behind scarred but healed new skin. A large patch of skin around his shoulder remained raw and red, where the burn had been most severe. The young man breathed more smoothly as the blood trickling from his lips ceased to flow.

Jared and Surina relaxed slightly, tension draining from their bodies. The worst of Quinn's injuries were healing, and his life was no longer in immediate danger.

"Gotta say, that was pretty stupid of him," Jared huffed, yet his tearful grin belied the scolding tone of his voice. Surina may not have been the most open with her own emotions, but the heartfelt relief that rolled off Jared was plain for anyone to see.

"I'll say. But he saved the Star..." Surina trailed off as she turned her gaze to the long object that now lay beside the unconscious young man. "It's strange, though. What on earth did he wish for?"

"I don't know, but with the wish made, we're in the clear for now. A new wish can't be made for another hundred years, at least."

A gruff laugh pulled their attention from the artifact near Quinn's body toward the now-kneeling and bound Arges. Even with only a single eye, the Cyclops' gaze was mocking. "Do you honestly think this is over?" he scoffed.

Jared moved to stand but was stilled by Surina's hand on his shoulder.

"I'll handle this, you keep watch over Quinn."

The Death God glared at the Cyclops but gave in to Surina's request. Perhaps her part-daimon heritage would loosen the giant's tongue.

৫১

Arges' single eye focused on Surina as she sauntered over to him and his captive brothers, her lips set in a hard line. "Well, for you it is," she stated, sneering. "After this stunt, you and your brothers are headed to the Labyrinth."

The Cyclops knew that he should feel afraid at her comment. It was true that their fate was sealed: the hive-like prison of the Labyrinth awaited them. It would be a hard life, but livable. Arges didn't have much faith in Scarlet coming for him and his brothers, but they had time on their side. He knew that Scarlet had several more moves left to make in their long and drawn-out game, and when that happened, an opportunity would present itself for him and his brothers to escape. Until then, he could wait.

"Doesn't matter," Arges shrugged in response to Surina's scorn. "It's only a matter of time before our brothers and sisters wipe out the vermin plaguing this planet."

"Brothers and sisters? You mean, other daimons," Surina stated.

"Perhaps," Arges answered as he avoided the question, though the confident look in his eye said everything for him. "I have to ask, how does it feel being a lapdog to the gods? Or perhaps *whore* would be a better term, hmm? It's a shame, really. Your mother would be so disappointed."

"Watch what you say!" The incarnation of Ares hissed, raising his fist to strike Arges from behind. Surina's hand intercepted the blow, but Arges could see that her whole body radiated with barely contained rage. It brought him a kind of sick pleasure.

Despite the mocking tone he had used with Surina, Arges' words held a note of sincerity. It truly was a shame, especially now having seen the demigod in action. She would have made a decent addition to their daimon ranks; after all, she was still a half breed.

"Leave him, he's not worth it," Surina spat, turning her attention away from her fellow daimons. "We've got more important things to worry about, like getting Quinn some medical help."

"You sure?" Ares pressed. Taking in the blood-tinged aura of the War God, Arges knew that Ares was just itching to take a swing at him. In a way, the whole thing was quite funny: a god following the orders of a daimon half breed. Perhaps this Surina Malik was more cunning than Arges had given her credit for in the past.

"Just get them out of here. I'm assuming you and the reapers can transport them to the Labyrinth?" the Cyclops heard Surina reply.

Ares glanced down at Arges and his brothers and sneered. "Shouldn't be too much of a problem."

"Then we should probably get going. Jared…"

The eldest Cyclops brother paid no attention to the chains securing his wrists. Instead, he watched as Surina turned to Thanatos, who now stood with the young man—*Quinn,* Arges reminded himself, for later—draped in his arms.

"I've got him. Let's get him topside," Jared replied, stepping closer to Surina, shifting his unconscious charge slightly in his movement.

Arges took a moment to examine the young man—the boy who had cost him the Star's wish. Quinn had evidently just reached adulthood, yet he had survived the initial burn of the Olympian fire. Had he been human, or even a demigod, the boy's dive through the flames would have completely incinerated him.

No, thought Arges calculatingly, this gangly man-child was no human, but a god. Regardless of his status, his actions had been foolish, but still, the boy lived, free, while Arges and his brothers remained shackled in chains. The thought enraged the eldest Cyclops as he raised his head toward the inky Erebus rafters. Quinn would never rest in peace again, as long as Arges and his brothers remained alive.

CHAPTER THIRTY-TWO

CLAWING HIS WAY back to consciousness, Quinn became aware of the burning along his right side and shoulder. It felt as if cotton balls now occupied the space where his brain should be.

Prying his eyes open took more effort than he expected, but the results were well worth it, as he was greeted with the sunlit blue walls of an unfamiliar room.

"And here I thought you would sleep for at least one more day."

Quinn turned his head and scowled at the young Seer sitting at his bedside. "You know, Surina was right—that can be a little irritating. How did you know I was awake?"

"I heard changes in your breathing," Sebastien replied.

"I see," Quinn replied, wincing as his head began pounding. "Where am I?"

"In one of the guest rooms of my penthouse."

"It's nice." Quinn groaned as he shifted, attempting to sit up. "What's wrong with my side?"

"I would refrain from moving about so much. Your side is still healing from the burn you obtained. Apparently, Olympian fire can cook you pretty quickly."

"The Star!" Quinn cried in recollection, snapping bolt upright up in bed, a movement he instantly regretted as he hissed with pain.

"Whoa, settle down. Everything is all right," the Seer assured him.

"All right? What happened? Where is the Star? Is everyone okay?"

"One question at a time. Yes, everyone is okay. As for the Star, it's right here."

Sebastien reached over to the bedside table and pulled an object from the drawer, before placing it on Quinn's lap.

Long, slender, and almost invisible, it took Quinn a moment to realize he was looking at a sword—a single-handed, xiphos short-sword, he guessed. The sleek weapon practically hummed as Quinn ran his hand over the flat of its blade, its crystalline edges gleaming in the dying afternoon light. A gold feathered guard curled around the hilt of the sword.

"*This* is the Star?"

"Apparently, it transformed the moment you touched it," Sebastien explained.

"I don't understand. I didn't make a wish," Quinn replied with a shake of his head.

"*Lo sé,*" Sebastien said with a shrug. "I get it. But the others don't."

"What do you mean?"

"They all believe the sword is the answer to a wish you made. The truth is, this is how the Star once looked in the hands of its rightful owner."

Quinn blinked up at Sebastien, before raising his hand to his forehead. "I just woke up. Maybe you could explain what you mean by that?"

Sebastien gave an amused chuckle. "I suppose. You see, before any of the other three Celestial Temples had ownership of the pieces of the North Star, it belonged to the Temple of Athena."

Quinn lowered his gaze, lost in thought for a moment. It wasn't that the idea hadn't crossed his mind, it was just a bit intimidating to find out that others would soon look to him for...well, guidance, he supposed. To be honest, he wasn't sure what he had to offer as a mentor.

"So Athena—I mean, *I* have a temple," he said slowly.

"For a time, yes. Magi of your temple were trained in many different types of combat, and much like you, learning came easily to them. Some believed that the Athenian temple acolytes could read the minds of their enemies. It made many afraid."

The words reminded Quinn of his thoughts just before he dove for the North Star. It had been as if he could predict every movement of his enemies and was able to dodge out of the way with ease as he approached his target. Was that the power Sebastien spoke of?

"What happened to them—my acolytes, I mean?" Quinn asked, a touch of worry colouring his words.

"Most people believe they were destroyed. But while the temple has been abandoned, I believe that there are followers of Athena out there still," Sebastien said.

"The Star is safe," Quinn murmured, though Sebastien knew the words were meant to reassure the young god himself. "And the temples?"

"They've been informed that the Star is now in the hands of the gods, and they appear satisfied."

Quinn gave a sigh of relief. He turned his head to gaze around the room and noticed a large pile of gifts, flowers, and cards sitting on a table nearby.

"Where did those come from?"

"I'm assuming you mean the tower of gifts. They're *Get Well* presents. Seems like they've come from all over the place. I believe that Justine sent the fruit basket, while Surina left some flowers.

James brought some tea and chocolate from Sofia, Joseph, and himself. Though I hear you should go light on the tea. Carter brought the newest editions of his temple's newspaper."

"Carter has a newspaper?" Quinn interrupted.

"Does that surprise you?"

Considering Carter's role as the God of Communication, it made quite a bit of sense. He shook his head. "I guess not."

"Oh, Jared left a few books for you, some of his favourite sci-fi novels, should you get bored. And much to my chagrin, Surina allowed Leo to deliver a crossbow as a gift. I believe he calls this one Charlotte. As for the rest: mostly cards from other gods, who heard of your heroism and wanted to thank you," Sebastien finished.

Quinn ducked his head, a light blush stealing across his cheeks. "They didn't have to do that."

"They wanted to," Sebastien replied simply. "You're family."

Those were words Quinn had longed to hear all his life. After all the years he spent moving from foster home to foster home, they warmed him more than he ever thought was possible. His breath caught for a moment as he tried to control the happy flutter in his chest.

"So, what happens now?" he asked.

"Well, to be honest, that's up to you."

"I don't know. Don't you think I should have some say in it?" rang out a familiar voice from the door.

Quinn turned his head and was greeted with a welcome sight. Leaning against the door frame stood Surina. Gone was her green bomber jacket, which she had removed in favour of a simple hooded sweater and a worn pair of jeans.

"Surina, you're okay!"

"And so are you—*despite* that bonehead move you pulled," she said, though the curve of her lips betrayed her satisfaction at seeing him awake and alert. She entered the room and Sebastien stood, gesturing for her to take the seat he had just vacated. "Thanks."

"I'll go make you some soup," Sebastien told Quinn, before exiting the room and closing the door behind him.

Now alone with Surina, Quinn could feel her eyes roving over his bandaged shoulder.

"So how do you really feel?" she asked.

Quinn winced. "It still hurts to move. But it'll heal, right?"

She frowned. "With time, you should get most of your mobility back, but we'll have to work on it."

"To be honest, I thought it would be much worse."

Surina fiddled with the edge of Quinn's blanket, the only sound in the awkward silence following Quinn's observation. He had made the comment in jest, but her odd pause unsettled him.

"Surina?"

"I want to apologize," she blurted out.

"Apologize?" *What on earth could the demigod have to apologize for?*

"I took a risk with your life."

Quinn shook his head. "It was my choice to come with you, just like it was my choice to grab the Star."

"That's not what I'm referring to."

"Then, what do you mean?" Quinn was on high alert, staring intently at his friend.

"The burns you suffered retrieving the Star were...much worse." Lines marred Surina's normally youthful face as she winced, recalling the state she had found Quinn in. "You were barely conscious...and barely alive. We didn't have time to collect a healer, so I made a decision. We were very, very lucky."

"Surina, you're not making any sense. What did you do?" Quinn pressed. Dread filled his chest, pressing down on his lungs and making each breath even more of a struggle than it already was. Surely, she hadn't forced Jared into saving his life.

Quinn suppressed a shudder, imagining another being dying so that he might live.

"Did you know that Gorgon blood is different from blood produced by any other species? The way that their—our hearts pump, changes the qualities of the blood depending on what side of the body it goes to. Taken from one side of the Gorgon donor, the blood acts as a powerful healing agent, whereas if the blood is collected from the other side of the body, it becomes a deadly poison. I made the wrong choice with Lear."

Quinn blinked, finally understanding his friend's turmoil. *"That's what you meant that night. You chose the wrong side, the poisonous side, when you tried to save Lear. But then, how were you taking a risk with me? Surely you knew by then which side was which."*

"In theory, but I'm not a full Gorgon. For all I knew, all blood flowing through my veins was poisonous. I took a leap of faith, using it to heal you."

He could see from her troubled expression just how much the decision had weighed on her. "And I'm here because of it."

"We were lucky," Surina argued.

"What else could you have done? You said it yourself, you didn't have time. I know that it must have been a hard decision to make, but I appreciate it," Quinn replied, gratitude reverberating through his voice.

Folding her hands on top of Quinn's blanket, Surina's lips twitched up into a smile. "I hate it when you do that."

"Do what?" he asked.

"When you're right. Reminds me of Sebastien."

"Hey, he's an okay guy."

"I suppose," she replied, her tone betraying her fondness for the Seer.

Quinn smiled, in many ways Surina was very much like himself. Seemingly rejected by her biological family, she was forced to forge bonds beyond those connected by blood. It seemed that he was finally starting to get the family he so desired and was more than happy to know that not only was Surina part of that but her family was growing as well. "So apparently, you have a say in what happens next?" he asked, changing the subject.

"Maybe I shouldn't have put it that way, *especially* since you technically have seniority."

"I feel as if I don't even know which way is up most of the time, so I'm open to suggestions."

"I want you to train with me—well, not just me," Surina corrected herself. "But I would be your primary instructor."

"Train me? You mean, in my duties?"

"Among other things. The truth is, Quinn, that this was not a clear victory. Yes, we got the Star back, defeated the Cyclopes, and got rid of Chimera and the Danaids, but others were involved. At the very least, we have a rogue Earthen magi we need to identify, and while this may be a setback for the Cyclopes' accomplice, I doubt they'll stop in their quest for chaos. Not after going through this much trouble."

"Do we even know who they are or what they want?" Quinn questioned, worry overwhelming his previously steady voice.

Surina's frown deepened. "Arges let it slip that other daimons were involved, which doesn't really surprise me. But until we know which particular daimons were responsible, it would be unwise, not to mention bigoted, to round them all up on a conspiracy theory."

"You're part daimon, aren't you?"

"Yes, though I'm not really part of their club," she hastened to concede. "I'm not saying that they're all bad people. Many of them have been quite helpful in the past. It's just that they've had time to nurse their grudges. A god's death and subsequent rebirth isn't only a punishment but also a cleansing ritual. Time can make you wise, but it can also make you bitter. It's not a bad thing to look at the world with fresh, new eyes."

Quinn nodded, his expression pensive. "You think they have a grudge against someone, specifically?"

"While you were unconscious, Arges spoke about 'wiping out the vermin that plague this planet.' I'm pretty sure he wasn't referring to cockroaches," she replied dryly.

"They wanted to kill someone?"

"More like they wanted to commit genocide."

Quinn shook his head. "But why?"

Surina shrugged. "Your guess is as good as mine. But I'd like you to be prepared when they make their next move. So, will you come train with me? I'm sure Jared and the others will come and help when they can."

Quinn paused for a moment, even though he was certain of his answer. "I will."

Surina shot him a genuine smile, a startling change from her common smirk. "Good."

He put his hand on the crystalline sword on his lap. "And hey, at least I've got my own equipment now. It's not exactly subtle, but I guess it'll do." As he said the words, the sword suddenly started to glow, and a strange power emanated from under his shirt.

Paying no heed to the initial concerns he had over revealing Gloria's last gift, Quinn pulled on the chain still around his neck to reveal the mostly empty pendant. Suddenly a bright beam of light shot out from the crystal sword, anchoring it to the pendant. The sword shrunk in size and shape, before snapping into place. The arrowhead frame of the pendant now contained a crystal prism. He blinked, wide eyed at the transformation. It seemed Gloria had had more than one trick up her sleeve.

Quinn removed the pendant from around his neck, a new understanding flooding his senses. Gripping the base of the arrowhead, he concentrated, and in another moment the pendant transformed once again to the blade he had just held minutes before. Sending forth another thought into the sword, it changed back again to a necklace, which he once again pulled over his head.

"Show off," Surina muttered as she gave him a friendly pat on his uninjured shoulder. "Well, I should let you rest up, because come next week, your ass is mine."

Quinn snorted in amusement, though his grimace betrayed his apprehension of the gruelling training to come. "Looking forward to it..." his voice trailed off as he sank further back into the pillows. "Has Jared come by recently?"

He felt silly asking the question, especially knowing that Surina was aware of his attraction to the Death God. Still, he wanted to know.

Luckily Surina decided not to tease him about his growing crush. "Don't worry, you'll see him soon. He's visited every day," she assured him.

Quinn smiled, the thought of Jared's visits warming his heart. He valiantly tried to keep his eyes open but knew he was quickly losing his battle to stay awake.

"I'll tell Sebastien to put the soup on hold. You get some sleep." Smirking at him fondly, Surina exited the room.

Quinn wanted to argue with her, but the softness of the blankets cocooned around his weary body pulled him into a much-needed, healing sleep.

❧

Surina closed the guest room door behind her and leaned heavily against the wood. She turned her head to glare at the figure slouching against the wall beside her, a cotton tote bag hanging off his wrist.

"He's probably already asleep—if you're thinking about going in."

"That's okay, I don't need to talk to him," Jared replied evasively.

"You've been checking in on him every day, and now, when you can actually speak to him, you're suddenly shy? I don't buy it." She frowned at the Death God as he refused to rise to her challenge. "Quinn told me about a dream he had," she continued, "about Seraphina and a figure in the dark. You and I both know why you're here, so why don't you just tell him?"

"What? So, I should just tell him that I was there when his father died? That his recurring dream is about me, and the night I came for his father's soul? Oh yeah, that sounds like a great idea," he sneered. "He'd never forgive me for what I had Seraphina do to him."

While Surina didn't have all the information on just what had happened the night Quinn lost his father, she knew the decisions made then had affected both him and Jared immensely. "Or perhaps he would realize the risk you took by letting him go," Surina reasoned back. "You knew what he was and what he was supposed to be. You knew you had to take him back to the elder gods. But you didn't."

"He was just a kid," Jared argued, a personal sadness colouring his words. She couldn't even begin to understand what kind of emotional toll reaping souls at such a young age had taken on Jared. The fact that he had wanted to spare Quinn of the heavy responsibilities showed her that Jared truly had good intentions that night.

"So were you." Surina sighed as she ran a hand through her dark tresses. "Listen, it isn't my place to tell him, but Quinn will find out eventually. I think it will be better if he hears it from you."

"I know."

"So, will you tell him?"

"I will, soon," Jared conceded. "But for now, I still, selfishly, want him to be my friend, and maybe by the time I'm ready to tell him, he'll be able to forgive me." He pushed himself from the wall and placed a hand on the guest room doorknob. "I just want to drop off a few more books."

"Well, if you're not gonna talk to him, try not to wake him," Surina replied, frowning.

Jared nodded and entered the room.

Surina shook her head as the door closed behind him.

True to Surina's words, Quinn was fast asleep, his right arm still swaddled in white gauze.

Jared moved to stand at the young man's bedside, the paleness of Quinn's skin reminding him of Alice for a moment. *But that was different,* he told himself. Quinn may be injured, but he'd recover. Well, for the most part. Jared still worried about how much movement Quinn would have in his damaged arm.

The sight of his friend reassured him, now that he knew Quinn had been awake and coherent. Jared knew that his young friend would soon grow restless lying in bed, so he thought it best to try to occupy Quinn's mind, though considering Athena's gifts, the books probably wouldn't keep him busy for long.

Jared stepped away from the bed and fished out a couple more tomes from the tote bag he carried. He knew that Quinn would enjoy the Underworld's personal library collection, which chronicled the history of the gods and their place in the Three Realms. Jared had often found the book's content to be dull, but he was sure that Quinn would soak up information like a sponge.

He reached into his bag once again and placed another item on top of the small pile of books. The worn, partially stuffed duck may not have been in the same condition as when Quinn had first owned it as a child, but Jared had been able to keep it in good repair over the past fourteen years.

The stuffed animal wasn't a complete confession, as it wouldn't be clear just who left it, but Quinn was clever. He would figure out the significance of the gift soon enough. And when that time came, Jared just hoped he could answer Quinn's questions, face his scorn, and still hold on to the bond forming between them.

CHAPTER THIRTY-THREE

ARGES LOOKED UP from his folded hands at the sound of the guard's footsteps approaching the Cyclopes' cell. Narrowing his eyes, he thought shrewdly to himself that the guard's steps were lighter this afternoon. He turned toward his brothers in their shared cell, but neither stirred from their cots.

Arges turned back to his small, barred viewing slot in the door as the new guard approached. He almost laughed out loud, emitting a dark chuckle as the pathetic creature came into view. Though she wore the traditional grey uniform of the feared Labyrinth guards, the mousy woman standing before his cell door commanded not a single ounce of authority.

The straight lines of the guard's uniform draped around her slim frame, and the cap sitting low on her forehead left her face in shadow.

The clinking of metal against the pottery balanced on the tray betrayed the slight tremor in her hands as the spoons within them rattled. Wisps of golden-brown hair, curling with sweat, were visible below her tightly wrapped bun.

The guard stood several paces away from the cell's bars with her head down, her body language betraying her unease. Arges snorted in amusement, his brothers finally waking and noticing their visitor, though neither seemed inclined to move from their uncomfortable beds.

"Our food's getting cold—think we can get it sometime today?" Arges growled.

The guard startled sharply at being addressed, but she complied, moving forward cautiously. She had just begun to slide the tray through the narrow food slot in the cell door when Arges, with a speed betraying his mammoth frame, seized the tray and pulled it from the woman's hands. She jumped back, fearful that the brute behind the bars might try to reach for her as well.

Arges and his brothers laughed at her fright as the eldest Cyclops brother passed the bowls to the other two. The spoons looked ridiculously small in the giant's hands and were soon discarded as the stew was devoured in a matter of seconds.

Arges growled at the sight of his empty bowl—the meagre portions in the Labyrinth never seemed to fill his belly.

He noticed that the guard was still standing a few steps from the cell, awkward in her silence. "What do you want?" he barked, once again causing the woman to jump.

"The tray and bowls, I need them back," came her shaky, and yet somehow familiar, voice.

"I need them back," he mocked, mimicking her tone. His brothers snickered behind him, the remnants of their watery stew leaking from the corners of their mouths. Brontes scooped up the bowls and spoons from the floor, placed them on the tray, and approached the cell bars.

G.E. White

He shoved part of the tray through the small opening, and with a nod, signalled for the guard to take it.

She moved forward hesitantly, but skittered backward as Brontes suddenly shoved the tray through the slot at breakneck speed. The move might have seriously harmed the guard had she been any slower in her retreat.

The three giants burst into laughter as the guard scurried about, gathering the scattered bowls and utensils.

With the tray now once more in order, the petite guard stood, her face still tilted downward, though now the rigidness of her spine spoke more of anger than of fear.

"You expecting an apology?" Arges said condescendingly as he watched the guard.

She shook her head. "No. I just wanted to see your faces as it happens."

"As what happens?" he asked, suspicion starting to nag at him.

A tight-lipped smile spread across the visible part of her face under her hat, filling Arges with a feeling of unease.

A throttled sound came from behind Arges, causing him to turn toward his brothers. Both Steropes and Brontes were hacking and coughing, their faces becoming swollen and purple as they struggled to draw in air.

Arges felt a growing tightness in his throat as his airways constricted. Poison—he should have known. He lunged at the guard, thrusting his arm through the slot in their cell in an attempt to grab her.

She stepped easily out of his reach as Arges slumped to the ground, barely able to breathe.

From his position on the floor, he could finally see their assassin's face. Dark-purple eyes, with an almost web-like pattern in the irises, smugly gazed down upon him from the face of a daimon who should have been his sister-in-arms.

"Arachne..."

Arges fought for each breath, but he knew this was a losing battle. He had to give her credit. With that scared little mouse bit, she truly had them fooled.

"Mother promised that she would take care of you and your brothers. And we daimons never forget a promise," Arachne said, her tone triumphant and without remorse.

Arges' eyes grew heavy as he took his final breath, Arachne fading from his view as his life left him. He should have known that Scarlet—Stheno—was never one to leave something unfinished.

☙

Arachne watched with some satisfaction as the light left the eyes of Arges and his brothers. The Cyclopes were brutes, through and through; they couldn't be trusted to keep her mother's secrets.

The gloves of the guard uniform she had stolen had kept her fingerprints from being left on any surfaces, so she was happy to leave the tray and bowls behind for the next guard to find. Keeping her head down, Arachne calmly made her exit. Once the bodies of the Cyclopes were discovered, the whole prison would be in an uproar, but she would be long gone by then.

Despite knowing that she had accomplished the job, a thorny thought pricked at the back of her mind. Word had gotten around that among the Cyclopes' apprehenders was Stheno's biological daughter, Surina Malik. Arachne sneered as she thought of the other woman. She hadn't seen the brat since their mother had shipped her off to the Lunar Temple. Arachne wasn't Stheno's biological daughter, but the Gorgon had taken her under her wing shortly after Arachne's real mother Achlys died.

She had been kind to Arachne when the new Queen of Spiders had no one else. For centuries it had been just the two of them, so when Stheno had finally given birth to a daughter of her own flesh and blood, it had hurt. Still, at least she could take some comfort that it appeared that Surina wasn't everything Stheno had hoped for.

Arachne thought for sure that the failure of the blood ritual and the subsequent abandonment of Surina at the temple would be the end of her mother's interest in the child, and yet...

Stheno's plans had many moving parts, motives, and desired outcomes. Arachne was more than determined to help see her mother's plans through, but she couldn't help the feeling of resentment that flooded her when she thought of her estranged little sister. Surina had no idea that much of what Stheno did was for her benefit. She just hoped the brat would be grateful in the end.

EPILOGUE

The Winged Herald Weekly

MISHAP OR MURDER? DEATH IN THE LABYRINTH
By Mavis Canterbury

A QUARANTINE AND investigation are underway in the Labyrinth, where three days ago, the Cyclopes brothers, Brontes, Steropes, and Arges, were pronounced dead after an unknown illness wracked their bodies.

The three daimons, who were apprehended earlier this month on charges of theft and conspiracy, were undergoing heavy interrogation procedures and had yet to name their accomplices.

There has been some speculation that the brothers may have been the victims of foul play, but so far, there are no leads in the investigation. Harmon Alecto, one of this generation's Erinyes and the warden of the Labyrinth, has given reassurances that, so far, no other inmates have shown signs of infection.

℀

Victor turned away from the computer screen to face Stheno, who sat hunched over her desk. She rested her head on one of her arms while her free hand spun around one of the Cyclopes' cuffs on the tabletop, her brows furrowed in thought.

"I assume that you had something to do with your daimon brothers' untimely deaths?" he asked.

Stheno shrugged. "I said I'd take care of them, and I always keep my promises. Besides, if even one of them had talked, any further plans would have been compromised."

"Of course," her partner deadpanned. He knew just how important it was that their plans go off without a hitch. So far, he had escaped any suspicion over being the Earthen magi informant. He would remain at his post as an instructor at the temple for a few months more before taking an early retirement. "I've got to ask, though, how did you manage it?"

Stheno pushed herself upright in her chair. "Arachne didn't tell you? I'm surprised, as the two of you have become rather close lately," she said with a knowing grin.

Victor figured he shouldn't be surprised. All of Stheno's agents, both daimon and otherwise, were devoted to the cause, even to the point of homicide. Still, it was hard to reconcile the woman who knitted him socks and flirted with him as she cheated at cards, with the Cyclopes' assassin.

"But perhaps she didn't want you to see all she is capable of," Stheno continued. "You might consider yourself highly skilled in such deadly arts, but I've found that Arachne is a true master of poisons—and needlework, of course," she commented as she lightly stroked the fine scarf draped about her shoulders.

Victor nodded. "I'm surprised that you're taking this defeat with such grace."

"It's not a defeat," she said. "It's a setback. The North Star wasn't the only way to get what we want; it was just the easiest. It's time to start calling in the heavy hitters. Creator knows you're not the only god who believes change is necessary."

Victor stiffened, the veins along his neck visible as he clenched his jaw. His newly discovered godhood was still a tender subject. The fact that Stheno had kept the secret long into their partnership had definitely created a rift between them. Still, it was good to know who he truly was: Lord Nemesis. It seemed almost a joke, what with him being the descendant of Lady Demeter, but the power of his magic and his desire for retribution could not be denied, and neither could the Soul Calendria.

"So you want me to start rounding up the troops?" he asked.

"Not yet, I'm hoping to receive a bit more information from our mysterious benefactor."

"Are you sure we can trust them? We don't even know who they are, let alone how they've come across this information." While Victor's nature urged him to put things to rights, he knew they would have to be careful going forward.

"We need information before we take our next step, and if anyone can find it, it'll be them. I've heard rumours that the Underworld is a treasure trove of dirty little secrets we could use, though it might take a while to get our ducks in a row. Lucky for me, I have nothing but time."

The dark-haired man scowled; Stheno had approached him early in his career as a magi for the House of Gemini. At first he was just keeping an eye on Surina for her, as she honestly seemed concerned for her daughter in her own distant way. Over the years Stheno had revealed to him the failures of the gods and the inequity that continued from generation to generation. He couldn't let that stand, so he had joined her cause. But even now, almost a decade into their partnership, Stheno had not let anyone else see the correspondence she had been receiving from their mysterious benefactor for the past seven years.

Though one thing was clear: only a god could have known the information they received. Itching to discover the identity of the mole, Victor couldn't help but wonder if the individual was a coward, frightened to get their own hands dirty, or a master manipulator, having Stheno seemingly following their lead.

He couldn't deny the tug he felt when she mentioned the Underworld; he was Lord Nemesis—Lord of Revenge and Divine Retribution—and the final judgement of the Underworld had always been part of his domain. Perhaps a homecoming was in order.

Yet as his mind drifted back to his own godhood and the Soul Calendria that had revealed his identity to him, guilt stabbed at Victor. The Soul Calendria had unfolded many other secrets to him. Truths others should know. He just hoped he would find the courage to tell her.

BOOK CLUB QUESTIONS

1. Which characters' storylines did you resonate with most in *Eyes of the Eternal?* Why do you think that you connected with those characters in particular?

2. How does Quinn's idea of family shift throughout the novel?

3. In what ways do you think Quinn will still have to change, in order to fully embody Athena's wisdom and patience?

4. Throughout the novel, G.E. White uses actual historical events to showcase the past lives of some of the characters (namely Quinn and Jared). These events include the Korean Imjin War, the Salem Witch trials, and World War I. What is the impact of these particular conflicts on the story?

5. How does Quinn's reincarnation help us think differently about our concepts of gender? If gender is tied to the physical body, what role does gender play when it comes to matters of the soul?

6. How does G.E. White bring a queer perspective to Quinn's journey?

7. How do you think Jared's role in Quinn's lost memories will affect his and Quinn's relationship in book two?

8. What is the significance of the North Star joining with the previous Athena's pendant?

9. With the mysterious Scarlet being revealed to be Stheno, Surina's estranged mother, what kind of complications could this pose in the future?

10. What exactly do Stheno and Victor hope to accomplish within the Underworld in book two?

11. What kind of quests do you think Quinn, Jared, and Surina might encounter in G. E. White's next novel? Do you have the gift of The Fates? Can you predict something of the companions' futures (like Sebastien could!) based on the hints G. E. White has left for you so far?

AUTHOR ACKNOWLEDGEMENTS

THIS BOOK HAS been a long time in the making—not once, but twice. When I originally self-published *Eyes of the Eternal* it was in no small part due to the love and support of my family and friends.

I can't thank my parents, Kathy and Bob, enough for all they have done for me. They have given me the security and opportunity to pursue my love of writing and have always had my back. I'm sure they've questioned themselves as to whether I would ever get this off the ground, and truthfully, I wondered the same, but they never wavered in their support. This book exists because of the work and sacrifices they made—from my dad handing me every newspaper article about writing he found, to my mother spending days combing through the book as one of my first line editors. Thank you both, so much.

I also have to thank my other early editors, critics, and sounding boards: my friends Corrie and Elisha, along with my sister Joanna and Aunt Arlene. You all kept me on the straight and narrow when it came to grammar and structure—the initial version of *Eyes of the Eternal* wouldn't have been what it was without it, so thank you once again.

My closest friend and biggest cheerleader, Kiran, has been a tremendous help in shaping the story and characters into the version you read today. She was always there to listen to my latest idea, or help steer me around a lingering plot hole. The newest forty thousand words wouldn't have been written without her. She also stood by me and supported me emotionally as I went through the journey of discovering who I was, not just as an author, but as a person. So, thank you, Kiran, for bringing my story telling and writing to a higher level, and more importantly, for being my friend.

To my amazingly talented cover artist, Hoàng Lập (Solan), you have been a joy to work with. The art you have created, not only for this book but for future books, just seems to leap off the page. You have brought my characters to life in a whole new way, and kept them true to what I imagined—thank you.

And of course, this revised and improved version of *Eyes of the Eternal* could never have been possible without the tireless efforts of my wonderful team at Doll House Publishing. Rebecca, you took a chance on an overeager writer with few to no bona fides—you saw the work and the promise it held and helped me run it over the finish line. For your confidence and commitment, thank you. To my dedicated editor, Theron, thank you for the countless hours you spent pouring over these pages, asking the hard questions and giving this book the polish it so dearly needed.

To my promotional manager, Christina, you have been my rock through the last couple months as we worked towards book launch. Your professionalism and dedication to a launch that not only got the book noticed but was true to who I was as an author is appreciated more than you could ever know. To my book designer, Frank, your knowledge, artistic eye, and clear understanding of the material made working with you both a breeze and pleasure, so thank you for all you've done. To my video specialist and editor, Robert, you were able to bring to life what I had in my mind, not only creating a beautiful and engaging book trailer but also walking the team through filming in multiple locations for our themes chat. Thanks also goes to France, another member of the promotion team who made my first interview a pleasure to take part in. I also want to give a little shout-out to our Doll House interns, Stephanie and Ainsley. While you may not have worked with us for very long, your enthusiasm and work ethic made up for it in spades. I wish you all the best as you move forward with your education and careers.

Finally, last but certainly not least, I want to thank you, the readers. Whether you read the original self-published edition, or are just picking up this title for the first time—thank you. I recognize that all of our time is precious, and for you to be taking some of your time to read this book is incredible. Those of you who have rated and reviewed this book, you are rockstars, and your feedback is worth more than you can imagine.

Cheers everyone!

~ G. E. White

Born and raised in Burlington, Ontario, G.E. White (Gillian or Jill to her friends) is a woman with a passion for all things fantasy and sci-fi. After receiving a Bachelor of Arts Honours in Professional Writing at the UTM, and earning a Graduate Certificate in Television Writing and Producing from Humber, she has since been a screenwriter, a video clerk, an actor stand-in, a YouTuber, and once impersonated an official from an Arboretum. When she's not writing, you can find her trying out for local musical theatre, or cuddling her cat, Harvey, and dog, Ruby.

Eyes Of The Eternal is her debut novel.

LIVES
OF THE
DEAD

G.E. WHITE

NEXT IN THE SERIES